My Ghosts At The Bottom Of The World

My Ghosts At The Bottom Of The World

Volume 1 - The Journey Begins

Scarlet Giesen

Dynamic Potential Press

Picture of Petone Wharf © Alfred Memelink used with his kind permission.

This paperback first published in 2022 by Dynamic Potential Press in Wellington, New Zealand.

You can connect with Scarlet Giesen on Facebook, Instagram, and Twitter.
@scarletgiesen

ISBN: 978-0-473-63100-0

CONTENTS

DEDICATION vii

1 Scarlet's Book 1

2 My Life: An Autobiography By Scarlet Giesen 9

3 Gidday! 11

4 January 2017 - My Ghost 14

5 How I Came To Be 20

6 1968 35

7 The Tea Lady 52

8 1969 54

9 1970 61

10 1971 74

11 1972 82

12 1973 103

CONTENTS

13 | 1974 123

14 | 1975 137

15 | 1976 154

16 | 1977 169

17 | 1978 188

18 | July 2017 - My Ghost Revisited 293

19 | Coming Soon 295

Dedication

A huge thank you to Sofia, Tresta, and Jacqui who have been instrumental in helping me get my book out into the World. I couldn't have done it without you.

Thank you also to the myriad of test readers, other helpers, and those who have believed in me throughout this project.

Love to you all,

Scarlet ❤

Scarlet's Book

Scarlet wasn't far from The Chocolate Fish café in Shelly Bay when the heavens opened, and torrential rain began to lash down. She instinctively took her foot off the accelerator and clicked on the windscreen wipers. Even on their highest setting they were fighting a losing battle against the sheer volume of water striking the car.

Mere moments before, Scarlet had opted to take the long way home and drive around the bays of the Miramar Peninsula rather than take the much shorter route to her house through the Miramar township. The skies had been overcast then, but nothing could have prepared her for the storm in which she now found herself.

"Typical Wellington weather!" Scarlet thought cheerfully. "Four seasons in one day."

The car radio grabbed Scarlet's attention as one of her favourite U2 songs began to play: All I Want Is You. Before the first verse had come to an end, she was forced to turn the volume down as the mobile phone mounted on the dashboard in front of her announced an incoming call.

"Hi darling," Scarlet said accepting the call and switching it to speakerphone.

"Hey babe," the caller replied. "Whereabouts are you?"

"Just coming around Shelly Bay now. Will be home in 10 minutes or so ok?"

"Sounds good. Just take it easy will ya? That weather bomb has hit, and it's really bucketing down now."

"Tell me about it! Why don't you put the jug on, and we'll have a cracking cuppa when I get in? Hey ... I love you, you know."

"Love you too babe. Jug's already on!"

"Tell our boy I love him too eh?"

"Will do, but you can tell him yourself in 10. See ya!"

"See ya."

Scarlet hung up the phone and turned the volume of the car radio up so she could continue listening to Bono's plaintive singing. By the time her eyes had returned to the road, the blue Subaru Impreza travelling towards her at almost twice the speed limit had lost control and was aquaplaning sideways across the road.

Time seemed to slow down. Scarlet knew instinctively she was about to be hit square on by the oncoming vehicle but could do nothing to avoid the inevitable. On impact, her head smacked sickeningly against the steering column, and everything went black in her world. The words "all I want is you" were the last sounds she heard.

Two boys in their late teens scrambled their way out of the wrecked Subaru; they were shaken up but otherwise unscathed. An older man driving a Ute behind Scarlet had pulled over to the side of the road and was now running towards the crash site.

"Quick!" the older man screamed at the teenagers. "Call 111, and get some help!!" He yanked at Scarlet's door, and after a couple of attempts managed to rip it open. Scarlet was slumped back in her seat, bleeding from a head wound as well as out of her nose. For a split second he thought it was Scarlet crying out "all I want is you" over and over before realising that music was blaring from the car radio. He was struck by the haunting quality of the song as it reverberated around him before being carried away across the choppy waters of Shelly Bay.

Momentarily taken aback by the sights and sounds before him, the older man then sprang into action placing his index and middle fingers over Scarlet's neck to the side of her windpipe.

"She has a pulse ... she has a pulse ... she's alive!" he shouted jubilantly. "Tell them she's alive boys ... and tell them to hurry."

Hearing Scarlet's cellphone ringing, the older man located it and answered with a hesitant "hello?"

The caller took a moment or two to reply. "My wife ... is my wife alright?"

"I'm sorry mate, she's just been involved in an accident. She's alive though, and we've called 111 ..."

Free of all pain or care or worry, Scarlet felt herself being lifted upwards. All around her was blackness, but a feeling of euphoria meant she wasn't alarmed or frightened. After an indeterminate period of time, she felt as though she was moving through a tunnel which then became a black empty void. Away in the distance she could make out the nighttime glow of a city; on flying closer to it, she recognised the city was her hometown, Wellington.

Scarlet found she could navigate around the city by thought alone and revelled in the joy of this for a time, visiting places familiar to her. She eventually found herself in front of two enormous bright golden doors where an older lady was waiting to greet her.

"Hi Scarlet," the older lady said in a reassuring voice full of love. "We need to talk. You have a choice to make. You can either walk through these doors with me and never come back or ... you can return to your body. However, if you choose to return, be warned that the Universe requires a price to be paid. The price is that when you return to your life, you will never be the same. You'll still have the support and love of your family, but things will be different."

"But I'll have love right?" Scarlet asked beseechingly.

"Yes you will Scarlet," the older lady replied.

"That's an easy choice then," Scarlet said without hesitation. "I choose **love**."

Without another word, Scarlet felt herself falling into darkness before suddenly waking up. And then the pain set in.

* * * * *

"How we doing this morning Scarlet?"

Dr. Michael O'Shea quietly sat in the chair beside Scarlet's hospital bed and watched as she turned from the window out of which she'd been gazing.

"Oh hi Doctor," Scarlet replied brightly. "Good thanks. I *do* feel a bit better today. The head doesn't hurt as much as yesterday ... or the day before that. What worries me the most though is not being able to remember anything ... will I ever get my memory back Doctor?"

"I suppose this means you haven't had any memories since we spoke yesterday then?" Dr. Michael replied.

"No, nothing ... there's just ... nothing there. Except for the memory you call a 'near death experience.' Other than that, it's as if I was born a 55 year old woman three weeks ago when I woke up here."

Dr. Michael nodded slightly. "The amnesia you're suffering from Scarlet – focal retrograde amnesia to be precise – has left you with no memory of anything that took place before your accident. Preliminary tests suggest there's little or no evidence of anterograde amnesia ... this means you're able to make new memories from the time of the car crash onwards. That's very positive."

"I get that bit Doctor ... that I can't remember anything that happened before my accident, and I'll be able to remember everything from now on. But what I don't understand is how come I can't remember people or events from the past, but I can remember how to do things. Like read and write and brush my teeth. I don't quite get that."

"Ah well, you've perfectly described the difference between your declarative and non-declarative memories," Dr. Michael explained. "Declarative memory is the memory of facts, figures and events. Non-declarative memory is the memory of how to do things, like the things you've described. What you're experiencing is quite common in amnesia cases."

Dr. Michael fell silent and looked as though he was reflecting on something. "You know what Scarlet?" he said slowly, as if picking his words carefully. "I've been coming to see you almost every day since you woke up from your coma and we've had quite a few chats by now haven't we?"

Scarlet silently nodded.

"I feel as though the time is right for me to tell you some things. Like the fact we've known each other for over 30 years and we actually work together. I've been your boss for the past 5 of those years, so I think it's ok for you to call me 'Michael' again!"

"Wow ... we've known each other all that time?" Scarlet said with a startled expression. She paused for a moment as if processing this information before continuing.

"Alright then ... Michael it is." Scarlet shifted uncomfortably in her bed. "It's just that it's hard to be familiar with someone you can't remember, even if I *have* known you for all those years. It's not just you though, I don't even remember my own family!"

"Hold that thought," Dr. Michael said kindly. He picked up his bag and retrieved an item from within. "I didn't think you were ready for this a week or two ago, but I feel you are now ... here you go Scarlet, here's your laptop."

Scarlet looked puzzled as Dr. Michael passed the device to her. "Thanks Michael ... but I'm not quite sure why you've brought *this* to me."

"Ok ... so fire it up and you'll find a document on the desktop. A very *special* document."

Scarlet turned the machine on, located the document and opened it. "Right ... so ... it looks like a book. Geez, it's a really long book! Let's see ... 'My Life, An Autobiography by Scarlet Giesen.' What? Wait ... that's me! What's going on Michael, I don't understand."

"A couple of years before your accident, you told me you were writing a book. Not just any book, but your memoirs. You told me that only three people knew you were writing it and that I was one of those three. You seemed to become ... how can I put this ... you were *obsessed* with your book and it began to take over your life. I became concerned when I saw you getting more and more run down both physically and mentally because you were working at the practice with me by day and then writing your book into the early hours of the morning. It got to the point just before your accident where you were so run down that I had to give you some leave so you could recharge your batteries."

Scarlet's eyes widened as the realisation dawned on her as to what she was holding. "Why the heck would I have written a book Michael? Don't get me wrong … it's great that I'll be able to read about myself and my life … but why did I write it in the first place? And who were the other people who knew I was writing it?"

"I don't know who else knew about your book unfortunately Scarlet. But you did tell me how you came to write it and that you were going to talk about that in the book. Personally, I couldn't get my head around your reasons at the time but I'm really pleased now that you wrote it because it may help you in your recovery. You've managed to bang yourself up quite well in that accident of yours, so you'll be in here for a few more weeks yet. There'll be plenty of time for reading while you get better!"

Scarlet was already lost in her book. "Look Michael, I've called the first chapter 'Gidday!' That's a bit odd isn't it?"

"I'd say that's your personality and sense of humour coming through," Dr. Michael said grinning. "You always had … shall we say … very *definite* ideas about how things should be done! If I know you, you're going to get an excellent sense of yourself from reading your story. I'll leave you to it ok?"

Scarlet looked up from her laptop. "Thanks for this Michael, I love it! Before you go, I have a very important question for you. No bullshit now … what was I like to work with?"

"You were *great* to work with," Dr. Michael laughed. "And that's no bullshit. I've always valued your honesty and no-nonsense approach … exactly as you've just demonstrated!"

Dr. Michael turned to go.

"Oh, one last thing Scarlet; you might need these." Dr. Michael rummaged around in his bag until he found a set of earbuds which he passed to Scarlet.

"Earbuds?" she said unsurely. "Why would I need earbuds to read a book?"

"You'll see!"

Dr. Michael said his goodbyes and left the room as Scarlet returned to her laptop. "Now ... where was I?" she said softly and started reading to herself.

"Gidday there and welcome to my book. My name is Scarlet, Scarlet Giesen ..."

My Life: An Autobiography By Scarlet Giesen

Gidday!

Gidday

gə'deɪ / exclamation / informal / New Zealand
Good day. Hello. Hi. Greetings. Welcome. Kia Ora.

Gidday there, and welcome to my book. My name is Scarlet, Scarlet Giesen, and I was born in 1963 in the Hutt Hospital in Wellington, New Zealand – a country right at the bottom of the world. Not so long ago, someone dear to me in life visited me from beyond the grave, suggesting I write the story of my life and times down on paper.

The end result, Dear Reader, is what you are now reading.

My story is written through the perspective of Me in my early 50s. Most of the time, I write about events that have taken place in the past, although sometimes I write in the present. I've organized the past events in chronological order by year which is why the titles of almost all of the chapters are years.

To separate one anecdote from another within each year, I use these symbols:

ε̌ ε̌ ε̌

This book is perhaps a little different from others you may have read. Throughout its pages, I have supplemented the written word with music and video which you should be able to access online via your favourite streaming website or service. References to music are simply in the form "artist – song" like this:

Artist – Song

Where I've made reference to a video, I've included the relevant video description – usually from YouTube – so you can search it up for yourself. You'll see these references prefaced by the words "YouTube" or the relevant video hosting site. I've included the length of the video in the description so you know when you've found the right one, just like this:

YouTube: Video description (1:23)

Sometimes I'll illustrate my stories with a reference to a specific website, or to Google, followed by some text which you can use to search online. These references will appear throughout the book like this:

Website: Description

You don't need to look at the online content of course, but I highly recommend that you do to get the most out of the experience of reading my book. This means you'll need some sort of device to access the Internet; perhaps a smartphone or tablet or something similar.

If you can, I recommend that you listen to the music and videos with a set of headphones. This is not only so you can get the full stereo effect but also so you can escape into your own world. Whether you use headphones or not, please stop reading the book while you listen to the songs and videos. Take a minute, surrender yourself to the music, focus on the video, and I'm sure you'll discern their relevance within the context of the part of the book you're reading.

I was brought up in the 60s, 70s, and 80s with what I believe was some of the best music ever made – perhaps I'm biased about that! Most of the songs in the book are my favourites, ones I've played throughout my life and right up to the present day. Sometimes they have helped me cope with a certain situation; maybe something paranormal, maybe to help mend a broken heart. Invariably, the songs evoke a feeling or recall a certain time in my life.

For me, that is the power of music – its ability to transport the listener immediately to another place or time or feeling. So as I write my story, I use the music to take me back to the events that have made up my life.

Just like the character in my first piece of music who hears an old familiar song and is immediately reminded of a past love called Marianne.

Why don't you put your headphones on and have a listen? I'm hoping the music will transport you along with me.

Boston – More Than A Feeling

Gidday and welcome to the story of my life. I hope you enjoy it!

4

January 2017 - My Ghost

"Scarlet, wake up.

"Scarlet, wake UP!

"SCARLET! WAKE UP!!"

I open my eyes and try to clear the sleep fog from my head. Standing silently beside my bed, I see the black and white slightly distorted image of My Ghost. I knew My Ghost well in life – I call her MG for short – and she exudes love and peace whenever she comes to me.

Although I hear MG talking to me as I rouse from my sleep, there is no auditory element to our communication. I never actually **hear** MG speak out loud and her mouth never moves when she talks. It's more like her words form in my head somehow, as if there's a transfer of thoughts between the two of us. Whatever supernatural process is at play, we're able to understand each other.

Or is it supernatural? Am I simply talking to myself and MG is actually some sort of psychological construct my subconscious has conjured up for an as yet unknown reason? I can't be entirely sure.

I sit up in bed and look at the time – it's 2 in the morning. Really? I can't say I'm totally unhappy to see MG, but it *is* 2am.

Rubbing my eyes, I look at MG and can't help but smile.

"Scarlet, you must start writing the book about your life *now*!" MG says in a loving but assertive tone. "Last year you promised you'd make a start on it at the beginning of 2017. Guess what? It's now the beginning of 2017."

I'm still half asleep and slightly annoyed. "Why is it so important I write a book about my life anyway? There's nothing that unusual about it."

"We've been over this a dozen times already," MG replies and her frustration is thinly veiled. "You always want to know the answers to everything and I can't give them all to you right now."

"It's just that I'm a bit busy at the minute to be writing a book," I say a little huffily. "On top of my day job and everything else I have to do, I have the Wellington Rugby 7s tournament at the Cake Tin this weekend – it's the last time *ever* that Wellington will be hosting it and my best friend is coming down from Auckland – I've already hired my Wonder Woman outfit. I've found a gorgeous, long dark wig and all the Wonder Woman knick-knacks, so I'm all set!

"After that, there's the Guns N' Roses concert to go to." An unsolicited mental image passes through my mind of me at the concert in my Wonder Woman outfit. I quickly discard the idea. Although ...

I try to reason with MG. "The last time Guns N' Roses was in New Zealand was 23 years ago and this time they're coming to Wellington! I can't wait!"

MG looks at me disapprovingly. "All I can tell you is there are dark times on the horizon, so you *must* write your book. Write about your life and the people in it, write about the events that took place around you and how they made you who you are. Write your book as if someone you don't know will read it. Above all else, write from your heart. You made a promise to start at the beginning of 2017, so ... start!"

Without warning, MG vanishes and I'm left pondering what she meant by "dark times."

"Ok, ok!" I say to the thin air. "I made a promise and I'll keep it. I'll start writing the weekend after the Guns N' Roses concert. Did I tell you it's been 23 years since they were in New Zealand last – and this time they're actually coming to Wellington?"

With no response forthcoming, I sit up taller in bed so I can look out the bedroom window, across Wellington harbour to my hometown of Petone.

Since the early 1990s, I've made Seatoun my home – a picturesque seaside suburb of Wellington situated at the harbour entrance. My house lies on the top of a hill with sweeping views of the harbour and Eastbourne to the east, Miramar and Mount Victoria to the west and my old stomping ground of the Hutt Valley and Petone to the north.

Looking out at the velvety night sky from the comfort of my bed, my mind drifts back to MG's parting words and how she won't leave me alone until I start writing the story of my life. MG has been at me for around a year now, visiting me from beyond the grave, urging me to start writing, in turns insisting, imploring, exhorting, sometimes agitated, but always at 2 o'clock in the morning.

My mind drifts further back in time and settles on one particular evening late in September 2016. I'm standing in my living room contemplating the strange situation in which I find myself. I've seen some odd stuff in my time, but I still can't quite bring myself to believe I'm being haunted into writing a book about my life.

So there I am, standing in my living room which also looks out across Wellington harbour towards Petone, and I say out loud, "MG ... if you're really serious about wanting me to write a book, then give me a sign."

I can't believe what happens next.

As if on cue, an unusually long, low rainbow appears outside which almost completely spans the entire window, framing my old hometown of Petone in the process. In the 25+ years I've lived in Seatoun, I've never seen anything like it.

The rainbow was captured by a number of photographers and even made it onto the stuff.co.nz news website. Take a look yourself – hopefully the one I saw that September day is still online; if not, you'll get the idea with what comes up.

Google: Photo of rainbow over Petone, Wellington

Rightly or wrongly, I take the rainbow as the sign I was asking for. "Ok, I get it," I say out loud. "I'll start writing the book. Next year. In 2017. The beginning of 2017. Ok?"

I don't see or hear from MG again until late January 2017. At 2am to be precise.

"Scarlet, wake up.

"Scarlet, wake UP!

"SCARLET! WAKE UP!!"

I received another telling off for not starting on my book.

Fast forward a few days and I'm at the Rugby 7s at Wellington's Westpac Stadium, lovingly dubbed "The Cake Tin" by some wag. My long dark totally unnatural Wonder Woman locks are flowing in the breeze. Ok, to be perfectly honest, they're positively wrapping themselves around my head – but apart from the wind, Wellington has put on a pretty good day for the festivities to come.

I hadn't been to the 7s for years, but 2017 was to be the last time Wellington would host the tournament, so my friends and I decided to go. It's tradition for people to wear themed costumes to the event and some have embraced the concept and run with it in all sorts of directions. There have been doctors, nurses, Smurfs, babies, aliens, fairies and cheerleaders. One year a group of guys wore mankinies; that particular item of clothing was promptly banned forever by the 7s Fun Police. My friends and I decided to play it safe and dress up as Superheroes.

Our New Zealand 7s team took a bit of a whipping in the quarter-finals at the hands of Fiji in that final Cake Tin tournament. We didn't really notice too much at the time though, as Wellington put on a cracker of a day and we were all a bit busy perfecting the art of the Mexican Wave.

Here is a highlights package of the first day of the tournament with a few shots of Wellington at the start of the clip.

YouTube: HIGHLIGHTS: Wellington Sevens 2017 Day One
(7:07)

When I returned home that night, I turned on the TV and was just in time to catch the late news. I had to laugh; the head doctor of the Accident & Emergency Department at Wellington Hospital was being interviewed about the medical misadventures of some of the revelers at the 7s Tournament. "If I see one more comatose Smurf or injured Superhero who thought they could actually fly, I'll go off my nut!" he said playfully.

Only in New Zealand surely. Luckily, hospital care in this country is free or it could have been a really expensive outing for those comatose Smurfs and injured Superheroes.

Everyone in my group had a great time over the two days of the tournament and we hit the town hard on the second night. We all got home safely, although I don't think my friend dressed as Superman – who totally overindulged in the pleasures of the Belgium Beer Bar – was exactly "The Man of Steel" in the department that mattered as he was last seen arm in arm with a very cute pink Fairy.

Not long after the 7s tournament, and with Superman's powers fully restored, Guns N' Roses came to Wellington for the first time ever. I think it poured with rain from the minute they arrived to well after their show had left town.

It rained so hard on the day of the Guns N' Roses concert that I was forced to abandon any residual thoughts of wearing my Wonder Woman outfit. Superman was likewise a little disappointed but at least he had his pink Fairy with him.

Despite the slightly inclement weather, we all had an awesome night with Axel and co. Secretly, I was relieved none of the boys on stage were electrocuted.

The clip of the concert below shows how much it rained that night. Kiwis are a pretty hardy bunch though; we definitely aren't made of sugar and it'll take a lot more than a little bit of rain to spoil our fun.

YouTube: 02.02.2017 Guns N' Roses in Wellington (0:58)

Dear Guns N' Roses: you rock! I wish you could have seen Wellington on a good day. Here's a song by a New Zealand band I sang for you when you came to town.

Dragon – Rain

A few days later is Waitangi Day, our national day and a public holiday. This particular Waitangi Day in 2017 is important to me not only because it's our national day. It's also the day I finally kept my promise to MG and started writing the story of my life.

I was awakened from a deep sleep in the early hours of that Waitangi Day morning. It was dark and quiet – darker and quieter than usual. I sat up in my bed, looked out of the bedroom window and my eyes were drawn upwards where I saw Venus in the night sky. The sight almost took my breath away as this little planet was shining so very brightly this morning.

Venus was named after the Roman goddess of love and beauty. It suddenly occurred to me that Venus stands for one of my most strongly held beliefs; that *love* is the meaning of life and one of the most powerful forces in the Universe.

As I was looking up at Venus and these thoughts were taking shape in my mind, I clearly heard MG's voice inside my head saying, "Scarlet, you've got this!" I looked around in surprise, but there was no one to be seen.

"MG ... where do I start my story?" I asked out loud.

"At the beginning!" MG replied. "Start with how you got here, then your earliest memory and carry on from there. You've got this Scarlet!!"

In that moment, gazing through my bedroom window at Venus twinkling brightly, I decided I was ready to start my story.

So here we go.

5

How I Came To Be

Still sitting in bed, I reach for my laptop, start it up and open a blank document. "Here we go," I say out loud, half expecting MG to answer.

Silence.

"What did MG say to start my book with?" I ask myself. "That's it – how I got here."

That shouldn't be too difficult. As a child, I was fascinated with stories of my family's history. My mother had a strong interest in genealogy and she was – and still is – the go-to person if anyone in my family had a question about this great-aunt or that cousin. Instead of reading me bedtime stories out of a children's book, Mum would tell me stories about our predecessors and relations.

So I place my fingers on the keyboard and ... nothing. Nothing comes. I can't seem to get anything to write about.

I glance out of the bedroom window and see Venus slightly higher in the sky than when I first saw her. I can't take my eyes off this little planet twinkling so brightly in front of me. I'm instantly filled with the most beautiful feeling of calm and peace, and above all else, *love*. I say the word "love" to myself and for the second time that morning make the connection that Venus stands for love ... and that love is all-powerful.

Instinctively I start breathing very deeply and very slowly. Little by little, images from my past begin to coalesce in my mind's eye and suddenly I'm a 9 year old girl getting ready for bed.

ぐ ぐ ぐ

"Scarlet, are you in bed yet?"

"Not quite Mum ... almost."

"Crikey girl, do you know what time it is? If you don't rattle your dags, that's the last time I let you stay up late to watch Love American Style."

"Ok, *OK*!"

"Tell you what. If you hurry up and snuggle down, I'll come in and tell you your favourite family history stories."

Now I'm motivated! I love hearing the stories about my family and how they came to New Zealand to make a new life. I cut a few corners in the bathroom and jump into bed calling out, "ready Mum!" at the top of my lungs even before I hit the pink candlewick bedspread.

I hear milk bottles clinking as my mother walks down the hallway towards my bedroom. I can hear her place the bottles – four I think – in the milk crate on the telephone stand and know I'm only seconds away from hearing my stories.

Mum comes into my bedroom and sits on the side of the bed. She closes her eyes for a moment or two as if she's meditating. Or channeling maybe. And then she starts.

"Ok Scarlet. Your great-grandfather was from a very wealthy and well-known English family. He did something pretty bad which brought disgrace on the family, so they put him on a ship with a sizeable amount of money and he was sent to the bottom of the world, to New Zealand, and was told never to return to England.

"They were tough back then in England, back in the 18th and 19th centuries. If you got caught stealing, say, and it might only have been a loaf of bread, you could get locked up on a ship and deported to the penal colonies in Australia. Your great-grandmother used to joke that Australia got sent all the convicts from England, and New Zealand got sent all the ratbags that had disgraced their families."

I have soooo many questions and interrupt incessantly. "Mum, what did my great-grandfather do to upset his family so much? It must've been pretty bad to be sent to the bottom of the world."

"Well, that part of the story hasn't survived, so nobody really knows. Perhaps he slept with someone else's wife, or something like that."

I don't get it. "How do you get in trouble for sleeping, Mum? That *does* seem pretty tough."

"Never mind, Scarlet. Let me get on with the story.

"Your great-grandfather arrived in New Zealand in the late 1800s and he settled right here in Wellington. He immediately bought a pub up the Ngauranga Gorge. You could tie your horse up outside this pub while you went inside for a drink. Then your great-grandfather married the prettiest girl in town and they had six children together."

Mum pauses and I get in quick. "I wish I could have known my great-grandfather. He sounds like he was loads of fun!"

"I think he *was* loads of fun," Mum says.

"One of those six children died of tetanus when he was a very young child after he was kicked by one of the horses tied up outside the pub. Your great-grandparents were devastated."

I can never help myself when Mum gets to this part of the story. I feel myself getting hot and tearing up. "That was really sad, Mum."

My mother gives me the eye to stop butting in.

"The eldest son was your grandfather and he fought in World War I – the Great War as it was later known. I can't say I ever found anything great about it though.

"When the English arrived in New Zealand in the late 18th and early 19th centuries, they learned a lot from the Maori in the arts of war. The Maori were excellent fighters, and the English noticed they dug complicated trench and bunker systems to defend their villages. It looks like the English adopted these techniques during World War I. The reason I'm telling you this Scarlet is because your grandfather dug trenches and bunkers during that war in a place called Gallipoli."

"Mum, I've heard of that place at school. But where exactly is Gallipoli?"

"That's actually a really good question. Gallipoli is in Turkey."

YouTube: Gallipoli: Drone video of WWI battlefield – BBC News (2.42)

"New Zealand suffered around 8000 casualties during the Gallipoli campaign," continues Mum. "That's 8000 Kiwis either killed or wounded trying to take a tiny strip of land. Luckily for you, your grandfather survived the fighting at Gallipoli, or you wouldn't be here listening to this story.

"When the Great War ended in 1918, your grandfather returned to New Zealand, but he wasn't in great shape. He fell terribly ill with tuberculosis which permanently damaged his lungs, but he was tough and he did get through it.

"When he returned to Petone, he got a job delivering ice. Back in the early 1900s, there was no such thing as a refrigerator, so people needed ice to keep food from spoiling. It was during a delivery one day that he met the prettiest girl in Petone – your Nana. They married soon after, late in 1918."

I'm bursting with a question I just have to ask. "Muu-uum," I start unsurely. "I've seen Nana heaps of times and I know what she looks like. Was she *really* the prettiest girl in Petone?"

Mum smiles and taps my nose. "Well, she used to be. But with all that bubbly blonde hair of yours, you are now!

"Your grandfather and Nana had four children, one of them being your father. Your grandfather died ten years after the end of the Great War because of the lung damage the tuberculosis had left him with. He died one day when he was delivering ice. It was all very sudden and your Nana was left to bring up four kids on her own. They virtually lived on honey sandwiches. Really."

It's imperative I interrupt with an absolutely crucial piece of information. "I *love* honey sandwiches, Mum!"

"Yes Scarlet," my mother replies. "I know you do. I wonder if you'd like them as much if that was pretty much all there was to eat, eh?

"Your father, who was raised on honey sandwiches, fought in the second great conflict of the 20th century, World War II. He fought in the Solomon Islands on an island called Guadalcanal. The fighting mostly took place in the jungle and it was one of the fiercest battles of the Second World War. Your father said it was a hell hole.

"The Americans landed on Guadalcanal in 1942 and the Kiwis, including your father, arrived a year later in 1943. He and his comrades were specially trained for the job and they fought alongside the Americans for a whole year. It must've been terrible ... your father doesn't talk about it much."

YouTube: The Battle of Guadalcanal: Anatomy of a Decisive World War II Victory (4:31)

"By the time I turned 21, I was married to your father. He was a bit older than me and on my 21st birthday he gave me a birthday card. I can still remember what he'd written inside that card:

> *Dear Jean,*
> *When I turned 21, I was fighting some bastard war*
> *in some bastard jungle. Happy Birthday!*
> *Love, Ken*

"Those were the exact words he wrote and he had the most beautiful handwriting. You know me though Scarlet; I'd never use words like that – swear words I mean. I think people who swear lack imagination. You'll never hear a swear word come out of *my* mouth!"

"Or mine!" I squeal excitedly.

"Yes I know," Mum says dangerously, "because if you ever did, I'd wash your mouth out with soap, or put mustard on your tongue."

I really don't fancy soap *or* mustard in my mouth, and I recall my brother putting his tongue under the tap in the bathroom one day when he got the mustard treatment for swearing. I make a decision then and there never to swear.

"Luckily for you again, Scarlet, your father survived fighting in Guadalcanal during World War II or ..."

"... or I wouldn't be here, yes I know Mum."

"It's around 1952 now, some years after World War II, and your father had finished sowing his wild oats. He'd travelled around New Zealand a lot and ended up in my hometown, Invercargill."

"What are wild oats, Mum? Do you have to sow them in a special way?"

Mum laughs and laughs. "I'll have to explain that to you one day Scarlet. But for now, I'll tell you a little about Invercargill."

YouTube: Invercargill New Zealand (Travel Guides: Baddo around the world) (1:33)

"Invercargill is New Zealand's southernmost city and is a lovely place. When I was a little girl during World War II, my father would take us kids down to the wharf and wait for the fishing boats to come in. If they were in season, Dad would buy us a sack of Bluff oysters and our whole family would sit at the end of the wharf and eat the oysters as fast as Dad could shuck them.

"In those days, you could buy oysters direct from the boats and a sack would cost around 10 to 15 shillings depending on how full the sack was. You can't buy oysters like that today. Now they're considered a delicacy, they're way more expensive."

I'm trying to get this straight in my head. "So ... you were brought up on Bluff oysters, and Dad was brought up on honey sandwiches?"

Mum chuckles. "Something like that."

"Oh ... oh ... Mum, tell me again how you and Dad met," I blurt out.

"Well, when your father first arrived in Invercargill, he stayed with one of his war buddies and I happened to be friends with this man's sister. So you could say the war brought your father and I together."

"Oooh, that's *soooo* romantic Mum," I coo.

Talk about perfect timing; my father walks into my bedroom to give me a goodnight kiss. He asks me where we're up to in the family history.

"Um, you've just finished doing some gardening, Dad." My father looks first at me and then at my mother with a quizzical look on his face. "You know, you were sowing some wild oats."

My father's eyes flash and he laughs heartily for a little before he picks up the story where Mum left off.

"When I first saw your mother Scarlet, I thought she was the spitting image of an American actress from the 1940s and 1950s called Ava Gardner. I thought then that your mother was the most beautiful woman I'd ever seen."

I see Mum smile as Dad kisses her on the cheek. "Is that why you sometimes call Mum 'Your Ava,' Dad?"

"That's exactly right Scarlet," he smiles.

My father gives me another goodnight kiss. "On that note, I'm off to the Petone Working Men's Club for a quick beer! I'll only be an hour or so."

"Yeah right!" says Mum in a fun way. She knows Dad only too well.

My father turns to me as he's about to leave my bedroom. "Not only is your mother beautiful Scarlet," he says, "but she also has the most beautiful singing voice. She might even sing you something if you ask nicely." He smiles mischievously and is gone.

After Dad leaves, Mum tells me my father is a very social person who enjoys having a couple of drinks with the boys at the Petone Working Men's Club in the evening.

"In fact," she goes on, "the Working Men's Club is his second home. Actually, his third home along with the Petone Rugby Football Club.

"You know I don't drink or smoke, don't you Scarlet? The reason for that is your father drinks and smokes enough for the two of us!"

We both have a little giggle over this. "Would you like me to sing you a goodnight song?" Mum offers.

I literally bounce up and down on my bed. "Oooh, oooh, yes *please* Mum!"

Mum sings one of her favourite songs, and I loudly join in at the chorus.

Doris Day – Que Sera Sera

After we finish singing, Mum tucks me in and smooths the bedspread over me. Everyone seems to be in a good mood tonight, so I try it on a little and plead with her to tell me more of the family story. Mum looks at her watch. "Well, I suppose I could. It is Friday night after all and it's still not *that* late."

"Yessss!" I think to myself. I decide to throw Mum a bit of a curveball. "Why did you pick Dad to marry?" I ask.

My mum replies without so much as a second's hesitation. "Because your father is Fun with a capital 'F' that's why! I suppose I did have a few suitors in my time, but you must remember this wasn't long after the war had ended and eligible young men were in short supply. Kiwi boys from all over the country went to fight overseas and many never came back. It was noticeable even in a small town like Invercargill – the family two doors down from us in our street lost their son. He was a pilot in the RAF.

"Anyway, of all the boys who were interested in me, I chose your father because he made me laugh – a lot!

"A little while after we got together, your father took me away from Invercargill and up to the North Island. I loved Wellington as soon as we got here. We came to Petone because your Nana lived here and we stayed with her to start with. I thought Petone was a step or two up from Invercargill, because nothing much was happening down there in 1952 that's for sure!

"Not long after we arrived in Petone, we were married at St. Augustine's Anglican Church. Your father got a job at a dry-cleaning factory. We never had more than a couple of brass razoos to rub together so we lived at your Nana's house for a few years.

"Buying our own house was pretty much out of the question, so we saved up to buy a car instead. It took us a while, but we got there – a second hand dark blue Morris Minor. After that, your father saved up for the swanky Possum fur coat of mine you love so much.

"It wasn't long before your eldest brother was born. It was 1953 and your father and I decided to name him after a very famous American movie star who we both really loved called Burt Lancaster.

"Burt was born around the time of Queen Elizabeth II's coronation in 1953. I remember that time really well, not only because your father and I were having our first child. On the morning of the Queen's coronation day, news arrived all over the world that a Kiwi, Edmund Hillary, was the first person ever to climb to the top of Mount Everest. That's the world's highest mountain, Scarlet. I remember the newspaper really clearly – half of the front page was about the coronation, the other half was about Hillary and Everest. We New Zealanders were so proud and the newspapers called it a coronation gift for the new Queen. She knighted Edmund Hillary soon after."

"What do you remember of the coronation Mum?" I ask curiously.

"Well, we didn't have television in New Zealand in those days, so if we wanted to see the news, we had to go to a cinema and watch a thing called a Newsreel … it was like the highlights of all the news stories from the last week or so. There was a special one just about the coronation. I remember it well – it had the coronation anthem 'Zadok the Priest' playing as we watched the footage. That anthem was written by the composer Handel for the coronation of King George II in the

18th century and has been sung at the coronation of every British monarch since."

YouTube: Handel's "Zadok The Priest" – British Coronation Anthem (5:44)

"A couple of years after Burt arrived, your elder sister was born. Your father named her Chrystal because he thought it was a beautiful name for a beautiful baby.

"Not long after Chrystal was born, your father received a promotion at the dry-cleaning factory. He was made Foreman and this was a significant event for us as the job came with a house. We could finally move out of your Nana's place and leave her in peace! It was heaven – at last we had our own home ... your father and I, Burt and Chrystal.

"I thought that was going to be it on the children front. How wrong I was! A few years after Chrystal was born, we had another son. Your father named your sister, so I thought it was only fair I should name our second boy. So I did ... I named him after a very handsome American singer and actor by the name of Frank Sinatra. Your father loved this entertainer and luckily approved of the name. Lucky for him I mean – not me – as I was going to stick with that name whatever happened!"

I smiled. "So *that's* how Frank got his name!"

"Then in 1963, your father and I had a daughter with masses of blonde curly hair. I've never been sure where it came from, as all our other children had been dark haired. That fourth child was you Scarlet!

"After you came along, I *really* did think that was going to be it on the children front. And it was – but only for ten years or so." My mother looks down and puts one hand under her pregnant belly resting the other hand on top. "This is what is called a 'Surprise Baby,' Scarlet."

"Did you and Dad have sex recently then, Mum?" I ask innocently. Mum does a pretty good job of hiding her surprise, but I can tell she's a little flustered.

"Actually Mum, I don't really know much about sex. It's just that ... well ... I overheard Burt talking to Chrystal the other day and he said he thinks it's disgusting you and Dad are still having sex in your 40s. Can you tell me what it is?"

Mum squirms a little. "Ask me that question again when you're older. All I'll say now is that sex is something people do when they love each other."

"But I'm really confused now, Mum. How did this 'Surprise Baby' get into your tummy in the first place? Or was that the surprise?"

Mum looks quite uncomfortable now. "Sort of ... kind of. I'll tell you more about sex when you're older, alright? You're only 9 and you won't understand most of it if I tell you now anyway. Ok?"

It wasn't really. I wasn't at all satisfied with Mum's answer. In fact, it only made me more curious. What wouldn't I understand? How complicated could it be? I made a mental note to ask Queenie about sex next time I saw her. Queenie worked at the factory with my dad, so I saw her most days. She'd tell me. She told me everything. Because nobody else around here gave me any straight answers!

Mum changes the subject. "I have a really strong feeling this baby will be a girl, Scarlet."

"That's *great*, Mum," I say excitedly. "I really hope it is a girl, because brothers are *soooo* stupid and annoying. Like what Frank said to me the other day. He said he was really enjoying being the youngest in the family and then I arrived and mucked it all up for him."

Mum chuckled. "I know brothers can be annoying Scarlet. I had three of them, remember? I actually wanted to talk to you about this and tell you that you can't keep smashing your brother whenever he teases you."

"But Mum, he teases me so much!"

"I know Scarlet. But you're almost 10 now and you need to start being more ladylike ... which means you *must* stop smashing your brother all the time."

I take this in and nod, but I'm thinking I'll definitely smash Frank the next time he annoys me. I swear my mother can read my mind though. "I really mean it Scarlet," she says quick as a flash. "It's time for you to become a young lady.

"Anyhow, it's well past your bedtime, so time to go to sleep now." Mum gives me a goodnight kiss and starts to get up.

"But Mum, you haven't finished your story yet," I protest. "You've only just had me!"

My mother sighs and sits down on the bed again. "When you were four, we moved into a bigger house in Petone that also came with your father's job at the dry-cleaning factory. Even though it was a little more run down than the last house, it was directly across the road from the factory. Do you remember when we first moved here and we called this the 'Big House?' We put butter on Snoopy's paws so he wouldn't run back to our old place."

I did remember. Snoopy was the family cat, an enormous ginger tom who loved being cuddled. All us kids knew how lucky we were to be living in the Big House. That was even though the toilet was outside and didn't have a light and the scrim on the walls used to get blown in and out when there was a decent wind outside – which happened a lot. To a little kid, it seemed like the walls were breathing and that used to scare the living daylights out of me. To make matters worse, the wind whistling through the gaps in the walls made a spooky "woo-ooo-ooo" sound that rose and fell in pitch. To me, this sounded *exactly* like the noise a ghost would make on a nighttime haunting visitation.

At these times, I'd hear my mum's voice in my head saying, "We're all so lucky to be living in this big house, Scarlet." I didn't feel that lucky sometimes. Especially when I'd hold on all night to avoid having to face the owner of the "woo-ooo-ooo" noise and go to the scary outside toilet. There were other frightening things about that house; I sometimes felt I was being watched – but I'm jumping the gun a bit now.

"The day we moved into the Big House," Mum went on, "you noticed a little girl with dark hair who was around the same age as you playing in her back yard next door to us. The two of you became fast friends almost overnight and everyone lived happily ever after. Good night! It really is time for sleep now Scarlet."

I can hear the weariness in Mum's voice as she kisses me goodnight again. "Sleep tight Scarlet, I love you."

"Love you too Mum," I yawn. I'm actually quite sleepy now. Suddenly a thought comes to me. "Mum ... Mum ... your story didn't have anything about *your* side of the family."

"No," she replies. "That's because all the interesting stories come from your father's side of the family tree. Actually, there is one quick interesting thing from my side ... my father was a really good rugby player and he was almost picked to play in an All Blacks side. But the team's management were split between picking him and another player and they couldn't decide between the two. So you know how they settled it? By the toss of a coin! Can you believe it – that's how they did it back then. My father was hugely disappointed when he lost the toss, but there you go.

"Good night now Scarlet. It's not quite the end of the night for me ... I still have some chores to do."

Mum pulls my bedroom door almost shut, just the way I like it, so the light from the hallway comes into my room a little. I was terribly afraid of the dark when I was young.

I hear milk bottles clink again as Mum picks up the milk crate from the telephone stand in the hall, opens the front door and places the crate in the letterbox outside.

When I was growing up, we used to put our empty glass milk bottles out at night. Sometime in the early hours of the morning, the milkman would come around, pick up the empty bottles and replace them with full ones. A pint of milk cost 4 whole cents when I was 9 and you would put either money or milk tokens in the empty glass bottles to pay for the new full ones. In my neighbourhood, it was a miracle if either the money or the milk hadn't been pinched during the night. I can still remember being sent out to the letterbox first thing in the morning to bring the milk in – fresh full cream milk with the cream in the top inch or two of the bottle. Yum!

Sadly, the Kiwi milkman is no more. This wasn't so much because glass bottles were replaced by cartons in the late 1980s. It was more that Supermarkets were allowed to become licensed milk vendors in 1987. By the mid-1990s home delivered milk had largely disappeared from the Kiwi landscape.

Take a look at the following advertisement. It's a marriage of two Kiwi icons – the glass milk bottle and the Instant Kiwi – a famous New Zealand lottery that's also no longer with us.

YouTube: New Zealand Instant Kiwi Milk Bottle (1:05)

My memory of that evening long ago has come to an end, but one thing about it stays with me. My mother was right about her fifth child, she *was* a girl. Mum and Dad named their final child Jane, after the actress Jane Fonda. Like all Mum and Dad's other kids apart from me, Jane had thick dark hair.

I look at the time. Dawn is almost upon me and I've been writing for a while now, but I decide to carry on with my story with my earliest memory, just as MG suggested.

"My earliest memory ... what actually is that?" I ask myself.

I glance out of the bedroom window over to the Wellington harbour, Eastbourne and my hometown Petone across the water. The first rays of the Sun are reaching out from the east and I can tell it's going to be a glorious day.

My eyes are drawn to a famous rock formation known as Steeple Rock which lies to the west of the harbour entrance. It rises 20-something feet above sea level, and is actually part of Barrett's Reef, one of the most dangerous reefs in New Zealand. You'd never know it this morning as it looks quite beautiful with the golden light of the Sun dancing across the multi-faceted surface of the rocks. The sea is as flat as a mill pond.

Many ships have met their end on Barrett's Reef. One of the worst shipwrecks was in 1968 when I was 4 years old and ...

Literally like a jolt of electricity, a flash of realisation courses through me and I have it, My Earliest Memory.

I'm immediately taken back to that fateful day almost fifty years earlier.

6

1968

"Oh Scarlet, *do* stand still while I'm trying to put your hair into a half ponytail," my mother scolds. "You're going to make me late for work."

My earliest memory is running in my head like a movie. In this movie, I am 4 years old and it is April 10th, 1968. Most New Zealanders of a certain age will remember this day vividly. And not only because it is Easter Friday eve's eve.

A little bit of background first.

As you've already seen, I come from humble beginnings. I don't know where all my great grandfather's pounds went, because neither Mum or Dad nor us kids saw any of that money.

In April 1968, we'd not long moved into the Big House – the house that had come with my father's job as Foreman of the dry-cleaning factory across the road.

Nowadays, it's very common for both partners in a relationship to have paid jobs. Back in the 1960s, this wasn't the case. The male partner would almost invariably have a paid job whilst the female partner would stay at home, do the housework and look after the kids.

Not in my house. With four kids to feed, clothe and everything else, both my parents had to go to work each day. My father had the higher paid job as he was a Foreman. My mother worked part-time in a factory in Petone, the Wills tobacco factory. There were a lot of factories in Petone back in the 1960s and they employed a lot of local people.

Take the Wills tobacco factory for example. My mother worked there alongside 600 other staff, mostly women. It's funny how times change, but when Mum was there, the tobacco factory was a prestigious place to work. It stood in spacious grounds, sported wide lawns, tennis courts and a large cafeteria. The factory put on free buses to get its workers to and from work; it was quite the respected business in Petone for a long time. The bonus was that the factory stood at the end of our street.

Even though both my parents worked, our family was still, shall we say, "not-so-well-off." This fact was reflected in the street in which we lived in Petone. Most of the houses were rented and a lot of them were run-down. Like our house.

No need to get your violins out just yet though, as I had a very happy childhood being not-so-well-off. Reflecting on things now as an adult, you don't really understand your family is poor until someone points it out to you. I guess I never really thought about it until I went to High School and met the Mean Girls. But that's all way in the future. Right then as a 4 year old growing up in Petone, I couldn't have been happier.

Some of this had to do with our neighbours. A few houses in our street were owned by the families who lived there, like the house right next door to our house. This house was one of the best houses in the street and in it lived a family with three children. The eldest was a girl who was around the same age as Chrystal; they became best friends. The next child was a boy who was around Frank's age and they became best friends. The youngest was a girl who was a year older than me and, you guessed it, we became best friends. My best friend from next door was called Matilda and she was very very smart – just like the titular character in Roald Dahl's famous book. I don't think my friend Matilda had telekinetic powers though; not that she showed me anyway.

Matilda was the best friend you could wish for. I can't recall ever having a cross word with her and she was very generous in sharing her toys with me. Matilda had the most amazing doll's house that had a number of rooms, all of which were furnished. In fact, Matilda's doll's house had more furniture in it than my entire house. Her dolls even had their own clothing which Matilda and I would spend hours playing with.

I had a few toys, but nothing like what Matilda had. Likewise, her house was way bigger than my house. Her house had five bedrooms, two living areas and a massive playroom in which Matilda's doll's house stood in pride of place. And Matilda's house had an inside toilet – two of them actually! Heaven. Sometimes, I'd hold off going to the toilet at my house and then go play with Matilda at her place just to use one of her inside loos. They certainly beat our drafty, dark, spider-infested outdoor dunny hands down.

Matilda's grandmother lived with her family in their huge house. As a young girl, I was genuinely scared of this eccentric old lady. Sometimes Matilda and I would be in the playroom playing with her doll's house. Matilda's grandmother would then shuffle in, glare at us both and point her walking stick at me saying in a big scary voice, "Scarlet … watch out for the spirits." I'd freeze until she left.

At other times she would say, "Scarlet! You know how sometimes you put something down in one place and it ends up in another? Well girl?!" I *didn't* know but would say "Yes" just to keep her happy. "Scarlet, that's the Trolls at work. They hide things and move them from place to place so you can't find them! Sometimes the Trolls do more than hide things; sometimes they *take* them and you never, ever see them again." She would then shuffle off, presumably trying to find something the Trolls had hidden or moved. Matilda and I would simply look at each other with wide eyes. I was convinced Matilda's eccentric old grandmother was bonkers!

I had cousins who also lived in Petone, only a matter of a couple of streets away from us. But it might as well have been the Moon where they lived. It was an impressive street and their house was so grand. Frank and Chrystal both told me they were envious of our well-off cousins. I told them I *wasn't* envious but this was because I didn't know what envious meant. I was also in the dark when Mum said my father's sister had married well.

My cousin Margaret was a few years older than me and she would give me all of her dresses when she grew out of them. Some dresses were better than others, and since my dad was the Foreman of a dry-cleaning factory, he'd have all of my cousin's hand-me-down dresses dry-cleaned and pressed perfectly for me to wear. I was 4, so of course by the end of the day, these perfectly pressed dresses would get trashed. That's how I earned my nickname "Bubs the Grubs."

That's it, we're up to date.

My mother has just dressed me in one of my cousin Margaret's hand-me-down dresses. I really didn't like this particular dress at all – a white number with blue polka dots and a matching blue cardigan, which I also didn't like. Mum is now trying to put my hair into a half ponytail and tie it up with a blue ribbon to match my hideous dress.

"You're going to make me late for work Scarlet," my mother growls.

"Please Mum, can I get changed into something else? I hate this blooming dress."

"Don't talk like that Scarlet! You look lovely in your beautiful white dress with blue polka dots. The matching cardigan is perfect too." Mum sees me screw my face up and as I'm about to say something, gets in first. "There's nothing wrong with your dress Scarlet. You're lucky to have such beautiful clothing handed down to you, so stop acting like a spoiled brat. And don't say words like 'hate.' 'Hate' is such a strong word."

"Ok, Mum, but I really want to put something else on. I hate this dress, it's yucky!" At the word "yucky" I stomp my foot on the floor.

My mum is getting worked up now. "I'm warning you Scarlet ... if you say 'hate' or stomp your foot one more time there will be consequences."

"Alright Mum ... um ... what are consequences?" I reply innocently.

"Don't worry, you'll find out!" my mother says in a very Don't Mess With Me voice. "Look Scarlet, I really don't have time for this. We must get going or else I'll be late to clock in for work at the factory. If I'm late for work, they'll dock my pay. And if they dock my pay, I'll be very angry with you. Now go and get that lovely Navy-blue coat Margaret gave you and we'll get going. Or do you dislike that coat too?"

I run into my bedroom and get the coat from my wardrobe. I take it to my mother who kneels down and hurriedly does up the shiny silver buttons.

"I like my coat Mum," I say. "It's just my dress I don't like."

"Oh Scarlet, can you please be on your best behaviour for once!" my mother says in an exasperated tone.

Mum finally manages to bustle me out the door and down the road where she deposits me at the creche around the corner from her factory. My creche teacher, Mrs. Barnard, walks briskly up to me as only Mrs. Barnard can. "Oh Scarlet!" she gushes. "What a beautiful dress and cardigan you have on today. Those blue polka dots are just the cutest!"

"Thanks Mrs. Barnard," I sulk back at her. "I really don't like my dress, but my mother made me wear it today."

"Oh really? But it's such a beautiful dress Scarlet. What don't you like about it?"

I look down at my dress and think for a moment. "I suppose ... I really don't like the blue polka dots."

Mrs. Barnard has a way of explaining things so little kids like me can understand. She ponders for a moment and taps her forefinger on her lips. "Well ... I guess you're just not a polka dot kind of girl Scarlet," she says thoughtfully.

I think she's nailed it – I'm just **not** a polka dot kind of girl.

It's now morning tea time. I love morning tea as all us kids get a glass of full cream milk and a Griffin's Gingernut biscuit. The idea is to dunk the biscuit into the milk to soften it up and infuse it with milky goodness.

Griffin's Gingernut biscuits are a Kiwi icon. The company that makes them was founded by John Griffin in Nelson in 1864. To put some context around this, the American Civil War was raging at the same time as John Griffin formed his company in the South Island of New Zealand.

Gingernuts are Griffin's most popular product, and Kiwis' favourite biscuit. It's been calculated that three Gingernuts are eaten every second of every day of every year. If I'd have known this as a little girl, I'd have said, "That's a lot of Gingernuts!"

Take a look at the following iconic Gingernuts ad.

YouTube: Griffins Gingernuts TV Advert (0:40)

The morning tea routine involves the creche teachers bringing around the milk and biscuits for us kids to eat and drink followed by wet flannels to wipe our sticky Gingernutty face and fingers. On this day though, I thought I'd save the teachers a job and use my dress to wipe away the Gingernut mush from my fingers – of which there was more than usual for some reason. I then finish the job off by wiping my face with my dress as well.

When Mrs. Barnard sees me, her face drops. "Oh, *no* Scarlet! You've got Gingernut all over your beautiful dress."

I look down at my dress and back up at Mrs. Barnard. "Don't worry ... my dad runs a dry-cleaning factory so he'll sort it out. He'll have this dress cleaned and pressed and back in my wardrobe in no time!

"Can I go and play with those new paints now please Mrs. Barnard?" I ask happily. "I want to paint a picture for my mum."

Mrs. Barnard looks at me suspiciously. "Alright, but I'll put a painting apron on you," she says warily.

"Ok," I reply cheerfully.

Mrs. Barnard goes away and returns with an oversize painting apron that looks like it would comfortably fit a 12 year old. "I'll tie it on nice and tight so you don't get any paint on that lovely dress of yours."

"Thanks Mrs. Barnard," I chirp.

I go over to the painting area to paint my mum a picture. I want to use lots of different colours. As I start working, I feel my painting apron is constricting my creativity, so I loosen it a little. Paint, paint, paint, still too tight, loosen, loosen, paint, loosen; this oversize painting apron is way too big and Mrs. Barnard has tied it on way too tight. So I make an executive decision to take the thing off altogether.

It's off now and I stand back to admire my art work. "Hmmm, more colours needed," I think. I dip my paint brush into a few different paints I haven't used yet. I've piled so much paint onto the brush that a few drops fall onto my dress. I look down and try to wipe the paint off, but it sort of smears a bit.

I then have a brilliant idea. If this paintbrush is going to drip paint all the time, I might as well use my hands to paint with. So, away goes the brush, and into the paints go my hands. I dip my fingers into the first colour and apply it to my painting. That works pretty well! I now want to use a different colour, so I wipe my hands on my dress and then choose another paint. Onto my picture it goes and it's starting to look really good. What a genius idea this is – I'm very happy! It's all working out so well, I decide to use as many of the paints as I can on my mum's picture. She's going to love it! My dress is actually turning out to be really useful as I use it to clean my hands before selecting a new paint colour to apply.

Standing back again to admire my Picasso, I hear Mrs. Barnard behind me. "Oh no Scarlet, no ... No ... *NO!*"

I look up at Mrs. Barnard and the smile that previously seemed to be a permanent fixture on her face disappears. "Where is your painting apron Scarlet?"

I smile sweetly up at Mrs. Barnard. "It came undone somehow so I took it off. It was far too big for me anyway."

Mrs. Barnard has a horrified expression on her face. "Your dress is absolutely *covered* in paint, Scarlet! Just stand there ... don't move and don't touch anything. I'll be right back with a damp cloth."

"No need Mrs. Barnard," I call happily after her. "I told you my dad works in a dry-cleaning factory. He'll sort it out."

As if by magic, my father walks into the creche. He **never** comes to creche. "Crikey, I must be in big trouble," I think. How did he know I'd trashed my dress and how did he get here so quickly?

I pretend nothing has happened and run up to him with the picture I've just finished. "Dad, Dad, I've painted this picture just for you!"

Dad looks at the picture, back to me, back to the picture. It's as if he's trying to figure out which has more paint on it. "It's a lovely painting Scarlet, but we'd better leave it here to dry. You can bring it home another day."

Mrs. Barnard hurries over to us with a wet cloth in her hand. She wipes my hands and face and does her best to sponge the paint off the disaster that is now my dress, shaking her head the whole time.

Dad picks me up and I wrap my hands around his neck and try to give him a big hug. He holds me in such a way so as not to get any of the paint that's still on my dress on his smart work clothes. "No wonder we call you 'Bubs the Grubs' ... look at the state of your clothes!" he says looking at my dress and laughing.

"I **hate** this dress," I inform my father.

"Why's that Bubs?"

"I'm just not a polka dot kind of girl Dad."

Dad smiles and chuckles. He looks outside and his smile disappears. "Well, that may be Scarlet. But right now I'm here to take you home."

"Yay," I squeal excitedly. "Home" means I can get changed out of this horrible dress. I can't wait to get home! I'm so excited that I squeeze my father tightly and repeatedly kiss his cheeks.

Dad is laughing all the way out of the creche until Mrs. Barnard stops him at the front door and tries to apologise for the Gingernut and paint that is plastered all over my dress.

"Don't worry Mrs. Barnard," he says. "I have a feeling Scarlet did this on purpose. But I run a dry-cleaning factory you know, and I'll have her dress cleaned and pressed and back in her wardrobe in no time!"

"It was just an accident Dad," I protest as Dad carries me out to his dark blue Morris Minor parked outside the creche.

I'm quite taken aback as I see my entire family already in the car; Mum is sitting in the front passenger's seat while Burt, Frank and Chrystal are in the back seat.

"Can I get out of this yucky dress when I get home please Mum?" I ask as soon as I'm in the car.

My mother raises her eyebrows, rolls her eyes and looks at my father. "Yes Scarlet, as soon as we get home."

"Yay ... finally!" I think.

As I sit down in the back seat of the car, Frank turns to me. "No school today because of this massive storm," he says.

I look out the car window. "What storm?" I ask in a shocked voice just in time to see a young boy being blown down the road like a tumble weed. For the first time today, I notice that the wind is really up and is blowing the shrubs and trees all over the place.

I remember thinking at the time that this storm is a lot more powerful than other ones I'd seen. It wasn't until years later that I learnt what was really going on, meteorologically speaking.

On the morning of Wednesday the 10th of April 1968, two huge storms met and merged right over Wellington City creating a massive cyclone. The winds created by this cyclone were the worst ever recorded here, gusting up to 275 kilometers per hour. That's around 170 miles per hour in the old money.

I didn't know it at the time, but as we watch this poor boy being pummeled by the wind, the Interisland ferry Wahine with 734 souls on board is in serious trouble at the entrance to Wellington harbour. More on this soon.

My father stops the car, helps the boy to his feet and bundles him into the back seat along with the rest of us. Now there are five kids in the back of this little Morris Minor. "Great," I think. "Another boy I have to deal with."

My father turns around in the driver's seat. "I'll take you home, lad. Where do you live?" Frank says hello to the boy as apparently they're in the same class at school.

"Did you see that massive tree fall onto the toilet block at school?" Frank asks him.

"Yeah, I did," the boy replies. "We won't be doing Number Ones or Number Twos in there for a while!"

"What are they talking about?" I say to no one in particular.

Mum turns around from the front to see our new passenger looking out the rear windows with round eyes at the mounting destruction being wrought on our neighbourhood. "It's really unsafe out there now," Mum says to him, "but we'll get you home ok. Fences and trees are being blown down everywhere and to make things worse, the power is out all over Petone. Maybe Wellington and the Hutt too. All the shops and schools and factories around here have been closed."

"I hope the power isn't out for too long," my father says worriedly. "I have a ton of work at the factory to do before the Easter break, and only a day and a half to do it in."

My ears prick up at the mention of Easter. "Easter, oh yay!" I say naively. "That means the Easter Bunny will be here soon. I hope he brings me one of those eggs with the chocolate buttons inside!"

"At the rate you're going Scarlet," my mum says, "the Easter Bunny won't be bringing you anything."

I'm really alarmed at this. "Why not, Mum? What have I done?"

"Well, for one thing, your father tells me you've trashed your lovely polka dot dress," Mum replies grumpily.

"Aww ... that was just an accident, Mum. I was painting you a beautiful picture."

Dad looks at me in the rear-view mirror. "I thought that painting was for ... never mind," he smiles.

Suddenly, Mum taps the car window drawing our attention outside. "Look over there – that man is being very kind." We see a man driving a smart Rolls Royce picking up kids that have been forced to walk home, helping them get there safely. "Isn't that amazing?"

"Wow, that *is* amazing," gasps Frank. "Burt, do you see that amazing Rolls Royce? I think it's a Silver Cloud."

Burt's face lights up as he watches the Rolls Royce park up, the man helping some more kids home. "I think you're right Frank – it could be a Rolls Royce Silver Cloud. He must be the richest man in Petone!"

Frank's schoolmate chimes in with a "Wow!" and all three boys follow the Rolls Royce with their eyes as it drives off.

"I've seen that Rolls Royce before ... driving around Petone," Frank says to Burt.

"So have I," replies Burt. "You can't miss it."

"It doesn't look like anything to me," I say.

"That's because you don't know **anything**," says Frank.

I don't reply, I simply dig Frank in his stomach with my elbow as hard as I can, making sure neither Mum nor Dad are looking.

"Aw Mum, Scarlet elbowed me in the guts!" cries Frank.

"Oh you liar, it's just that we're all squashed up in this car," I protest.

I don't know how all four of us kids managed to fit in the back seat of Dad's Morris Minor, let alone squeezing another person in. Back in 1968, we didn't have to wear seat belts, so when the car went around a corner, the person who was at the end of the seat would get squashed by everyone else. It always seemed to be me who got the end seat, so I got squashed a lot.

Mum turns around to face me with a stern look on her face. "Scarlet, I'm warning you. Remember about consequences. We're all trying to get home safely – it's very dangerous out there."

I look over at Frank and he gives me this smarmy look he makes whenever I'm in trouble and he isn't. I just know I'll have to smash him by the end of the day.

We get to Frank's schoolfriend's house and watch him wave to us as he walks safely inside. Mum visibly relaxes in her seat. "He's home ok ... that's a relief."

"That's a relief alright," my 4 year old mind thinks. "Only two boys to deal with now ... and a heck of a lot more room in this back seat."

Dad turns the car around and we head towards our street. I didn't know what Armageddon was back in 1968, but that's how I'd describe what I was seeing if I did. Fences had been blown down and broken up, trees had toppled over and most dangerously of all, bits of corrugated iron were whipping through the air like frisbees.

As we drive slowly down our street, Frank is turning his head this way and that, trying to take in all the carnage outside. "All the fences have been blown over, just like a stack of dominoes!" he says in wonder.

Dad drives the car up our driveway and we see the fence between our house and Matilda's has been blown over and is now lying flat on the ground. "This is great news!" I think looking at the fence in ruins on the ground. "It'll be much easier for me to get to Matilda's house now. I can just walk *over* the fence instead of having to go all the way out to the pavement, down the road and in through her front gate."

Looking up at our house, a part of the roof has started to lift at one corner and this worries Dad. "That roof's a bit of a concern," he says. "The whole thing could get ripped off."

I was far too focused on getting out of my awful dress to be worried about the small matter of our roof being blown off.

Dad opens the back door of our house, and I'm first in. I race to the bedroom I share with Chrystal, barely making it before dumping my polka dot dress right in the middle of the floor and changing into something more comfortable. I can't recall exactly what that was, but what I can say is I never wore the polka dot dress ever again. Maybe even Dad couldn't get the paint stains out.

After I change, I'm so happy! I join the rest of my family who are all sitting quietly around our large kitchen table. I know something is up.

Dad has taken the radio down from its home on the mantelpiece above the coal range and placed it on the table. He switches it on and I hear music playing. "That's 'Communication Breakdown' by Roy Orbison!" says big sister Chrystal.

Roy Orbison – Communication Breakdown

We all listen to the song playing on the radio in silence. For a room usually full of life and fun, the mood is very somber in our kitchen today.

The song finishes and I hear a man talking as though it's a news bulletin. We all move closer to the radio – I don't think I've ever seen my whole family sitting around the radio like this before.

I ask Dad why we're listening to the radio and why we don't just turn the TV on. "Power's out," Dad says sharply. "Only the radio is working. Sssh, Scarlet. Something important is happening."

I don't quite get it all from the commentary on the radio, but I eventually piece it together by listening to what my family is saying. A ship has run aground and capsized on Barrett's Reef at the entrance to Wellington harbour. People are in the water and swimming for their lives.

The ship is the Union Steam Ship Company's roll-on roll-off passenger ferry "Wahine" – a Maori word meaning "Woman." The Wahine's captain made the ill-fated decision to enter the harbour from the open sea in the early hours of the morning, but shortly after got into trouble as Cyclone Giselle suddenly intensified. The ship was sailing blind; it had lost its radar and visibility was very poor. At some point the order was given to drop anchor, and the Wahine drifted up the harbour past Fort Dorset. Eventually, it ran aground on Barrett's Reef and started listing to starboard. Water had flooded the large open vehicle deck and was forcing the ferry further and further to one side.

Despite the Wahine being relatively close to shore and in shallow waters, the extremely bad weather initially made it impossible for rescuers to reach it. By 1:15pm, the vessel was listing alarmingly and the captain gave the order to abandon ship. The extreme list to starboard left the four lifeboats on the port side high and dry and unable to be used. Only the four on the starboard side were launched. One of these capsized shortly after and many people were drowned, including children and elderly passengers.

The crew did their best to get as many passengers as possible into the remaining lifeboats and inflatable life rafts. When these were full, hundreds of passengers and crew were forced to jump into the cold, churning sea and take their chances.

Years later, I heard of a story where a baby was thrown like a basketball by its mother to someone in one of the life rafts. Fortunately, the baby was caught and survived the disaster, as did her mother.

Others weren't so lucky. Some clung onto the inflatable life rafts for as long as they could before being ripped away. Many of these poor people drowned, as did many others trying to swim to either the eastern or western sides of the harbour. Some managed to make it to the rocky eastern side of the channel, south of the little settlement of Eastbourne, only to be dashed to pieces on the rocks.

Reaching the shore on that eastern side still wasn't a guarantee of survival. Many passengers who struggled through the waters to reach the shore alive needed urgent medical attention. But that area south of Eastbourne was largely unpopulated then and it took hours for rescue teams to travel by road – some of it gravel – to get to the survivors. For many it was too late and they succumbed to their injuries or exposure on the shore.

Of the 734 souls on board the Wahine that day, 51 were killed at the time and a further 2 died sometime later.

In the days and weeks that followed what became known as "The Wahine Disaster," many tragic stories were told. Equally however, many stories of heroism, bravery, unselfishness and self-sacrifice came to light. Stories of deliverance were common too.

There was one lady who was in a life raft right next to the hull of the Wahine. She had recently watched the 1953 film "Titanic" which showed rafts and people being dragged under the water as the ship sank. Worrying this would happen to the life raft she was in, the lady pushed hard against the Wahine's hull with her legs and the life raft was propelled out to sea away from the doomed vessel. She later said that when the life raft was being tossed around in the open waters, the visibility was so bad she couldn't see land on either side of the harbour. In fact, she had no idea in which direction the life raft was facing at all. She and her fellow passengers made it safely to shore on the Seatoun side of the channel and was shocked to find how close the Wahine was to land.

Another story surfaced about a man who had been picked out of the water by one of the life rafts. This man was very distraught and told the people who'd saved him he didn't want to be rescued because his wife was gone. But rescued he was and as the man was later walking up the beach having reached shore, he noticed a woman running down the beach towards him. It was his wife.

The capsizing of the Wahine was not New Zealand's first maritime disaster nor was it the last. It wasn't even our worst in terms of lives lost. But the events that unfolded that day were listened to on radio and later watched on TV by Kiwis from Cape Reinga to Bluff. It was perhaps the first disaster to be reported in real time in our young country's history. Film footage was even flown overseas and the disaster was reported all over the world. Here is some of that grainy black and white film from fifty years ago.

YouTube: Wahine footage 1 (13:00)

My family was one of the many thousands of Kiwis who listened to the radio commentary as the disaster was taking place that gloomy April day. We largely listened in silence, looking at each other from time to time, shaking our heads, even sobbing quietly as the scale of what was happening became apparent.

Suddenly, the power comes back on. My father, who seems stunned by what he is hearing, leaps up from the table. "I've got to get back to the factory!" he says impatiently. "The Easter break is coming up and we have lots of deadlines."

I'm distressed at what my father has just said and my bottom lip starts to quiver. "Daddy, where are all the dead Lions?" I whimper. "Were they on that ship?"

Everyone in the room chuckles; it's as if the tension has been relieved a little.

My dad picks me up and cuddles me. "Scarlet, it's coming up to the Easter break and everyone wants their dry-cleaning done by the end of tomorrow. We have tons of overalls from General Motors, Manthel Motors, the Colgate factory, Todd Motors, Gear Meat works and all of it needs to be cleaned and folded and then delivered. Not to mention all the clothes from Mr. and Mrs. Joe Blow that have to be done and then delivered to all the depots in the Hutt and Wellington. Can you believe we even have an Easter bride's wedding dress to be cleaned and pressed along with all the wedding party's clothes? There's so much to do."

My father sighs and turns to Mum. "I really don't know what time I'll be home. Looks like we'll be working all night." He leaves reluctantly taking Burt with him who has volunteered to help him at the factory for a bit of extra pocket money.

As Dad and Burt walk out the door, I realise I'm still none the wiser as to where all the dead Lions are.

Nobody *ever* gave me a straight answer when I was a kid.

🦌 🦌 🦌

It's funny how memories work. I can remember a lot of the events of the day the Wahine capsized, but next to nothing of the day before, the day after or the day after that.

As I'm writing this story of Me aged 4, I'm really quite embarrassed by my behaviour that day. I acted like a spoiled brat especially when it came to the white dress with blue polka dots. All I was concerned about was getting home so I could get changed while hundreds of people were fighting for their lives in the rough seas of Wellington harbour.

Every year on April 10th, I walk from my house down to the Wahine Memorial Park located not far from where survivors of the disaster were washed ashore at Seatoun. Part of the Wahine's anchor chain is there, at rest now for almost fifty years.

I then quietly stand at the end of the Seatoun wharf where I toss some freshly picked rosemary – long associated with remembrance and death – into the shallow waters.

YouTube: Dronie @ Seatoun in Wellington (0:33)

As I watch the rosemary drift away, I remember all of the passengers aboard the Wahine on the 10th of April 1968 and in particular those who perished only meters from where I stand. I hope they are at peace now.

I also can't help but remember that 4 year old brat and the white dress with blue polka dots.

7

The Tea Lady

Movement in the doorway of her hospital room caught Scarlet's attention and she looked up from her laptop to see a tea trolley being pushed towards her.

"Hi Scarlet!" the tea lady said in a friendly voice. "Could I interest you in a cup of tea and a biscuit this morning?"

Scarlet looked thoughtful as she closed her laptop and placed it to one side.

"Actually ... have you got a Griffin's Gingernut? And a glass of milk if that's not too much trouble?"

"A Gingernut biscuit eh," the tea lady smiled brightly. "I have a packet of those here somewhere ... yes, here they are. Good choice Scarlet! Gingernuts and milk are a perfect combo! In fact, Gingernuts are Kiwi's favourite biscuit."

"Yes, I know that," Scarlet replied. "I also know the Griffin's company was founded in Nelson in 1864 ... at the same time as the Americans were fighting their Civil War."

The tea lady stopped what she was doing and looked at Scarlet in surprise. "Wow – I didn't know that one! Are you starting to remember things?"

"Nah, I just read it in my book!" Scarlet said playfully.

"What book is that then?" the tea lady asked, pouring Scarlet's glass of milk. "A history book about New Zealand?"

"No, it's not a history book. There *are* stories about the history of New Zealand in it, but it's actually a book I wrote about my life before my head injury ... before I lost my memory. I'm reading it now and learning all about my past ... and about New Zealand."

"That's incredible!" the tea lady said excitedly. "What made you write a book about your life?"

"Looks like a ghost told me to," Scarlet replied. "That's what I'm getting from the book at least."

"A ghost?!" the tea lady exclaimed, a shocked expression on her face. "Whoa! That's a bit Twilight Zone isn't it?"

"If by that you mean 'strange,' then you can say that again!" Scarlet said a little unsurely. "Anyway, this book has all sorts of stuff in it. I've just been reading about the history of my family and the Wahine disaster and now I'm up to Me aged 5 in 1969. That's how I got the idea to have a Gingernut biscuit with a glass of milk."

"All I can say is you're lucky you wrote that book Scarlet, whether a ghost told you to do it or not! I wonder what you'll get up to as a teenager ... reading your book will be like filling in a blank slate eh?! Anyhow, I'd better get cracking on. See you this arvo, ok?"

Scarlet thanked the tea lady, dunked her Gingernut in the glass of milk and held it in for a few seconds before taking a bite.

"Oh, that *is* yum!" she thought.

Retrieving her laptop from the bed, she opened it and found her place in her book. "That nice lady was right, this *is* like filling in a blank slate," Scarlet said out loud. "I wonder what I got up to as a teenager as well ... "

8

1969

started school as a 5 year old as most Kiwi kids do. School years in New Zealand start at the beginning of a calendar year right after the Christmas holidays, usually in late January or early February. As my fifth birthday was in December 1968, I started school at Petone Central School at the beginning of the new school year in January 1969. Nowadays that first year is called Year One, but in my day it was called Primer One.

What a great first day I had – I remember it vividly. I was playing with some older kids in the playground at lunchtime and the subject of Christmas came up. "What presents did you get for Christmas?" the older kids asked me.

"Well ... Santa brought me ..." I started to reply. Before I could finish my sentence, an older boy butted in. "What a baby! She still thinks Santa is real!" Everyone started laughing ... but I wasn't. I couldn't believe what I was hearing. Of course Santa was real, you *idiots*. It was obviously Santa who gave us our presents; it was Santa who filled up our stockings; it was Santa who drank the glass of beer we left out for him on Christmas Eve. Wasn't it?

Doubt began to creep into my mind. What if the older kids were right? I suddenly became dizzy with the implications of that possibility – however remote – and I had to sit down on the ground.

Growing up with two older brothers, I knew how to put on a brave face when something hurtful was said to me so they couldn't tell they'd upset me. I stood up, faced the older kids and said defiantly, "Santa is *so* real. I don't care what you think!" I stomped off as one of the older girls called out after me. "Ask your mother then if you don't believe us!"

With the sound of their laughter still ringing in my ears, I strode off. I didn't want to give them the satisfaction of knowing I'd heard them, but I remember thinking to myself, "I'll ask my mother alright, don't you worry!"

I couldn't wait to get home from school that first day. I ran all the way, which is no big deal really as my school was only around the corner from my house. I'm a fourth child, so I had no mother standing outside my classroom waiting for school to finish like some other kids did. Mum had walked with me to school that first morning, but she told me I was to run home by myself as soon as school finished. So that's what I did. I burst into the kitchen where I found Mum calmly sitting at the table with a cup of tea having just returned home from work. How could she be sitting there so calmly if it was true Santa didn't exist?

"Mum!" I blurted out before she could say anything. "Mum ... the big kids at school said Santa Claus isn't real and made fun of me for saying he was. He is real, isn't he Mum! Isn't he?"

Now, before I tell you what my mother said in reply to this, you need to understand something. My mum was a pretty busy person. She worked five hours a day at the Wills factory, had the house to manage, the dinners to make and probably the most time-consuming job of all, four kids to look after. And a husband to organise. I was the fourth out of four kids Mum had raised at that point. I look at it like this; the first child, he or she gets all the attention from doting mums and dads – it's a given, they're the firstborn. The second child is still pretty special and gets molly-coddled a fair bit. Even the third child is indulged to a certain extent. But that seems to be the limit. By the time the fourth child comes along, parents have been there and done that and I think they're a bit over it.

I'm not saying for a moment I wasn't loved as much as my siblings – of course I was. And I'm not complaining either; I loved being Mum and Dad's fourth child and all the experiences that brought me.

With that in mind, back to my question about Santa Claus. "He is real, isn't he Mum! Isn't he?"

Mum looked at me over the top of her cup of tea. "Those kids are right Scarlet," she said matter-of-factly. "There is no such person as Santa. He isn't real."

My mother had probably been asked that question on at least three separate occasions in the past and I think she was tired of perpetuating the Santa myth and everything that went with it.

I stood where I was, incapable of movement, looking disbelievingly at my mother and feeling like someone had just whacked me over the head with a piece of 4 by 2. This couldn't be happening! "Where is Snoopy?" I thought. "I need a cuddle with Snoopy!"

Christmas presents for me growing up in Petone in a not-so-well-off family meant a collection of Summer fruit in a brown paper bag, perhaps some plums and cherries, and a few lollies thrown in for good measure, all arranged decoratively at the end of my bed. There would also be a small gift from Santa under the tree in the lounge. All the same, I loved Christmas and all its trappings and I was absolutely devastated to find out, as a 5 year old on my first day at school ever, that Santa Claus wasn't real.

Looking back now, I wonder whether my mother couldn't have – well – told me some believable untruth and played along with the Santa thing for a few more years?

I eventually found Snoopy and we had the biggest cuddle together. I'm sure he felt the whole thing wasn't entirely fair as well.

🦌 🦌 🦌

Not long after I started school, my class went on a field trip to the General Motors plant in Petone. At that time, the factory assembled car brands such as Chevrolet and Pontiac, but it is probably best known for the Holden range.

I didn't know this at the time of course. To me then, a car was a car was a car. But when we arrived at the massive plant I suddenly remembered the day the Wahine went down and recalled Frank and his schoolfriend gushing about the Rolls Royce Silver Cloud they'd seen.

When the guy who was showing us around the factory asked if there were any questions, I put my hand up and in front of my whole class asked forthrightly, "Do you make Rolls Royce cars here?" The man laughed and laughed and soon my whole class was laughing. I bet they didn't have a clue why he was laughing. Nor did I really, so I just laughed too.

༄ ༄ ༄

The thing I liked the most about going to school were the breaks, morning and afternoon tea and lunchtime, as this was when I could go and play in the playground. I loved mucking around on the monkey bars and jungle gym in particular.

Nowadays, monkey bars and other bits of playground gear are designed with safety features such as soft ground padding. Back in my day, the only padding underneath the monkey bars was concrete. I recall many cases of kids falling off the bars resulting in grazes, twisted ankles and even some broken bones. I had my fair share of accidents, but I never got badly hurt; a few grazes and bruises were the worst injuries I suffered – I never broke anything thankfully.

There was a boy at my school called Digby who wasn't so lucky. He was quite good on the monkey bars and I remember him practising a manoeuvre which would start with him hanging from the bar upside down by the back of his knees. He'd then start swinging, a little at first, then more and more, higher and higher, swinging and gaining speed before releasing, executing a flip and ... bang! ... landing perfectly upright with both feet planted on the ground. This boy was what we kids back then called a "bighead," as he was always showing off. For example, when he'd completed the monkey bar trick and nailed the landing, he'd hold both arms outstretched to the heavens with a flourish, just like gymnasts do.

I remember looking at him and thinking, "Show off!"

I'd seen Digby complete his trick a few times when there were only a couple of kids around, but the day came when he felt he was finally ready to show it off to the world. This day, he rounded up as many kids as he could calling out, "Hey everyone, come and watch this trick I can do." Just like the Pied Piper, he led a bunch of kids to the monkey bars; kids of all ages flocked to his call and eagerly followed him, from the very young ones who were cuddling their teddies and stuffed toys for reassurance through to older kids.

Like the bighead he was, Digby stood in silence in front of the monkey bars and started breathing deeply. He then straightened his shoulders, cracked his knuckles for one last effect and then climbed onto the bars. With great showmanship, he leaned backwards and was now hanging upside down on the bar; at this there was an audible collective intake of breath from the kids watching on. As Digby started swinging, it was too much for some of the audience as they half covered their faces with their hands, or looked away briefly, only to be drawn back as Digby continued to swing backwards and forwards, higher ... faster ... higher ... faster ... until suddenly ... release ... flip and ... bang! Digby landed perfectly ... perfectly flat on his face on the ground. He couldn't have been flatter if he was a pancake run over by a steamroller.

Digby rolled over on the ground, slowly got up on his knees, groaned and held his nose from which blood was gushing in spurts. It ran down his face and onto his immaculately cleaned and pressed white shirt. Pandemonium ensued. Kids started screaming. Some cried out "Oh no!" or "Teacher, teacher come quickly," or simply "Aaaaaahhhh!!" Some of the younger kids were rooted to the spot, mouthing words but unable to speak, watching Digby with a look of horror on their faces as they patted and stroked their stuffed toys for comfort.

I couldn't believe what I was seeing and remember cocking my head to one side and thinking, "Digby's nose looks a little off." It turned out that Digby's nose had been broken. Fortunately, nothing else had and he was back at school the next day. He was still the bighead he was before, but he no longer played on the monkey bars.

❣ ❣ ❣

Apart from the Santa Claus debacle on my first day at school, my most vivid memory from Primer One took place on July 21st 1969, New Zealand time.

Just after morning tea time that Monday, the teacher of my Primer One class took us all outside to one of the concrete play areas. We had no idea what was going on. Only one of the defining events of the 20th century as it turned out.

I remember it was a fresh but clear Winter's day. My teacher pointed to the sky and spoke with as much gravitas as she could. "This is a very important day children. For the first time in history, there are men up there ... on the Moon." We all went "oooh" and "aaah" but I don't think as 5 year olds we really grasped the significance of the occasion.

Everyone was making a big deal out of it though. Even Mum and Dad made all us kids sit down in front of our black and white television that evening to watch the news. First story up was grainy footage of Lunar Module *Eagle* on the Moon and Neil Armstrong stepping down the ladder onto the surface saying those famous words, "That's one small step for [a] man, one giant leap for mankind."

YouTube: First Moon Landing: NASA Releases New Video
(1:52)

I clearly remember there was some white text on the TV screen flashing on and off saying something like "Live from the Moon." I learned as a teenager that the landing had actually taken place on the morning of July 21st our time and the footage we were watching that evening had only just reached New Zealand having been flown in from Australia. I felt a little ripped off when I found this out; up to that point in my life I thought I'd actually witnessed the first Human Beings ever walking on the Moon, *live*.

The news story must have made an impression on me. I remember going outside to our spider infested open-air external toilet as part of my bedtime routine that night and looking up at the Moon.

Two things went through my mind. First, I wondered why I couldn't see the men walking around on the Moon. After all, the Moon was so small and men were so big.

Secondly, I was grateful for the first time ever that our loo was outside, so I could gaze up at the Moon as I was having a pee.

1970

On to the 70s, one of my favourite decades.

Learning what the 60s were like in later years, there must have been some pretty outrageous parties on New Year's eve 1969. You've probably heard the quote "If you can remember the 60s, you weren't really there." I can't recall much about the 60s in general, and have absolutely no memory of that last night of the decade in particular. But I had only just turned 6.

I was now in my second year of Primary School. As usual, the school year started after the Christmas holidays and I found I had the good fortune to be in the same class as Digby. One day, he was proudly showing off his collection of Matchbox cars to all the boys and girls in the classroom who would listen.

I watched Digby as he played. "My brother Frank has cars like that," I said innocently.

Eventually, the other kids drifted away. Digby waited until they'd all gone, then looked me straight in the eye. "You'd better steal one of your brother's cars and bring it to me tomorrow or I'll give you a hiding after school," he said menacingly.

I looked straight back at Digby. "You want me to steal one of my brother's cars from his collection and give it to you. Is that right?"

"Yeah Scarlet, that's right!" Digby replied with a mean look on his face.

"Have you seen the size of my brother, Digby? He goes to this school you know."

Digby's eyes grew wide. He never mentioned Frank's Matchbox cars to me again, but I don't think he got the message long term. Last time I heard, Digby was serving a stretch in jail for stealing real cars.

🐾 🐾 🐾

My next memory is not a good one.

It must have been around July or August as it was frosty cold in the mornings – unusually so for Petone. I remember walking past the clothesline on my way to school and all the washing left out overnight had frozen solid. For some reason, I specifically remember it was a Monday.

When I arrived at school, I noticed one of my friends, a little girl called Tui, had bruises and welts up and down her legs. Of course I asked her what had happened. I was only 6 at the time, but Tui answered in a way that gave me the distinct impression this wasn't the first time this had happened to her. She told me her stepfather had been in a really bad mood after some rugby league game had been lost. This guy got a golf club out and gave her a hiding with it.

I visualised what had happened to her as Tui was telling me the story and I felt sick to my stomach. I felt so badly for this little girl who was in such a mess. Not long after this, my teacher saw Tui's injuries and she was taken out of our classroom. I found it difficult to concentrate on my work that day, thinking about her and where she'd gone.

There is some good news to this story. Tui never came to school looking like that again. A little later she told me in hushed tones that her *whanau* [extended family] had dealt to her stepfather in their own way. He didn't live with Tui and her mum anymore. I can only imagine how happy Tui felt about this; I was over the Moon and gave her a big hug.

🐾 🐾 🐾

After the experience with Tui, and all the way through my formative years, I felt very lucky that my parents never used physical violence on us kids. The worst punishment I'd ever get – usually after I smashed my brother Frank – was to be sent to my bedroom with the light switched off. I was scared of the dark when I was younger and my bedroom was pretty dark at the best of times, even during the day. I couldn't reach the light switch when I was little, so the worst I could do was scream the house down until Mum eventually let me out. I found I could scream for a very long time.

When my mother rescued me from my time-out, she'd always say, "Scarlet, you're not allowed to hit your brother ... you hurt him you know. Go and say you're sorry." Which I would, knowing full well I'd hit Frank even harder the next time he annoyed me. Tell-tale!

Sometime during my sixth year I realised I could reach the light switch in my bedroom, so my mother had to find somewhere else to use as time-out. She found the back doorstep was quite dark so she'd put me there whenever I was naughty – which was quite a bit. I actually didn't mind that particular spot as a punishment because at night-time light came through the kitchen window which ruined the effect my mother was after. I was quite happy to look up at the stars and make wishes. One night, I remember wishing on a star that I could be as beautiful as my big sister Chrystal when I grew up.

There was another punishment my mother would use when I was naughty, and I think a lot of people can relate to this one. "Scarlet!" she would say in a loud voice. "Just you wait until your father gets home!"

This was the best punishment I could get for whacking big brother Frank. When my father *did* get home, he'd walk up the driveway and see me sitting on the back doorstep. If I saw him early enough, I'm sure I'd see the start of a smile on his face. He would come over to me, all the while trying hard to keep a straight face. "Scarlet, have you been hurting your brother again?" he'd ask.

I'd stand up, push all of my blonde curly hair away from my face, put my hands on my hips and look up at him. "Well, yes I did, but *he* started it!" I'd reply.

Dad would try not to laugh. "That may well be the case," he'd say kindly, "but you're not to hurt your brother anymore, ok?" He would then shut the outside door and walk into the kitchen leaving me on the doorstep – I knew I wasn't allowed back inside until I got the all clear from Mum. Next, I'd hear Mum and Dad talking inside and if I put my ear right up to the door, I could make out what they were saying.

"Did you tell Scarlet off?" my mum would say.

"Of course I did," Dad would reply, followed by a few seconds of silence. "Oh, alright, no I didn't. How am I supposed to tell that sweet little girl off?"

"That 'sweet little girl,'" Mum would reply in a mocking tone, "is a baby-faced assassin. She's always lashing out at her brother and she really hurts him!"

My father would then come back outside and give me a pretend telling-off, saying in a half-hearted playful way, "Scarlet, you are a ... *very ... naughty ... girl*!" He would always have to turn around and walk off quickly so I couldn't see him crack up with laughter.

There was something in the way Dad spoke to me on those occasions that made me think he was impressed I stood up to my older brother as I did. I felt some sort of tacit approval from him that I didn't take any rubbish from Frank.

At some level though, part of me knew it wasn't right to hit Frank. But I had all this energy inside me that I had to let out somehow.

My brother Frank and I are the closest siblings in terms of age; maybe that's why we had so many fights compared to my other brother and sisters. But we were very close also – and still are – and had loads of good times together. Many more good times than bad.

Frank and I both loved the music of the late 60s and early 70s. Because Frank worked a bit at the dry-cleaning factory after school, he earned a little money – enough to buy the odd record. In 1970 he bought his first 45 single. We would put this single on the family stereo in the living room and sing our hearts out to it over and over again. We must have driven everyone mad! Frank has a great singing voice and to this day he and I still sing along to this song.

The Mike Curb Congregation – Burning Bridges

There is an interesting Kiwi – and Wellington – connection to the song "Burning Bridges." Pretty much everyone who lived in New Zealand in the 1970s and 1980s have heard of the "20 Solid Gold Hits" series of compilation LPs. The first came out in 1972 and over the next ten years, more than thirty records in the series were made. Ask any Kiwi old enough and you'll probably find at least one of these records in their collection.

The idea behind them was the brainchild of a guy by the name of John McCready who was then manager of Philips Records in New Zealand. He looked over the Tasman and saw the success K-Tel was enjoying in Australia by marketing compilation records using television advertising and he wanted to do the same here in New Zealand. As television advertising didn't come cheap, he worked out a record would break even if it sold 30,000 copies. 50,000 copies would generate a healthy profit.

Taking a huge risk, he ordered a pressing of 30,000 copies of the first 20 Solid Gold Hits compilation LP and nervously visited the major record outlets in Wellington on the Friday night it was released. His first stop was the James Smith record bar in Cuba Street where he saw crowds of people waiting to be served at the counter. They were all buying 20 Solid Gold Hits. That record went on to sell 90,000 copies, and a Kiwi icon was born.

Guess what song was Track 1, Side 1? Frank's favourite song, Burning Bridges by The Mike Curb Congregation.

۴ ۴ ۴

One day at school straight after lunchtime, my classmates and I filed back into our classroom to find our teacher already standing at the front of the room. Once we'd all sat down at our desks, she informed us we'd be doing art for the rest of the day. Some of the kids less enamoured with art – like Digby – let out a little groan. I could all too easily hear their thoughts: "No way ... two hours of art?!" Add in that our teacher was a bit of a Dragon Lady and I'm not sure there were many of us kids who were looking forward to what the afternoon would bring.

In lofty tones, our teacher then proceeded to give us instructions as to the sort of painting she wanted us to draw. As it was straight after lunch, and I was full of honey sandwiches, I must have zoned out momentarily as our teacher gave us the all-important briefing about the particular type of painting she was after. I zoned back in only in time to hear the teacher say with a flourish, "Alright children ... off with your paintings!"

Rather than risk looking dumb and asking the teacher to repeat what she'd asked us to do, I thought I'd say nothing and try to work it out from what the other kids were drawing. Having sneaked a look at a couple of my classmates' work, I thought I'd figured it out and started on my own painting with zeal.

After half an hour or so, the teacher started walking around our tables, stopping to give suggestions or words of encouragement. I thought my painting was coming along swimmingly and I'd receive my fair share of praise – just as the teacher stopped at my desk and inspected my work. I remember looking up at my teacher with a smile on my face, only to see her scowling angrily down at me. "Uh-oh," I thought. "Maybe I haven't picked the right subject after all."

This was confirmed very soon after. "Come with me, Scarlet Giesen!" my teacher said brusquely. I knew from experience that when teachers used your whole name, you were definitely in trouble.

The teacher grabbed my unfinished painting and, turning on her heel, strode purposefully to the front of the class. I followed from what I thought was a respectful distance behind.

"Attention children ... attention please," the teacher said dramatically when I'd joined her at the front of the class. "Put down what you are doing and face the front, *now*!" When she was sure every single child was focussed on her and her alone, the teacher suddenly produced my painting from its hiding place behind her back and held it up high above her head for maximum effect.

"Look at this painting, children. Just look at what this ... this ... *idiot* is drawing. This is a prime example of what happens when someone doesn't listen to instructions."

The teacher didn't expand further, so I was still in the dark as to what I should actually have been drawing. Many of the kids in my class were sniggering and of course it was Digby who was sniggering the loudest. But to their credit, a fair number didn't betray any reaction. Perhaps they were thinking it could very well be them up there next time. Perhaps they'd been humiliated in a similar manner once before.

And humiliated I was, having to stand in front of my peers and watch them laughing at me because of heaven knows what. That wasn't the end of it though, oh no. My teacher had a gift for the dramatic and sent me to one of the far corners of the classroom to stand looking at the walls for the rest of the afternoon. I initially felt very ashamed standing in the corner looking at nothing but the drab cream of the walls. My shame quickly turned to disappointment; I became upset because I actually enjoyed art – especially painting.

This incident has obviously left its mark on me as I can still remember a lot of detail about that afternoon. I even remember crying all the way home from school at the end of the day, only wiping my eyes when I walked up the driveway so no one in my family could see I'd been upset.

Not paying attention to the teacher would become a recurring theme for me throughout my schooling. I think I eventually got the hang of it though – towards the end of my time at High School.

To this day, I still don't have the faintest clue what my painting *should* have been about.

❧ ❧ ❧

I have an even worse memory from around this time … or should I say, a *series* of even worse memories.

The bedroom my big sister Chrystal and I shared was at the front of our house, pretty much right on the street. Our bedroom was across the hall from the bedroom shared by Frank and Burt, also on the street front.

Quite often in the weekends, our usually quiet little street in quiet little Petone would come alive with someone hosting a not-so-quiet party. Chrystal and I would hear, and feel, the all-too-familiar "doof doof doof" bass sound as someone's stereo a few doors away was cranked up to the max.

Sometimes, late in the night or early morning, these parties would spill out into the street and end up in a brawl – it sounded like it was happening right outside our bedroom window. I found these fights really scary and upsetting and I'd climb under Chrystal's bed with a blanket. I'd stay there until the police turned up to calm things down.

I'd climb *under* Chrystal's bed because somehow my beautiful sister could manage to sleep through the whole thing; raised voices, then shouting, then fight, then police sirens, the lot. When I'd speak about it next day, she'd be blissfully unaware that anything untoward had happened. I wished I could be like that, as did Frank and Burt who would witness the whole thing from their bedroom also.

Sometimes the brawls were exceptionally violent. If you've ever seen the final fight scene in the Kiwi movie "Once Were Warriors," the one between Jake the Mus and Uncle Bully, you've got the idea.

❦ ❦ ❦

Those fights were pretty scary, but there was one thing scarier than that to me aged 6; Matilda's eccentric grandmother who lived next door.

She was the one always pointing her walking stick at me and saying in a big scary voice, "Scarlet, watch out for the spirits." She was also forever asking me if I could help her find something the Trolls had either taken or hidden. I'd try and help her find whatever it was she'd lost this time and I couldn't help but think she was absolutely bonkers. She told me there were Trolls all over the place and as a 6 year old I believed her. Every time I was over at Matilda's house I found myself looking here and there, peeping out of the corner of my eye, wondering whether I'd catch a glimpse of a Troll. I did want to see one, but at the same time I didn't.

Spoiler alert: I never did.

Apart from the Trolls, there was one other thing Matilda's eccentric old grandmother used to talk to me about whenever she saw me. She would tell me about her famous relation who was a Hollywood movie star. It must have been around 1970 she told me he had a major part in a 1965 movie called "The Greatest Story Ever Told." It was quite a few years later before I got to see that movie on TV and sure enough, there he was. Matilda's grandmother was very proud of this relation, as was the rest of her family. Over the years either Matilda's grandmother, or Matilda's mother, or Matilda herself would tell me about every one of the movies their relation was in. Sometimes all three would tell me on separate occasions, but I didn't mind. I liked that they were proud of him and I'd celebrate his successes along with them.

I thought Matilda was lucky as she had two living grandmothers, even if the one that lived with her was bonkers. I only had the one living grandparent when I was growing up and that was my father's mother. I called her Nana. My Nana was a very kind lady and I loved staying at her house which wasn't far from ours. She had a huge Grandfather Clock in the hallway, the type that would chime every quarter of an hour. The chime was a little different each fifteen minutes so you always knew what time it was. She would wind the clock up every Sunday lunchtime with a special key and even from a young age she'd let me wind it up if I was around. That made me feel very important!

In the weekends, Matilda and I would sometimes go to the movies together. The Petone State Picture Theatre wasn't far from my house and we'd walk there together to watch the Saturday matinee. I remember it cost 15 cents for admission to the movie and for a further 5 cents I'd buy some lollies. My parents always seemed to manage to rustle up the money for me whenever I wanted to go – maybe it was nice for them not to have me around for a couple of hours on a Saturday afternoon; I could be a bit of a handful sometimes.

I can clearly remember when – shock, horror, scandal – the price of admission went up to 20 cents; my mother complained bitterly about this price rise and that for 20 cents we "should be served a lunch as well." This price hike was bad for me as I didn't always get the extra 5 cents for lollies. If not, my awesome friend Matilda would share her sweets with me.

She and I would pay our admission, buy our lollies and excitedly take the seats the usher led us to with a torch. The Petone State was a movie theatre in the grand old style; it had an ornate ceiling and huge, thick curtains hung over the screen which would open dramatically as the movie was starting.

Then as now, New Zealand is a member state of the Commonwealth of Nations, previously known as the British Commonwealth. Most of the 53 states that currently comprise the Commonwealth were once territories of the British Empire. When I was young, movie theatres would play "God Save the Queen" before a movie started, and everyone was expected to stand and sing the first verse of the anthem.

It seems so quaint now – that tradition is long gone. Here is the verse I remember singing along with everyone else before those huge, thick curtains would open to reveal the day's excitement.

YouTube: God Save the Queen – 85th birthday of HM, Queen Elizabeth II at Westminster Abbey (2:20)

Matilda and I would dutifully stand to attention and sing God Save the Queen at the top of our lungs. We learned very early on not to start on our lollies until *after* we'd sung the anthem as we found it was quite hard to sing with a mouthful of sweets.

❦ ❦ ❦

One day, for a special treat, my father took me into Wellington city on the train to see a movie at the Embassy Picture Theatre. This theatre is at the end of Courtenay Place which is a fair walk from the Wellington Train Station. I had possibly been to the city before, but this was the first memory I have of walking through the city streets, looking up at all the impossibly tall buildings along our route. My father called them "sky scrapers" and they really did seem to me to touch the sky. I remember looking up and seeing the clouds race past the buildings and it seemed for all the World that they were actually standing still and it was me that was moving.

We arrived at the theatre and for a special, special treat, my dad bought us both ice creams *and* a box of Jaffas to share. As we took them into the theatre and found our seats, I really did feel like the Bees Knees. God Save the Queen came through the speakers, so Dad and I stood up and sang as usual. When the film started, I was absolutely blown away, particularly with all the vibrant colours in the movie. It was hands down the most amazing film I'd seen up to that point and for some years after. It made a massive impression on me and I raved on about it for days to Matilda. I think she got sick of me going on about it until she finally saw it and was blown away too. It was great once she'd seen the movie as well, as we could rave on about it to each other after that.

I loved this movie so much. It had everything; strange creatures, singing, dancing, and best of all, Mama Cass. The movie was, of course, "Pufnstuf."

Mama Cass Elliot – Different

I'll never forget the day my dad and I went to the city on a train, saw those incredibly tall buildings and then that amazing film. It was a perfect, hot, clear day so it must have been towards the end of the year. It's true the movie was awesome, but the thing I remember most about that day was spending some quality time with my father. He was a really busy guy after all what with being a member of the Petone Working Men's Club **and** the Petone Rugby Football Club.

🐾 🐾 🐾

Even though my mother had a lot on her hands when I was young, she was very generous with the small amount of time she had for herself. She was always taking me to feed the Ducks at Percy's Reserve, or pushing me on the swings at one or other of the many playgrounds around Petone, or taking me on some other outing. Sometimes we simply stayed at home and baked a recipe together out of that Kiwi icon, the Edmonds Cookbook.

On hot Summer days, Mum would take all of us kids swimming down at Petone beach. I remember one occasion in particular when I was swimming in the sea and Frank started shouting, "Scarlet ... shark ... shark!!" from the beach at the top of his lungs. He reckoned he'd never seen me move so fast as I rushed out of the water and hurried back to the safety of the shore, only to find Frank cracking up laughing at his hilarious "joke." Even Big Sister Chrystal and Mum had a giggle at that one.

"Brothers!" I thought with disdain as I chased Frank up the beach so I could smash him a good one.

"*SCAR ... LET!!*" yelled Mum after us, knowing I was determined to thump Frank.

𝓮 𝓮 𝓮

My last memories from 1970 are from Petone Central School. Right before Primer Two had ended, I was reading a book called "The Hungry Lambs." It was from a series of books that included "The Stars in the Sky," "Boat Day" and "The Donkey's Egg." But if you were up to "The Hungry Lambs," you knew you'd made it on the reading front!

Then there was the Petone Central School end-of-year play. I'd been entrusted with a major role, a role my teacher told me could not *possibly* be performed by anyone else. It was a tree. It wasn't to be *any* old tree mind you; I played the *only* tree. I had no lines to speak, but I did have to shake my arms – or should I say "branches" – around a bit at pivotal points in the story.

Afterwards, my parents told me I'd been a "super amazing" tree, the best performance of a tree they'd ever seen.

I was stoked!

10

1971

I'm now in my third year of Primary School.

Back in the day, the first two school years were called Primer One and Primer Two. By the third year, I'd started in the "Standards;" Standard One through to Standard Four. After that it would be goodbye Primary School and on to two years at Intermediate School. Following that, five years at High School.

As usual, I celebrated my birthday during the Christmas school holidays. Now a 7 year old, it was my job after school every day to pick up the two loaves of fresh bread my mother had pre-ordered and paid for at a dairy in Jackson Street, the main street of Petone. My family would go through two loaves of bread a day with no trouble at all.

There was a menswear shop next door to the dairy that was owned and run by an ex-All Black by the name of Bob Scott. I would pick up the bread from the dairy, and then pop into Bob's store to say hello to him and his assistant, a young guy called Andy Leslie who would go on to successfully captain the All Blacks a couple of years later.

Many still consider Bob Scott to be one of the greatest All Black fullbacks of all time. At the time, I had no idea how famous he was and the high regard in which he was held. I just knew him as "Bob," a lovely man who always made time to talk to me. I had first met him through my father who had deep connections with Petone rugby.

Although rugby was well settled as the Kiwi National Pastime by the early 1970s, it would be another two and a half decades before the sport turned professional. Every one of the All Blacks back then had day jobs and had to earn a living on top of training and playing what is an extremely demanding sport. Bob and Andy worked in a store. Many All Blacks were farmers. I know of at least one who was a doctor, another a dentist, another a policeman. They all did what they had to do in between representing our country at rugby at the highest level around the world.

One last thing about Bob Scott. At the time of his death in 2012, Bob was then the oldest living All Black; he was 91. It's fitting his mantle then passed to long-time friend Wally Argus who was also 91 years old. Each was the Best Man at each other's wedding. Isn't that amazing?

Rest in peace Bob Scott, you were always so lovely to me.

YouTube: All Blacks Hall of Fame: Bob Scott (1:48)

After visiting Bob and Andy, I'd walk down Jackson Street and window shop. I was particularly interested in the clothing stores. There was one clothing shop in Petone that sold jeans and I would stand outside the window display for ages and dream of owning a pair of Levi's. Once I even plucked up enough courage to walk into the shop and look at the price tag of the women's jeans displayed in the window. If I remember rightly, it read "$30."

I really didn't have any conception of how much that was, so when I got home, I matter-of-factly told my mum what I'd been up to and that I wanted a $30 pair of jeans.

Seriously, I thought Mum was going to have a fit! Initially she couldn't talk at all and then could only manage "30 bucks, 30 bucks, *only* 30 bucks?!" When she had recovered sufficiently and regained the power of normal speech, she explained to me that $30 was a lot of money – for that she could put food on the table for a family of six for a whole week and still have something left over for the power and telephone bills.

The Home Economics thing went over my head a little, but what I did take out of what Mum was saying was there was no way I was going to get that pair of Levi's. All I could do was to continue wearing my cousins hand-me-downs. It was lovely she gave those clothes to me, but there definitely were outfits I liked better than others.

Carrying on with my after-school routine, I'd place the bread I'd brought home on the kitchen table and then run across the road as fast as I could to Dad's factory to find Queenie. When I found her, she would get me to climb on a bench behind her work station, ask about my day and get me to sing to her. Well, she *usually* asked me to sing to her; if she didn't, I'd sing anyway.

Queenie was a Maori lady who lived not far from the factory. From as far back as I can remember, she was like a second mother to me and I absolutely adored her. She'd often tell me stories about the Maori myths and legends; about Ranginui the Sky Father, Papatuanuku the Earth Mother, Tane the God of the Forest and Tangaroa the God of the Sea. Her stories absolutely fascinated me and in hindsight were one of my first glimpses into the realm of the supernatural.

Queenie was an amazing woman by any standard. She was well-respected not only in the factory but in the Petone community as well. If Queenie said something, everyone listened. She was one of my dad's most trusted employees and because of this, she was solely in charge of cleaning and pressing all of the most expensive clothes; top end suits, ball gowns that sort of thing. Not only that, but she was the only person my dad trusted with the repairs of the most expensive items of clothing.

Sometimes for a laugh, Queenie would put one of those beautiful ball gowns up against me as I was sitting on the bench behind her. She would turn her head slightly to one side and say, "Hmmm, what do you think of this dress, girl?"

To me, they were all beautiful and I quickly realised they probably cost a little bit more than $30. "Wow ... this dress is amazing, Queenie!" I would say.

"Scarlet, I know things you know," Queenie said mysteriously one day. "I bet you'll own a beautiful dress like this one day eh? Many beautiful dresses actually."

"I'd just be happy with a pair of Levi's!" I replied.

Queenie and I laughed and this became something of a catch phrase between us.

Queenie would always look at the labels of the clothes she was working on to see who the designer was, and every once in a while you'd hear her say, "Ah," or "Oh," or "A-ha!" She was always really on to it. The names on the labels she read out to me didn't mean much at the time though – I wish I could remember those names today. But there was only one item of clothing and one label I was interested in right then; the item was a pair of $30 jeans and the label was Levi's.

I loved mucking around with Queenie. I'd sing songs to her while she was working away at a massive press that let off clouds of hot steam. There was always loads of steam in the factory and it was permanently hot and humid in there regardless of the time of year. In the Summertime, the workers would open all the windows and doors to get a bit of a draught through the place.

🐜 🐜 🐜

Queenie was very dear to me and there was something I'd wanted to do for her for a while; I wanted to sing a song for her. Not like I had in the past, singing in a quiet and small way. I wanted to really open up and sing from the heart powerfully and with passion.

I'd already chosen the perfect song to sing. One of my father's favourite artists was Cilla Black, the songbird from Liverpool. Mum and Dad loved Cilla and had quite a few of her records. Cilla's TV show was a feature of Sunday night television in New Zealand in the early

1970s and my parents would faithfully tune into it on our black and white television set every week.

We Kiwis didn't have much choice as to TV viewing back then. From the early 1960s to 1975, our fabulous country at the bottom of the world could boast only one television channel. This meant Cilla had a captive audience until the advent of TV2 when it was rolled out across New Zealand in 1975 and 1976.

The Cilla song I had in mind to sing to Queenie was "You're My World" which had been a Number One hit for Cilla in the 1960s. I'd been singing this song in my head and quietly around the house for quite a while now, but I'd never had the opportunity to practise it out loud as our house was usually alive with activity.

Walking home from school one day, I was hoping against hope that Burt, Chrystal and Frank – especially Frank – wouldn't be home when I got there so I could practise my song in peace and quiet. The last thing I needed was for Frank to be there as I knew exactly what would happen if he were home. As soon as I'd start to sing, he'd yell out, "Oh shut up, Scarlet!!" after which I'd probably go and smash him one and then it would be me in trouble. I knew Mum would be home at this time of day, but that was ok; I didn't mind practising with her in the house.

As soon as I walked in the back door of our house, I said "hello" to Mum who was pottering around in the kitchen. I asked her who was home at the moment and she said only she and I were in. "Yesss!" I thought. "Today is the day! Here is my chance to practise my song while annoying brother Frank isn't around to give me grief about my singing. Perfect!"

I shut the door between the kitchen and living room leaving Mum looking a little puzzled. I made a beeline for the stereo, turned it on and then found the Cilla Black album with "You're My World" on it. On went the record, up went the volume and off I went. I knew all of the words of the song off-by-heart from the countless times I'd sung it in my head and quietly out loud.

One thing was missing though. When I'd seen Cilla Black perform this song on her TV show, she'd had a microphone in her hand with a big black cable leading away from it into the distance. I wanted to mimic this, but how could it be done? I had it! The power cable on our TV wasn't long enough to reach the wall socket, so my dad had bought an extension cord which plugged into the wall and led to the back of the TV where it met the TV's power cable. I quickly unplugged the power cable from the extension cord and held the female end of the extension cord to my mouth – now I had my make-believe microphone complete with big-ass cable!

I started the track again and belted the song out to the empty living room, singing into the plug of the extension cord and wafting the cable this way and that. When I'd finished, the living room door opened, and there stood my mum. My first reaction was, "Oh-oh, am I in trouble for having the stereo on so loud?"

To my surprise, my mum smiled. "Wow Scarlet!" she said. "Your singing voice is actually pretty good. Well done!"

Coming from my mother, this was high praise indeed.

Encouraged by my mum's words, I wanted to sing my song for Queenie straight away, so I decided to head across the road to the factory immediately. I was so excited and as soon as I found Queenie, I ran up to her and gave her a big hug.

"Crikey girl, what's this for?" laughed Queenie as I latched onto her like a limpet.

"I want to sing you a *special* song Queenie," I said.

"A *special* song is it Scarlet?" replied Queenie in mock surprise. "But you sing to me most days don't you?"

"Yes I do, but today is going to be different," I replied.

"Alright then," said Queenie picking me up and standing me on the bench behind her work station. "Off you go with your special song!"

I stood on the bench a little self-consciously for a few moments before Queenie said, "Just take your time Scarlet, ok?"

For some reason, this totally relaxed me and I started singing "You're My World" *a cappella*. I put every ounce of feeling I had for Queenie into that song. As I sang, I could see the factory workers in rows behind Queenie stop working one by one and stand away from their presses in silence so they could watch me. For a while, the air was no longer filled with the ubiquitous clouds of hot steam; likewise, the never-ending hissing sound made by the presses was silenced for a time.

It was a magical if not slightly terrifying moment. I was now the centre of attention for those nearby and everyone was focussed on my singing. I really hadn't expected this – I'd simply wanted to sing to Queenie but now I had a dozen or so clothing pressers as my audience as well. Singing my song, I looked out at them all and could see some of them were smiling, some had surprised but happy looks on their faces, some turned to their neighbours with wide eyes or raised eyebrows. It was a little off-putting, but I carried on singing as I knew Cilla would have done.

Cilla Black – You're My World

I'd almost come to the end of my song. I closed my eyes to deliver the final few words with as much feeling as I could muster and when I was finished, reopened them and looked around. There was silence for a second or two and I started to doubt myself. Maybe my mum was being nice and my voice wasn't that great after all.

But then I saw the happy faces of the factory workers looking back at me; most of them were smiling or nodding with approval. Then I looked over at Queenie. She had a huge grin on her face. "Geez girl, that was the best *waiata* [song] anyone has ever sung for me. Thank you!"

"That was my song to you Queenie," I said happily. "I've wanted to sing it for you for a while now."

"Well ... I loved it girl!" Queenie replied, clearly chuffed.

The factory workers slowly turned back to their presses and the steam and hissing returned. But the atmosphere in the factory wasn't as it was before; there seemed to be a lightness now and here and there I could see workers swaying or tapping their feet to a song only they could hear.

Queenie went back to her press also. I sat down on the bench behind her work station as I always did and watched her work. Queenie had a huge smile from ear to ear that didn't leave her face for the rest of the day. I felt so proud of what had just happened and before long I was wearing a huge smile too.

All too soon, it was time to go home. Before we went our separate ways for the day, Queenie turned to me and gave me a big hug. "Scarlet, you've given me a memory I'll never forget ... thank you!" she said.

Queenie paused before continuing. "You know what Scarlet?" This has given me an idea. Tomorrow I'm going to talk to the bosses and see if they won't let us get a better radio for the factory floor. The one we have at the moment is really old and we can hardly hear it."

"That's a great idea Queenie," I said. "I'll start work on Dad tonight over dinner shall I?"

Queenie nodded and smiled.

Guess what happened after that? By the end of the week, Queenie had her brand new radio and the factory was filled with music every day from then on.

11

1972

One of my fondest memories of 1972 is the day Best Friend Matilda had saved up enough pocket money to buy the 7 inch single of "Puppy Love" by Donny Osmond.

Matilda shouted over the now repaired fence between our houses for me to come over. As soon as I got there, we hurried to her living room where she'd already fired up the record player with Puppy Love ready and waiting on the turntable. Instant heaven! We both loved that Donny Osmond song and we'd play it over and over again in Matilda's living room, singing as loudly as we could.

Donny Osmond – Puppy Love

When Mum called me home for dinner, I sang the song to her while she was working in the kitchen. Frank wasn't particularly keen on Donny Osmond. I heard him yelling from the lounge, "Oh shut up, Scarlet!!" whereupon I stomped over to where he was and whacked him a good one. I had plenty of time to think about the wisdom of that as I was banished to the back doorstep, waiting for my father to come home.

As I was sitting on the doorstep making wishes and looking up at the stars, I could hear some of the conversation drifting through from the kitchen where Mum was preparing dinner. She was trying to explain to

Frank how things were regarding my singing. "There are two types of singers in this world," she said. "There are the ones that only sing in the shower ..."

"But Mum, we don't have a shower ... we have a bath," Frank interrupted, trying to be smart. I rolled my eyes in the darkness.

"... or the bath," Mum continued impatiently. "Then there are the ones that sing everywhere. Scarlet is one of those singers that sing everywhere."

I was pleased Mum was sticking up for me. At least I *think* she was sticking up for me. That was how I took it at the time anyway.

My mother had always told me I could sing long before I could talk properly. She said the first song I sang that she could make out both the tune and the words was "Happy Birthday." Apparently I sang this song to anyone and everyone, all the time, even before I was 2 years old.

🐌 🐌 🐌

One Saturday evening I was over at Matilda's house for a sleepover. We were draped over her couch, in heaven listening to Puppy Love and discussing an extremely important issue. Matilda's eccentric grandmother appeared at the doorway, paused and then shuffled in with the help of her walking stick. Matilda and I stopped talking as we watched her grandmother scanning the living room as if looking for something.

"I wonder what the Trolls have taken this time," I thought.

The record came to an end and there was an uneasy silence before Matilda's grandmother pointed her walking stick towards the fireplace. "The spirit of a lady is standing right there, by the fire," she said.

Matilda and I looked at each other with eyes as big as saucers. It seemed for a little while that Matilda's grandmother was going to start talking to the lady we couldn't see. Instead, she simply turned to us and said, "Nothing to worry about girls, it was just a bypass."

With that, she shuffled out of the living room as if nothing in particular had happened. Trying to regain some sort of normality, Matilda started Puppy Love up again. Comforted immediately by the sound of teenage Donny Osmond's singing, I thought to myself for the millionth time that Matilda's grandmother was absolutely *bonkers*. I never ever said this to Matilda though.

A strange energy remained in the living room after Matilda's grandmother left, so Matilda and I quickly continued with our very important conversation. The pressing topic of that conversation, and many more like it after that, was which one of the two of us was going to marry Donny Osmond. I was pretty sure it was going to be me but Matilda assured me it would be her.

As it was a Saturday night, Matilda and I were allowed to stay up late. With her grandmother supervising, we watched the classic 1950s horror movie "The Fly" on TV. I don't know who the genius was who put this scary old lady in charge of an 8 and 9 year old watching a horror movie. I mean, she had both Matilda and I on edge throughout the movie because at regular intervals she'd peer around the room as if she was tracking something. "Just another bypass, nothing to worry about girls," she'd say. I was scared out of my skin watching the movie, let alone watching it with the scariest person I knew.

If you watch that movie now, there's nothing particularly frightening about it. But I was only 8 when I saw it with Matilda and it scared the absolute you-know-what out of me. The worst part of it is right at the end when the white-headed fly – the fly with the human head – gets trapped in the spider's web and screams those famous words "Help me! Help me!" as the spider moves closer and closer towards it. Now that's pretty chilling even by today's standards.

YouTube: The Fly (1958) Help Me! Help Me! (0:52)

When the movie had finished, Matilda and I started to make our way out of the living room to go to bed. We were both pretty frightened, so it didn't help when Matilda's grandmother pointed her walking stick at me and said in a really scary voice, "Remember to watch out for the spirits, Scarlet." I said I would and rolled my eyes while looking at Matilda, trying to make light of the situation; secretly though, I was petrified.

I think Matilda was too, so it was lucky we had each other. I remember we topped-and-tailed in her bed and talked nervously for hours. At one point in the conversation, Matilda told me if I stayed awake long enough, I'd see something weird happen in her bedroom. She said around the same time every night the atmosphere in her bedroom would suddenly change and it would get unusually dark. This just about sent me over the edge, but at the same time I was fascinated to see this strange thing happen. I questioned her a bit more about "The Darkness" as we called it. Matilda said The Darkness had started up around the time her grandmother moved in with her family; before that, her bedroom had been like any other.

Whatever the cause of The Darkness, we both tried to stay awake long enough to see it happen, but eventually we fell asleep. I stayed over at Matilda's quite a lot growing up and I did get to witness The Darkness once when I was much older. The Moon was full that night but the room went completely dark sometime in the early hours of the morning. It was really spooky.

Matilda told me something else the night we watched The Fly movie. She said other strange things had happened when her grandmother came to live with her family. Like the very day her grandmother moved in. Matilda was watching her grandmother unpack her things and at one point the old lady placed a beautiful antique silver hair brush on her dressing table. Matilda couldn't take her eyes off the brush because she'd never seen such a beautiful thing in her life and remembered thinking it was very solid and heavy looking. She wanted to pick it up and have a play with it and perhaps even brush her hair with it. Her grandmother asked her to help unpack a few other things and when they'd finished, Matilda asked her grandmother if she could look at the silver hairbrush again and perhaps even hold it.

"Of course, Matilda," her grandmother said, "we can have a look at it. It's exquisite isn't it? It's very old too … it's been in my family for many generations."

They both turned to the dressing table where Matilda's grandmother had put the brush only a matter of minutes earlier. It was nowhere to be seen. Matilda's grandmother's first reaction was to ask Matilda where she'd put it. Things got a little heated between them when Matilda was adamant she hadn't laid so much as a finger on it. "Well, where is it then?" Matilda's grandmother said irritably. Matilda swore on the bible that she hadn't touched it and didn't know where it could have gone. She reasoned with her grandmother that they'd been together unpacking as soon as the brush had been put on the dressing table and neither had left the sight of the other after that.

Matilda's grandmother had to admit this was true, so the two of them turned the bedroom upside down looking for the brush. They also searched the hall, the living room and Matilda's bedroom for good measure, but the brush had disappeared. It was as if it had literally vanished into thin air. To this day, neither Matilda nor her grandmother, nor anyone else in her family for that matter has seen hide nor hair of that antique silver hair brush.

Matilda told me that after the brush went missing, her grandmother spoke to her about the Trolls for the first time – mischievous beings that took things, or moved them from place to place. Matilda didn't entirely believe her grandmother at the time, but she had to acknowledge the lost brush did make her stop and think.

Matilda said the hair brush was only the start. From then on, things went missing all the time. Sometimes the missing items would turn up later in a different place, but sometimes they never turned up all at. Her father started getting multiple keys cut of all the important locks for the house and car as they'd lost whole chains of keys as well as individual ones here and there. Losing things inexplicably was simply a fact of their life and they needed to take precautions whenever they could.

Matilda said she now believes her grandmother when she talks about the Trolls taking or moving things; they've simply had too many things happen for there to be a "normal" explanation.

❧ ❧ ❧

My mother has told me many times that I looked like Shirley Temple when I was little. This would have largely been because I had naturally blonde hair which was really curly. For some reason, looking like Shirley Temple inspired my mother to enrol me in Tap Dancing lessons. She would cut my hair with her sewing scissors to keep it around the same length as Shirley's – something like this:

YouTube: Shirley Temple – On The Good Ship Lollipop.avi
(3:31)

I went along with the Tap Dancing lessons to please my mother, but what I was really interested in was gymnastics. I learned how to do cartwheels and flick-flacks from the girls at my school who went to gym lessons and I loved practising them.

I remember my creche teacher once telling me that I wasn't a polka-dot kind of girl. Well, I really wasn't a Tap Dancing kind of girl either, but I did stick it out for a year or so and I did work really hard at it to please my mother. I sat the first Tap Dancing exam after a year of lessons and I got an honours pass – the highest mark possible.

Getting that pass was a **big** mistake on my part. Huge! Mum was so proud of my achievement that she signed me up with the dance school for another year. When I found this out, I pleaded with Mum to drop out of Tap Dancing and change to gymnastics instead. "But Scarlet, you're so good at Tap Dancing," Mum said to me in a well-meaning way. "Maybe if you weren't so good at it I'd let you change. But you've just received the top pass in your first exam so I can't possibly let you leave now."

All of a sudden and for some totally unfathomable reason, I wasn't good at Tap Dancing anymore. The way I explained this sudden loss of form to my mother was that the second year was a lot harder than the first, but I think Mum could see through this rather lame excuse.

Luckily for me, Mum eventually capitulated. "Ok Scarlet you win," she said one day. "You can go to gymnastics."

"Yippee!" I thought. "No more Tap Dancing ... gymnastics here I come!"

Even better was an unexpected by-product of cancelling Tap Dancing; my mother never attacked my blonde curls with her sewing scissors again.

🐞 🐞 🐞

As far back as I can remember, my father was a rugby coach at the Petone Rugby Football Club. He was about as mad keen on the game as you could get and when the All Blacks played a test match at Wellington's Athletic Park – a ground sadly now gone – he'd take Frank and I along. Over the years, Dad coached quite a few boys who ended up playing for the All Blacks and he would always point them out to me.

At one test match Dad took Frank and I to, I had to sit next to a teenage boy Dad used to coach. I didn't know this boy, so Dad introduced us. "Scarlet, this is Alan, Alan Hewson." I reluctantly said hello because I was of an age when I thought most boys were yucky and annoying.

During the game, my father pointed to the action on the field and enthusiastically said to this boy, "That'll be you out there playing for the All Blacks one day, Alan."

The man sitting next to Alan said to my dad, "I hope so!"

"Wait a minute," I thought. "I've heard that voice before!" I leaned forward to get a better look at the man who had just spoken and when I did I snapped straight back in my seat. It was Mr. Hewson, the headmaster of the school I went to. I realised Mr. Hewson and Alan must be father and son. Boy, was I ever on my best behaviour for the rest of that game!

Meanwhile, Frank was sitting on the other side of me and talked to Alan Hewson across me constantly throughout the game because he knew Alan was an up-and-coming player. I found this intensely annoying and eventually I got Frank to swap seats with me so I could watch the game in peace.

Eventually, that boy – Alan Hewson – *did* become an All Black. His test debut was at Carisbrook in Dunedin, another ground sadly now gone, in June 1981 when the All Blacks played Scotland. The All Blacks won that day 11-4. The following week, Alan was in the All Black side that pummelled Scotland 40-15. But it is for his performances in the three tests against South Africa in August and September 1981 that Alan Hewson's name will forever be remembered in All Black folklore. More about this later.

Whilst it's true I learned to enjoy watching rugby as a result of all the games my dad took me to, I've always thought one of the most exciting parts of going to an All Black's test match is the *haka* the team performs before the match starts. In Maori culture, the *haka* is a ceremonial dance or challenge that was commonly performed as part of battle preparations. The *haka* is also used to recognise great achievements, to welcome guests and is also performed at special occasions and funerals. New Zealand sporting teams, the All Blacks in particular, have been performing the *haka* for over a hundred years.

This is one video you have to watch; the *haka* is very impressive.

YouTube: The Greatest Haka EVER? (2:24)

One of the things I didn't enjoy so much about going to a test match was having to fight the traffic to get home to Petone. Cars were bumper to bumper trying to get out of Wellington after the game and it would take ages to get home. Dad's Morris Minor didn't have the best heater in the world, so my dad would put blankets in the back seat for us kids to snuggle into during the trip home. Sometimes I'd even use the time to have a wee nap provided Frank and I weren't fighting in the back seat. If we were, all it would take from my father was a "Hey, hey, hey," in a way which commanded respect and we'd both stop having a go at each other. For a while.

Sometimes, Frank and I would sing the jingle to our favourite TV ad as we drove home from Athletic Park:

YouTube: 1970s KFC Advertisement (Hugo & Holly) (1:08)

Dad never did get the hint to stop and buy KFC unfortunately. He just thought it was a funny tune.

During the club rugby season, the Petone teams would play every Saturday. This was invariably followed by either a celebration or commiseration party at the Petone Rugby Football Club clubrooms. Whichever flavour party it was, Frank would call these get-togethers "piss-ups." The first time he used this term, I had to ask him the obvious question.

"What's a 'piss-up' Frank?" I asked innocently.

Frank replied without hesitation. "A 'piss-up,' Scarlet, is a social gathering that involves alcohol. Lots of alcohol."

"Oh," I replied, not any the wiser for Frank's explanation.

Having a father who was a rugby coach wasn't all test match glamour. For example, every Sunday morning, Frank and I would help Dad tidy up the Petone Rugby Football Club clubrooms after the piss-up – as Frank would have called it – the night before. Our "payment" was a small bag of chippies and a bottle of soft drink.

Most Sundays, it looked as though a bomb had hit the clubrooms. There were ashtrays full of cigarette butts everywhere. There were half empty jugs and 7-ounce glasses of beer dotted around the place. The entire clubrooms stank of stale beer and cigarettes. It was gross.

Dad would give Frank and I a bucket each to empty all of the leftover beer and wine into; you cannot imagine the distinctive aroma of that concoction unless you have experienced it yourself. Then we'd take the empty glasses up to the bar where Dad would wash them by hand. Once our buckets were getting full, we'd tip the disgusting contents down the drain outside.

Next job would be to pick up all the rubbish and empty the overflowing ashtrays into rubbish bins. That job was more gross than it sounds. Frank and I would then get a bucket of hot soapy water and wash down all the tables, on which a surprising amount of horrible smelling, warm, flat beer had accumulated during the previous night's festivities. Finally, it was Frank's job to vacuum all of the carpets in the clubrooms, while I mopped the lino around the bar area. We got pretty good at our Sunday morning job, and the three of us could knock it out in just over an hour.

Frank and I would then receive our reward; a small packet of chippies and a bottle of soft drink of our choice. I always chose a bottle of Fanta while Frank always chose Coca-Cola.

Once we'd finished our tidy-up, Dad would usually have some meetings with other club members. Frank and I would pass the time by playing in the sawdust in the club gym. It was a great environment for me to practise my gymnastics moves as the sawdust made for a soft landing if I mucked something up. Another memory I have is Frank and I pushing at the massive pads of the scrum machine, trying to make it move forward.

When we got home, I'd continue practising gymnastics by working on my cartwheels along the top of the fence between our house and Matilda's. The original corrugated iron fence had blown over during the Wahine storm a few years earlier and had been replaced with a 1970s basket-weave type fence which had a wooden railing running along the top. This rail was about the same width as a beam used in gymnastics, and it was around the same height off the ground too. Sometimes as I was practising my cartwheels along the fence rail, I'd fall off and hear laughter coming from the kitchen window. Of course it was Frank. "Brothers," I'd think. "What's the point of them? They're *soooo* annoying."

During the rugby season, I would quite often go with my dad on a Saturday to watch the team of boys he was coaching at the time. Dad would pick up one of the vans from the dry-cleaning factory and we'd drive to the Petone Rugby Football Club clubrooms to pick up the boys in the team. These boys were much older and bigger than me, and there always seemed to be heaps of them. Dad would squeeze them all into the back of the van and we'd be off.

I clearly remember one particular day when we travelled further up the Hutt Valley to play one of the Hutt rugby teams. We had more than a full complement of players this day; 18 or 19 boys had been squeezed into the back of the van all looking forward to a game of rugby.

When we got to the ground in the Hutt, all the Petone boys piled out of the van and were met with a pretty pathetic sight. Only a handful of the Hutt boys had turned up to play, certainly way short of a team of fifteen. An adult from the Hutt team came across to dad and apologised for the turnout. Clearly a formal match was not to be had and the Hutt team had to forfeit. The guy from the Hutt remained upbeat though. "Well, we could still make your trip worthwhile by having a friendly match if some of your boys joined our Hutt team," he suggested to Dad.

I looked up at my father and will never, ever, ever forget what he said next. "There is no way on Earth I'm taking any of my Petone boys back home to their parents to tell them they played rugby for The Hutt – they play for Petone, full stop." The way Dad said "The Hutt" was all you needed to know about the depth of feeling for Petone rugby my father possessed. With that made crystal clear to the somewhat startled Hutt team guy, the Petone boys were told to get back into the van.

If I didn't know it before that day, I knew then my dad was passionate about Petone rugby.

Although disappointed, the boys were of like mind with Dad and they all piled back into the van. The best they could do was to go back to the Petone Rugby Football Club grounds and practise on one of the fields adjoining the clubrooms. They looked so disconsolate about missing out on a game; I felt sorry for them. But above everything else, they simply couldn't believe how their Hutt counterparts hadn't turned up for a game of footy.

One of the Petone boys who missed out on a game that Saturday went on to become an All Black. He also remembers the day well and he told the story so much better than I have when he got up to say a few words to the congregation at Dad's funeral many years later.

The story brought the house down and there wasn't a dry eye in the place. The ex-All Black told the tale brilliantly and I nodded thinking, "Yep, that was my dad, the coach who wouldn't let his boys play for the Hutt even for a friendly game."

A proud Petonean my dad was; Petone through and through.

🐾 🐾 🐾

I remember another of those trips in the van with my father driving his Petone rugby boys to a Saturday morning game. The boys are sardined into the back of the van as usual and Dad is driving out of Petone. One of the boys was leaning on the back doors and hits the door handle by mistake. The doors suddenly pop open and the boy spills out of the van and onto the road.

Dad screeches the van to a halt and races around to the hapless boy who is picking himself off the tarseal. Dad helps him to his feet, dusts off his rugby strip – can't have his Petone rugby kit looking shabby can we? – and eases the boy back into the van. Dad gets back behind the steering wheel and hurriedly continues on his way. Fortunately, we are still in a built-up area so the van wasn't going very fast when all this happens.

From the front of the van Dad yells out, "Are you alright mate?"

The boy yells back, "Yeah I'm alright Dad."

I then realise it's my brother who'd fallen out of the van. "Blast!" I thought. "If I'd known it was Frank sooner, I would've told Dad to carry on driving!"

All jokes aside, it was lucky Frank hadn't been hurt. You wouldn't get away with any of this these days, but there was no such thing as "Health and Safety" back then.

🦌 🦌 🦌

On the weekends, if I wasn't going to rugby with my dad, or cleaning out the clubrooms, I'd either be practising my gymnastics or hanging out with Matilda.

Matilda's family were extremely religious and they all went to St. Augustine's Anglican church just around the corner from our houses every Sunday morning. One day, Matilda asked me if I said my prayers before I went to sleep at night. "No, I don't," I replied naïvely. "What do you pray for?"

"Scarlet, you don't pray *for* something, you thank God for every-thing you have!"

"But I don't really have anything," I replied.

"Oh yes you do. You have a roof over your head, a loving family and you need to thank God for all the food you have every day."

Matilda was way smarter than me and I generally did what she suggested to do. "So ... I should pray each day before I go to sleep to thank God for all of those things?"

"Yes, that's absolutely right," Matilda replied authoritatively.

From then on, I would kneel down at the side of my bed and pray as part of my going-to-bed routine.

A few weeks later, Matilda asked me whether I'd been saying my prayers as we'd talked about a while back.

"Yes Matilda, I've been praying every night since then," I said proudly.

"That's great Scarlet!" enthused Matilda. "Do you want to give me an example of what you say at prayer time?"

"Oh yes, I'd love to!" I said, always wanting to impress my best friend. "Ready?"

"Ready!" Matilda said eagerly.

"Ok, here goes," I said, clearing my throat, standing up straight and trying to sound important.

"Dear God. First of all, thank you for all the food I've had today. Today at breakfast I had Skippy cornflakes and milk with a tiny little bit of sugar. Then for lunch my mum made me luncheon sausage sandwiches and they were yummy, believe me. For dinner, we had lamb chops with mashed potato, swede, peas and Wattie's tomato sauce. I'm not particularly keen on the swede and peas but my mum says they're packed with vitamins and are soooo good for me so I smother them in tomato sauce and eat them. So thank you for them too I suppose. I think that's all the food … oh, no, thank you for the two Vanilla Wine biscuits I had at suppertime. Thank you God for my loving family, but if you could possibly get a message through to my brother Frank to stop being so annoying, that would be much appreciated. A special thanks, God, for the roof over my head because it does rain here quite often. My mum tells me the rain is why our grass is so green, so thanks for the lovely green grass too. And thanks for everything else. Thank you God. Amen!"

I was so proud of my prayers, but during the course of saying them out loud to Matilda, I noticed the smile on her face fade and a frown appear in its place. By the end of my speech, she'd folded her arms and was tapping the floor with her foot.

"No Scarlet … you haven't got the hang of this at all," Matilda said shaking her head and rolling her eyes.

I was actually quite taken aback, thinking I'd done a pretty thorough job. I was particularly proud of adding in the bit at the end where I talked about the grass, because Matilda hadn't mentioned anything at all about thanking God for the lovely green grass. I'd come up with that one all by myself, but from Matilda's reaction it seemed as though you didn't have to include things like grass in your prayers at all. I was taken aback *and* confused now.

One of the reasons for this was that my family didn't go to church much; if we had, maybe we'd have learned how to say our prayers properly. We all identified as Anglicans or Church of England, better known in New Zealand as C of E. If someone asked us what religion we were we'd say, "Oh, we're C of E." Except for my dad who'd say, "We're C *and* E." When asked whether he meant "C *of* E" he'd say, "No, 'C and E' – Christmas and Easter." I got the joke when I was a bit older.

Truth be told, my father's real religion would better be described as "C of R" – the Church of Rugby – whose congregation met every Saturday night at the Petone Rugby Football Club.

On the odd occasion my family did go to church, my mother would let me wear my best dress which, of course, was a hand-me-down from my cousin. Unlike the polka-dot number from a few years earlier, I really liked this dress; it was Navy blue velvet with a big waist belt that tied up at the back. The dress came with a matching Navy blue coat which I also loved. I wore the dress and coat with white tights, shoes and hat. I loved dressing up in these beautiful clothes and I'd finish it all off with a white handbag complete with Navy blue handkerchief.

One Sunday, I remember my whole family was at church – it must have been the rugby off-season as Dad was there with us. My family pretty much took up one pew all to itself and I remember looking down the line at all of us dressed up in our Sunday best. My mother in particular looked very smart in her flash Possum fur coat and red lipstick.

When we all sat down in the pew, I wasn't quite sure what to do with the white handbag I had with me, so I took my cue from Mum. I looked over at her and saw that she was sitting up straight with her handbag placed on her knees and her hands placed lightly on top of the handbag. I knew my mother would know how to sit properly; she was always a real lady and was very well-mannered. I copied what she was doing.

I couldn't possibly know that day at church as I was admiring my elegant mother in her fur coat that one day, way in the future, she would give it to me. "Here, Scarlet," she would say. "Take my Possum fur coat to keep warm." My mother is such a selfless woman that she'd give her children anything and everything she had.

There was one thing I really liked about going to church when I was young and that was the ridiculously handsome Vicar's son. He had blond hair like me and we'd position ourselves in the church so he and I could look at each other and silently smile and flirt. I did feel a little bad about doing this whilst his father was telling the congregation that we would all go to hell if we didn't live righteous lives.

On this particular Sunday, the Vicar was making a very good case for going straight to the second circle of hell if we had lustful or impure thoughts. I wasn't entirely sure what the second circle of hell was, but it sounded pretty awful so I stopped eyeing up the Vicar's son just in case what the Vicar was saying was true. Instead, I sat up as straight as I could in the pew and faced the front of the Church. "I'd better start paying attention because I really don't want to go to hell," I thought.

In retrospect, that Vicar was of the "Old School" variety and he was a big-time believer in the Ten Commandments. His sermon that Sunday was all about those Commandments, what they meant and how we should live by them.

I came away from church that day a bit rattled and worried that I might be a candidate for hell because I was so interested in the Vicar's son. As soon as I got home, I wrote down the Ten Commandments I'd just learned on a large piece of paper and pinned them up on my bedroom wall. "These are the rules I'll live my life by," I thought looking at the Commandments up on the wall. Hell really didn't sound like a heck of a lot of fun, so I wanted to avoid it if at all possible.

When I'd pinned the Commandments on the wall, I asked my mother to come to my bedroom to have a look and go through them with me so I was on the right track. After we'd worked through them all, I looked up at them thoughtfully. "Mum, I don't think I have to worry about some of these Commandments," I said.

"Oh really?" Mum said suspiciously. "Which ones did you have in mind?"

"Well," I replied, "take Number Nine for example, 'Thou shalt not covet thy neighbour's wife.' Now that you've explained what that one means, I certainly won't be lusting after our next-door-neighbour's wife!"

Mum laughed, but then continued in a semi-serious tone. "You should be focussing more on Number Four Scarlet, 'Thou shalt honour thy father and mother and stop smashing your brother when he annoys you.'"

"Yes Mum," I replied, knowing I'd continue to smash Frank if he continued to annoy me.

I looked back at the list of Commandments pinned to the wall. "There sure are a lot of things you're not allowed to do, Mum," I observed. "But there really is nothing in the Ten Commandments that says anything about not smashing your brother, is there?"

Mum shook her head slowly as she laughed a little laugh. She smiled as she began to walk out of my bedroom. "You're such a literal little thing aren't you Scarlet?! I'm glad you've got the Ten Commandments on your wall, because it's time for you to start behaving like a young lady now you're almost 9 years old."

"Yes Mum," I said in a tone that must have had a little more attitude than I intended, because my mother stopped walking out of my bedroom and turned back to me. "I mean it Scarlet. I will turn you into a young lady if it's the last thing I do." With that, she walked out of my room and off down the hallway.

I looked back up at the Commandments. "They don't say anything about being a young lady either," I thought. I then mimicked my mother's voice and spoke out loud. "I'll turn you into a young lady if it's the last thing I do. Woooo!"

"I heard that, Scarlet," my mother called out from the hallway. I swear she had eyes and ears on the back of her head.

❦ ❦ ❦

It's Saturday the 2nd of December 1972 and there is great excitement in our house.

In the small hours of the following morning, the first ever overseas sports event to be broadcast live via satellite in New Zealand will be shown on TV. Fittingly for rugby-mad New Zealand, that first sports event is the All Blacks test match against Wales to be played at Cardiff Arms Park.

As it's a weekend, and an important event in New Zealand sport and TV history, I'm allowed to watch the game with my family. The downside is I have to go to bed an hour earlier than usual and then Dad will come and wake me up before kick-off. I don't really mind; I just want to see the game.

I'm not too clear on what all the fuss is about initially – we watch rugby games on TV all the time. I guess the difference with this one is it's in the middle of the night? Chrystal has to take me aside to explain the finer details to me.

"The reason the game is on in the middle of the night here in New Zealand," she explains, "is that you're going to be watching the game *as it happens* on the other side of the world in Wales. That's what the word "live" means. Over there, it'll be the middle of the afternoon. Usually we get to see these sorts of games days later, when the film has been flown to New Zealand. This time, we're going to watch the game as it actually takes place because of a satellite."

I understand most of this, even the bit about it being midnight here and afternoon over there. But the satellite thing is still a bit of a mystery to me. I've heard the word "satellite" before, back in 1969 when my teacher took all of the kids in my class outside, looked up at the sky and said, "Neil Armstrong is up there on the Moon, children."

"Chrystal, what has the Moon got to do with this?" I ask.

Chrystal laughs. "Well, you're right, Scarlet. The Moon is a satellite of Earth. But the satellite we're talking about here is a man-made one. The TV signal filmed in Wales is fired up into space, then bounced off that satellite and then beamed to our TV sets here in New Zealand. What we see on our TV screens will have taken place in Wales only a fraction of a second earlier."

Chrystal always has a way of making me understand things. I don't fully appreciate the technology involved, but I certainly get a strong mental image of a TV signal flying up into space, hitting the satellite and then flying back down to Earth where it's picked up in New Zealand and beamed directly into our very own living room. "That's pretty cool!" I say to myself. It's amazing to think we can do this and it all adds to the excitement of the occasion.

It's a bit of a waste of time sending me to bed earlier than usual though. I end up laying awake for an hour or so, thinking about the game to come. Or is it I'm worried Dad will forget to come and wake me up before the game? Or is it the soup in a cup that has just hit the supermarkets which Dad has bought specially for the game? I chose tomato and Dad chose beef; apparently all you do is add boiling water to the soup mix in a cup and ... and ... I eventually drift off.

Dad shakes me awake, careful not to wake Chrystal who didn't want to ruin her beauty sleep for a game of rugby. I didn't think she needed the beauty sleep; I think she's beautiful already.

Dad and I creep down the hall to the living room where Mum, Burt and Frank are already watching our black and white TV. On the grainy screen, I see images from across the world where, right now, it's twelve hours or so earlier. It's a lot to take in, but incredible nonetheless.

It's a good game by test match standards of the day. Quite a few points are scored and the All Blacks just come out on top 19-16. Both teams score only one try each and the difference in scores at the end of the day is our five penalty goals to Wales' four.

I go to bed after the game tired but happy. Not only have I seen my first live rugby match on TV from across the world, but it's my first live rugby match on TV full stop. The first of many.

🦌 🦌 🦌

There are two things I particularly remember about watching that test match at the end of 1972.

The first has nothing to do with rugby; it's the soup in a cup Dad and I make up at half time. My tomato soup was ok, but it was nothing like my mum's homemade soup. I don't try soup in a cup for years after this. In his haste to get back to the TV as quickly as possible, Dad didn't mix the hot water into his soup properly and ended up with a big brown blob of raw soup mixture. He had to go and make up the second sachet and barely got back from the kitchen in time to watch the second half kick-off. He actually liked the result second time around though.

My second memory is the only try scored by the All Blacks. It was scored by tighthead prop Keith Murdoch whom my dad called a "tough bugger." Dad also said he was "built like a brick shithouse. You have to be big and tough to play in that position, physically tough and mentally tough," Dad said.

"Have you ever met Keith Murdoch, Dad?" I asked my father.

"No, I haven't," Dad replied, "but I know people who have. They say he's a man of few words."

Neither Dad nor I could know it at the time, but what happened after that test match would change try scorer Keith Murdoch's life forever.

Exactly what took place at the Angel Hotel in Cardiff in the early hours of the Sunday morning following the All Black's win over Wales is murky at best. What is thought to have happened is that Keith Murdoch was hungry, went looking for some food but was told there was none to be had at that hour of the morning. Somehow a security guard got involved with whom Keith had an altercation, the security guard coming off second best. For his part in the incident, Keith was sent back to New Zealand, the only All Black ever to be sent home from a tour in those circumstances.

The press were waiting at Auckland airport for him, but Keith had other ideas and never arrived. He had switched planes along the way, flown to Australia instead and headed to the Outback for a life of nomadic obscurity. He is said to have returned to New Zealand from time to time to visit friends and family but was always able to slip under the radar.

Various members of the press tried to find him from time to time over the years; those few that actually succeeded were sent off with a flea in their ear. The mates he made along the way in Oz never knew about his rugby past. To this day, many members of the All Black squad in which he played, including legendary captain Ian Kirkpatrick, regret they didn't do more to keep him from being sent home.

It's unclear why Keith Murdoch never came back to New Zealand after that fateful incident at the Angel Hotel. Maybe he was ashamed of being sent home. Maybe it was his shyness and not wanting to be confronted by a media scrum. What is clear though is a few fleeting moments changed the course of Keith Murdoch's life forever. For me, his story remains one of the saddest and strangest in New Zealand rugby.

There's a highlights package of the All Blacks v Wales test match played in 1972 on YouTube. Have a look at the 7:45 mark or so in the video below to see Keith Murdoch score the only points he would ever score as an All Black.

YouTube: 1972 Rugby Union Test Match: Wales vs New Zealand All Blacks (highlights) (24:50)

I read somewhere that Keith Murdoch is invited to all of the All Black reunions. At these dos, his rugby mates apparently leave an empty chair out for him in case he should turn up.

He never does.

12

1973

Some of my favourite childhood memories revolve around the Petone Rugby Football Club annual picnic. This picnic was always held in Summer because none of the rugbyheads at the club were ever going to organise anything like that once the rugby season started later in the year.

Frank and I looked forward to these picnics and would run riot. We'd both enter all of the running races we were allowed to and then try and outdo each other. To my surprise, I'd win one or two of the races I entered. Some of the prizes I won were pretty cool and I enjoyed taking them back to show my parents in the giant marquee that had been set up for the occasion. My mother would give me a nice cold glass of Raro orange juice she'd prepared earlier using one of Dad's beer flagons.

In 1973, the rules of the picnic were changed. My father told me if it rained on the Saturday set down for the picnic, it would be cancelled outright instead of being postponed to a later date. When I heard this I was disturbed. "Oh NO, it *can't* rain," I thought. "The Rugby Club picnics are amazing and we all have so much fun. I'll have to do something about this."

Taking my cue from Matilda, I decided to get God involved. Each night from then on, I'd ask God in my nightly prayers to make sure it would be a perfectly hot, sunny Summer's day for the Petone Rugby Football Club picnic that year. My prayers went something like this:

"Dear God. First of all, thank you for all the food I had today. Matilda told me I don't need to go into detail about exactly *what* food I had, but just to thank you for it, so thank you God for the food I had today. Tonight, my prayers are going to be a little different than usual, because I really need to ask you to do something special God. Matilda told me I should never ask you for anything in my prayers, or ask you to do anything, and I never have. Oh, except for the time I asked you to get Frank in trouble for being mean to me. And the time I asked you for the Vicar's son to notice me at school. And that other time ... well, they weren't very important things and this thing is so *very* important God. And I'm not really asking it for me, well, not *just* me, it's for all the other children too including Frank I suppose, so you see God this is very, *very* important. The thing I need is this ... The Petone Rugby Football Club annual picnic is coming up really soon and everyone loves that picnic and it's so much fun for everyone. But Dad says if it rains that day, the picnic won't happen and it won't get changed to another day, so you see God, it just can't rain that day, it just *can't*. It's got to be the best weather we've ever had in Petone ... in Wellington really. It's got to be hot and sunny and fine and hot and warm all day until around 5 in the afternoon and then it can rain if it really needs to. Because Mum tells me the rain is why our grass is so green – and thank you very much for the lovely green grass God, but Matilda told me I don't actually need to thank you for the green grass either, but I'm going to anyway – but there will be lots of other days you can make it rain so the grass can be green. It can't rain on the day of the Petone Rugby Football Club annual picnic, that's all. I'll even stop smashing Frank if you could keep the rain away for that one day. Well, unless he annoys me too much that is. And thank you for everything else. Thank you God. Amen!"

As the day of the picnic closed in, and the fine weather held up, I started to get worried. I had thought if it was going to rain, it should rain in the days leading up to the picnic so the day itself would be fine. In my perfect logic, I reasoned all these fine days in a row made it *more* likely rain would come on the day of the picnic and I couldn't have that. So I decided to step things up and say my prayers *twice* a day; once when I woke up in the morning and once again in the usual timeslot as I was getting ready for bed.

New Zealand is a funny place weather-wise. Our country consists of two narrow islands; the one to the north is called "The North Island" while the one to the south is called "The South Island," just in case people get them muddled up. At times we can get tropical storms – such as the one that devastated the Wahine – and at other times large parts of the country can go without rain for months creating drought conditions.

Just ask Guns N' Roses how terrible our weather can be in Wellington. The whole time they were here in 2017, it rained. And that was in Summer. Our weather is so unpredictable we can get more rain in Summer than in Winter. So you can see why I was worried rain would ruin my fun come picnic day.

The days before the picnic seemed to drag by and the weather held ... and held ... and held. In fact, it did more than hold; we had one of the finest and driest Summers for years.

Finally, the day of the picnic arrived. I woke up early that morning, early enough to see the sun rise into what turned out to be an almost entirely cloudless sky. It was 20°c before 8am. While I was eating my Skippy cornflakes for breakfast I looked up at the ceiling and spoke very quietly out loud. "Thank you thank you thank you thank you, God. And thank you for my Skippy cornflakes that I've put a tiny little bit of sugar on."

After breakfast, I was walking down the hallway towards my room when Frank intercepted me. "I heard you thanking God when you were having breakfast this morning Scarlet. Why did you do that? You don't believe in God do you?"

I knew something Frank didn't. God clearly was real because He'd listened to me and kept the rain away on picnic day. I remembered my promise about not smashing Frank and instantly regretted it, but at least I had my magnificent sunny day.

"Yes I do actually," I said to Frank.

Frank countered with a tried-and-true response. "If there is a God, where is he then? How come I can't see him anywhere?"

I wasn't really up for a theological discussion concerning the existence or non-existence of a Devine Being on the day of the Petone Rugby Football Club annual picnic, so I told Frank what Matilda had always told me. "God is everywhere Frank ... everywhere at all times." With Frank's mind blown, I went to my bedroom to get ready for the day's fun.

All ready for the picnic, I went to the kitchen to wait impatiently for the rest of my family to arrive. I sat down at the table where my big sister Chrystal, now a teenager, was sitting alone. Mum was working by the kitchen sink, making up a batch of Raro orange juice in one of Dad's beer flagons. When it was made, she put it in the freezer so it would stay cold for as long as possible at the picnic.

"Good luck with that," I sniggered to myself, knowing it was an absolute scorcher outside and I was the one who made it happen. With God's help of course.

I noticed Chrystal was still in her pyjamas and wasn't in a hurry to get ready for the picnic. Chrystal saw me looking at her and worked out what was on my mind.

"I'm not going to the picnic this year with you all Scarlet," she said. "I'm staying at home. Matilda's big sister is coming over soon and we're going to listen to my David Cassidy records."

I was disappointed initially. But then I remembered how strangely Chrystal had been behaving lately. She'd started going to the pictures with boys and had even been kissing them. Ew yuck! So I wasn't too upset the whole family wasn't going to be at the picnic this time around.

As well as that, I knew Chrystal's secret. She'd told me a while back after I'd caught her kissing David Cassidy's picture on one of her LPs that she was in love with him and they'd probably end up getting married. I thought I'd share my secret with her, so I told her I was in love with Donny Osmond and would probably end up getting married to him – although Matilda was quite certain it would be her who married Donny. Chrystal screwed her face up. "Matilda? And Donny? No way, Scarlet. He's much more your type."

"I love my big sister Chrystal," I thought.

Chrystal had left High School and started working as a clothes presser in the factory Dad managed. Chrystal worked right next to Queenie which made me extremely happy. Now, after school, I had a captive audience of *two* to listen to my singing.

After working for a little while, Chrystal saved up enough money to buy a little mono record player which she kept in our bedroom. She loved listening to records of the 60s and 70s with Matilda's big sister while they shared a cigarette. I'd caught them smoking heaps of times and Chrystal owed me big time for not telling on her to Mum or Dad. Chrystal had also confided in me that she was saving up to buy herself a horse, but asked me not to say anything to our parents about this. My big sister was the best Big Sister I could ever wish for, so her secrets were always safe with me.

Finally, everyone was ready for the picnic and we piled into Dad's Morris Minor. As we drove off, I could already hear Chrystal's record player playing this song:

David Cassidy – I Think I Love You

When we arrived at the picnic, Mum and Dad unpacked the car and started putting up the giant marquee that would become party central when all the running races and other activities had finished. Frank and I took off immediately, found the officials who looked after the races, and entered as many events as we could. We even entered the novelty events like the sack race and three-legged race. I wasn't so keen on that one as it meant Frank and I had to race together with a leg tied to each other.

The formalities completed, Frank and I walked back towards the tent. On the way, we passed a man who said, "Hello Scarlet." I said "hello" in return in a friendly manner.

Frank's eyes almost exploded out of his head. "Scarlet, do you know that guy?" he asked disbelievingly.

"Yes, why?"

"Oh, no reason really," Frank replied sarcastically. "I suppose it's just that he's … he's *an All Black!*" Frank could barely get his words out and he looked as though he was about to go into shock.

"Yes, I know he is," I replied casually. "I've met him heaps of times with Dad. It's no big deal you know Frank."

"Well, it *is* actually Scarlet … he's a blinking *All Black*! How come I haven't met him?" The irritation in Frank's voice was obvious.

"How should I know?" I said. "Maybe you're not important enough."

As the running races were held throughout the day, Frank would always watch me race and cheer me on and I would do the same for him. At the end of the day, we were family and as Dad always said, "Blood is thicker than water, kids." Whatever that meant.

After I was awarded the prize for winning a race, Frank and I ran back to the tent to show Mum and Dad what I'd won; a really neat set of paints complete with brushes and palette. Dad took one look at them and smiled. "I've got just the outfit you can wear when you use those paints Bubs," he said with a twinkle in his eye. "A nice white dress with blue polka-dots." We all laughed remembering the day of the Wahine storm and how I'd ruined that dress because I'd disliked it so much.

"What's next then Bubs?" Dad asked me.

"I think it's the novelty races," I said. "First there's the sack race, then the three-legged race and the egg-and-spoon race is last."

"Alright then – your mother and I will come over and watch you. Those races are always good for a bit of a laugh … somebody always ends up falling arse over kite."

Mum fixed Dad with one of her famous death stares. "I mean 'head over heels,'" Dad said quickly correcting himself.

I felt really chuffed my parents were going to watch me in the sack race and that gave me a lot of confidence and motivation to try my best. I hardened my resolve and I decided I really wanted to win that race.

Dad gave me some words of advice as we were walking over to the race. "Remember Scarlet, not all sacks are created equal." This was Dad's way of saying I needed to choose a sack that was exactly the right size for me. If it was either too large or too small, I'd never create the momentum necessary to get over the finish line first.

I chose a sack that looked right for the job and glanced over to my father. He gave me a surreptitious thumbs up and I knew I'd chosen wisely. As I walked over to the starting line and climbed into the sack, I spoke to it under my breath. "Come on sack! We're going to do this ... we're going to win this race, just the two of us. Our strategy is to go on the attack from the word go, ok? We're a team now sack, so you give me your best and I'll give you mine!"

Waiting for the race to start, I could see Mum, Dad and Frank standing at the side of the track cheering me on. I looked at the other racers to the left and right of me and even though I was smaller and younger than most, I remember gritting my teeth and saying very quietly, "Come on sack! We can do this."

As soon as the starter's pistol sounded, sack and I took off down the track as fast as we could go. We were going great guns and didn't look back until ... I overextended myself and landed face first on the ground. Ground that had been baked hard and the grass burned brown by weeks of no rain. No rain, caused in my mind at least, by me. I heard laughing coming from the spectators on the side of the track; this was bad enough until I looked over and saw it was my father and Frank who were laughing the hardest. Mum was trying not to smile and, always the lady, managed not to break out into open laughter.

I heard Frank yelling at me. "Come on Scarlet, don't be such a piker!" That stung a bit, knowing in Kiwi slang that a "piker" is someone who gives up easily.

I sat up and with my hands firmly on my hips shouted, "Dad! Frank!"

"Sorry Bubs," my dad called back at me. "It's bloody funny, that's all!"

I wasn't having any of this, so I picked myself up, rearranged sack and took off after the rest of the field. It was all too late however and I eventually came in across the line dead last. Dad came over to console me and said I showed a lot of game to get up after such a bad spill and keep going.

I looked up at my father. "I just didn't want to be a piker Dad," I said.

"That's my girl!" Dad replied, a hint of pride in his voice.

All up, Frank and I won three races each at the picnic that year, including the three-legged race which we won together. I remember the prizes I won were pretty good; the painting set, some writing paper, coloured pencils and envelopes and a garden Gnome. I always thought the Gnome was a bit of an odd prize, but seeing how Frank and I had won it for coming first in the three-legged race, perhaps it was fitting – a novelty prize for a novelty race.

Frank and I placed the Gnome on the small front lawn of our house when we got home. It happily remained there until it was stolen sometime in the late 1970s when that sort of thing was all the rage. Groups of young lads would sneak around the neighbourhood in the middle of the night pinching and relocating Gnomes in a practice known fittingly as "Gnoming." If your Gnomes had been stolen, or you found a bunch of Gnomes on your lawn in the morning where none had been the night before, you had been "Gnomed."

Mum and Dad must have thought I was an ok runner after winning those races at the picnic because they encouraged me to enrol in the Petone Athletics Club. This club met every Saturday morning in the Summer at the Petone Recreational grounds opposite Dad's second home, the Petone Rugby Football Club. So enrol I did and then I had two activities on the go – athletics and gymnastics. I loved them both.

The picnic finished, 5pm came and went and ... no rain. No rain came the next day either; or the next, or the next. In fact, there was no rain for weeks and weeks after the picnic and finally the Government declared an "Adverse Weather Event" in the Wellington region – in other words, a drought. All the houses in the greater Wellington area were on water restrictions, meaning we were supposed to have quick showers or shallow baths and weren't allowed to water our gardens or wash our cars. A lot of Kiwi homes at the time had Para Pools in their backyards. Their owners complained they weren't allowed to fill them up with water to gain some small respite from the hot weather.

As the drought wore on, I became more and more convinced I'd been the cause of it. God really must have listened to me when I'd asked for hot sunny weather, but missed the bit where I'd asked for it not to rain *only* on the day of the picnic. It was now weeks later and still there was no sign of rain. I thought it was all my fault. I was particularly upset when the story hit the nightly television news bulletin about the Para Pool owners who weren't allowed to use them. I saw the disappointment on their kids' faces and thought it was all because of me.

It got to the point that I thought I'd better add a segment into my nightly prayers to see whether I couldn't organise some rain. When Matilda had taught me how to pray, she said I should thank God for everything I had. That list was getting quite long now, what with the recent addition of the paints, writing paper etc, so my prayers were taking quite some time. But I added a new bit at the end where I asked God to please make it rain as the grass was no longer green. I made sure I asked for a "little bit of rain" because knowing how powerful my prayers were, I thought we'd end up with a flood unless I was very specific about how much rain we actually needed. It must have done the trick, as the drought broke soon after.

This whole experience put me right off asking God for anything in my prayers, and I stopped doing that not long after the rain came. Maybe this was why Matilda had told me prayers were not for asking God to do something in particular – they were for thanking God for the things I already had. So I went back to doing just that and I didn't ask God for anything again until I was fifty years old and in the middle of a dark chapter in my life's story.

Unless you count the time I asked God to bring back Freddy Mercury because I missed his music so much!

🐚 🐚 🐚

My mother was pregnant with her fifth child – the one my parents called their "Surprise Baby." I've already mentioned that my eldest brother Burt thought it was disgusting our parents were still having sex in their 40s when Mum became pregnant. I didn't know anything about sex and nobody would tell me anything, so I was in the dark as to how this Surprise Baby had got into my mother's tummy.

One day, I decided to ask Queenie. "She'll tell me," I thought as I ran over the road to the dry-cleaning factory.

When I asked her, she looked at me sideways. "Go ask your parents eh girl," she said.

"But Queenie, they won't tell me anything ... that's why I'm asking *you*," I protested.

Queenie would only say what my mother had said. "You'll just have to wait until you get a bit older, little one." The mystery around how this "Surprise Baby" came to get into Mum's tummy would have to remain a mystery a while longer it seemed.

When it was time for Mum to be taken to hospital, I stayed at my Nana's house. I loved staying with my Nana and one day she took me on the bus to see Mum in the maternity ward at the Hutt Hospital. Back in those days, mums stayed in the hospital with their new-born babies for up to two weeks.

I was over the Moon when I found out my mother had been delivered of a baby girl. When I saw Jane for the first time, I thought she was very cute and she had lots of thick dark hair right from the start.

The day finally arrived for Dad to bring Mum and Jane home from the hospital. There was great excitement and anticipation in our house over this momentous occasion. Given it was a Saturday, Chrystal suggested we put together a Welcome Home Afternoon Tea for mother and baby.

I was particularly excited as this was to be the first time I'd welcome a new arrival into the household. "Chrystal, Chrystal," I blurted out overeagerly, "shall we bake a cake to have for afternoon tea?"

"I don't know if you've noticed Scarlet," Chrystal replied, "but I've never spent any time in the kitchen ... I've been way too busy riding horses. But you've given me an idea. We could get Burt and Frank to pop down to the Petone Cake Kitchen and buy a plain sponge. You and I could then cover the sponge with raspberry jam and lots of whipped cream and – voila! Instant cake! What do you think about that?"

I thought this was a great idea. While Burt and Frank were fetching the sponge, Chrystal and I prepared the cream. I knew from watching Mum countless times that she added a teaspoon of icing sugar and some vanilla essence whenever she whipped up cream, so Chrystal and I followed suit.

By the time Burt and Frank arrived home with the sponge, Chrystal was ready to cover it with a thick layer of jam and the cream mixture. The finished product looked amazing and as a finishing touch, Chrystal sprinkled a generous amount of hundreds and thousands over the top.

At around 3pm, Dad announced he was going to pick Mum and Jane up from the hospital. As soon as he left, there was a flurry of activity in the kitchen as we prepared everything for the afternoon tea. With the sponge in pride of place on the kitchen table, we awaited Dad's return.

Soon enough, we heard Dad pull into the driveway followed by the sound of footsteps. Any second now, Mum and Jane would walk through the kitchen door where she'd be greeted by her loving family, a cracking cuppa and a beautifully finished sponge cake.

It was right at this moment I noticed a fly buzzing around the room that then started to circle around the sponge cake. I shooed the fly away a couple of times with my hand, but each time it returned, edging closer and closer to the sponge. At the exact moment Mum walked through the kitchen door, the fly looked as though it was on final approach to land directly on the sponge, so I gave it one last massive backhand swipe.

The unimaginable then happened. I totally misjudged how close my hand was to the sponge and I ended up making perfect contact with it. Bits of sponge cake, cream, raspberry jam and hundreds and thousands were immediately distributed throughout the kitchen ... including all over my mother who by now had walked a couple of steps in through the back door.

Mum was instantly covered in cake and accoutrements as was the blanket in which she'd wrapped Baby Jane. Dad had been spared a splattering given he was a couple of steps behind Mum, but had nevertheless seen the whole unfortunate incident play out in front of him.

Chrystal was the first to start laughing. "Of course it had to be Bubs the Grubs, didn't it?!" she managed to say between fits of hysterical laughter. One by one, each member of my family joined in the laughter with the exception of Mum who was literally dripping with sponge cake.

Fortunately, my mum came to see the funny side of things. "Thanks Scarlet ... you just can't keep anything nice, can you?!" she joked.

While everyone was roaring with laughter, I felt terrible about the whole thing. To add insult to injury, Frank told me I'd better start cleaning up the kitchen before the cake mixture set on the walls.

While Mum went off to the bathroom to get herself cleaned up, I made a start on the kitchen. Big Sister Chrystal came to my aid and helped me in this mammoth task. "What a lovely sister I have," I thought as I wiped cream off the floor.

It wasn't quite the Welcome Home Afternoon Tea I'd imagined, but nevertheless was destined to remain in our memories forever.

🦎 🦎 🦎

Life gives and life takes away.

Not long after Jane was born, my Nana died suddenly. Now I had no grandparents at all. I was very sad because Nana was such a lovely grandmother.

The Grandfather Clock she'd let me wind up sometimes came to live at our house soon after she passed. Often as I lay in my bed waiting for sleep, I'd listen to the chimes and always knew what time it was. When they rang out during the night, I'd think of my Nana and the times we'd had together.

I wish I'd had more time to get to know her better.

❦ ❦ ❦

My eldest brother Burt was now a full-time fireman based at the Petone Fire Station. Burt still lived at home as he was saving the money required to buy a yacht together with three of his friends. He and his mates all shared the same dream; to buy a yacht and sail around the world together.

I didn't see Burt all that much – he was always working. On his days off from his job at the Fire Station, he worked for extra money at the dry-cleaning factory. Burt seemed to work all the time; either that, or he was out with his mates making plans for the yacht. When I did see Burt and asked him how he was, he'd always give the same light-hearted reply: "I'm buggered, Scarlet!"

Burt had loved the sea from Day One. He joined the Sea Cadets in Petone as soon as he was allowed to and went to their parades every week like clockwork. I always thought he looked very smart in his Navy uniform.

One December, Mum wanted the whole family to go to his final parade for the year. This parade was open to family and friends and prizes were to be given out. I remember it being a hot Summer's evening, and all the boys were standing to attention in front of the clubrooms right by Petone beach.

Burt received the Outstanding Sea Cadet award that year. As he saluted the officer presenting the award, we were all very proud of Burt, but none more so than my mother. I was still very young at this point, but watching my mother watching Burt, I had my first inkling he was Mum's favourite child. I remember looking up at my mother with her red lipstick, wearing her best dress on this balmy evening. "It's ok if Burt is your favourite Mum," I thought. "I know you love me too."

The other thing Burt was mad keen on was his job as a fireman. I remember once there was a huge chemical fire that broke out in one of Petone's many factories. Even though the unit of which Burt was a member consisted of professional firefighters, there was never enough gear and equipment to go around everyone. This included the breathing apparatus and the firemen had to take it in turns to use what apparatus they did have. This meant that at any given fire, one or two of the boys had to work without breathing gear. Of course, this would never happen today with the big emphasis on workplace health and safety. But things were done differently back in the 1970s.

The day of the chemical fire happened to be Burt's turn to go without any breathing equipment. When he got home that evening, he was coughing and spluttering and eventually started to cough up thick black goo. Mum was extremely concerned for him and Burt was sick for days afterwards.

After what seemed like an age to me, Burt finally returned to full active duty. It was good to hear Burt's favourite music blasting out of his bedroom once again; Burt was a gigantic Led Zeppelin fan.

Led Zeppelin – Immigrant Song

A quick observation. Over the years following Burt's time in the Fire Service, it seemed like the men he worked alongside at the Petone Station passed away before their time with alarming regularity. Some of them didn't even make it to the age of sixty.

At the time I'm writing this story, I'm pretty sure most of Burt's workmates are now sadly gone.

ё ё ё

Towards the end of 1973, a frightening movie was released. It was all the more frightening because it was supposedly based on real-life events. The buzz around this movie was everywhere; on the TV news, in the papers and magazines, everywhere. And guess who had a major part in it? Matilda's famous relation. Unfortunately – or perhaps fortunately – the film had an R16 rating in New Zealand meaning Matilda and I couldn't go to the theatre to watch it. I'm not sure I would have wanted to anyway; I'd found The Fly scary enough.

The film I'm speaking of is, of course, *The Exorcist*. It did very well both at the box office and at the 1974 Academy Awards where it was nominated for ten Oscars, winning two. It was the first Horror movie to be nominated for the Best Picture award. I know all of this because Matilda told me. So did her mother. And her grandmother. Multiple times. They were very proud of their relation even if they did wince a little at the subject matter of the movie – being so religious and all.

Chrystal and Matilda's big sister went to see the film together in Petone one night. When Chrystal came home after seeing the movie, she went straight to bed and pulled the covers up over her head.

"What's wrong, Chrystal?" I asked worriedly. "How was the movie?"

"Scarlet," she said, her voice quivering, "promise me you'll never watch that movie, never, ever. It scared the absolute shit out of me!"

I promised and have never seen it. Never will. Because a promise is a promise.

ё ё ё

Chrystal worked hard at the dry-cleaning factory and saved the $120 she needed to realise her dream of buying a horse. This was quite a sum in 1973 but Chrystal told me the horse she'd had her eye on was a really good jumper and good jumpers didn't come cheap.

She came clean with Mum and Dad the day before she bought the horse; needless to say they were none too pleased Chrystal was spending all of her hard-earned cash on an animal. They didn't exactly say "no" to her purchase, but that could have been because Chrystal said she was buying it whether they liked it or not. She was strong like that, my big sister. Still is.

What she didn't tell my parents was that she was going to save up her money for her next purchase – another horse. That would have gone down like a lead balloon, so she kept her powder dry on that one for a while. I was chuffed she told me though.

Chrystal found a place to graze her horse in Horokiwi, a semi-rural northern suburb of Wellington not far from Petone. On Saturday mornings, I'd watch her get ready for a day's riding and she'd get me to play this or that 45 from her ever-enlarging record collection. This next song was usually the first she'd ask me to put on:

The Monkees – Daydream Believer

After a few weeks, I noticed Chrystal was putting something on her eyelashes. One morning as I was watching her getting ready for horse riding, I had to ask the question.

"Chrys-tal," I said slowly, "what the **heck** is that black stuff you're putting on?"

Chrystal stopped what she was doing. "Well Scarlet," she said like a schoolteacher, "it's called 'mascara' and it makes your eyelashes look much longer and thicker than they already are."

"Oh, ok," I said. I wasn't entirely sure why it was necessary for her eyelashes to look longer and thicker when she went riding, but I guessed the horses must have liked Chrystal wearing mascara.

Once in a while, Chrystal would take me with her up to Horokiwi to feed and brush her horse. She even taught me how to ride a little and how to make the horse jump. She didn't take me with her every Saturday, but I felt very lucky on the occasions that she did.

I loved Chrystal's horse. He was very good natured and she named him after one of the longest rivers in America, the Colorado. Back in the early 1970s, it was legal to ride a horse along the Old Hutt Road and around the streets of Petone. There weren't a lot of cars back then, but how times have changed. You definitely couldn't ride a horse around those streets now given the volume of traffic – nor would you want to.

Just before Christmas 1973, Chrystal had saved up enough money to buy her second horse. He was only half the price of Colorado – $60 – as he wasn't quite as good at jumping. But he was a big, impressive looking animal and Chrystal named him after America's mightiest river, the Missouri. Chrystal spent a lot of time with Missouri and soon had him jumping almost as well as Colorado.

Mum and Dad didn't say much about Chrystal's latest purchase; maybe this was because they didn't want to bring a sour note to the time of year, but more probably it was because Chrystal would have pushed back hard and it didn't seem to be worth the fuss. She had shown herself to be a committed and competent horsewoman – it wasn't a passing fancy for her.

As it turned out, I reaped some of the benefits of Chrystal's love for all things equestrian. My big sister gave me the best Christmas present I've ever had in my life – a memory that will last a lifetime.

Chrystal had got up really early on Christmas morning and brought the two horses down from the Horokiwi hills, along the Old Hutt Road to our house in Petone. I had no idea Chrystal was doing this, but my mother did. She said I should keep checking the street outside our house because Chrystal would be coming home soon.

I kept looking out along our street, expecting to see Chrystal walking towards our house. Soon though I heard the sound of horses hooves trotting along the road and I realised Chrystal was riding her new horse with Colorado in tow behind. I was so excited! Chrystal rode right up to our front gate, dismounted and gave both horses a drink of water and a chance to rest for a bit.

"Scarlet, this is your Christmas present! We're going to ride together down to Petone beach and then along the seashore."

I was over the Moon and must have had a smile from ear to ear. Soon, all of my family and all of the neighbours had gathered around and were giving the horses a pat. I was especially proud when Matilda came outside with her family and I told her I was about to go for a ride along the beach. Even back then, you didn't see horses in the streets of Petone often, so Colorado and his new friend were definitely the stars of that Christmas Day.

Chrystal climbed up onto Missouri, and I pulled myself up onto Colorado as Chrystal had taught me; both reins in my left hand, left foot in the left stirrup, push up with my right leg, right leg over and ... I'm in the saddle. With that, we were off and rode down the road single file at a slow trot. It was the best moment ever! When we got to the beach, we formed up side-by-side and rode across the sand at a canter. We saw a large log in the distance close to the water line that had washed up on the beach. We picked up the pace and both jumped our horses over the log before riding into the surf a little. I think Colorado enjoyed it as much as I did.

Thank you so much, Chrystal. I've never forgotten riding Colorado along Petone beach on Christmas Day 1973. What a memory! And what an amazing big sister you were to me as we were growing up.

🦐 🦐 🦐

My birthday is two days after Christmas Day. I recall my mother asking me what I'd like for my birthday in 1973 given it was a bit of a milestone – my 10th. What I really wanted was a pair of Levi's jeans, but I knew Mum and Dad were constantly broke and this year was worse than usual as their "Surprise Baby" had arrived earlier in the year. Mum had also had to give up her part-time job at the Wills factory so she was now a full-time stay-at-home mum.

I really didn't mind not getting much for Christmas or birthdays. As my birthday is so close to Christmas, I was used to getting a "joint" Christmas/birthday present. I didn't mind this either; I think the less you have, the less you expect. That's why I was so rapt with the Christmas present Chrystal gave me that year – it was so thoughtful and you could tell it came from the heart.

So when my mother asked me what I'd like for my 10th birthday, I tried to think of something really simple and cheap. After a bit of thought, I had it. "I'd just like a coconut Mum. That's all, a coconut." I know it sounds odd now, but it was the simplest thing I could come up with on the spot.

When Mum gave me a heavyish round thing wrapped in birthday paper on the morning of my 10th birthday, I kinda knew what it was. I thought a coconut would be easy to get, but apparently not. "I really hope you enjoy your coconut Scarlet," Mum said. "I had to walk up and down the streets of Petone trying to find you one!"

I took the coconut next door to Matilda's place and we had loads of fun with it. First, we placed it on an old wooden apple box and threw tennis balls at it, trying to knock it off. It was never in any danger of being hit, so we ended up making a hole in it and shared drinking the milk within. Then we took turns trying to smash it on the concrete path in Matilda's back yard. We found out those things are pretty tough and it was ages before it broke into pieces. Once it did, we ate the bits of coconut until it was all gone. I loved sharing that coconut with Matilda.

After we'd finished with it, Matilda gave me a huge bar of chocolate – this was her birthday present to me. We shared it as well and collapsed in a satisfied heap on her bedroom floor once we'd eaten the whole bar.

Life was simple back then. But it was good too.

As Matilda and I were experiencing the sugar high that came from eating the coconut and huge chocolate bar all in one sitting, we could hear voices and music coming from Matilda's big sister's bedroom.

Chrystal was in there with her and they were playing the records of their new love, David Bowie.

They had moved on from David Cassidy now, finding him and his music a little immature for their sophisticated teenage tastes. Matilda and I could hear them debating which of the two would be the one to marry David.

We looked at each other and laughed.

Matilda's big sister and Chrystal both still love David Bowie to this very day, so I guess it must have been true love after all.

David Bowie – Life On Mars?

13

1974

Once I'd turned 10 in December 1973, my father offered me an after school job at the dry-cleaning factory he managed. The job involved folding up all the overalls once they'd been cleaned; they had to be neatly folded in a special way so they looked the same and then sorted by the factory they belonged to.

There were a lot of overalls – and I mean *a lot*. My wages were actually pretty good – $5 per week for just over an hour's work each day after school. To put this in perspective, I could go to the pictures around 20 times on that money, or buy 25-30 pretty big bags of lollies. I felt very rich!

But it wasn't the movies or lollies I had in mind when I jumped at the chance of taking up the job. What I wanted to buy first with my newfound wealth was ... yes, you guessed it ... a pair of Levi's jeans. If I saved all of my wages each week, I figured it would take only six weeks before I had enough money to buy a pair. Then I could ditch my cousin's dresses and just wear my jeans – no disrespect to my cousin of course. Some of her hand-me-down dresses were very nice, but jeans were the item of clothing to wear in the early 1970s and I desperately wanted some. It would be a dream come true.

I reasoned I was at the factory pretty much every day after school anyway, singing to Queenie or Chrystal or both. Now, I could sing while I was folding up the overalls, either to myself or anyone who would listen *and* get paid while I was at it. I thought it all worked out really well.

Like a lot of workers back in the 1970s, everyone at the factory received their pay in cash. I remember feeling very proud when the pay lady pushed her trolley full of brown envelopes over to where I was folding up overalls and asked me to sign for my very first pay. As soon as the admin was complete, I enthusiastically ripped open my envelope to reveal the pristine orangey-red $5 that lay waiting within.

All sorts of thoughts went through my head. I was tempted to go straight to the corner dairy to buy Matilda and I the largest bag of mixed lollies. But discipline prevailed and I ran to the clothing store with the jeans in the front window to put a pair of Levi's on layby. I tried on a few pairs before I found the perfect fit. They were a striking dark blue colour and, as was the fashion of the day, flared. As in *hugely* flared. But they were the height of fashion! If you ask anyone who was around in the 1970s to come up with words to describe that decade, "flared jeans" would almost certainly be high up the list.

"Now listen … you have six weeks to pay these Levi's off," the lady in the clothing store said in a solemn voice. "Six weeks at $5 per week equals $30. Can you manage that?"

"No problem!" I said confidently. There was no way on Earth I wasn't going to own those jeans in six weeks' time.

Six weeks absolutely dragged by. Every payday Tuesday I'd trot down to the clothing store and deliver my week's wages. After a couple of weeks, I didn't even bother opening the little brown envelope; I simply handed it over to the lady in the store.

Come the final instalment, I sprinted down to the store and couldn't get those jeans on fast enough. I thought they looked fantastic and luckily I had a couple of hand-me-down tops from my cousin that went perfectly with them. From that point onwards, my jeans and I were inseparable. I wore them 24/7 apart from bedtime and bathtime and Mum had real difficultly getting them off me when it was time to give them a wash. I'd reluctantly allow her to do this, but only once she'd promised to get them back to me again as soon as was humanly possible.

As you know, I was my parents' fourth child. Mum now had a fifth to care for also. I think she was getting a little tired of having to fight me every time my jeans needed a wash. Eventually, Mum told me it was high time for me to learn how to do my own washing. She took me into this foreign room called the laundry where our rather large and intimidating agitator washing machine complete with electric wringer lived.

Washing the clothes in the agitator part of this monstrosity was no problem but I soon came to understand the meaning of the phrase "to be put through the wringer." Literally. To be fair, Mum warned me not to feed the clothes too far into the wringer because you could easily get your fingers caught in the twin rollers. They did part a little if your hand was caught between them, but you'd still end up with some nasty bruises. That happened to me a bit in the beginning.

I wasn't really that concerned about my fingers though. Mum always told me to tie my long hair in a ponytail if I was going to be doing the washing. She had heard stories about people getting their hair caught in the electric wringer and being scalped by it. This absolutely scared the you-know-what out of me, so I always made sure my hair was in a high ponytail when I did my washing after I heard that story.

I managed to survive the wringer to tell the tale though, only to then be confronted with new technology – the mighty Hoovermatic Twin-tub Washing Machine.

The agitator washing machine had simply passed its best-by date. My parents couldn't afford to pop down to Smith and Brown's and buy a new piece of whiteware, but what they could do was to buy it on Hire Purchase and spread the payments over three years. So that's what they did.

One day in the school holidays I came home planning to do my washing and ... there it was, sitting proudly in the laundry. The new Hoovermatic. No more painful rollers to contend with now. The Hoovermatic did come with its own challenges however. For example, how were you supposed to get the sopping wet clothes from the washing tub into the spin-drying tub without flooding the laundry?

I remember being very excited about the purchase of our new appliance, so I ran outside and called over the fence. "Matilda ... Matilda ... are you there? Come and look at our new washing machine!"

"What sort of machine is it?" Matilda called back.

"It's a Hoovermatic Twin-tub," I proudly informed her.

"Geez Scarlet, we've had one of them for ages now!" she shouted.

My bubble burst.

I asked Mum to show me how this shiny new piece of kit worked. The Hoovermatic was a quirky little machine. Whilst the washing tub was quite smooth and quiet, the spin-dry tub sounded like a 747 Jumbo Jet taking off when it really got going. If the clothes in the spin-dry tub got unbalanced during the spin cycle, the whole machine would vibrate violently and bang against the laundry wall. Quite often the machine would be in one spot at the start of a wash cycle, and end up in a completely different spot by the time it had finished spin-drying.

The other trick with the Hoovermatic was to make sure there was nothing in the sink into which the drain-hose was placed. If an item of clothing had found its way in there by mistake, it would block the sink and flood the laundry as the machine was emptying. I did that a couple of times, much to my mother's irritation.

Whether we were using the agitator machine or the Hoovermatic, my jeans would still have to go on the clothes line to dry. This could take hours, sometimes days if the weather wasn't good. One day I had a brainwave. It had been raining for days and my jeans needed a wash. I was going out to the cinema that evening with Matilda to see American Graffiti – "It's directed by some guy by the name of George Lucas," Matilda had told me – and they needed to be dry by then. So I washed them, put them straight into a bag and ran across the road to the dry-cleaning factory. I asked my dad if he could "please, please, *please!*" put them into one of the enormous industrial sized tumble dryers that lined part of the back wall of the factory and which were going virtually all day. Surely there was room for a little pair of jeans.

My father teased me while I was waiting for them to dry. "Scarlet, do you sleep in those things as well?"

I smiled and shook my head. "Very funny, Dad."

When my jeans were dry and I put them back on, they were tighter and shorter than they had been. I learned the hard way that the downside of the tumble drying process was that it made certain clothes shrink. I looked like a bit of a dick wearing jeans which were now too short when Matilda and I went to American Graffiti that evening, but I figured I'd be sitting down the whole time anyway.

"Oh dear," I thought. "I'd better start saving for a new pair of jeans."

🐜 🐜 🐜

Once I'd bought another pair of jeans and a couple of new tops, I had $5 to spend each week. I loved music, so the natural thing to do was to buy some records. I started off with 45s which I think were 90 cents or so when I first started buying them.

My first 45? Donny had been sidelined a little in favour of a very famous Scottish boy band which seemingly came out of nowhere and very soon were everywhere. This was the first 45 I bought with my own money – the first of many:

Bay City Rollers – Shang-A-Lang

As well as records – and lollies of course – I'd usually have an item of clothing on layby that I paid off over a period of time. Looking back, I did go a bit berserk buying all those clothes with my newly-found wealth. Mum and Dad let me go for a while, but eventually suggested I save at least some of my weekly wages.

The tension between spending and saving was only to get more intense as time went by. Eventually, Mum and Dad's suggestion I save some money became an order that I do so. It all came to a head one day when my mother pointed out I now had more than enough tops to go with my jeans and I must save at least half of my wages each week. I reluctantly agreed, but can't say I ever saved *half* of my wages. I figured if I saved at least a little bit each week, it would get Mum and Dad off my back.

༒ ༒ ༒

I was now in Standard Four at Petone Central School – my last year in Primary School before moving to Intermediate. Fortunately, Petone Central had Primary and Intermediate Schools in one, so I'd simply move to where all the big kids hung out when the time came.

One day after school, I mentioned to Queenie that all the kids in my Standard Four class were working on research projects that we had to present to the whole class. I said I wasn't sure what my project would be about, but I'd started some research on Greenland and might write about that.

"Did you know, Queenie," I said, "for six months of the year it's light in Greenland and for the other six months it's dark? And Greenland isn't actually a country, it's a part of Denmark? And it isn't even green either."

Queenie laughed and said she didn't know much about Greenland. "Does your project have to be about a country?" she asked.

"No, we can do whatever we want, as long as it's 'informative,'" I replied.

"Hmmm," said Queenie thoughtfully. "I might have the perfect story for you, girl. It's definitely informative and something I don't think many *Pakeha* (non-Maori) will know about."

I was very excited about this. I loved Queenie's stories which were largely about the Maori creation stories, myths and legends. But she assured me this particular story was absolutely true.

Queenie told me her story quite a few times over the next couple of weeks as we both worked at our stations at the factory. After work each day, I'd go home and write a little bit more down on paper until I finally had the whole story. I then read it back to Queenie, exactly as I planned to present it to my class the next day. Once she'd helped me with a few changes and corrections, we had the story down pat.

Walking to school the next day, I remember being extremely excited about the prospect of reading my story out to my classmates. I even wore my best – and only – Poncho that my mum had made for me out of squares she'd crocheted and joined together.

Here is the story I presented to my class in Standard Four as a 10 year old – thanks so much for your inspiration and help, Queenie.

The Removal of the Wahine from Wellington Harbour

When the Wahine capsized at the entrance of Welling-ton Harbour that fateful day in April 1968, few would have thought it would take over five long years before the last pieces of the stricken vessel were finally removed from the waters in which she lay.

Even though the Wahine was only 400 metres off the Seatoun coast, and had remained relatively intact after she capsized, she was deemed a hazard to navigation and plans were quickly drawn up to salvage her. At first there were high hopes that valuable items could be removed from the ferry before refloating her, salvaging what remained and then scuttling her in Cook Strait. The floating crane Hikitia and excavation dredge Kerimoana were brought in for the job. Another ship, the Holmpark, was anchored nearby and provided accommodation for the salvage workers.

As the plans to salvage the Wahine were being made, local Maori told the salvagers their plans would ultimately meet with failure unless a Maori painting, located in the ship's entryway, was found and removed. The painting was of a Maori woman, a Wahine.

Nobody took any notice of what local Maori were saying and salvagers continued with their plans. Much preparatory work had been accomplished despite constant setbacks caused by bad weather which hampered progress on a regular basis. Progress was made nevertheless and it was hoped the refloating could take place in May 1969.

Mother nature had other plans though as she sent a violent gale through Wellington on the 8th of May, almost on the eve of the refloating. In the aftermath, it became clear the Wahine had been broken up into three large pieces. She looked like she had been sliced open by a huge can opener. Not only that, but thousands of dollars of salvage equipment and months of hard work had been wasted. Plans to raise and refloat the Wahine were now abandoned in favour of merely breaking up what remained and selling it for scrap.

Again, local Maori told the salvagers the Wahine would not be able to be removed from Wellington Harbour until the Maori painting was found and taken to shore. Again this advice was ignored.

Efforts to break up and remove the now wrecked Wahine continued over the next few years, although storms would frequently ruin the work of months leaving salvagers no choice but to start again. Tragically, a diver was killed in the salvage operation.

After years of frustration, it was decided to heed the words of local Maori and efforts were made to locate the painting they'd spoken about at the outset of the salvage plans. After some searching, the painting was found and removed. Salvage workers were amazed in the change in weather that occurred almost as soon as the painting was taken to shore.

No longer did storms and high seas hamper their work; instead the sea was calm and fine weather became a regular feature of Wellington Harbour once more.

Work was able to continue at pace now and the salvage operation was not hindered by a single storm from that time onwards. Work was finally completed after five long years in 1973. The salvagers managed to realise $4.5m for the scrap metal they recovered, a figure that paled in comparison to the salvage costs.

After I'd finished telling my story to the class my teacher spoke. "Scarlet, I can remember the difficulties the salvage people faced with the storms that always seemed to arrive at crucial times. Stories about the progress of the salvage operation were on the evening news for years after the Wahine capsized. Thank you very much for your story – can I ask you how you came to know about it?"

"A really lovely lady told me the story Miss," I said proudly. "She's a Maori lady called Queenie who works at the same factory as my father."

My teacher smiled at me and nodded.

I then sat down at my desk and remember thinking how I totally believed Queenie's story to be true. I still do.

༄ ༄ ༄

In the house directly across the road from ours lived an old man. I remember him as a nice old man who lived alone. Neighbourhood scuttlebutt had it that some people knocked on his door one day and asked to buy his house. When he asked what they intended to do with it, they replied they wanted to turn it into the Petone Spiritualist Church.

"Bugger off!" was the old man's reply. According to gossip that is.

What wasn't gossip was the nice old man died suddenly not long after this and his family duly sold his lovely house ... to people who turned it into the Petone Spiritualist Church.

Frank and I found this new Church directly across the road from us very mysterious. For a start, they'd meet on a Sunday evening. "At least you don't have to ruin a Sunday-morning lie-in to go to their Church," Frank observed. He and I would hide behind our front fence on a Sunday evening and watch as carload after carload of Spiritualist Church-goers would arrive, park their cars down our very narrow little street and walk to the Church.

One Sunday evening, Frank and I popped our heads above the fence palings and looked directly into the Church across the road. On this particular Sunday, the curtains were open and the lights were on inside. Frank and I could clearly see a giant banner with thick black writing which said:

THERE IS NO DEATH!!

"What does that mean Frank, 'There is no death?'" I asked. "If there is no death, what happened to the nice old man that used to live in that house?"

Frank shrugged his shoulders. "Yeah, he seemed as dead as a door nail to me when they carted him off in that bloody big wooden box," he replied. "It's all a bit weird for me Scarlet. I don't even believe in God and here is this outfit saying there is no death."

"You may not believe in God Frank, but you'd better live by the Ten Commandments to make sure you don't go to hell," I said officiously. "I'll help you Frank. I'll write the Commandments out for you. You can put them on your wall. Remember what Matilda says: 'God is everywhere.'"

In hindsight, and as my understanding of Life, the Universe and Everything has evolved, I realise I really didn't need to write the Ten Commandments down for Frank. He was, and is to this day, a very honest person with integrity to burn.

We popped our heads above the fence palings again and this time the curtains were drawn.

"What the heck goes on in there?" I asked Frank in hushed tones.

Frank replied in equally hushed tones. "The only thing I've heard is that they do séances in their Church."

"Oooooooh ok," I said.

Silence.

Frank continued to spy on the people filing into the Spiritualist Church.

"Frank?"

"What is it Scarlet?" Frank said irritably.

"What's a 'séance?'"

Frank stopped looking across the road, sat with his back to our fence and turned to face me. "It's where a group of people get together and ... and ... conjure up dead people."

The thought of 'conjuring up dead people' terrified me, but it interested me too. Probably in equal measure. Queenie had told me stories from Maori culture involving spirits and supernatural occurrences, so I was familiar with the concept – if not a little uncomfortable with it. She'd also told me a story from her own family line of a long-deceased family member who suddenly appeared to warn his *whanau* that something bad was about to happen.

I was emboldened by Queenie's stories to find out more from Frank. "So ... how do they do it Frank? Conjure up dead people I mean?"

"I really have no idea Scarlet," Frank said turning back towards the Church. There was something in his voice and manner that suggested he really didn't **want** to know either.

I also had no idea. The difference was that I **did** want to know.

Not long after the Spiritualist Church opened its doors across the road, strange things started to happen at our place. And I don't mean for a little while after, I mean for **years** after. The first inkling I had that something strange was happening was that I started to feel like someone was watching me in our house, especially when I was alone in my bedroom. It wasn't a nice feeling either – it was creepy.

Unbeknownst to me at the time, this was only the beginning.

❧ ❧ ❧

At the end of each year, the factory my father managed put on an amazing Christmas party. These parties were one of the most anticipated occasions on my social calendar. In fact, I'd have to say I loved the factory Christmas parties more than the Petone Rugby Football Club picnics, certainly as I grew older. My father was the ultimate party guy and I think a little of that might have rubbed off on me.

The Christmas parties were a veritable hive of activity. There was loads of singing and dancing and there was always a whole pig roasting on a spit outside in the courtyard that someone was constantly turning by hand and basting. When it came time to serve up, I loved the hot pork sandwiches which came complete with crackling and apple sauce.

Pork was such a rarity in our house. Most of the roasts we had were of the lamb variety as sheep were ubiquitous in the 1970s. At this time, there were around 60 million sheep in New Zealand and only 3 million New Zealanders. That's 20 sheep for every Kiwi. Those numbers have dropped drastically nowadays. There are now around 30 million sheep and 4.8 million New Zealanders making the ratio around 6 sheep per Kiwi. That's still a lot of sheep. Add in around 10 million cattle – beef and dairy combined – and for a small country, that's a lot of animals being farmed.

With so much lamb around in the 1970s, it was a real treat to have something different. Chicken was out of the question; it was so expensive and I'd only ever had it at Matilda's house on special occasions. So the annual hot pork sandwich at the factory Christmas party was a rare treat and something to look forward to.

Frank and I loved the Christmas party for another reason. Everyone there partied in the same way the members did at the Petone Rugby Football Club during the footy season ... except on this occasion he and I didn't end up having to clean up the huge mess the following day.

We didn't actually know who ***did*** clean up the huge mess the following day, but Frank and I sure did feel sorry for them.

A Maori boy who worked at the factory had the most amazing singing voice and also played the guitar. This boy was much older than I was and with the benefit of hindsight, he could have been Cliff Curtis' double. It was no secret at the factory that I loved singing, so as soon as Cliff Curtis started playing guitar he'd yell out, "Scarlet, get over here!"

This is one of the songs he played and everyone at the party would sing along to. I think we sang this song at every Christmas party – every one I can remember anyway. It became a Kiwi classic and can still be heard at Kiwi parties today.

Engelbert Humperdinck – Ten Guitars

Needless to say, the factory Christmas parties were legendary. Everyone was invited; the workers, their families as well as the people who lived in the houses close by the factory. Matilda and her family came along every year too.

By now, Burt had found himself a beautiful girlfriend who had a smile that could light up a whole room. There was only one thing bigger than her smile – her heart. I adored her and we called each other "Sister." Her name was as beautiful as she was; Waimarama which means "Moon Over The Water."

Waimarama worked as a seamstress at a factory called Haines which mainly made tee shirts. In their lunch breaks, the Haines' workers were allowed to use the fabric off-cuts that would otherwise have been thrown away to make clothing for themselves or family. I didn't know it at the time, but Waimarama had been busy making me tee shirts and jackets and I was about to receive another memorable Christmas present.

This Christmas, Mum and Dad had bought a huge pine Christmas tree which stood in pride of place in our living room. One of the presents under this tree was a large box wrapped in Christmas paper addressed to "Scarlet, from Burt and Waimarama."

I couldn't wait for Christmas morning. When it finally came, I made a beeline for the large box, unwrapped it and opened it up. It was absolutely chock-a-block full of the clothes Waimarama had made for me. The first item of clothing I pulled out was a tee shirt that was mainly white with an orange and navy blue stripe across the front alongside the words "Detroit Tigers." I didn't know who the Detroit Tigers were, but I loved that tee shirt. It went so well with my jeans.

The next thing I pulled out of the box was a red jacket with a tartan stripe that went down the length of both sleeves. "Wow, a Bay City Rollers jacket!" I squealed with delight. I was in clothes heaven! Waimarama had made me lots of other tee shirts and jackets to wear with my jeans – she knew how much I loved them. Everyone did actually, but Waimarama did something which enhanced my enjoyment of wearing them and I have never forgotten her most generous of gifts.

I couldn't thank Waimarama enough; she was so kind.

Now I had so many more things to add to my list when I said my prayers at night.

14

1975

In late January, I started the first of my two Intermediate School years at Petone Central School. Back then it was called Form One. Now it's known as Year Seven.

I remember my first day in Form One really clearly for not such a good reason. Everyone in my class was getting settled into the classroom for the very first time. We had all been given a few minutes by our new teacher to put our schoolbooks and stationery tidily away in the desk that had been allocated to us.

For some reason, I couldn't get my desk to close once all of my books and pencils and pens were inside it. I lifted up the lid of my desk and rested it on top of my head so I could rummage around inside, rearranging the contents first this way, then that.

Without warning, my teacher strode over to my desk, pulled the lid way open and away from me and then slammed it back down again – right on the top of my head. This really hurt and within a couple of minutes a painful lump had formed on my head. But the worst thing was the shock of it; why had my teacher done this to me?

I told my mum what had happened when I got home and she promptly complained to the school. Big mistake. From then on, this teacher picked on me every chance she got. I was always in trouble, especially at Maths time because I struggled with Maths.

My unpleasant Form One teacher was an older woman called Miss Armstrong and she was universally disliked amongst the Intermediate kids at Petone Central School. She had been for years apparently. Someone a long time ago had given her a nickname which had stuck down through the years; the nickname was "Legweak," a play on her surname, "Armstrong." All us kids thought this nickname was absolutely hilarious and everyone used it behind her back. I suppose it was our small way of getting back at her for being so mean.

One of the meanest things Legweak did wasn't to me as such, but rather to my whole class. One extremely hot late Summer's day, she gave me some money and told me to go and buy a Crazy Joe Cola Ice Block and can of Lemonade from the Dairy that was right next door to our school. I dutifully did as I was told and on my return, was told to sit with all the other kids on the mat at the front of the classroom. Again, I did as I was told. As I took my place with my classmates, I wondered whether Legweak had bought the Ice Block and drink for us kids as some sort of prize or reward on this sweltering hot day.

My thinking couldn't have been further from the truth. This teacher of mine proceeded to take great pleasure in demolishing first the Ice Block and then downing the gorgeously cold can of Lemonade in front of all the kids in my class. We all looked on and then at each other in disbelief as we suffered in the heat of the classroom, forced to watch Legweak enjoying her cool refreshments. What made it worse was every one of the classroom's windows and both doors were shut so there was no breeze at all to help cool us down a little.

I was pretty disgusted with Legweak and as I watched her licking that icy-cold thirst-quenching frozen Ice Block, a thought flicked through my mind that perhaps I should become a teacher. I would be a kind and lovely teacher who would always let her kids open the windows and doors in the classroom when it was hot. Furthermore, I'd buy Crazy Joe Cola Ice Blocks for the entire class on stinking hot days like this. They were only 7 cents each after all.

I couldn't understand how someone could be so mean to little kids – especially a teacher.

☙ ☙ ☙

The research project my Standard Four class had been assigned the year before had been a great success and it had been decided by the Powers That Be that it would be rolled out as part of the Intermediate School curriculum.

I was quite happy about this. "Yay!" I thought. "I can make use of the research I started on Greenland last year and make that my project topic this year."

"Oh no you won't!" Legweak informed me with great glee when I told her what I was planning to do. "Your project this year must be on an historical aspect of **New Zealand**. Last time I checked, Greenland isn't part of New Zealand, Scarlet. It's a whole different country."

Legweak abruptly walked away with a smug look on her face.

You know those moments in life where you almost kick yourself because you weren't quick enough to come back with something smart or witty when talking to someone? This was one of those moments. Watching Legweak walk away with that smug look on her face I wish I'd been able to say, "Actually Miss, Greenland isn't a country – it's a part of Denmark." By the time the thought had come to me however, the moment had passed and Legweak had gone.

Looking back on this incident now, I'm actually glad I **wasn't** quick enough to get my little dig in. Who knows what gruesome punishment Legweak would have dreamt up for me for talking back to her? In any event, it was back to the drawing board in terms of my research project. Greenland would have to wait for another time.

That evening, I mentioned my school project to my mother. She immediately came up with a brilliant idea for a topic: the 1855 earthquake that shook Wellington and the lower North Island.

"I'll help you if you like Scarlet," Mum offered. "We can go to the Petone library after your job tomorrow and do some research."

I was thrilled at both the subject and the thought my mum would help me with my schoolwork. As planned, we visited the Petone library the very next day. Here is a summary of what we found out.

The 1855 Earthquake and Tsunami

Just after 9pm on January 23rd 1855 – Wellington's Anniversary and 15 years to the day after the first European settlers stepped ashore at Petone – a violent magnitude 8.2 earthquake hit the Wellington region. Lasting around 50 seconds, the earthquake is now recognised as the most powerful recorded in New Zealand.

The earthquake caused a tsunami in Cook Strait and a four metre high wave overtopped the Rongotai isthmus and entered Wellington Harbour, flooding buildings along Lambton Quay. A surge of water travelled up the Hutt River, destroying the wooden Hutt Bridge.

While damage was widespread, fatalities were fortunately few. The main legacy of the earthquake was that the Wellington region was lifted and tilted, exposing new areas of useable land. Many blocks of Wellington's modern-day CBD were below sea level before 1855. A new road and rail route between Wellington and the Hutt Valley was made possible by land raised from the harbour.

The earthquake also had the beneficial effect of draining previously swampy parts of the region, including the area now occupied by the Basin Reserve.

Mum and I put a lot of time and effort into researching the 1855 earthquake and tsunami and I enjoyed learning about our region's history. I wrote four pages on the topic and duly presented it to my class.

My mum was proud of my work and I received a good response from my classmates.

But not from Legweak. She gave me one of the lowest marks in my year group.

❧ ❧ ❧

The Petone Central School Talent Quest was approaching fast, and for the first time I decided to enter. Most of the other girls in the contest were going to sing Abba songs so I thought I'd do something a bit different. I'd bought a 45 single of a song I liked not long before and I played it in my bedroom a lot. I'd pretend I was singing it to a boy in my Form One class that I had a gigantic crush on. He looked a bit like Donny Osmond and probably had no idea I liked him. He probably had no idea I even existed. I'm pretty sure about this, as I never – as in *ever* – initiated a conversation with him; I was way too shy. I would gaze at him adoringly from across the classroom and then sing him this particular song when I got home in the evening.

I'd been doing this for a while when the posters for the Talent Quest went up all over the school. I decided quite quickly I'd enter and sing this song, if for no reason other than it was already very well-rehearsed. The only bit of the song I really needed to work on was the part where the band whistles the lead riff. I practised whistling this bit over and over again while I was folding overalls at the factory after school. One day, Queenie heard me whistling and came over to my work station. She knew I was practising for the school Talent Quest and gave me some tips and coaching. With her help, I soon had the whistling part down pat also.

The day of the Talent Quest arrived, and it was my turn to stand up on stage and deliver. Up I climbed in my Levi's jeans and Detroit Tiger's tee shirt – still not knowing who they were – with my Bay City Roller's jacket over the top. I belted out this song and pretended I was back in my bedroom, singing to the boy in my class who I had a crush on.

The song I sang was an anti-war anthem and was very big at the time. Here it is.

Paper Lace – Billy Don't Be A Hero

If you attended Petone Central School in 1975, looked a bit like Donny Osmond and your initials were P.J., that song was for you!

Legweak expressed her opinion on my effort the minute I returned to the classroom after the Talent Quest had finished. She informed me – and everyone else within earshot – that she didn't like my choice of song and I didn't have a very good singing voice in any case. She finished her expert critique of my performance by saying she wasn't at all surprised I didn't get anywhere in the contest and then laughed as she walked away.

The Talent Quest was won by a girl who I thought was the best female singer at our school. She sang an Abba song that had just hit Number One in the New Zealand charts.

Abba – I Do, I Do, I Do, I Do, I Do

Well done Bridget, you sang that song beautifully!

🐞 🐞 🐞

One day, for no reason other than a bit of fun, Burt took Frank and I for a ride in his Ford Valiant to pick up Waimarama at the house where she lived with her foster parents. We didn't really know exactly what had happened in Waimarama's family which led to her living with a foster family, but we were soon to find out she was looking for a sibling named Tane. She had found her other two siblings, photos of whom she'd placed on the mantelpiece in the living room of her house. Now she was trying to find the last sibling to get the whole family back together again. She had a picture of this third sibling as a younger boy on the mantelpiece as well.

Frank and I had absolutely no idea of this at the time. Being such a Nosey Parker, Frank walked over to look at the photos on the mantelpiece and picked one up. "Who is the boy in this picture Waimarama?" he asked. "He looks like a boy in my class called Tane, only a bit younger."

I truly believe some things in life are meant to be. Frank and I weren't supposed to be at Waimarama's place that day – we randomly wanted to go for a ride in Burt's car. It turned out Frank had identified the sibling Waimarama had been looking for as a boy he went to school with. Waimarama was so excited that she now knew where to find her youngest brother and soon all of her brothers and sisters were reunited.

I was so happy for Waimarama. I had a smile from ear to ear as she rushed over to Frank and I with tears in her eyes and gave us both a tight hug. You could see how much it meant to her.

🜲 🜲 🜲

Meanwhile, both Chrystal and Matilda's big sister were still mad keen on David Bowie having moved on from David Cassidy a year or so earlier. Between them, they had all of his records and they'd play them whenever they had a chance. Ziggy Stardust, Aladdin Sane, Diamond Dogs, I know these three albums in particular very well if not off-by-heart due to the amount of play each one of them received.

David Bowie – The Jean Genie

One evening, I was sitting on my bed watching Chrystal getting ready to go out and listening to "The Jean Genie" on the record player in our room. Chrystal seemed to be taking quite a long time to get ready this evening, so I asked her what she was doing.

Chrystal looked at me for a few seconds and then put her make-up down. "I'll tell you if you can keep a secret," she said very quietly.

"Oh *yes* Chrystal, I can keep a secret!" I replied eagerly.

"Well then," Chrystal started. "I met a boy at Horokiwi a couple of years ago and we've been secretly seeing each other since then. He owns a couple of horses, just like I do and he's a really amazing rider. I'm going to meet him now outside the Petone Railway Station, and we're going to go to the pictures this evening."

I collapsed flat on my back on my bed and swooned. "That is *soooo* romantic, Chrystal!"

I turned on my side and propped my head up on my hand so I could watch Chrystal apply the final touches to her mascara via her tiny hand mirror. I thought she looked really beautiful in her make-up, Amco jeans and high-heeled boots. A colourful top and jean jacket finished her outfit perfectly.

"Why is it such a big secret?" I asked.

"Let's just say ... I'm not sure Dad would take the news of me going out with a boy particularly well."

I'm not sure I really understood what Chrystal meant at the time. Looking back now though, I realise my dad makes Robert De Niro's character in the Focker's movies look like the perfect father-in-law.

"Do you want to hear about the very first movie we ever went to see together?" Chrystal asked.

"Ooh, yes *please* Chrystal," I said enthusiastically. "I bet it was really romantic!"

Chrystal told me her boyfriend David was a real cowboy and loved horses as much as she did. The first movie David took her to see was called "100 Rifles" and it was a western. Chrystal had a little laugh as this wasn't quite as romantic as she'd pictured her first movie outing with her first real boyfriend, but she'd enjoyed the evening nevertheless.

100 Rifles had some big names in it: Raquel Welsh, Jim Brown and Burt Reynolds to name a few. Have a look here at the romantic movie David took Chrystal to see on their very first date.

YouTube: 100 Rifles – Trailer (2:58)

Chrystal told me 100 Rifles had rather set the scene for her relationship with David movie-watching wise. In the two years they'd been seeing each other, they'd only ever seen westerns together.

"How do I look?" Chrystal asked, finishing her preparations. Before I could answer, she glanced at her watch. "Heck, I'd better go, I'm running late. I'll be back later tonight but you'll be asleep by then. See ya Scarlet!" With that, my big sister hurried off.

I tried to stay awake long enough to see Chrystal come home, but eventually I drifted off to sleep. I woke up when she arrived home later that night and barraged her with questions about the movie and her "new" boyfriend. It was very exciting for me to hear the story of her evening.

Once I'd asked all my questions, Chrystal told me she'd invited David to our house the following week so he could meet everyone. It was about time really – she'd known him for a couple of years after all.

I was so excited!

🦌 🦌 🦌

The day David was due to arrive I was peering out of my bedroom window – I didn't want to miss a thing. "What does your boyfriend do for a job?" I asked Chrystal while she was getting ready behind me. Chrystal told me David was a builder and worked for his father who owned his own building company. She said David was a couple of years older than she was, but that didn't matter to her. He was 20, she was 18; it wasn't a big deal.

As we were talking, we heard a car pull up outside. Chrystal dashed to the window, squealed "Here he is now!" and rushed outside to meet David.

David pulled up in a dark blue Ford Escort with expensive looking mag wheels. He got out of the car to greet Chrystal and I can remember to this day what he was wearing: dark blue flared Amco jeans, tan coloured platform shoes, cream shirt with tan pattern running through, all finished off with a tan coloured suede jacket with tassels down the length of the sleeves. He was the height of mid-70s Kiwi fashion and with his tanned skin and longish light brown hair, I thought he was gorgeous and perfect. "Go, sister!" I thought when I'd had the chance to take in the whole picture.

From the very first day David arrived at our house, I just loved him. From that day onwards, David would come over to our house almost every night. He and Chrystal would mostly sit in our living room, listen to music – David Bowie of course – and smoke cigarettes. Sometimes I'd catch them kissing and tease Chrystal by saying, "David is your kissing darling!" Chrystal would laugh and reply, "That's right Scarlet, David *is* my kissing darling." I figured those two must have truly been in love, as I caught them kissing a lot.

David would never turn up empty handed. If he wasn't bringing gifts for Chrystal, he'd bring a load of wood off-cuts for our fireplace. David was a genuinely nice guy.

Like Chrystal, David was a fan of Bowie, but he was also into The Beach Boys. So when David arrived on the scene, I got a bit of a break from David Bowie.

The Beach Boys – Wouldn't It Be Nice

With David now a fixture, we had quite a full house every evening. Along with Mum, Dad, and us five kids, Matilda and her older sister would come over, as would Waimarama and David. It seemed there was a party almost every evening at our place. Even if Burt was working, Waimarama would come over anyway. She loved our family and we all loved her.

Par for the course for the 1970s, every other person seemed to be a smoker. Dad smoked, as did Matilda's older sister, Chrystal, David and Waimarama. Luckily our house had 12 foot ceilings all over, so the cigarette smoke would sit way up above the light shades over our heads and the non-smokers could get some cleaner air down below. A little thing like cigarette smoke didn't deter me from wanting to be in the thick of it; above all else I wanted to listen to the music.

I wasn't always the perfect little sister. I loved getting into all of Chrystal's things and I remember the time David gave Chrystal a matching pair of beautiful Maori dolls with long dark curly hair. One day when no one was around, I decided I'd restyle their hair with my mother's sewing scissors. It would be fair to say the hairstyles I had in my mind's eye didn't quite end up being replicated on the dolls. They finished with hairdos Frank called "kina heads."

Chrystal was much less impressed and I was in her bad books for days over that one. When David saw the dolls, he just laughed. "That's little sisters for you," he said.

Chrystal still has those dolls and loves bringing them out from time to time to show people what her perfect little sister did to them. Everyone always laughs and so does Chrystal now.

On another occasion, David bought Chrystal a jewellery box which had a glass top. I managed to drop the box by accident and, of course, the glass top smashed. It really was an accident, and when David saw what had happened, he went out and bought another one. Unfortunately, David couldn't find an identical replacement for the one I'd broken, but the new jewellery box he ended up buying was equally as beautiful. What a guy!

David, you are truly one in a million, a Star, so here is your song:

David Bowie – Starman

I was getting ready for bed one night and headed to my bedroom where I found Chrystal and Matilda's sister puffing on a cigarette.

When I walked into the room, Chrystal looked at me mischievously. "Would you like to try a drag, Scarlet?" she asked.

I'd always looked up to my big sister, and thought if she could do something, then so could I. Naturally I replied, "Yes, of course Chrystal."

Chrystal passed me her cigarette and showed me how to hold it and take a drag. "Breathe it in, right down into your lungs – that's how it's done Scarlet," she told me. "You don't just suck a bit into your mouth and blow it out again."

Not one for doing things by halves, I took a colossal puff of smoke and breathed it in. "That's right Scarlet ... well done," Chrystal said encouragingly. "Now try another one, breathe it in, right down into your lungs."

As soon as I took this second puff, I knew something wasn't right. I started feeling really hot and dizzy. Not long after that, a strange feeling began to rise up inside me and I knew I was going to be sick ... violently sick. I dropped the cigarette I was holding and dashed out of the bedroom towards the bathroom. I didn't quite make it unfortunately as someone had shut the door and I couldn't get it open in time.

Chrystal got in big trouble when my mother came to investigate what the noise was all about only to find vomit up and down the bathroom door. I was sent to bed with my tail between my legs and Chrystal was given the job of cleaning up my mess. Ooops ... sorry about that one big sister.

Something good came out of this experience though. I've never touched another cigarette between that day and this. In fact, just the thought of taking a puff brings that queasy feeling straight back to me and I'm 11 years old again being offered a cigarette by Chrystal in our bedroom.

Thanks Chrystal. You helped me dodge a big bullet a lot of my peers didn't.

🐛 🐛 🐛

The next present David gave Chrystal seemed to arrive out of the blue – a little like David himself appearing on the scene only a few months earlier.

I was in my bedroom at the time when I heard the familiar sound of many people talking at once in the living room. Not wanting to be left out, I raced down the hall and into the lounge to see everyone looking at Chrystal's finger. David had given Chrystal a ring with loads of sparkly diamonds.

"Wow," I thought. "David must quite like Chrystal to give her such an amazing ring." It took a few more minutes for me to realise what everyone else must have known right from the start – David had asked Chrystal to marry him and this was the engagement ring he'd offered her. From all the congratulatory pats on the back and hugs, I took it Chrystal must have said "yes." My big sister was going to get married! I was so excited for them and ran over to give them both a kiss and a big hug.

"You're just looking forward to having that bedroom all to yourself!" teased Burt as he cracked open a bottle of beer and filled everyone's glasses. The thought hadn't actually occurred to me yet – that Chrystal was going to move out and live with David. I didn't know whether to laugh or cry. I'd never had my own space before.

Mum put paid to that idea straight away. "When Chrystal gets married, Jane can move into your bedroom with you, Scarlet. She can have Chrystal's old bed."

Oh well. Easy come, easy go.

But it wasn't really the thought of who was going to sleep where that was racing around my mind right then. I was mostly thinking that I wasn't at all looking forward to Chrystal not being around all the time. Things were changing a little too quickly for my liking.

Realising that the penny was dropping in my mind, Chrystal tried to reassure me. "Don't be upset Scarlet. When I'm married, I'll still be working at the factory so I'll see you every day. Besides, the wedding won't be for ages."

And yet, in what seemed like the blink of an eye, it was November and there we all were, lining up outside St. Augustine's Church in Petone about to celebrate Chrystal and David's nuptials. I'd known of couples in our street who had been engaged for two years or more before they were married. You can't say Chrystal and David wasted any time in that department; from the time David arrived on the scene until the time they were married, barely six months had passed by.

They certainly picked a great day for the wedding. It was a flawless fine and hot late Spring day with absolutely no wind. I was chuffed to be one of Chrystal's four bridesmaids. Mum had made all the bridesmaids' dresses and guess what colour Chrystal had chosen? That's right – Scarlet!

Chrystal made a stunning bride in her ivory wedding dress. After the wedding photos had been taken at Percy's Reserve gardens, the wedding party headed off to the reception held at the Petone Working Men's Club. In those days, the club was quite the venue as it was housed in a grand old building on Campbell Terrace before it moved to its more modern location in Udy Street in 1977. I remember the very flash bubbly wine served to all the guests that day – Marque Vue. When the adults were drinking their bubbly wine and making toasts, I thought it was the height of sophistication!

This was the music that was played as Chrystal and David took their first dance together as a married couple:

Sonny & Cher – I Got You Babe

Later in the evening, Frank and I sneaked out of the reception to fix a "Just Married" sign on the back of David's Ford Escort.

One of the collateral advantages of Chrystal marrying David was there was far less cigarette smoke in the living room every night. Ever since my "cigarette episode" I couldn't stand the smell of smoke, so that was a bonus.

An even bigger bonus was that Chrystal had left her record player behind in my bedroom for me to use. My little sister Jane had now moved into my bedroom, so now I was the big sister. I was determined to be just as good a big sister to Jane as Chrystal had been to me.

Chrystal and David now lived in a hill suburb of Wellington called Ngaio where they rented one of the flats owned by David's parents in Heke Street. For a wedding present, I'd bought them an oversize wooden fork and spoon carved with ornate Maori figures and motifs. David made a fitting for them and hung them up in pride of place in their kitchen.

Chrystal was quite right about seeing her every day. She would drive down the hill from Ngaio to Petone very early every morning and come in and see us all before she headed across the road to the factory. I would also see her after school when I went to work. Chrystal drove the Ford Escort around and David drove his father's work Ute, so the Escort really became Chrystal's car. I got so used to the sound of it that I could hear it coming a mile away and I'd dash outside to meet Chrystal at the curb.

There were lots of benefits to Chrystal being married, but I would have swapped them all to have had Chrystal living back at home with us. Mum said this was simply the way of the world, that the chicks all leave the nest eventually.

One evening, Chrystal and David turned up at home unexpectedly with a big leather bound photo album full of photos from the wedding. Everyone piled into the living room to look through the portfolio. "Now before I start," laughed Chrystal, "see if you can see something in common in almost all of the photos."

She began turning the pages and before long we realised the "thing in common" was me! I'd managed to appear in almost every single photo. This was a little unusual for me, as I didn't like having my photo taken at all. But at the wedding I'd been in a silly mood and this translated into me ending up in most of the photos.

Back in 1975 there was no word for what I'd been up to on the day of the wedding. Today there is – "photo bombing." Whenever we talk about Chrystal's wedding day, she always says I was ahead of my time in photo bombing my way into almost all of the photos taken that day.

❦ ❦ ❦

The Christmas holidays were fast approaching and so was the social occasion of the year – the Annual Factory Christmas party. The party was always held on the evening of the last day of work for the year. After the party wound up, the factory closed down for three weeks, and everybody took their year's allotment of annual leave. That was the way things were done back then. In fact, it seemed the whole of New Zealand closed down in the last week of December and the first two weeks of the following January. Being the last day at work for three weeks meant everybody was in extremely high spirits and absolutely in the mood for a party.

Not too long into the festivities, the Cliff Curtis lookalike struck a few chords on his guitar and took to the makeshift stage. As he did every year, he yelled out, "Hey Scarlet, get over here!" This year, he'd learned to play a Tony Orlando song that had been around for a while. I knew this particular song well as my father was a bit of a Tony Orlando fan. Dad would play this song in our living room in the evening when we were having our private parties and we'd sing and dance along to it:

Tony Orlando & Dawn – Candida

A lot of the partygoers knew the words to Candida as well and the song nearly lifted the roof off the old factory!

After a couple of songs, gorgeous Cliff and I went in search of the food table which we found groaning with hot-off-the-press pork sandwiches with crackling and apple sauce. In between devouring the sandwiches, we would talk about the songs we'd sing together next. I was in heaven and I didn't want the evening to end.

If you'd like to take a look at the actual Cliff Curtis, check out the clip below.

YouTube: Exclusive: Cliff Curtis reveals what it feels like to play a Maori hero fighting Zombies (4:56)

Hey Cliff – I think you're gorgeous, eh!

15

1976

At last I've come to my final year at Petone Central School. I'm now 12 years old and the following year will be my first at High School. "I'd better make the most of this year," I thought to myself on my first day in Form Two. "It's all business at High School."

I had the best teacher ever for my last year at Petone Central School. I felt so lucky because the year before had not been a good one for me at school. My new teacher on the other hand was the perfect fit for me as he and I shared a lot of the same interests, for example singing and running. He introduced me to the world of long-distance running which I still enjoy to this day.

But the best thing above all else about this teacher was that he was great at helping me with my Maths. He had a way of explaining things in innovative ways that made me understand whatever it was we were working on at the time. He was one of those teachers who made a difference in your life and who you never forget. I was really lucky to have him.

He was also very skilled at the guitar and had a fantastic singing voice. He introduced me, along with my whole class, to his favourite band – the Eagles. He used to play his guitar and sing "Take It To The Limit" all the time and he taught my class to join in like the HomeTown boys below – not quite as proficiently of course, but we gave it a good crack!

*YouTube: HomeTown – Take It To The Limit (The Eagles
Cover) Crookedwood Studios Session (4:05)*

The Eagles weren't completely unknown to me – I'd heard of them as Frank had a Greatest Hits album of theirs. Like Chrystal, Frank and Burt had a record player in their bedroom and I'd started going in there when they were both out to surreptitiously check out their albums. Their taste in music was slightly rockier than mine at this stage in my life – for example, I've already mentioned Burt was a gigantic Led Zeppelin fan – but I did really enjoy playing their records on the sly.

🎵 🎵 🎵

The time had finally come to ask my mum to help me buy my first bra. I was still doing athletics and gymnastics which involved lots of running etc, and I had these ... boobs. I think you can get the rest. Mum and I went to Farmers in Petone where we bought a few bits and pieces; the bra, a new gymnastics leotard and some new gym shoes.

The gym shoes were special shoes made of white leather with a rubber sole which tightly hugged your feet so you could grip onto the gymnastics beam. The beam was my favourite piece of equipment at gym. Second favourite was sprinting up to the springboard and bouncing off the vault to execute somersaults and twists and land on the mat to finish gracefully – hopefully.

I may have been no Olga Korbut or Nadia Comaneci – I loved watching those girls at the 1972 and 1976 Olympic Games – but I was an ok gymnast. I loved the sport and worked hard at it. But then I started growing up and things were ... getting in the way ... so to speak. Have a look at any good female gymnast and you'll see they're stick thin all over – which I no longer was unfortunately.

Not to worry.

The Universe was about to make another physical activity known to me.

🦂 🦂 🦂

Looking back on it, I loved growing up in Petone. I just didn't really appreciate what I had at the time. Our house was close to work, close to the main shopping streets of town, close to the train station and best of all, close to the beach. Matilda and I would often walk down to the beach to play when we were kids. It was like our own personal playground.

We were getting older now though and our "play" turned to other things like sunbathing. On a nice day, we would walk down to Petone beach with our bikinis on under our clothes. Once there, we'd lay out our towels, strip off to our bikinis, smother ourselves with coconut oil and read magazines. There was no "slip, slop, slap" Sunsmart type campaigns in those days – we wanted to get as brown as we possibly could as quickly as we possibly could. Pale was very uncool in 1976, so on went the tanning oil!

Matilda always had the latest magazines and we loved reading them and talking about the stories. We'd outgrown "Jackie" and "Princess Tina" which were more comic-like with romantic stories of boy-meets-girl, boy or girl loses girl or boy, boy or girl regains girl or boy, boy loses interest in girl and cheats on her – and every other permutation you could possibly imagine.

Now we were reading sophisticated grown-up women's magazines such as Cosmopolitan and Cleo. In these magazines we learned extremely valuable things that all young women should know such as, "what men like," "what men don't like," "how to get a man," "how to keep a man," "how to recognise the red flags," "how to get your man back when your best friend has stolen him," (Matilda and I swore a solemn oath we'd never *ever* do this to each other) "secrets of being a good kisser," and "tips for great oral." Matilda and I skipped that last article as we figured we were already quite good at talking to boys.

I wasn't able to contribute much to the pool of magazines available to Matilda and me. After the arguments I'd had with my mum over money, I was allowed to buy the odd record and pay off an item of clothing on layby with my wages from the factory, but I had to save the rest. Mum would *never* have let me buy such a frivolous thing as a magazine. She said if I wanted to read something, she would give me the newspaper after she and my dad had finished with it. I can't remember ever taking her up on that offer.

One Sunday morning in late Summer, I was down at the beach waiting for Matilda to finish Church and join me. I was sunbathing at our usual spot and I noticed a group of Karate students who were older than me dressed in their Karate Gis and black belts. They were working with their Sensei on a series of moves or "kata" which they were performing in perfect unison.

I was absolutely mesmerized by those Karate students and the movements they were making; one moment they'd be stepping and turning, the next, punching or kicking. Everything was done with such precision and discipline whether it was a fast move or a slow one. It was simply amazing!

I couldn't stop watching these students at work and I was sure with a little training I'd be able to do what they were doing. I had a background in gymnastics and athletics after all. Another thing I noticed about the group – there was only one single female student in the whole bunch of a dozen or so. I couldn't help but wonder why that should be.

Although I loved gymnastics and athletics, Karate looked far more exciting to me. I decided then and there I wanted what those Karate students had – especially the Sensei with his exquisite control and fine movements. I knew exactly what I had to do. The little Karate I'd seen that morning screamed discipline and hard work. I realised straight away I didn't have the time to do everything, so I made the difficult decision to give gymnastics and athletics away and focus everything on Karate.

Karate looked challenging and it filled me with excitement. I was sold; all I had to do now was to get my parents on side with my decision.

As soon as Matilda arrived at the beach, she unpacked her bag and took out a small transistor radio so we had some music to listen to. I pointed out the Karate students not far away along the beach and we both watched them for a little while. After a few minutes I couldn't contain myself any longer so I hopped up and tried to mimic the kata movements the students were practising.

Matilda was very impressed. "Wow Scarlet!" she said excitedly. "You're doing it exactly the same as those Karate guys!" I wasn't sure whether this was what Matilda really thought, or whether she was being a good friend. Maybe it was both.

"I love you Best Friend Matilda!" I thought.

That Sunday morning was one of those pivotal moments you have in your life from time to time, one of those moments you look back on in later years and can recall in vivid detail. I remember the Karate students practising their kata with precision and beauty; I remember the magazines Matilda and I read and talked about; I even remember the songs playing on the radio – they were all songs Matilda and I loved.

In particular, I remember singing this song together with Matilda while it played on her little transistor radio as we sat on our towels at Petone beach that sunny Summer's Sunday:

Barry Manilow – I Write the Songs

When I arrived home from the beach that afternoon, I enthusiastically ran up to my mother and asked if I could drop out of gym and athletics and learn Karate. I got quite the surprise when this request didn't go down at all well with Mum. In fact, she had a blue fit. She went on and on about the new gymnastics gear she'd only just bought me and that she'd recently paid the fees for the term. Mum was really wild, but eventually calmed down and we were able to have a rational discussion about the whole thing.

Mum's concerns were twofold. First, she didn't think Karate was very ladylike and she'd been worried for some time whether I'd ever behave like a young lady should. Secondly, she didn't like the fact I still hit Frank whenever he annoyed me, which to be honest was a lot. In her view, learning Karate was only going to make me more aggressive towards Frank, not to mention more dangerous when I lashed out at him.

I saw an opportunity here, so I reasoned with my mother. "Ok Mum, if I promise to act like a lady and promise to stop smashing Frank, will you let me do Karate?"

Mum thought about this for a little while. "Well Scarlet, if you can promise those two things, you can ask your father when he gets home."

"Yessss!" I thought and almost punched the air. My father would be really easy to get on board with this Karate thing and I couldn't wait for him to get home.

If I was surprised at Mum's reaction, I was positively dismayed with Dad's. He simply didn't want me to learn Karate *at all*. He was so against it, even more so than my mother. He pretty much had the same concerns as Mum did, so she and I talked him through the agreement we'd discussed earlier. I even added I'd pay for my own Gi and the first term's tuition out of my own money if they'd let me start Karate straight away.

Eventually they both agreed and the deal was done. I was to become a young lady, I dropped out of gymnastics and athletics and I started Karate. And I was to stop smashing Frank. Even I wasn't too sure how that one would play out.

I bought my first Gi with my own money as I'd promised and made sure I bought one a size or two too large so I could put it in the drier at the factory and not grow out of it in six months' time. I'd learned those lessons the hard way after buying my first couple of pairs of jeans. I also paid for the first term's Karate tuition out of my savings.

The day finally arrived for my very first Karate lesson. I was so excited! At the dōjō, I noticed a boy who sat on the sidelines for the whole class. Whilst he was dressed in his Gi, he sat to one side, watching. As soon as the class was finished, I went up to him and asked why he hadn't taken part in the class. He explained how his mother hadn't been able to pay his fees yet and until she did, he wasn't allowed to join in.

"Crikey!" I thought. "I'd better make sure my fees are always paid up on time." I made a mental note to draw money out of my own bank account if my parents didn't have enough for fees because I didn't want to miss a single lesson. Sometimes I did have to draw on my own resources when times were tight.

I absolutely loved Karate and I'd practise it all the time in my back yard. I'd practise the kata movements over and over again until they became second nature and automatic. I found out that the Karate beach session which had inspired me to start Karate was a special lesson our Sensei put on for free, but only for the best, most passionate and dedicated students. The elite. It became my dream and my goal to make the Sunday beach squad one day.

It wasn't long before I'd earned a black tab to go on my white belt, my first progression through the grades of Karate. My gymnastics and athletics training really helped and before long I'd mastered the double kick and I was awarded an orange belt.

My Sensei was very big on fitness. Like huge. He had us running all over Petone in our Gis and bare feet. This was all part of toughening us up and I loved it. I couldn't understand it when a girl my age who had started at the same time as me dropped out because she didn't like running in bare feet. When the other Karate kids heard about this, they called her a "big time piker."

I was used to running around in bare feet anyway because I could never bring myself to ask my parents to buy me a pair of running shoes. I suppose I sensed they were already financially stretched, so I didn't even bother to ask the question. I think being a fourth child made me more accepting of my situation and grateful for the things I did have.

🐾 🐾 🐾

Not long after they were married, Chrystal and David welcomed a new addition to their family. It's not what you're probably thinking though; it was neither a baby nor a horse, but a small white fluff ball of a Samoyed puppy. Chrystal and David named him "Kemo Sabe," the term of endearment Tonto used for The Lone Ranger in the TV show. We'd heard somewhere that "Kemo Sabe" translated to "trusted friend," and whether or not this was true, "trusted friend" is what that adorable fluffy dog quickly came to mean to our entire family. Just as quickly, Kemo grew from being a small white fluff ball to a rather large white fluff ball.

YouTube: thats Right Kemosabe (0:20)

From then on, Kemo would accompany Chrystal in the Ford Escort each morning to be entertained by Mum and Jane while Chrystal was at work at the factory. Chrystal had a real way with animals and she introduced Kemo to Snoopy in such a way that they became good friends, sometimes even snuggling up with each other for a snooze.

This gave Chrystal the confidence to make a second addition to her family shortly after the first. This time it was of the feline variety – a long-haired ginger-and-white Persian tomcat Chrystal and David called Eugene. Kemo and Eugene grew up together and it seemed as though they thought they were brothers because they got on extremely well with each other. Chrystal said the only downside to her growing family was she now had even more fur to clean up around her house.

When Kemo arrived at my place in the morning, he'd make a beeline for my bedroom and next thing would be all over me. Every morning Chrystal would have to say, "Down boy, leave Scarlet alone!" and every morning Kemo would ignore her. I didn't mind, I loved that dog. I think Mum did too, but she got the job of cleaning up after him. Invariably, there was white fluff all over the house by the time Chrystal got back from the factory each afternoon.

Kemo was always very excited, but was very clever too and we all trained him to do little tricks. He also knew the meaning of the word "walkies;" whenever anyone said that word, Kemo would run to his lead and sit there waiting expectantly for someone to take him for a walk. It wasn't long before Chrystal had Kemo well trained and he even became a champion Show dog.

Ever since the Petone Spiritualist Church bought the house across the road, strange things would happen in our house. I often had the feeling an unknown presence was watching me, but I could never see anything or put my finger on exactly what was going on. Now Kemo Sabe was coming to our house almost every day, he picked up on "the unknown presence" straight away. When he came bounding into my bedroom, the first thing he'd do would be to jump up all over me wanting a bit of love. After that, he'd face the eastern wall in my bedroom – the wall directly facing the Spiritualist Church – and bark and bark and bark. There was clearly nothing there, but this didn't stop Kemo barking the house down until someone finally led him to another room. It was very strange and not a little disconcerting.

Everyone in the house saw Kemo do this but didn't think too much of it. But Chrystal and I did and we spoke about it often. This was fine until Chrystal went home to Ngaio and I was left to go to bed in my room with only a 2 year old for company.

Snoopy had also picked up on "the unknown presence" straight away. As a little girl, I loved that he would sleep on my bed sometimes and he'd often be seen during the day in my bedroom. All that changed when the Spiritualist Church arrived. Snoopy would no longer come anywhere near my room. Even when I'd carry him in and put him down on my bed for a pat, he'd run straight out of the room.

As Matilda was slightly older than me, she was now at High School. We still had sleepovers at each other's houses regularly and when I was staying over at her place, I'd watch as her scary grandmother roamed around the house looking for all the things the Trolls had taken or hidden. If anything, the level of activity in Matilda's house seemed to have taken a step up and her grandmother was forever going on about "the bypasses."

While I was still of the view that Matilda's grandmother was bonkers, the presence of the Spiritualist Church across the road did make me wonder whether it had anything to do with all the weirdness going on in both Matilda's house and mine.

🐜 🐜 🐜

I was thoroughly enjoying my Form Two year. Not only did I have a fantastic, motivational teacher, but when the research project was announced for the year, we were allowed to pick any topic we wanted ... anything at all. I was *finally* able to complete the research I'd begun a couple of years earlier on Greenland and went all out to do the best job I could.

I supplemented my presentation to the class with pictures and diagrams and my teacher awarded me one of the top marks in my entire year group. I was stoked!

Towards the end of the school year, the Petone Central School Talent Quest kicked off again. I was wondering whether I was going to enter and what I might perform when, out of the blue, a girl from my class called Bridget came up to me and asked whether I'd like to sing with her. I was quite chuffed, as this was the same Bridget who'd won the Talent Quest the previous year – the girl who I'd always thought had the best singing voice in our whole school.

When Bridget and I told our teacher we were going to sing something together, he thought we'd make a good team because Bridget had a mezzo soprano voice and I had a soprano voice. I didn't have a clue what that meant; I just knew Bridget had dark hair and I had blonde hair and in our universe there was a fundamental law of nature that went:

Blonde Hair + Dark Hair = Abba

So we had no choice really but to sing an Abba song. We picked the one that had just been released in New Zealand and was racing up the charts, eventually reaching Number One.

The two of us practised together for weeks leading up to the Talent Quest; before school, lunchtimes, evenings, whenever we both had a spare moment. We also practised all of the Abba moves.

On the day of the Talent Quest, I asked my mother if she could help me iron all the curls out of my long blonde hair. I explained to her I simply *had* to look like the blonde singer in Abba, and she definitely didn't have any curls. After Mum ironed my hair straight, I got all the other stuff I needed together. I'd borrowed a dress from best friend Matilda – a short, backless dress which tied up at the back of the neck. Matilda called it a "halter neck" dress and it looked just the part. I also borrowed Matilda's boots that laced up the front, just like the blonde girl in Abba wore. I was all set!

When I walked into the kitchen dressed in my Talent Quest outfit, my mother did a double take and had a very surprised expression on her face. She looked at me up and down, made me turn around again and again and then looked at me up and down again.

"Scarlet!" she said in a stunned tone. "I've only ever seen you wear jeans and tops for the last couple of years, never a dress."

The way Mum was looking at me, I thought I'd done something wrong, or put my dress on back to front.

"I'm amazed!" Mum continued. "You look like a proper young lady."

"Wow," I thought. "So this is what Mum meant all those times she said she wanted me to be a lady. I just had to wear a dress!"

"Thanks Mum," I said and took off to the bathroom to have a proper look at myself in the tiny 6 inch by 12 inch mirror inlaid into the medicine cabinet door.

Later at the Talent Quest, I saw Mum and Jane sitting in the audience. I can't recall being nervous – more excited to get up on stage and show everyone how hard Bridget and I had been working on our performance.

Finally it was our turn. "You girls have fun up there, ok?" our teacher said and we took our places. Both Bridget and I loved our teacher, so we took his advice and had fun.

We stood up on stage with our backs to the packed audience and waited for the music to start. We'd each used a microphone to practise with, which was just as well as the long thick cord tended to get caught up and twisted if you weren't careful. No wireless technology back in 1976. As the music struck up, we stole a glimpse at each other, smiled, turned around to face the audience and gave the performance of our young lives. We had such fun singing and dancing, trying to match the Abba girls in the music video we'd seen on TV as closely as we could.

Abba – Dancing Queen

To this day, I think Dancing Queen is one of Abba's finest creations – if not ***the*** finest. Whatever you may think of them, Björn Ulvaeus and Benny Andersson were craftsmen, masters of the pop song form. Their genius in Dancing Queen was to put the chorus right at the start of the song rather than the usual verse-chorus-verse-chorus structure. But it only worked out so well because the chorus is so good – one of the best of all time. That first chorus is a statement of intent and the rest of the song does not disappoint. Every time I hear Dancing Queen, I think it is a perfect piece of pop confectionery.

At the end of the Talent Quest, our Headmaster Mr. Hewson hopped up on stage to announce the winners. The whole audience fell silent with anticipation. He was handed a microphone, flicked the switch and the familiar mains hum came through the school's PA system. Right at that moment as you could almost cut the atmosphere with a knife, my little sister Jane called out to me across the hall in a loud voice. "Scarlet, look!" she yelled. "I have a new tote!" She meant "coat" of course and the whole hall erupted in laughter.

I wasn't embarrassed really and I had a pretty good laugh myself. From that point onwards, when anyone in my family wears a new coat, that line comes out from someone; "Scarlet, look! I have a new tote!"

The Headmaster had a bit of a job on his hands to quieten everyone down after my sister's antics, but eventually there was quiet across the hall once more. There were prizes for first, second and third place and he started to announce the winners in reverse order. Bridget and I were far more nervous waiting for the results than we were performing our song.

Mr. Hewson announced third place. It wasn't us. He announced second place. It wasn't us. At that point we knew we'd either won the whole shebang, or come nowhere at all. Mr. Hewson then announced the winners. "Bridget and Scarlet for their tremendous rendition of Dancing Queen by Abba."

The audience cheered and I saw my mother stand up and applaud. I felt so proud as I turned and hugged Bridget who was smiling broadly. Somehow we'd pulled it off and won the Petone Central School Talent Quest for 1976. The Headmaster asked if we could perform the song one more time and of course we did. I think our second performance was better than the first – what pressure there was on us before was now gone. Bridget and I had a ball and everyone in the audience seemed to be singing along with us. It was such an amazing occasion to be a part of.

As Bridget and I left the stage, we had to walk past Legweak, my teacher from the year before, who was giving me a series of filthy looks. Just as we were passing Legweak, I turned to Bridget and said in a loud voice, "Come on Bridget, I'll shout you a Crazy Joe Cola Ice Block at the Dairy next door. It's really hot today!"

For some reason I can't recall, the Talent Quest for 1976 was a lot later in the school year than usual. I think it was only a matter of a few days before school broke up for the year and I'd finished my time at Petone Central School.

Bridget, who'd sung so brilliantly with me at the Talent Quest, was Catholic so she was off to an all-girls Catholic High School as a boarder the following year. I never saw her again.

There were a few girls from my school who were going to the same High School as I was. They were nice girls, but we never met up outside of school like Matilda and I did.

I still had a crush on the boy who looked a lot like Donny Osmond. I never did summon up enough courage to go and talk to him, but on the very last day of school he came up to me and we had a quick chat. He asked me which High School I was going to in the new year and he told me he was going to an all-boys private High School. I was absolutely devastated. I don't know why, but I'd always assumed he and I would go to the same High School. It was not to be though and when we parted that day, I'd never see him again either.

Speaking of people I'd never see again, Digby wasn't going to go to the same High School as me either. It wouldn't have mattered though – even if we were going to the same school, I wouldn't have seen much of him as he was destined for a life of crime. A pretty unsuccessful life of crime as it turned out.

I never entered another Talent Quest after the one in my Form Two year in 1976. But I still get a warm and fuzzy feeling whenever I recall the moment the Headmaster read out my name and Bridget's as winners of that Talent Quest over forty years ago.

I did still sing whenever I got the chance though. That year at the legendary dry-cleaning factory Christmas party, I got up on the make-shift stage with the gorgeous Cliff Curtis lookalike when he gave me the "Hey Scarlet! Get over here!" call. We sang a song that was very well known in New Zealand at the time and which the party-goers seemed to enjoy. This song was on Volume Two of the 20 Solid Gold Hits series of compilations, so everyone knew it and sang along. In fact, it went down so well that Cliff Curtis and I sang it at many factory Christmas parties after that.

Mouth and MacNeal – How Do You Do

As the curtain was falling on the year's Christmas party, I found a quiet moment to reflect on the year that had been – and it had been quite a big one for me. The thing I was most thankful for was I'd been very lucky to have had such a great teacher to end my Intermediate schooling off with. My Form Two year had eclipsed most of the bad memories from my first year at Intermediate School which were largely due to Legweak who had so disliked me for some reason.

Mr. F, in the unlikely event you read my book, you were awesome! I consider myself very fortunate to have been in your class in my final year at Petone Central School.

My thoughts then turned to the following year and how I was about to start at a new school which would take me through to my late teens. The thought was a little daunting, but for the most part I was excited at what this new chapter in my life would bring.

16

1977

Excitement. Trepidation. Anxiety. Anticipation.

All of these emotions and more bombarded me during the Summer of 1976-77 as I prepared to start High School in late January. I wouldn't say it ruined my holiday break exactly, but it was a thought that cast a shadow over everything I did and was never far from my mind during those long Summer days.

In addition to this, I'd become a teenager during the Christmas holidays and Mum often commented that "her nice little girl had gone and been replaced by a surly one." I didn't really know what Mum was on about. I didn't think I was surly at all and certainly didn't feel any different now I'd turned 13. Maybe Mum was right though and the hormones had started to flow.

Mum and I went shopping for my school uniform at the sales which invariably followed Christmas. As we were walking to the Petone shops to buy the various uniform items I needed, Mum let me in on her strategy. "I can only afford to buy you one High School uniform, Scarlet, so we're going to buy it really big so you can grow into it, ok?"

As Mum said this, I wondered how big this uniform was going to have to be, as I was growing up fast now.

Turns out it had to be very big indeed. My skirt was well below the knee and I had to turn up the cuffs of the white blouses that were part of the school uniform. I didn't say anything of course as I knew how expensive uniforms were and how tight things were financially at home. Mum bought everything I needed though, including a smart pair of black leather shoes with a seam running along the top; these were all the rage in 1977. She also bought me a special pair of blue shorts I needed for PE – physical education or "physed" for short.

There wasn't any room in the budget for running shoes and I didn't have the heart to ask for any as Mum was stressing all the way home from the shops that my uniform had wiped out the small amount she'd been able to save. I didn't mind about the running shoes of course; my feet were getting really tough now with all the bare foot running and kicking practise I was doing for Karate. There was no way a lack of running shoes was going to affect me as it had the girl who bailed out of Karate because she didn't like running in bare feet.

"What a piker!" I thought.

My High School was called Hutt Valley Memorial Technical College, a co-ed school. I already knew a few people who went there – Matilda did for example, but she was a year ahead of me. Frank was also a student there, although he didn't really count.

Once I'd started at my new school, I quickly fell into a morning routine. At 7am, Dad would play one of his songs on the stereo in the living room to blast Frank and I out of bed. I'd usually already been woken up by then by my little sister Jane who had a knack of waking up at the crack of dawn, whatever time that was. I swear, as soon as her eyes opened in the morning, she'd bounce out of bed and go running to find Mum. I'd then roll over and try to get another hour's sleep or so.

I loved my dad's music, so when I heard the stereo start up at 7am on the dot, I'd race out of bed to join him in the living room. For as long as I could remember, Dad would get me to stand on his feet and we'd dance around the living room to one song or another. Now as a teenager, I was definitely too big for that, but we still had a dance together.

My dad loved Tony Christie – and I mean he really *loved* Tony Christie. Chances were if you turned up at our house at 7 in the morning, you'd be greeted by Tony Christie playing on the stereo with Dad and I having a little dance.

Here is one of our all-time Tony Christie faves.

Tony Christie – Is This The Way To Amarillo

Dad and I played this song countless times in the morning, so often in fact I can still remember all of the words off-by-heart forty years later.

After a quick dance and singsong, Dad would head across the road to the factory and light the giant boiler which generated most of the factory's power. Straight up – when he lit that boiler, you could hear and even feel the rumble of it all the way across the road in our house.

After Dad left, I'd get some breakfast and get ready for school. Hutt Valley Memorial Technical College was a good 45 minute walk away, so I'd need to be out the door by 8am at the latest to get there comfortably in time for Period One.

All Summer, I'd run movies in my head of Matilda and I merrily walking to and from school each day and I was really looking forward to it. For my first day at school, I'd arranged to meet Matilda at my front gate at 8am sharp. From there, we'd walk the 45 minutes to school in a leisurely manner chatting about this and that.

So there I was at 8am, dutifully waiting for my friend and ... nothing. No sign of her. 8:05 came and went. 8:10 came and went and I was starting to get very nervous. "Hey Matilda," I yelled in the general direction of her house, "get your A into G ok?" In Kiwi Speak this means, "get your Arse into Gear," or more politely, "get a move on!"

A minute or two later, Matilda came running out from her house. "Come on Scarlet, what are you waiting for?!" she said cheekily. We were off!

"Nothing leisurely about this first trip to school," I thought as Matilda and I jogged the whole way there. Not exactly the way I wanted my first morning at a new school to go.

My first day at school was actually pretty good as first days go and I made friends with a girl in my class called Tracey who was very good looking and had lovely long dark hair. I didn't know it at the time, but Tracey was to become a good friend. That first day was a little overwhelming however, as everything was so different to what I'd been used to at Primary and Intermediate School. I sensed this feeling wouldn't last long though.

After school, I ran all the way to the factory for my after-school job. I went straight up to Queenie and stood in front of her with a smile on my face. She took one look at me in my oversized school uniform and took a step back from me. "Woah, Scarlet! What is up with that big as uniform? I need to sort you out don't I girl?"

"Thanks Queenie," I said. "I was hoping you would!"

After a quick examination, Queenie said she could easily nip and tuck my school uniform here and there to shorten it in such a way that it could be let out again as I grew into it. She was in charge of making all the alterations to the most expensive pieces of clothing at the factory, so I knew I'd come to the right place.

I was rapt. In no time, Queenie had taken my skirt up to just above the knee so now I looked like all the other girls at school. I was so thankful to Queenie; she was always so lovely and caring towards me and I truly looked on her as a second mother.

"Thanks Queenie," I said appreciatively when she'd finished altering my uniform. "You're the best!"

🐫 🐫 🐫

I very quickly realised Matilda was genetically wired to be late for school. Every. Single. Morning. I'd never noticed this about her before, but she got later and later each morning in spite of me yelling at her from the front gate to get her A into G. Things got to the point where I finally had to suggest we find our own way to school in the morning. I'd always disliked being late for any kind of meeting or appointment and I found I doubly disliked being late for school. Matilda had extra-curricular activities to attend once school had finished and I had my job to get to, so we very rarely walked home from school together either.

Matilda was a true academic and enjoyed the extra classes she took after school. One of the extra classes was French and it turned out she was very good at it. Within a couple of weeks of the start of term, Matilda tried to convince me to take French in the after-school class with her, which I eventually did. After the weekly French class, Matilda and I would walk home practising French on each other.

"Parlez vous Français?" I'd ask her. [Can you speak French?]

"Oui je peux," she'd reply. [Yes, I can.]

🐛 🐛 🐛

Not long after the school year had begun, and as Summer was start-ing to fade into Autumn, the Hutt Valley Memorial Technical College Athletics Day was held. I'd been looking forward to this day as I wanted to test myself athletically against a wider pool of girls than I was used to at Petone Central School. I'd been one of the fastest female runners at Primary and Intermediate School, but High School was different and I didn't know what I'd be up against.

I entered into quite a few races that first Athletics Day and somehow Frank always managed to be on the sidelines cheering me on. I really don't know how he managed it, but he was always there. On reflection, he'd always been a very supportive brother like that, even if he was also the most annoying boy in the Known Universe.

The first race I entered was the 400 metres. I lined up on the track looking at all the other girls slightly ahead and behind me and realised they all had running shoes; I was the only girl to be running in bare feet.

My heart was racing so fast I thought it was going to jump out of my chest. When the starting pistol went off, my training kicked in and I took off. I remember one of my old athletics coaches saying the 400 metres was a unique race. "You have to sprint the first 200 metres and then you have to sprint the last 200 metres as well," he'd said. That's what makes the 400 metres so tough – you've got to run full tilt from start to finish.

I ended up coming second in that race – I was pretty happy with that. The winner of the race was a very good looking girl called Aroha ("love" in Maori). She came up to me after the race and shook my hand. "Good race," she said assertively. "What's your name?"

"Scarlet," I said. "What's yours?"

"Aroha," she replied. "Nice to meet you Scarlet. You're very fast and I only just beat you."

"I don't know about that," I said. "You were so much faster." Aroha smiled and ran off. "I think I may have made another friend," I thought.

Frank came running up to me after Aroha left. "Scarlet, you would've won that race if you had some running shoes." I said the same thing to him as I had to Aroha – that I wouldn't have because Aroha was much faster than me – but Frank was convinced I was the better runner.

You know what my lovely big brother did after that? He bought me my first ever pair of running shoes with some of the money he'd saved from working at the factory during the school holidays. The next time I raced Aroha I had my new running shoes on, but the result was the same. That girl could run like the wind. The difference was I now had a newly-found respect for Frank. I've never forgotten how generous he was in buying me those running shoes and how generous he was with his time in always cheering me on from the sidelines at athletics – and later Karate.

I started to appreciate Frank more after that and I came to the realisation that I actually had an awesome brother. Annoying but awesome. In 1977 I was only starting to realise how amazing Frank was, and this realisation only grew as I got older and matured. I couldn't know it then, but Frank would always cheer me on whatever I was doing and look after me throughout my life in good times and bad. I'm so lucky to have Frank as my big brother.

As for Aroha, we *did* become good friends and she invited me on a number of occasions after school to the house in Petone where she lived with her grandmother. Her house was a turn-of-the-century villa like mine, but extremely well kept and maintained. It was amazing compared to my house. For one thing, it didn't have scrim on the walls that would blow in and out and whistle in the wind like my house had.

Once I'd seen how great Aroha's house was, I was way too embarrassed to ask any of my friends back to my place after that. Our house was too run down and in desperate need of a paint job – at the very least – to have friends over.

❦ ❦ ❦

Frank was now in his mid-teens and having developed a keen interest in hunting, eventually secured a firearms licence. His first purchase was a .22 calibre air rifle he bought using the rest of the money he'd saved from working at the factory over the school holidays. His air rifle fired slugs (pellets) and Frank would take me up to Horokiwi to practise firing at tin cans. Frank taught me how to handle the rifle and the Number One rule around firearms – always treat a weapon as though it's loaded. After a few weekends with the air rifle, both he and I were getting to be pretty good shots.

One afternoon, Frank and I were at Horokiwi practising with the air rifle and the farmer whose permission we'd obtained to shoot on his land approached us. He'd been watching Frank and thought he was very responsible around guns for a boy his age and a good shot as well.

The farmer asked Frank if he'd like to try his hand at rabbit shooting around his property. He said he was having a lot of trouble with rabbits around the paddocks where he ran some cows. He was experiencing a lot of cases where his cows were breaking their legs in the burrows dug by rabbits and then the cows would have to be put down. The farmer said he could really do with a hand in controlling the rabbit population and he'd supply all the slugs Frank needed. He also said he had an air rifle I could use if I wanted to shoot some rabbits too.

Frank and I jumped at the opportunity and we went off rabbit shooting straight away. I was a bit of a waste of time to be honest as I found I couldn't bear to actually shoot any of those cute little bunnies, even if they were a pest. I would point and aim the rifle at a rabbit, but I just couldn't bring myself to shoot the poor little thing even though I could hear Frank shouting, "Scarlet … shoot! … pull the trigger!!" But I never could.

Frank shot quite a few rabbits that first day. On our way home he spoke to the farmer. "My sister is good at shooting tin cans, but useless at shooting rabbits." They both laughed. "But my best mate is a good shot and he has his own air rifle as well. Should I bring him up next weekend for a shoot?"

The farmer thought this was a great idea, and so it was that Frank and Matilda's brother would head up to Horokiwi for a shoot almost every weekend, either first thing in the morning or late afternoon when the rabbits came out to feed. I would still go up occasionally but I wasn't interested in shooting the rabbits – only tin cans. I do recall actually shooting at a rabbit once, but ended up only parting its fur. I still couldn't bring myself to shoot that cute little bunny.

One of the by-products of Frank's shooting expeditions was he'd bring home two or three rabbits each time he went up to Horokiwi. The farmer showed Frank and Matilda's brother how to skin and dress the rabbit for cooking. It was a great deal all round and everyone got something out of it. Frank and Matilda's brother got to hone their hunting, shooting and skinning skills all pretty much for free. The farmer lost less cows and got a few bucks each for the rabbit pelts, especially when they were thicker in the Wintertime. Best of all, my family would get a delicious rabbit dinner courtesy of Mum.

It's a funny thing; I could never bring myself to shoot a bunny rabbit but I sure as heck didn't mind eating one. It made a nice change from lamb that's for sure. I thought rabbit tasted a little bit like chicken, which I'd tasted once or twice at Matilda's house, only gamier and richer.

Mum was very creative in the cooking department and she knew only too well how to cook up a bunny. My favourite was rabbit pie with super amazing puff pastry Mum would make from scratch and which I'd smother with Wattie's tomato sauce. Yum! Dad loved rabbit casserole with lashings of mashed potatoes and suede.

🐇 🐇 🐇

After years of saving, Burt and his three sailing friends had finally got together the cash they needed to buy their yacht. The boat needed a lot of work, but it wouldn't be long before they'd be ready to embark on their round-the-world trip. First stop was to be America where they wanted to watch the 1977 America's Cup yachting final at Rhode Island between the US defender, "Courageous" and the Australian challenger, "Australia."

Mum was extremely sad Burt was soon to be leaving home. It was no secret in our family that Burt was her favourite child. None of us other kids were remotely upset or jealous about this; it was simply one of the laws of the Universe in our family – that was just the way it was. In fact, rather than getting our knickers in a twist about it, we all used to make jokes instead.

For example, at dinner time one of us would yell out to Mum who would be pottering around in the kitchen. "Come on Mum, everyone's at the table … come and sit next to The Favourite Child." Mum would quietly walk over and sit down next to Burt, smile and giggle a little. She would never deny Burt was her favourite either. "There's something special about your first born," she'd simply say. "You'll find out." And that was that, done and dusted.

The day finally came for Burt and his mates to leave on their sailing adventure. Burt walked into my bedroom that morning with his hands behind his back and with a flourish handed me an album he was hiding.

"Hey Scarlet," he said, "can you look after this for me while I'm away? I know you'll take good care of it." The album he gave me was Goodbye Yellow Brick Road by Elton John. Burt knew I loved that double LP because he was forever having to rescue it from my room and take it back to his.

I was stoked when Burt gave me his record and that he thought enough of me to know I'd take care of his things. After all, he wasn't going to be away for a month or two. It was probably going to be at least a couple of years before we saw him again. I jumped up onto Burt, thanked him for the record and gave him the biggest hug. "Please come home safely to us Burt," I said. As he left my bedroom, I could see in his eyes how excited he was about sailing around the world with his mates. I was happy for him; he'd worked and saved hard for this opportunity and he deserved it.

My whole family drove over to the Seaview Marina in Petone where Burt's yacht was berthed. His friends were already there with their families – it was quite the farewell party. Mum and Waimarama were holding each other just as they were holding back the tears.

A song had got stuck in my head from the Goodbye Yellow Brick Road album Burt had given me earlier. I was singing it softly to myself as we watched Burt and his friends slowly motor out of the Marina and into Wellington Harbour on their way to the adventure of a lifetime.

Elton John – Goodbye Yellow Brick Road

Every one of us stayed and watched as Burt and his mates' yacht got smaller and smaller and eventually disappeared into the distance altogether. Waimarama finally lost it and started to cry hard out, which set Mum off, which set me off. Pretty soon most of the farewell party were sobbing as we walked back to our cars.

In the months after Burt left, Waimarama hung out at our house with my family and me a lot. I think being around us made her feel closer to Burt. For our part, it was great having Waimarama around. She was truly one of the family and she and I felt as though we were sisters.

I can clearly remember Waimarama was at our house on that terrible day in August 1977 when news broke Elvis Presley had died. It was one of those "you remember where you were when it happened" moments. We all huddled around the TV that evening to watch the news and pretty much the whole hour was devoted to the life and death of this amazing artist.

I couldn't quite believe Elvis was gone. As a music lover, his records were very familiar to me. His last ever single release, "Way Down," had made its way to the New Zealand charts literally only weeks before his death and I had it in my collection. It was sad for me to think there would be no more new music from this most original of artists. I also loved his movies which were fun to watch.

I recall the following music clip was played during the newshour on TV the night after Elvis passed.

YouTube: Elvis Presley last song ever 1977 (3:01)

Sleep now Elvis. You thoroughly earned your title, "The King."

🐾 🐾 🐾

I practised my Karate as much as I could all through 1977. "Practice makes perfect" goes the old saying, and by the end of the year I'd been awarded my green belt. I was particularly pleased with my progress because I put a lot into my Karate. It would be a rare occurrence for me not to practise at least once a day, sometimes more. I found my gymnastics background was hugely helpful, not only in getting the moves right, but also in the discipline required. Practising Karate was never a chore – I really loved doing it.

It was an ongoing source of disappointment to me that Mum and Dad weren't at all enamoured with my Karate exploits. If anyone supported me, it was Frank who came to watch me at the dōjō from time to time. But as for Mum and Dad, I knew they weren't happy with all the time and effort I was spending on a martial art. I think they were hoping Karate was a fad and I'd grow out of it soon enough. Mum was of the firm opinion that Karate wasn't something a lady should be doing and for some reason my father didn't like it either.

I kept to my side of the bargain in that I was trying to act more like a lady – when Mum and Dad were watching at least – and I made a genuine effort to stop smashing Frank. I think Mum and Dad were pretty happy with this, so I was allowed to continue with Karate even if they preferred that I do something else. I hope at least they respected the effort I was putting into my Karate studies.

From Day One, my Karate Sensei had taught all of us students never to tell anyone we were learning Karate. His reasoning, based on his own experiences, was that if people knew you were a student of Karate, there were some who would try to pick a fight with you to see what moves you had. I knew there was no danger of Mum and Dad telling absolutely anybody about my Karate as they were way too embarrassed about the whole thing. For example, my father would ask me in a fun but pointed way, "Why can't you learn ballet, or join the Girl Guides or something?"

"I'm just not a ballet kind of girl, Dad!" I'd reply and we'd both have a good laugh.

🐱 🐱 🐱

My first year at High School had come and gone so quickly and I'd enjoyed almost every minute of it. Maybe I'd enjoyed it too much because my Third Form school report was terrible – absolutely *terrible*.

I can remember one comment in particular made by my English teacher. The mark she'd given me for my year's work was a 7D, where the "7" was on a scale of 1 to 10 – 10 being the worst – for academic results and the "D" was on a scale of A to E – E being the worst –

for effort. The comment she wrote in my report card went something like, "There are times to work and times to play. Scarlet has a bad sense of timing."

Ouch.

Without a great teacher who'd taken an interest in me as I'd been blessed with the year before, my Maths result wasn't much better. It was a 6C.

It's not that I went into my Third Form year with the conscious strategy of being a slacker, but I definitely remember thinking there was no real need to work hard that year because nothing was riding on it. Same for the Fourth Form year to come. The important year was the Fifth Form where I'd be studying for School Certificate exams – I'd definitely work hard in that year. But for now, no need to bust a gut really.

That's why when I read my English teacher's terrible mark and comment in my end-of-year report, I initially thought nothing more of it. In fact, I actually thought it was funny and laughed out loud. For that matter, I thought nothing of my whole terrible report.

Then two things happened.

The first was when I attended the Third and Fourth Form Prizegiving ceremony along with Mum and Dad in the school hall one evening. It seemed like most of my friends, Tracey, Aroha and Matilda for example, received some sort of award that evening be it for excellence in this or diligence in that. Matilda, of course, received a bucketload of awards in the Fourth Form categories. She received so many awards and trophies the teachers had to find a box for her in which to cart them all home. In my naivety, I actually thought my name would be read out for something or other during the ceremony and was a little miffed when it wasn't. But in retrospect, how could it have been? I simply hadn't put the effort in during the year and I didn't deserve recognition of *any* kind. Except maybe the "Third Form Massive Underachievers Award For 1977" that is.

If that experience didn't burn, the second one certainly did.

When we arrived home from the Prizegiving ceremony, my father quietly came into my room. All he said was this: "Scarlet, I've read your report and I think you're selling yourself short. Way short. You can do much better."

This was all Dad said before disappearing back down the hallway. Boy, that hurt! It hurt because he was absolutely right. I had a mini epiphany – the scales fell from my eyes. I'd mucked around the whole of my Third Form year and the truth was in black and white in my terrible report. I *had* sold myself short, I saw that now.

Right then and there, I resolved that things were going to change. From then on, I was going to work at my studies and put my best foot forward. If I didn't get good academic marks after that, at least it wouldn't be for the want of trying.

One of the things I did to make a change was to go and talk to Frank. He was extremely good at Maths – it was his best subject in fact – so I asked him if he could help me the following year because I wanted to improve on my Third Form mark.

"What mark did you get for Maths this year?" Frank enquired.

I put my head down. "6C," I said quietly.

"Whoa!" Frank shot back. "I didn't know our marks could go that low!!"

I had to laugh.

"I thought you were getting better at Maths," Frank said. "You certainly seemed to be getting it more last year at Intermediate School than you had been."

"Yeah, that's right," I replied sadly. "I had a great teacher that year who spent a lot of extra time helping me with my Maths. But I didn't have that this year and I guess ... I guess I just mucked around and I've slipped back down again. Can you help me get my mark back up, Frank? Please!"

"No problemo Scarlet," Frank said brightly. "I can help you get a way better mark than a 6C! I'll be able to show you some new and different ways to look at Maths that I've learned that will help you a lot.

But you've got to put the work in ok? That's the only real trick with schoolwork – you have to be prepared to put the hours in."

"Absolutely I will, thanks Frank," I said with relief and appreciation. Maybe things were looking up on the Maths front. Who knew the answer had been in front of me the whole time in the form of my brother. To be fair, Frank was always helpful like that. Even if he was annoying.

༄ ༄ ༄

The friend I'd made on my first day of school, Tracey, was starting to become more important in my life and we did a lot of things outside of school. One Saturday afternoon in early December, we met up at the Petone Railway Station to make the journey into Wellington to watch a movie everyone was talking about. For some reason, this movie hadn't come to the State Theatre in Petone, so we had to make the trek into Wellington to see it. We weren't disappointed.

The movie Tracey and I went to see was directed by George Lucas, the guy who'd made American Graffiti. We'd first heard about it when a boy in our class had returned from a holiday in Disneyland around the middle of the year. He told us he'd seen an amazing movie when he was in LA and was blown away by it. America was going mental about this movie and it was one of the first to take advantage of its popularity by selling merchandise based on the characters. The boy didn't think it would be long before it got to New Zealand. He was wrong about that one however, as it took around six months after it was released in America before it came to NZ. The buzz certainly hit here not long after its release in the States, but the film didn't actually make it to our shores until December of 1977.

The movie I'm talking about is, of course, Star Wars.

YouTube: Star Wars Theme – Disco version (3:33)

Tracey and I absolutely loved Star Wars. By this I mean we loved Mark Hamill and Harrison Ford. Actually, that's a little unfair on the movie – we did enjoy the whole thing. Star Wars still has a special place in my heart and I'm a big fan to this day.

❦ ❦ ❦

Now school had finished for the year, Dad asked whether I'd like to work at the factory during the Summer holidays. He said I could work from 8:00am to 4:30pm with a half hour lunch break Monday to Friday and earn $30 per week. My mind went straight to "That's a pair of jeans a week!" My second thought was I could now buy my family some really nice Christmas presents. So of course I jumped at the opportunity.

I'm sure my dad could read the look in my eyes as I was thinking about all the new clothes I could buy, because he told me that I *must* save a big chunk of my wages. "You can't spend it all on clothes alright Scarlet?" he'd said.

"Of course, Dad!" I replied in mock outrage. "The thought of buying new jeans and tops never crossed my mind. Or shoes. Or records."

Possibly because he wasn't convinced by my protests, Dad made me promise I'd bank "most" of my wages if he took me on for this job. As I made this promise, I thought about how loose the word "most" was. How much was "most" of $30 per week? It had to be over half I reasoned, but would $16 count as "most"? I decided the better thing to do was to come clean, so I told my dad I needed to buy at least one new pair of jeans for the coming year, a couple of tops, two or three 45 records and some nice Christmas presents for the family. After that, I'd bank the rest. Dad was happy with this arrangement and so it was that I bought a new pair of Levi's with my first week's wages.

One thing I hadn't banked on though was how tiring a full eight hour day at the factory could be. Up to then, I'd only worked for an hour or so after school every day. Now I was working more than an entire week's worth of after-school work in a single day. Every day. Once I got home, practised Karate, had dinner and helped clean up, I could hardly keep from falling asleep on the couch in front of the TV.

This was more of a bummer than you might at first appreciate. Because it was the school holidays, I was allowed to stay up a bit later at night than usual. And because of this, I was able to watch my favourite TV show at the time.

YouTube: Love American Style Intro (1:06)

By the time the show came on around 8:30pm, I could barely keep my eyes open and often fell asleep during the programme. I missed most of my favourite show during those Summer holidays in this way although I did get to see a couple of episodes all the way through. I loved that show, and so did Frank. As I watched the stories each time, I'd dream of going to America one day.

🦎 🦎 🦎

Around the start of the school holidays, a noisy bunch of people moved into a house across the road from us who were forever throwing rowdy parties. Dad called them "as rough as guts," meaning in Kiwi Speak they were unpolished or unrefined. Occasionally these parties would end up in a street fight and the Police would have to be called to quiet everything down.

Like Chrystal before her, little sister Jane managed to sleep through these regular events. Frank and I couldn't do that and we'd meet up in the middle of the night in the bedroom he used to share with Burt and peer out of the window to see what we could see in the dimly-lit street outside.

There were quite a few of these fights in the Summer at the end of 1977, so when Matilda invited me to join her in a visit to her non-scary other grandmother who lived up on the Kapiti Coast, I couldn't wait to go. As soon as the factory closed down for the Christmas break, Matilda and I headed off on our holiday.

The house Matilda's non-scary grandmother lived in was absolutely beautiful. It was set up on a hill and had views out towards the sea and Kapiti Island. To get to it, you drove up a long sweeping driveway that had been cut into the bush. The house itself was also surrounded by native bush. It was a magical place.

I'd been there before for a day or two at a time, but this visit was to be the longest yet. We were allowed to stay there for a couple of weeks, so of course Matilda and I packed as if we were going away for a month.

Unlike Matilda's scary other grandmother, her Kapiti grandmother was very normal. And very interesting. She'd been a schoolteacher for over forty years but had now retired. I think she saw Matilda and I as her final teaching assignment as she was always telling us interesting things about geography and history and the like. She had a really engaging way about her that made everything she told Matilda and I come alive. We were never bored.

In quiet moments, I loved to stand in the west-facing living room of the house looking out across the bush, out to sea and over to Kapiti Island. Matilda's grandmother pointed out that Kapiti Island looks a little like a crocodile lying in the water. Have a look at this clip and you'll get an idea of what I was looking out at.

YouTube: New Zealand – Paraparaumu, Kapiti Coast (3:56)

When I'd first looked out of the huge floor to ceiling windows to take in the vista, I made a promise to myself that went something like this: "Scarlet, one day you will live in a beautiful house like this, set up on a hill with amazing views of the sea, where there are never any scary street fights outside at night."

I had no idea how I was ever going to pull this off. But this was my dream and I'd make a point of repeating this promise, almost like a mantra, every day that Summer holiday at Matilda's grandmother's house. I couldn't believe what a tranquil and peaceful feeling the house had. It was nothing like my house in which I was constantly feeling watched by whatever Kemo Sabe could see but I couldn't.

Matilda and I had the best Summer holiday together with her grandmother. We hardly watched any TV the whole time – except for Love American Style that is. At night Matilda and I played Scrabble and sometimes Monopoly with Matilda's grandmother. When we went to bed, we'd read the books Matilda's grandmother encouraged us to dig out of her prodigious library which took up an entire room.

The days all blurred together and Matilda and I lost all track of time. One morning at breakfast, Matilda's grandmother surprised us. "Happy New Year girls!" she said with a flourish. "Did you make any resolutions?"

Matilda and I laughed. At first we thought Matilda's grandmother was going the way of her other grandmother – loopy in other words – but then we realised she was right. It was indeed a new year and such was the magic of the house in the bush that neither Matilda nor I had realised we'd gone to bed the night before in 1977 and woken up the next morning in 1978.

Excitement. Trepidation. Anxiety. Anticipation.

I'd experienced all of these emotions and far more during 1977. As I ate my breakfast that New Year's Day morning, I couldn't help but think what wonderful things were going to take place in the year to come. Later in the morning, I stood in my spot in the living room, looked west out across the sea towards Kapiti Island and dared to dream how amazing it was all going to be.

Little could I know just how wrong I was.

17

1978

978. A year I shall never forget.

It's been a couple of days since I finished writing the 1977 chapter. That year finished off with a wonderful, magical holiday at Matilda's non-scary grandmother's house on the Kapiti Coast. I still have dream-like recollections of that holiday, as one day merged into the next in that most beautiful and peaceful of houses.

Then my mind moves to the events of 1978 and the images of Kapiti are shattered.

"I can't put off writing this year forever – time to get stuck in again," I think. I open my laptop, start a new document and type "1978" at the top.

That's as far as I get. I make the excuse it's late and I'm tired, save the document, shut down the laptop and go to bed. I fall into an uneasy sleep.

Wouldn't you know it? At 2 in the morning, just like the good old days ...

"Scarlet, wake up.

"Scarlet, wake UP!

"SCARLET! WAKE UP!!"

I wake with a start to see MG's insubstantial form standing beside my bed.

"You must carry on with your book Scarlet," MG says, her words forming in my mind. "I know some difficult things happened in 1978, but you've got to push through and keep going."

I sit up in bed and wipe my eyes. "Nice to see you too MG," I say gently mocking her lack of pleasantries. "Tell me again why it's so important that I write my story?"

MG sighs. "All I can say is you'll find out one day. Dark times are coming Scarlet. You *must* keep moving until the job is finished. I can't tell you any more than that ... you'll just have to trust me. Have faith in your book Scarlet. There is no time to lose."

Before I can so much as open my mouth to form my next question, MG vanishes and I'm left wondering – not for the first time – whether she was here at all. I lay back down and look at the full Moon shining through my bedroom window. I notice Jupiter is only a few degrees away from the Moon tonight and is also shining brightly.

My mind wanders for a little, but suddenly latches onto something ... Jupiter. When MG appeared to me earlier in the year and pushed me to start writing this book about my life, Venus had appeared in the sky. Her association with *love* had resonated with me so deeply that I was inspired to begin my story there and then.

Now I'm having a little trouble with moving onto a year in which I know some challenging events took place and suddenly Jupiter appears brightly in the night sky. I remember there is a relationship between Jupiter and Venus in that they were known traditionally as the "benefic" planets – planets which were believed to bring good fortune and happiness. Venus was the lessor of the two being given the title "Fortuna Minor" while Jupiter was "Fortuna Major." I recall how Jupiter stands for confidence, optimism, faith and trust.

With a start, I make the connection between Jupiter's meaning and MG's final words about *trust* and *faith*. I get out of bed and look through the bedroom window at Jupiter, marvelling at how bright she is tonight. Not even the light of the full Moon can outdo her. It truly is a magnificent sight and I resolve right there to pick up my story again.

I reassure myself that 1978 wasn't all bad.

❦ ❦ ❦

Frank had now left High School. He'd passed his School Certificate exams at the end of the previous year and decided there was no real point in going back to school to sit University Entrance. After all, he didn't have any intention of going to university; he wanted to be a Tradesman – an electrician to be precise. And for that, you needed to do your time as an Electrical Apprentice.

Frank was lucky and quite easily found a qualified Electrician who needed to take on an apprentice. So at around the same time as I started the new school year as a Fourth Former, Frank started work.

What this meant for the morning routine in our house was "business as usual." Frank had to get up at the same time as I did so he could get ready for work on time. So, at 7am on the dot, my father would continue to blast us both out of bed by playing his favourite songs on the stereo.

One morning, I bounced out of bed as usual as soon as I heard the 7am wakeup song cranking up on the stereo. I wanted to have a quick dance and singsong with Dad before he headed across the road to start up the boiler in the factory. The day before, I'd gone shopping with Matilda in Petone at a department store called McKenzies. Because I'd been pretty good with the money I'd earned over the Summer holidays, I'd treated myself to a long white satin nightdress with matching white satin robe.

I trotted out into the living room wearing my new nightdress and robe, expecting my father to say something complimentary such as, "Wow Scarlet, look at you in your new sleepwear!"

Imagine my disappointment when Dad took one look at me and shot me a dead pan look. "Have you saved any money yet Scarlet?" he asked.

"Yes Dad ... actually I have. These are the first clothes I've bought all Summer."

Dad looked at me dubiously, but I looked him straight in the eye with my hands on my hips almost as if I was daring him to challenge what I'd said. Which actually happened to be true, unless you count the Levi's I'd bought right at the start of the holidays. And those tops I'd bought to go with the jeans. And two or three records.

Dad's face broke out into a smile and he lifted the turntable stylus back to the start of the record he was playing. "Alright, come on then!" he said. We had a little dance and sang along to the music and all too soon Dad had to leave to go to work.

Here's another of my dad's favourites. It was played so often that the words are burnt into my memory.

Tony Christie – I Did What I Did For Maria

❦ ❦ ❦

Frank was a very protective brother. He'd always warn me when the Mongrel Mob were roaming the streets of Petone. We had to be particularly wary as the Mob had a house only a couple of streets away – everyone in Petone knew to stay clear of that street.

One afternoon, I was about to leave the house when Frank came running in the front door in a very flustered state. When he saw I was about to go out, he firmly said, "Scarlet, I can't let you leave this house unless you have a shotgun with you!" This was his roundabout way of saying that I shouldn't leave the house at all.

"Why Frank, what's going on?" I asked.

"The whole of the Mongrel Mob are hanging out at the end of our street!" he said dramatically. "Listen, I'm being straight up now. If you ever see so much as a *single* Mob guy, just run Scarlet run! Ok?"

I didn't really know what would happen if the Mongrel Mob got hold of a little 14 year old girl like me, but I didn't think it would be anything good. Years later, Frank's words came back to me when I went to see the movie "Forrest Gump" and Jenny tells Forrest to "Run, Forrest, run!" That's what Frank used to say to me and I took his words seriously.

In fact, it wasn't long after this incident that I saw some gang members sitting on a low brick fence in a street not far from my house. There were four of them just sitting there as I walked past them on the other side of the road. When they saw me, they all slowly stood up, but I wasn't hanging around to see what they'd do next. I heard Frank's words in my head yelling, "Run Scarlet run!" and I swear my feet didn't touch the ground until I got home. Again, I wasn't sure what they'd wanted with me, but I had a feeling it wasn't to share a slice of pizza and a bottle of Fanta.

So I got out of that one ok. But the problems I faced in 1978 were all about to start. My biggest problem, one that would continue for many years, was to be something I couldn't even see.

🐈 🐈 🐈

Frank and I were getting on really well now. I'd kept to my word that I'd stop smashing him, and try to act like a lady. In return I was allowed to continue learning Karate.

Everything was going so well until one day, Frank thought it would be hilarious if he put a small piece of squished up paper into his air rifle and shoot me with it as I was practising Karate in the backyard. My back was to Frank so I had no idea what he was up to until ... **wham** ... he got me fair on the bottom with what was a pretty good shot. It actually hurt like crazy!

Frank was laughing so much he'd momentarily lost control of his motor functions. I stomped straight over to him and he could see I was pretty angry. He pulled a towel off the washing line and held it up in front of him like a mock shield, all the while laughing uncontrollably.

This made me even more wild, so I aimed a Karate kick at the towel to move it out of the way so I could have it out with Frank face to face.

I executed a perfect kick and … ***whack!!*** … I made contact with the towel. The only problem was that I'd underestimated how far the towel was away from Frank's face. Thinking it was further away than it actually was, I'd managed to kick Frank fair and square on his nose and the towel at the same time. Frank's laughing turned to wailing within a nanosecond or two and he went down in a heap on the ground – exactly at the moment my mother appeared from around the side of the house with a washing basket in her arms.

Of course the only thing Mum saw was a very angry Scarlet standing over her brother who was helpless on the ground, holding his nose and crying out in pain. Blood was streaming from his nose which now looked … oddly … bent. Mum flung her washing basket to the ground and ran over to where Frank was thrashing around.

"What have you done now?" Mum cried angrily. She helped move Frank and propped him up against the house while shouting at me. "You are in so much trouble Scarlet … I knew this would happen as soon as you started Karate … you've broken his nose you little madam!"

I tried to protest it was an accident and I'd been aiming at the towel, not Frank's face, but this didn't cut any ice at all with Mum in the state she was in. I decided the best thing to do was to shut up and help out as much as I could.

Mum raced inside and re-emerged with a wet towel that she wrapped around Frank's face to try and stem the flow of blood. Once it had slowed a bit, we all went inside and sat at the kitchen table. Frank wanted to lie down on the couch, but Mum said it would be better for him to sit up so the blood didn't run down the back of his throat. Mum showed Frank how and where to pinch his nose so as to slow down the bleeding.

"You'll be fine soon if you keep doing that," Mum said reassuringly. "How about I cook you your favourite dinner tonight – curried sausages with tons of mashed potatoes?"

Frank gave Mum a thin smile. "That would be great," he said weakly.

I felt so bad about what had happened. When Mum went to get a clean towel, I turned to Frank. "I am *soooo* sorry Frank," I said apologetically. "I never meant to hurt you. It really was an accident."

Frank looked over at me and I could tell he was in a lot of pain. "Yeah, I knew you were aiming for the towel and it was an accident Scarlet. Thanks for not telling Mum I started it all by shooting you with my air rifle."

I realised I'd quite forgotten that part of the story already, and was only worried about what I'd done to Frank and how I could make things right. I thought I must be growing up as it hadn't even occurred to me to try and shift some of the blame onto Frank by telling Mum about the air rifle.

Mum came back into the kitchen, fixing me with her death stare as she gently placed a packet of frozen peas on Frank's nose, holding it in place with the new wet towel. I knew I was in deep, deep trouble because Mum wasn't saying much.

After about an hour's worth of attention, Frank had stabilised and the bleeding had all but stopped. "Sit upright now Frank," Mum said, "and gently hold the packet of peas against your nose with the towel – it'll stop the swelling. Don't move until Scarlet and I get back."

I looked up with a start. "Are we going somewhere, Mum?"

"Yes, Scarlet, we are," Mum said slowly and menacingly. "We're going to see your teacher at that blessed Karate place and I'm telling him you're dropping out as of now!"

Tears welled up in my eyes but I knew there was no point in protesting. I'd never seen my mum so angry and we walked in silence together through the streets of Petone until we got to my dōjō. All the way, I was hoping against hope there would be no-one there, giving Mum a chance to cool down and me a chance to plead my case. But as we got closer and closer, it was clear the dōjō *was* open.

"Maybe Sensei won't be there," I thought as we passed a window just in time to see him inside, practising a kata alone. "Bummer!" I said under my breath.

"Hello Scarlet," Sensei said in his usual cheerful manner as Mum and I walked into the dōjō. "It's not your class this afternoon is it?"

"No," Mum said forcefully before I got a chance to say anything. "And it won't be her class any other afternoon ever again, ever."

Sensei stopped his kata immediately and faced both of us with a quizzical look on his face. He didn't get a chance to say anything either before Mum opened up both barrels on a rant the likes of which I hadn't heard in all my 14 years. I don't remember all of it, mainly because Mum went on and on and on for what seemed like ages. If I wasn't embarrassed enough about how I'd contributed to the situation, Mum's ranting embarrassed me even more. She didn't seem to breathe the entire time she was talking and I thought at one point she was about to pass out. But she did get through it all – in time.

Here is my best recollection of what my mother said.

"You know what she's gone and done don't you? Have a guess. She's only gone and broken her brother's nose hasn't she? Didn't like something he said or did I expect and went up to him and ... *bang* ... Karate kicked him in the face and broke his nose. Right in front of me. I was right there and I saw her do it with my own eyes. Just kicked him square in the face and broke his nose. I've had brothers you know, rugby playing brothers and I've seen enough rugby injuries to know a broken nose when I see one. I knew this would happen, didn't I? Didn't I say, Scarlet, that I knew this would happen? That you'd use your Karate against Frank one day and really hurt him. Well, it's happened hasn't it? Just a matter of time really. She's only gone and broken Frank's nose, hasn't she? You've made her into a weapon you have, a dangerous weapon, with all those kicks and punches and things you're teaching them here. It wouldn't have happened in my day, oh no. If I'd said to my parents I was going to learn Karate, Father would've said, 'Over my dead body you will.' And Mother would've said, 'Father's right, it's not what a lady would do, is it?' And it isn't is it? It's not ladylike in the slightest. Look at her, does she look like a lady to you? Always wearing jeans, never nice skirts and dresses like a young lady should. And always running around and practising kicking and punching and all of that business and getting hot and red in the face and sweating all over the place. She never sits up nice at the table, or anywhere else for that matter. Never uses a knife and fork properly. Always slouches around … don't you Scarlet … in your jeans and running shoes … the running shoes your brother bought you! The brother whose nose you've just broken no less. What a way to repay him. What a way to say, 'thank you for buying me those running shoes, Frank – come here and take this.' **Whack**! … right in the face. Wasn't doing anything, just minding his own business and you go up to him and kick him in the face. Poor Frank, he'll have a funny looking nose from now on, you mark my words. Lucky he didn't end up with brain damage."

Throughout the whole of Mum's diatribe, Sensei stood quietly, listening, hands together at his front, nodding from time to time, never interrupting once. This seemed to have a calming effect on Mum and eventually she finished and the dōjō fell silent.

Sensei nodded again and turned to me. "Do you have anything to add Scarlet?"

My mind raced through all the things I could say to deflect the responsibility of the events that had taken place in our backyard, or at least mitigate my role in them. It all seemed so lame to me though and I merely said, "It's all true Sensei. But it was never my intention to hurt Frank, it was all a terrible accident and I'm so sorry."

"Ok Scarlet, could you please wait outside the dōjō while I have a quick word with your mum?" Sensei said calmly with another small nod.

I left the dōjō and started pacing up and down the street outside. I couldn't hear anything of the discussion taking place inside. Sensei and Mum seemed to talk for ages.

Eventually, Mum walked out of the dōjō in the direction of home and motioned for me to join her. Although she seemed to be a lot calmer than before, I could tell she was still pretty angry. After a while, Mum stopped walking and turned to face me. "You are *so* lucky, Scarlet," she said. "Your Sensei convinced me to give you one more chance. He said you are one of the most dedicated and passionate students he has at your level and it would be a real shame if you had to stop your training now."

"Mum, I'm ..."

"Just listen Scarlet!" Mum said shutting me down. "I meant what I said in there about you not being a lady. And it's something we've talked about time and time again. I know you've been trying though and that's part of the reason I'm prepared to give you a second chance and let you continue Karate. But you will try harder now. I've told your Sensei my condition for you to carry on your training is that you'll learn to be a lady. If you don't, then Karate is all over. Got it?"

"Yes, Mum."

"'Yes, Mum' is right alright!!" Mum hadn't finished. "You can start tonight by sitting up nicely at the table and holding your knife and fork properly. I bought you a lovely skirt a while ago and you can start wearing that as soon as we get home. And if I so much as see you holding a cup of tea the wrong way, Karate is all over. Ok?"

"But Mum," I protested. "I didn't even know there's a right and wrong way to hold a cup of tea."

"Alright then," Mum said in an enthusiastic manner that started to get me worried. "I have some books on etiquette at home you can read. Not a quick flick through mind you, a proper read that I'll ask you questions about as you go."

"Ok Mum." I thought I'd got off relatively lightly considering. I could still go to Karate and all I had to do was read some books on etiquette and wear a skirt once in a while. Don't get me wrong though; I was genuinely remorseful for what I'd done to Frank.

My pleasure wore off as soon as we got home and Mum brought out the "lovely skirt" she'd talked about earlier. It was hideous, revolting. No, "grotesque" is probably closer the truth. It was this beige thing, not unlike the colour the New Zealand cricket team was forced to wear in the early 1980s for one-day matches. It wasn't only the colour that made it unappealing – when I put it on, this thing reached mid-way between my knees and ankles. There was just so much material to it! I don't know how to describe how truly awful it was. But if wearing it was going to keep me in Karate, then "so be it" I thought.

If the skirt wasn't bad enough, Mum then produced the etiquette books she required me to read. And be tested on. The first book was called "Lady behave: A guide to modern manners" by Anne Edwards and Drusilla Beyfus. To me, this thing was positively ancient, although it had only been published in the 1950s. The second book was the "updated" version, "Lady Behave: Guide to Modern Manners for the 1970's."

These books were truly revelatory to me. Apparently, there were different ways to place your cutlery on a plate if you wanted to say "I'm still eating," or "I'm finished," or "That was yummy." Who knew? And who knew all these years I'd been saying "That was disgusting" after eating the food my mum prepared, just by the placement of my cutlery? I must admit I found some of it quite interesting, but at the same time I wondered how I was going to remember it all.

I practised some of what I'd learned at dinner that night. I wore my new beige skirt, sat up straight on my chair – bottom on the edge not pushed to the back – and said things like "Mmmm, these curried sausages are delicious Mother," and "One is very much enjoying dinner this fine evening," in a very posh voice.

Frank had a huge dark brown sticking plaster that went from one cheekbone, across his nose and all the way to the other cheekbone. He was in stitches watching me trying to be a lady. Mum had a "you're not quite getting it, Scarlet" look on her face, but I think she appreciated that I was trying.

Dad had no idea what was going on. He wore a bemused expression on his face as he looked around the dinner table at us one by one. I was wearing the horrendous beige skirt and acting a bit strange, Mum wasn't saying anything but was just plain grumpy and Frank had a huge dark brown plaster across his face. Finally Dad spoke up. "Would someone like to tell me what the heck has been happening today?"

"Oh no," I thought. "Wrong question Dad."

Like a dam bursting, Mum started channelling a version of the rant she'd directed at Sensei earlier in the afternoon, complete with hyperventilation.

"You know what Scarlet has gone and done, don't you? Your wonderful daughter. Have a guess. Frank will have a wonky nose now for the rest of his life ..."

And on it went.

I put my cutlery down on my plate with a clatter in the "I'm still eating" position, folded my arms and looked up at the ceiling. "Here we go again," I thought. Frank was just about falling off his chair with laughter – he hadn't heard Mum's rant of course. He was laughing so hard I thought his nose was going to start bleeding again.

Dad's jaw dropped and dropped and dropped as the story of the afternoon's events slowly unfolded. Dad didn't get to say anything. How could he? He couldn't get a word in edgewise.

The rant completed, Mum started breathing again. Frank had totally spent himself laughing so much. We all ate our curried sausages and mash in silence after that.

Straight after dinner, I went to my bedroom and changed out of my hideous beige skirt into something more comfortable. I was so relieved I was allowed to carry on with my Karate studies and I decided to celebrate by playing a relevant song. I turned my little record player on and picked out an appropriate 45 from my collection. "Phew ... that was close!" I said placing the stylus on the single spinning on the turntable.

I then celebrated my good fortune by practising my favourite kata to this song:

Carl Douglas – Kung Fu Fighting

🐨 🐨 🐨

Straight after school the next day, I changed out of my school uniform as usual, put on the ugly beige skirt Mum said I had to wear and ran to my afternoon job at the dry-cleaning factory. I went straight up to Queenie's station and stood in front of her without saying a word.

Queenie looked up at me from her work and involuntarily recoiled a little when she saw what I was wearing.

"Woah girl, what is up with the bigass *skirt*?" she exclaimed loudly.

"It's part of my punishment for breaking Frank's nose," I replied matter-of-factly.

Queenie's eyes widened. "Well ... I'd say you got off lightly then."

She got me to do a twirl and I held the skirt away from my body so she could see how big it was. "Jeepers, looks like a whole bolt of material went into making that thing. It's massive, girl! At least when you've finished with it you can make it into a tent or something."

We both laughed and laughed. Queenie had said what I'd thought the day before – that I'd got off pretty lightly considering. When I was finally able to stop laughing, I saw the huge pile of overalls waiting for me at my station to be folded and sorted. I began to sing as I walked over to my station to start work for the afternoon. I resolved to buy Frank a box of Continental chocolates – his favourite – with my pay for that week to say sorry.

🐨 🐨 🐨

One weekend as I was walking home from the Petone shops, I saw a couple of girls from my High School walking the opposite way on the other side of the road. They were in the same year as me and both said "hello" as I started down the driveway of my house. I said "hello" back and they asked me if this was where I lived. I told them it was and I saw them both giggle a little as they went on their way.

I didn't think any more about this incident until I got to school on Monday. During morning break those same two girls came up to me and said, "Scarlet, you live in a dump of a house!" It wasn't said in a nice way. Both girls had a good laugh and then ran off before I could say anything.

From then on, whenever those girls saw me, they called me "Dump Girl," or asked, "how's it going at the dump," or something equally as witty with the word "dump" in it. I tried hard not to let it bother me, but as time went by, their mean words really upset me.

I decided one day to talk to best friend Matilda about it after school. She was not only the best friend a person could ask for, but she was whip-smart too. If you have a friend in your life as lovely as Matilda, you are very lucky indeed.

As soon as I'd finished work at the factory that day, I ran straight to Matilda's house. I told her all about the two girls and how they were always teasing me about my house and calling me Dump Girl.

Matilda's response surprised me. "Scarlet, those girls are just jealous of you," she said.

I thought about this for a moment before replying. "But why would they be jealous of me when I live in such a dump? They're actually right about that you know. Our house is a bit of a dump."

Matilda smiled. "No, that's not what I mean. Have you looked in the mirror lately Scarlet?"

I didn't have a clue what possible connection Matilda was trying to make. "No, not really," I said. "We only have the one mirror in our house and that's in the bathroom. You know ... the tiny mirror in the medicine cabinet door."

"You're really not following me are you Scarlet?" Matilda said light-heartedly.

I really wasn't.

"You need to go and have a look at yourself ... really look at yourself. My brother thinks you're gorgeous. He said to me he wants to marry you when you both get older. He goes on about it all the time. I think you have the biggest heart out of anyone I know and beauty on the inside makes you beautiful on the outside."

I had no idea what Matilda was talking about.

"I know one other thing about you Scarlet," Matilda continued. "You sure do have a lot of curly blonde hair. In fact, you're *all* blonde hair!" Matilda started laughing which set me off laughing too. At the same time, I was now really confused.

Matilda saw my frown and stood up. "Come with me Scarlet, I want to show you something." She lead me out the back door of her house, along a skinny concrete path which went past the garage, past the washing line and finally ended up right at the back of her section. I'd never been that far back before and believe me when I say it was all a bit creepy. There were tall trees back there and a high fence, all of which blotted out the sun so that it was dark and cold. In keeping with this creepy ambience, an old dilapidated wooden shed stood close to the fence line.

When Matilda pushed on the shed door, it creaked all the way open, just like you knew it was going to. I half expected to see Matilda's scary grandmother inside adding ingredients to a cauldron in a fireplace, but quickly looking around found the shed to be empty. Empty of people that is. On the other hand, it was stuffed full of old furniture and bric-a-brac. Some of the bigger items had white sheets covering them, but mostly things were out in the open, gathering dust. There didn't seem to be much organisation to the way things were arranged. It really looked as though whoever had shifted the things in had pretty much dumped them so they could get out of there as quickly as they could.

"This stuff is mostly my Grandma's," explained Matilda. "Some of it belonged to her best friend who ..." Matilda's voice trailed off and she drew closer to me. "... who was put into a loony bin and died there," she whispered.

I looked at Matilda with a shocked expression on my face. Matilda nodded. "So some of this stuff has been here for a long time."

"I had no idea," I said. "This is the first time I've ever been out here."

"Yes, well, I don't like coming out here," Matilda said nervously. "I'm sure I've seen something out of the corner of my eye here a couple of times. Place gives me the creeps."

"Gee, thanks for bringing me here," I said sarcastically. "I thought you were trying to make me feel better about what those Mean Girls keep saying to me."

"Oh, that's right," Matilda said as if she was waking up from a dream. "I wanted to show you something."

Matilda took me right to the back of the shed where a white sheet was covering something tall and skinny. It would have been at least six feet tall if not more. She ripped the sheet off to reveal a charming old fashioned full-length mirror resting on a stand. Matilda asked me to help her move the mirror so it was in a clearer part of the shed. The mirror had an ornate wooden border and the first inch or so of the mirrored glass had a frosty appearance – I figured this was because it was so old.

Matilda gave the mirror a quick dust with the sheet that had been covering it. "Here Scarlet, have a look," she said. "I wanted to bring you to this full-length mirror to show you this." She placed both hands on my shoulders and manoeuvred me in front of the mirror. "Right then, what do you think?"

I stood in front of the mirror with Matilda behind me and peered through the gloom of the shed until my reflection finally came into focus. After everything Matilda had been talking to me about ... after all the trouble of getting to the shed and finding the mirror ... I was expecting to see something pretty amazing.

"Wow Matilda!" I said in mock amazement. "You're absolutely right ... I am all blonde hair aren't I?"

We both cracked up laughing and immediately felt a lot better about being in this dark, cold, creepy shed. "My hair is such a mess," I said still laughing. "I'll have to get something done about that!" Matilda thought this was just the funniest thing.

"Look," Matilda said once we'd finished cracking up. "The reason I brought you out here was so you could look at yourself in the mirror and see the beautiful girl outside ... and inside. Have you ever heard the expression 'the eyes are the windows to the soul,' Scarlet?"

Matilda said this in such an eerie, mystical way that it sent a shiver coursing down my spine.

"Um, no, not really," I answered, a little spooked.

Matilda continued in her best impersonation of her scary grandmother. "What it means is that when you look into someone's eyes, really look into them, you can see the real person inside. So when I look beneath all that blonde hair of yours and into your eyes, I can see the beautiful person inside. That's what those Mean Girls are jealous of and that's why they have to find something to try and make you feel bad about. Don't be upset they call your place a dump, Scarlet. A house is just a thing after all. What's important is the kind of person you are on the inside. If those Mean Girls were beautiful on the inside, they wouldn't say mean things to you and call you 'Dump Girl.' If they say someone or something is ugly, then they're really the ugly ones."

I was blown away. My friend was so inciteful and had figured all of this out from the little I'd told her. "Boy, she's so smart!" I thought. I didn't know what to say so I simply said, "Thanks Matilda."

Another shiver went right through me. "Can we get out of here now please?" I said. "This place gives me the creeps!"

"Absolutely," Matilda said happily. We moved to the shed door which somehow had managed to close itself without us noticing or hearing anything. Slightly alarmed, we looked at each other as Matilda stepped forward to pull the door open. It was jammed. She pulled and pulled turning the doorknob this way and that, but there was no opening that door. Fear started rising up inside me as Matilda's efforts became more and more frantic.

Suddenly, the door flew open to reveal Matilda's scary grandmother framed in the doorway. Matilda and I got such a surprise to see her there that we both let out full-on screams.

Matilda's grandmother seemed to be just as surprised to see us there as we were to see her and she clutched her chest. "Oh my goodness gracious girls," she said in a shaky voice. "What on Earth are you doing in here? You gave me quite the fright."

Once we'd all calmed down, Matilda explained that I didn't have a decent mirror at home so she'd shown me the old full-length one which was stored in the shed.

"Actually Grandma," Matilda said thoughtfully, "if you're not using that mirror, could Scarlet borrow it and keep it at her house?"

That was a nice thing to ask for, I thought.

Matilda's grandmother replied without hesitation. "Well, of course, if you'd like to take it, you're only too welcome Scarlet. In fact, it's only collecting dust out here and nobody else has ever shown any interest in it. It used to belong to a friend of mine you know. If you'd like it, let it be my gift to you."

"What ... I can take it for good you mean?" I asked Matilda's grandmother.

"Yes, of course," she replied. "My friend won't be needing it anymore. She passed away quite a few years ago."

I looked at Matilda to find she was looking back at me with wide eyes.

I was excited at the prospect of having my very own mirror. More than this, I was touched by the kindness Matilda's grandmother had shown in giving it away to me without a second thought. I said "thank you" over and over while giving Matilda and her grandmother several hugs.

"Now, I must go girls," Matilda's grandmother said in a serious tone. "I was in the middle of looking for something those troublesome Trolls have taken from the kitchen when I heard noises coming from the shed."

"Kind, but still bonkers then," I thought.

Matilda's grandmother turned to go. "Maybe the Trolls have hidden it in the shed," I said trying to be helpful.

With the aid of her walking stick, Matilda's grandmother turned slowly to face me with a look I thought said, "Don't be so stupid Scarlet." Instead, she raised an eyebrow and broke into a wide smile. "Yes, yes of course … good thinking Scarlet! The little blighters, that would be the logical place to hide something, wouldn't it?"

I didn't think logic had much of a part in the old lady's Universe, but off she went into the shed looking for whatever it was she'd misplaced this time. Matilda and I followed her in, picked up the full-length mirror between us and started to carry it out of the shed.

"Are you ok in here, Grandma?" Matilda asked.

"Yes dear, quite alright thank you. I'll see you at dinner shortly."

Watching Matilda's grandmother for a moment or two, it seemed to Matilda and I that her search for whatever the Trolls had taken had been replaced by her reacquainting herself with the things packed away in the shed. She looked only too happy pottering around, picking up this and that and muttering to herself all the while. So Matilda and I continued to cart the tall mirror out of the shed and back along the skinny concrete path.

As soon as we got the mirror to my house, Matilda said she'd better get back home for dinner. I thanked her again for being such a great friend and she was off.

I proudly showed the mirror to my mother who thought I was very lucky to have been given such a lovely thing. Mum suggested I use hot soapy water to clean the frame and turpentine to clean the glass. She said the best way to clean glass or mirrors was to use newsprint, so I grabbed last night's newspaper and used that.

As Mum watched me cleaning the mirror, she said in a cheeky way that it was great to see I was finally getting some use out of the newspaper. It took me a moment or two to realise my mother had cracked a joke – an actual joke. To be fair, my mum did have a good sense of humour and would crack the occasional joke. When she did, I'd always say the same thing: "That was quite a good joke for you Mum!" and we'd both have a little giggle.

Once I'd finished cleaning my new mirror, I placed it and the stand carefully in a corner of my bedroom. It looked quite the part, and I could see myself from top to bottom. Now the mirror was clean, I'd somehow acquired even more curly blonde hair.

I played my latest 45 while I was mock-posing like a model in front of the mirror, pushing my hair this way and that and putting on my best pouty looks.

10cc – Dreadlock Holiday

🐾 🐾 🐾

The next morning, Kemo Sabe came bounding into my room as usual when Chrystal arrived. This morning however, instead of barking at the wall after he'd finished jumping all over me, he stood in the middle of the room and looked at my new mirror. He stood there looking bemused for quite a few seconds – and then all hell broke loose. He began barking like he'd never barked before – he went absolutely mental! He was way more animated than usual. Chrystal thought it was the funniest thing, but I wasn't so sure.

Hearing the racket, Mum hurried into my bedroom. "What the heck is going on in here?" she asked above the din. All three of us stood in silence watching Kemo for a while. Chrystal and Mum thought maybe he was disoriented by seeing his reflection in the mirror and thought no more of the incident. On the other hand, I was left with an uneasy feeling.

A few nights later, the creepiest thing happened to me. I woke up from a nightmare in the middle of the night to the feeling that someone or something was pulling me down my bed. The feeling is hard to describe as I couldn't feel any hands on me, but I was definitely being pulled by some unseen force down my bed. I tried to shout out for help, but nothing would come out. It was like I'd lost the power of speech. If this wasn't bad enough, I realised I could hardly move either; it felt like my body was made of lead making any movement extremely difficult. I remember being reasonably calm considering the situation in which I found myself, but at the same time I desperately wanted to get away from whatever was doing this.

It's difficult to say how long the experience went on for. It seemed like ages, but was maybe only a minute or so. All of a sudden, the episode was over. I was able to speak and move again and I shot out of bed as fast as I could. I didn't cry out as I didn't want to wake anyone. There was absolutely no one else in my room apart from Jane who'd slept through the whole thing – of course.

My mind was racing – what the heck had just happened? At first I tried to convince myself it was only a dream, but then again I was pretty sure I was conscious all the way through it. I then realised I must have been awake as I remembered looking over at Jane in her bed when the "thing" was happening and saw her clutching a doll I'd bought for her. Looking over at her once more, she was lying in exactly the same position, clutching that doll.

I think I was more scared afterwards than when the "thing" was actually happening. I really wanted to go and wake my parents up and tell them what had happened but I knew this would make me very un-popular. I was still in the dog box after having broken Frank's nose and I didn't want to make things worse. In any case, I knew exactly what my parents would say if I went into their bedroom and woke them up. It would be something like, "Oh Scarlet, there's no war on, everything is fine. Go back to bed."

I eventually snuggled back into bed and tried to get back to sleep.

Of course that wasn't going to happen after what I'd experienced and I lay awake for the rest of the night listening to the sound of my Nana's clock chiming. First 3 o'clock ... then 4 o'clock ... then 5 o'clock ... not to mention all the quarter hours in between.

By the time morning finally came, I'd decided not to say anything to my parents or family about what had happened. I was more and more convinced it was part of a nightmare and thought it better to say nothing.

I had to accept it ***wasn't*** a nightmare when the exact same experience happened a couple of months later. The pattern was identical: waking up from a bad dream ... the sensation of being pulled down my bed ... not being able to speak or move ... everything returning to normal a short time later. Everything about it was the same as the time before. Right down to my Nana's clock chiming three o'clock right after the episode had finished.

Having this "thing" happen to me twice now in identical circumstances had me worried. My gut was telling me this experience had something to do with the paranormal, as unappetising as that prospect was. On top of this, a pattern was starting to emerge and it was probably only a matter of time before the "thing" happened again. I had to consider the possibility this was going to be a regular thing now – maybe it was going to get worse. I had to talk to someone about it, but who?

Then it occurred to me. Because the experience was really scary, I asked myself the question "who is the scariest person I know?" That was easy – Matilda's eccentric grandmother. "She loves this kind of stuff," I thought. "I'll talk to her." I resolved to go and speak to Matilda's grandmother straight after I finished my after-school job at the factory that very day.

Who could have known our conversation that afternoon would play such an important role in defining the path my life's work would take?

❧ ❧ ❧

After work that day, I ran straight to Matilda's house. I didn't want to get Matilda involved in all of this, so I decided to go and see her grandmother alone. I knew Matilda was back at school taking one of her extra lessons. I also knew I could rely on her to take her time getting home after the lesson had finished, so I should have plenty of time to talk to her scary grandmother. Even though I'd been in Matilda's grandmother's company many, many times, I was still a bit scared of this old woman and more than a little nervous about talking to her alone.

When I got to Matilda's house, I walked through the front gate and then down the path beside the house that lead to the back door. I figured if I went to the back door, I wouldn't have to stand at the front door and risk being seen. I stood with the back door in front of me, composed myself and then raised my right hand to knock on the door. No word of a lie, but before I had the chance to knock, I heard Matilda's grandmother call out from inside the house in a loud voice. "You can come on in Scarlet. And there's no need to be nervous."

I almost jumped out of my skin! I tried to calm myself with a couple of deep breaths, opened the back door and went in.

Matilda's grandmother was sitting at the kitchen table knitting while listening to her large old fashioned valve radio. I can clearly remember walking through the kitchen towards her and hearing this Fleetwood Mac song playing:

Fleetwood Mac – Dreams

Matilda's grandmother put her knitting in her lap and turned the radio off. She motioned me to sit down.

"What do you want to talk to me about, Scarlet?" she asked.

How could she possibly know I wanted to talk to her and that I wasn't here to see Matilda? Was she psychic or something?

I must have had a frown on my face because before I could say anything, Matilda's grandmother began to explain. "I know you're here to see me, Scarlet. Matilda has an extra class today at school and you would have known that. So you didn't come to see her, did you?"

Oh, I got it. "She's good!" I thought.

"What, did you think I was psychic or something?" Matilda's grandmother chuckled.

I took another couple of deep breaths and told her the whole story of what had happened to me in the middle of the night. Matilda's grandmother seemed to be taking this seriously because she stopped me once in a while to ask for some detail or another. I thought this was quite comforting. I'm not sure I would have received the same response from my parents, definitely not from my mother who was a firm non-believer in anything she couldn't see or touch.

Matilda's grandmother was most interested in my description of the feeling of being pulled down my bed, that it wasn't a hand exactly, more like a force. She asked lots of questions about this. When I'd finished describing the two episodes, I went on to tell her about the feeling I got at home quite often – the feeling I was being watched. Then I told her about how Kemo went nuts in my room and lately he'd taken to barking at the mirror she'd given to me.

When I'd come to the end of my story, Matilda's grandmother fixed me with a stare and spoke in a very scary voice. "Scarlet, you must never *ever* talk to anyone else about this alright? Because if you do, the man in the white coat will come to your house, put you in a straight jacket and take you away to the same place they took my friend – the loony bin. You know who I'm talking about don't you? The friend whose mirror you now have at your house. And once you're in the loony bin, you'll be lucky to get out."

Matilda's grandmother looked at me intently and continued in her best scary voice. "Do you understand Scarlet? You need to promise now."

If I was scared before, I was freaking out now. I nodded rapidly. "I won't talk to anyone other than you about this, I promise!" I said nervously.

"That's good then! Now, if this should ever happen to you again – and it could – the best thing you can do is *not* give in to fear. Human emotions are very powerful and are a strong source of energy that the supernatural can latch onto. But that energy can go either way; it can be positive when created by love, kindness and happiness, or negative when created by anger and fear. Negative supernatural entities will feed on fear, so be strong and don't give whatever is doing this to you anything to feed on. Don't give in to the fear. Do you understand?"

I did, sort of. "It's really hard though ... when you're in that situation and you're scared ... it's really hard **not** to be scared ... and not to give in to the fear. You know?" I hoped I was making sense. "I'm only 14 years old ... how can I be strong and not give in to the fear?"

"Ah, well it's not as hard as you might think," replied Matilda's grandmother. "All you have to do to negate fear is to create a thought that is the **exact opposite**. What's the opposite of fear for you?"

"Um ... to me ... the opposite of fear is happiness," I said.

"Well there you have it," smiled Matilda's grandmother. "Happiness it is then. And what makes **you** feel happy, Scarlet?"

"Oh, that's easy," I replied. "Singing. Singing makes me really really happy. Instantly."

"Alright then. So now you have your strategy. If anything like this happens again, sing. Sing out loud, sing in your head, it doesn't matter which. Sing and the fear will go away. And if the fear goes away, you starve whatever this thing is of the energy it needs. Do you understand, Scarlet?"

I did. In fact, it was like a lightbulb going off in my head. It made total sense then and it makes total sense now. I've used Matilda's grandmother's advice so many times down through the years, in so many different situations. To negate **any** bad feeling or emotion – not only fear – simply create a thought that is the exact opposite and focus on that.

Something unexpected happened that afternoon during my talk with Matilda's grandmother. At some point during the conversation, I found I wasn't scared of her anymore. She was just a kindly, old and very wise lady. I warmed to her like I never had before.

I stayed and chatted with Matilda's grandmother for a little while longer about all sorts of things. I no longer thought she was bonkers at all – eccentric maybe, but not bonkers.

In fact, one of the things we spoke about at length concerned that very distinction. Matilda's grandmother was adamant that in the past, many people had been locked up in what she variously called "mental institutions," or "the loony bin," or "the funny farm," because of the supernatural. These people had experienced some sort of supernatural event, told their story to someone in a position of authority and ended up being admitted to an institution for their troubles. That's why she'd made me promise right at the start of our talk not to tell anyone else about the things I was experiencing.

I sat in my chair digesting this for a moment. "How can you be so sure these people were locked up because of something supernatural?"

"Because my friend was one of them," Matilda's grandmother said dramatically. "My friend whose mirror you have. We'd been friends for years and years and one day she told me her house was full of the spirits of the departed, and that these spirits talked to her."

"They ... talked to her?" I said incredulously. "What about?"

"Mostly they wanted my friend to pass on messages to their loved ones. She told me some of the people she had messages for would listen, but most thought she was ... well ... bonkers."

I couldn't help giggling when I heard Matilda's grandmother say "bonkers."

"Oh, no, it's no laughing matter Scarlet. I told my friend to stop doing what she was doing or one day she'd live to regret it. And you know what happened don't you?"

I shook my head.

"She lived to regret it. One of the people she had a message for turned on her didn't he?" Matilda's grandmother slowly shook her head. "One day out of the blue, the man in the white coat turned up on her doorstep, strapped her into a straight jacket and took her to the loony bin. She never got out and eventually she died in there. I really tried to help get my friend out of that place. But in the end they were never going to listen to me and I couldn't help her. It was so sad. To this day I wish I could have done something for her."

Matilda's grandmother looked down and was quiet for a while. Eventually, she looked back at me and tapped her temple with one of her fingers. "So as I said before Scarlet, be smart and keep this business to yourself. Nobody else has to know."

Matilda's grandmother didn't need to tell me again – I was convinced. "That's not a very nice story," I said sadly.

"No, it's not is it? When my friend told me she could see spirits, she said anyone can do it. It's a question of being open to it and not being afraid. You could do it too if you wanted to."

I smiled nervously. "You know, it's not that I'm not interested in the supernatural. I am interested actually ... quite a lot. It's just that it scares me so much. Take the Spiritualist Church across the road from us. Frank says they do séances over there. I'm interested to know what goes on in a séance, but I'm frightened too."

"Nothing wrong with being a little frightened Scarlet ... keeps you on your toes it does. Now, about that church over there. Don't get me wrong, they're all well-meaning people who go there, but I think a lot of them might be a bit on the inexperienced side. If they do séances over there, I really hope they close them down properly. If they don't, who knows what manner of things are left roaming around? One thing I'm pretty sure of – that church is the reason there's so much more activity around here lately. Do you know what I mean?"

I did and nodded animatedly. Strange things **had** been happening more frequently lately, from the feeling I was being watched, to Kemo's barking and now the episodes that had brought me to Matilda's grandmother in the first place.

"Yes, I thought so," Matilda's grandmother said in a knowing way. "Listen carefully Scarlet. What people like those churchgoers across the road may not realise is if you hold a séance, or you fool around with a Ouija board or **anything** to do with the supernatural, it stirs up a lot of energy. It's like turning on a light that can only be seen on the Ethereal Plane and suddenly all manner of entities flock to that light ...

like moths to a flame. Now this isn't a problem in itself, it's just the way things work. But once you've finished the séance or whatever you're doing, you have to send the spirits back, otherwise they could decide to stay a while ... and if it's a bad one ... well ... let's not think about that shall we?"

I swallowed hard and shook my head.

Matilda's grandmother looked at me in silence for a little. "I can see you're interested in the supernatural Scarlet. I have a strong feeling it is your destiny to be involved in it in some way in the work you'll do as an adult. You're a very empathetic person ... you can sometimes feel what others are feeling can't you?"

This took me by surprise. It was true – for a long time I'd recognised I was able to instinctively sense what someone was feeling ... almost as if it were an invisible sort of energy they gave off and I could pick up on.

"It's your destiny Scarlet," Matilda's grandmother said again as she rocked back and forth in her chair. "Maybe you'll become involved with helping people like my friend. Whatever it is, follow your path."

I didn't really know what Matilda's grandmother meant by this. "But how can I help people like your friend?" I asked.

"That, me dear, is something you'll have to work out for yourself!"

My eye was drawn to the kitchen clock on the wall and I realised with a start that Matilda would be home soon.

I said thank you to Matilda's grandmother for the amazing conversation and promised to come back regularly for more. I was about to walk out the back door, but turned and stepped a couple of paces back into the kitchen. There was something I had to ask her.

"Um ... when I first got here," I said unsurely, "I didn't have to knock on the door – you knew it was me and you called for me to come in. You also knew I was nervous and you told me not to be. How could you possibly know that?"

Matilda's grandmother gave me one of her inscrutable, mysterious looks. Her face then broke into a smile. "I knew it was you, Scarlet, because I saw you walk past the kitchen window over there to get to the back door. I knew you were nervous because you're always nervous around me. But not anymore, right?"

I laughed and looked up at the ceiling in disbelief. I was expecting Matilda's grandmother to divulge she'd used some special teaching she'd learned somewhere on her travels. Or maybe a spirit had told her – something along those lines. As it turned out, there was absolutely nothing paranormal about how Matilda's grandmother had known those things. It was down to good, old-fashioned observation.

"Right?" Matilda's grandmother repeated.

I looked at her one last time before heading off. "Right!" I said. "Not anymore."

It's fair to say I was a little shaken by the events of the afternoon. Fear slowly crept over me as I walked home but then I remembered what Matilda's grandmother had said; when you want to negate a bad emotion, create a thought that is the exact opposite. It occurred to me I could choose to have negative thoughts that would make me feel freaked out and scared – which would only draw negative things to me – or I could choose positive thoughts that would make me feel happy and strong and thereby attract positive things. I decided I was going to be happy and strong.

Doing my best to think good thoughts only, I was home now and remembered the latest addition to my 45 collection I'd bought the week before. The song's title was so relevant to the way I'd felt during the course of the afternoon that I couldn't wait to get to my bedroom to play it. As soon as I got there, I turned on the little record player Chrystal had left for me, played the new 45 already on the turntable and lost myself in the music as I sang and danced to this song:

Chic – Le Freak

Singing and dancing to Le Freak, I found happiness had replaced fearfulness, just as Matilda's grandmother said it would. I decided if the experience of being pulled down my bed happened again, I'd sing and create happy thoughts.

I couldn't know whether it would happen again, but now I was prepared.

🐛 🐛 🐛

One afternoon not long after my meeting with Matilda's grandmother, I was walking home by myself having finished my after-school French class when I heard a boy's voice behind me call out, "Hey Scarlet ... wait up!" The boy came running up to me and I immediately recognised him from the French class we'd both just attended. He asked me whether it would be ok if he could walk with me as we were heading home in the same direction.

"Yes, of course," I replied politely.

He noticed my schoolbag was bulging with textbooks, so he offered to carry it for me.

"That would be great," I said.

"What's with all the textbooks?" he asked. "Your schoolbag is chocka with them!"

"My older brother is helping me with my Maths," I explained. "So I have to take them home with me every day."

"Right," the boy mused. "Hey, I'm not bad at Maths ... I could help you if your brother gets too busy."

I looked up at the boy and remember thinking how tall, dark and good looking he was. I smiled. "Thanks, that's very kind of you," I said.

The boy turned out to be a year older than me and was in the same schoolyear as Matilda. He said his name was Matt.

Matt and I chatted about this and that as he walked with me to the corner where my street met the main road. Once there, we stopped briefly as he explained his house was in a different road. He handed my schoolbag back to me and started to walk away.

After a couple of paces, Matt turned and smiled at me. "Bye Scarlet," he said softly. "I might see you tomorrow then?"

I stood on the street corner like a stunned Mullet. "Bye Matt," was all I could get out. Even at the time I thought how pathetic my response was. Walking the rest of the way to my place alone, I quietly chided myself. "Nice one Scarlet! Is 'bye Matt' the best you could come up with? You'll have to do *way* better next time!"

From then on, Matt would often come running up behind me and call out his trademark, "Hey Scarlet … wait up!" He would even walk me home on days we didn't have French class. He'd always carry my heavy schoolbag and we'd always part where my street branched off from the main road. He was such a gentle, caring boy and it wasn't long before I realised I'd developed a massive crush on him.

Matt had a very positive effect on my French studies. Up to then, I was only luke-warm about learning the language. I found Matt was much better than me at French – easily as good as Matilda was. I decided I'd pay attention during class and actually do some work and even practise in the evenings so I could impress him.

Matilda would join Matt and I on our walks home from time to time and eventually I told her that I really really liked him.

"No way Scarlet, *really*?" she said in a playfully mocking voice. "I would never have guessed that in a million billion trillion years!"

"What do you mean Matilda?" I asked, puzzled.

"Geez Scarlet, it's kinda obvious," Matilda replied. "Whenever Matt is around, you have a ginormous smile glued to your face. And you get all shy and lose the ability to speak for a while."

I looked at my friend and went bright red in the face. "Is it really *that* obvious Matilda?"

"It is to me," Matilda said in the voice she reserved for when she wanted to come across as Miss Smarty Pants. "But don't worry," she said softening her tone. "Matt probably has no idea. He is a boy after all."

On the days Matt walked home with me, we'd practise our French on each other. During one of these walks, Matt dropped into the conversation that he played a lot of tennis.

"You do?" I said. "That's interesting."

When I got home from work later that day, I sprinted over to Matilda's house who I knew played a bit of tennis and had all the gear.

I ran into her bedroom excitedly. "Matilda! Matilda! How would you feel about a game of tennis with me? Today. Now. Like … right now."

"Don't tell me," Matilda said in her All Knowing voice. "Matt plays tennis and you want to get good at it in case he asks you for a game. Am I right?"

"Gee, you're smart!" I thought. That was exactly the reason.

"We'd need to change into some gym gear," Matilda went on. "But yes, we can play right now if you really want?"

Woah, did I? Of course! I raced next door to my house, got changed at light speed and shot back to Matilda's house, all in the time it took Matilda to start to get the tennis rackets out of her wardrobe. She could be soooo slow sometimes! But soon she'd changed as well and we were off.

Nowadays, almost every school has a tennis court marked out somewhere in its grounds. But back in my day, you pretty much needed to join a club to get access to a decent court. Matilda and I were happy to play tennis in the narrow lane that ran parallel with our road immediately behind our houses. The lane was so narrow that when a car drove towards us, it took up the whole road and we had to move to one side until it had passed. This didn't worry us though and we spent many an hour hitting the ball to one another in that lane. I don't know if you could exactly call it "tennis" though.

We also practised by hitting tennis balls against a large wooden roller door that belonged to a building not far from the dry-cleaning factory. Once when Matilda and I were there, a carload of young guys pulled up and told us their band was going to practise in the building. Matilda and I stood and watched as these guys unloaded all of their gear; guitars, a drum kit, amps – the works.

Before long, Matilda and I heard the band of young guys practising a song we both knew over and over again. We put our tennis rackets down and started singing and dancing to the music right outside the wooden roller door. I remember thinking these guys were really good as the song they were practising sounded almost exactly like the original.

YouTube: Paul McCartney – Ob-La-Di, Ob-La-Da (Diamond Jubilee Concert) (2:04)

I realise this isn't the original, but I love the version of Ob-La-Di, Ob-La-Da Paul McCartney performed at the Diamond Jubilee Concert – especially when all the other performers join in later on in the song. Every time I hear it, I'm immediately taken back to the day Matilda and I were singing and dancing outside the practice building to the music the young guys were making inside.

🐌 🐌 🐌

My Fourth Form English teacher was great, she made the subject so much fun. I actually listened in her class for a change, because I wanted to impress her. She was also a netball coach and one day asked me whether I'd like to play in her team. I said I wouldn't mind, but I hadn't so much as picked up a netball ball before. She said she'd organised a friendly match at lunchtime and if I was interested, I should come along to the netball courts.

I thought about this during the periods before lunch and thought I'd give it a whirl. Who knows – I might really like netball.

I almost instantly regretted my decision to play as soon as I got to the courts. The two Mean Girls who were the bane of my life were there. I'd simply been ignoring them up to now, but here they were on the same team as me. Sigh. Of course they didn't say anything mean to me while my English teacher was within earshot, but as soon as she wasn't I got the full treatment. "Hey, Dump Girl." "You live in such a dump, Scarlet." And so on and so on. But only when the teacher wasn't close by and couldn't hear what they were saying.

I totally ignored the Mean Girls, but this only seemed to spur them on. At every opportunity, they told my teammates I lived in a dump and that's why they called me Dump Girl. Pretty soon, I was getting it from everyone on the court.

My lovely teacher was totally unaware of what was going on. During the first quarter break, she told the girls in my team to pass the ball to me because I hadn't received a single pass during that whole quarter. This only made things worse. I was rarely passed the ball and I got "Dump Girl" all game.

At half time, I decided to change my strategy. Instead of waiting for a pass, I did my best to get the ball off the opposition whenever they were down my end of the court. I was quite successful at this, but it rankled I then had to pass the ball to girls who wouldn't pass it to me and didn't have the moral strength to stand up against the Mean Girls.

As soon as the game was over, I quickly left the courts. I was so upset and had been holding back the tears all game, but I wasn't going to give the Mean Girls the satisfaction of seeing they'd got to me.

When my lovely English teacher saw me later that afternoon, she hurried over to me. "Scarlet, why did you leave the game so quickly at lunchtime?" she asked.

"Netball is not really for me, Miss." I said.

She looked at me with a disappointed look on her face. "That's a real shame because you were one of the fittest girls out there and showed lots of potential. I couldn't believe it was the first time you'd ever played netball. I thought you were a natural."

Her words made me feel good, but I couldn't imagine playing a sport where all the girls in the team were constantly at me. I smiled at my teacher. "Thanks ... but it really isn't me," I said. "Karate is my thing."

"Oh really," my teacher said with interest. "I didn't know you studied Karate. That would explain why you're so fit. What belt are you up to?"

"I'm a blue belt," I said very proudly. "I have a couple more belts to get and then I'll be a black belt. I'm really focussed on getting my black belt by the time I'm 16."

My teacher seemed impressed. "Good for you Scarlet, you stick at it."

"I will Miss," I replied.

I never told my teacher what had happened on the netball courts that lunchtime, even though it really upset me. My teacher's words had helped, but I was terribly unhappy and was holding back tears all afternoon. As soon as school ended, I quickly ran out of the school grounds and all the way home. I didn't even want Matt to see me this day as I knew I was going to cry eventually.

As soon as I got home, I went straight to my bedroom, lay on the bed and cried my eyes out. I simply couldn't understand how all those girls could be so mean. What had I ever done to them?

My mother knew something was wrong as soon as I got home. After a few moments, she followed me into my bedroom and stood beside my bed as I sobbed and sobbed. Mum sat down on the edge of the bed, gave me a big hug and asked why I was so upset.

I told Mum the whole story; how it had started with the two Mean Girls, to everything that had happened at the lunchtime "friendly" netball game.

My mother's face dropped and dropped as I spoke to her. She didn't say anything and I could sense she was upset too. After a little while, she stood up and walked to the hallway where she picked up the telephone book from the hall stand. I could see exactly what she was doing as the telephone stand was right outside my bedroom door. "Mum, what are you doing?" I asked, half knowing what the answer would be.

"I'm looking up your school's telephone number and then I'm going to call them and make a complaint," she said gruffly. "This house may be a dump, but it's our *home* and we can't afford to live anywhere else.

I'm going to ring your school and tell them it's not on that you're being given a hard time because of our house."

Mum started dialling the number for my school. I quickly jumped off my bed, ran into the hallway and pushed the phone's flash button to cut Mum's call off.

"Mum, if you make a complaint to the school, it's only going to make things *way* worse for me," I said to her. "Please don't."

"Scarlet, I'm furious about those girls calling you 'Dump Girl.' Let me go now, I'm going to call your school to complain." Mum was adamant.

I could easily visualise what would happen to me at school if Mum did complain. So I pleaded and reasoned and pleaded some more for her not to call the school. I told her I'd ignore the Mean Girls in future, although I knew in myself I hadn't been doing a great job of that all year.

Finally my mother relented. "If I don't complain Scarlet, you have to promise me you won't use your Karate on them. If you do to them what you did to Frank ..."

"Oh come on Mum. Don't you think I'd have used my Karate on them by now if I was going to? I've told you this has been going on for a while now. And anyway, you know our Sensei teaches us never to use Karate as a weapon, only for self-defence. He's very big on that and anyone who disobeys that rule would get kicked out of the dōjō."

Mum sighed and shook her head. "I don't know," she said.

"The only person I'd ever use my Karate on is Frank, and I've promised not to do that because I'm a lady!" I thought making light of the situation might help.

Luckily Mum recognised this for the joke it was meant to be and finally agreed not to complain to the school. I kissed her, thanked her for understanding and took off across the road for my job at the factory.

As soon as Queenie saw me, she knew I'd been crying. She asked me what the problem was and I told her the whole story, even the bit about Mum wanting to make a complaint to my school. As I was telling her the story, I couldn't help but relive the emotions I'd felt during the netball game and before long my eyes were full of water.

Queenie reached out to me with her arms. "Oh Scarlet, bring it in for a hug girl," she said compassionately. Queenie gave the best hugs and I instantly felt better. While she was hugging me, Queenie whispered in my ear. "Do you want me to smash those Mean Girls for you?"

I looked up at her and realised she was having a laugh.

Queenie continued in a more serious tone as we got on with our work. "Actually, I could have a little chat with my nephew Rangi – he goes to your school eh? He could go and have a gentle word with those girls and I'm sure they'd see the wisdom of never bothering you again. What d'ya think, Scarlet?"

"That's ok Queenie," I replied. "I've seen what happens when Rangi has a 'gentle word' with someone. At Sports Day last year we were all lined up for some race or other and a boy pushed in front of him. Without a word, Rangi picked this boy up like he was a dry twig and spun him 360 degrees around in the air before dumping him in a heap on the grass."

"Our Rangi is a big boy eh?" giggled Queenie before launching into one of her patented bouts of laughter. "He just never stopped growing! But he's a gentle soul really."

"Right," I said with a hint of scepticism as I visualized the boy who had pushed in front of Rangi flying through the air and crunching on the ground.

"Thanks for the offer anyway Queenie," I said, "but I need to sort this out myself. She'll be right!"

🐱 🐱 🐱

That evening at the dinner table, Frank surprised me by asking whether I'd like to go into the bush for a night with him and Matilda's brother. They were planning to hunt deer in the Orongorongo Valley in the Rimutaka Ranges to the east of Wellington and stay overnight in one of the huts. I looked at Frank, then at Mum, and back at Frank again and I could tell Mum had told Frank about my day. This was his way of trying to cheer me up. "Yeah sure I'd love to go," I said.

After dinner I went next door to see Best Friend Matilda. I told her the whole story of my netball game ... and I started welling up again.

"I've told you about those girls before Scarlet," Matilda said. "When people are mean, it's because they don't feel good about themselves. Being mean in some strange way makes them feel better ... perhaps it's because they feel they have the power over you to make you feel bad. So don't feel bad! And don't worry about them, they're dumb. Literally – they're not very bright you know.

"When you get home," Matilda continued, "go and take another look at yourself in the mirror Grandma gave you. Really *look* at yourself. You are such a kind person and have the biggest heart. Go and have a look at that person."

I did as Matilda said as soon as I got home. I looked at myself up and down in the mirror to check whether anything had changed since I'd got myself ready for school that morning. Nope. Nothing was different. I looked exactly the same. All I could see was Scarlet from Petone who lived in a dump of a house.

It hadn't been a great day.

With the benefit of hindsight, there is a song I love that perfectly sums up what Matilda was trying to tell me about the Mean Girls. If this song had been around in 1978, I'm sure Matilda would have played it to me on the spot. I had to wait until 2005 before the wonderful Sugababes released it, but I hope you agree the wait was worth it.

Be sure to listen to the lyrics, but take a look at the video if you can – both are amazing.

Sugababes – Ugly

The next weekend, I went deer hunting with Frank and Matilda's brother. We walked into the Orongorongo Valley for about an hour with full packs on and after crossing the Orongorongo River, we walked for another half hour or so before reaching the hut we were to stay in that night. The bush we walked through was absolutely magnificent and the hut was very comfortable.

While we were settling into the hut, I overheard Matilda's brother talking to Frank outside as he was organising a campfire. "I'm really surprised at Scarlet, Frank," he said. "She didn't complain once on the way here and she could easily keep up with us even though she was carrying a full pack."

"You don't have to worry about Scarlet, she's pretty tough," replied Frank. "She's a pretty good shot with a rifle too. I doubt whether she'd shoot a deer though – you know she can't bring herself to even kill a rabbit which is why I asked you to come with me to Horokiwi to help that farmer out with his rabbit problem."

Both Frank and Matilda's brother had a laugh at my expense.

They were right though. I wasn't interested in the slightest in shooting a deer, although I'd happily eat a venison steak if they got lucky and bagged one. Which to my surprise, they did. A good sized one too. Later on, all three of us went into the bush a wee way and had a little target shoot. That was the best part of the trip for me.

Here is a flavour of our experience in the Orongorongo Valley.

*YouTube: Rimutaka Forest Park – Catchpool Valley and
Orongorongo Valley (9:05)*

The next day, the two boys took it in turns to carry the deer on their shoulders out of the bush, while I helped carry their heavy packs. We finally made it out and back to the carpark where we all collapsed absolutely spent, but happy.

"Good on you for carrying those packs out Scarlet," Matilda's brother said to me. "There's no way in a million years Matilda would've done that without complaining all the way!"

Frank may have invited me into the bush that first time as a way of cheering me up after my experiences with the Mean Girls. But the many invitations after that were solely based on my abilities and willingness to pull my weight on the weekend hunting trips. The three of us went on numerous deer hunts, and although the boys didn't get a deer every time, we always had a lot of fun. The target shooting was always my favourite part of those weekends.

Frank was proving himself to be quite the provider in our family. He still brought home plenty of rabbits from Horokiwi and now he supplemented that with deer from time to time from the Orongorongo Valley.

Mum was equal to the task in preparing the venison for the table. As with the rabbits, my favourite was venison pie – smothered in Wattie's tomato sauce of course – whilst my father preferred his casseroles with loads of spud and swede.

🦌 🦌 🦌

After the high of that first hunting weekend, Monday morning dawned and it was back to the routine of school for me and work for Frank. It must have been 7am because Dad had cranked up the stereo, blasting Frank and I out of bed. I looked up at the ceiling and couldn't believe the weekend had flown by so quickly. I glanced over to Jane's bed, but she was long gone, probably in the kitchen with Mum.

Dad's music was always so infectious and uplifting and this day was no different. I leapt out of bed, pulled on my satin robe and raced into the living room for a quick dance with my father before he had to leave for work. What was he playing this morning?

Dean Martin – King of the Road

A bonus to start the week – Matt walked home with me after school. I tried to impress him with my French, but his was always much better than mine.

"Comment était votre journée, Matt?" I asked. [How was your day, Matt?]

"Très bon, merci Scarlet," he replied. [Very good, thank you Scarlet.]

I was the happiest girl in the world when I walked home with Matt. He never judged me. If I completely stuffed something up in our French conversations, he'd gently laugh and then tell me what I should have said.

One day as Matt and I were walking home from school, he turned into my street instead of saying goodbye at the corner and carrying on along the main road towards his house. I got quite a shock at this and felt the panic rising up in me – panic because I didn't want this nice boy seeing the dump of a house I lived in.

As we continued walking down my street, I felt my stress levels approaching critical so I made a split-second decision. Matt didn't know which house I lived in, so I decided that when we got to my place, I'd simply carry on walking as if it were any old house. And that's what I did – I walked right past my house as if I didn't live there.

Once past my house, my brain started to work overtime; what do I do now, what do I do now? I barely heard what Matt was saying, I needed to get myself out of this situation. And then I had it. We walked to the corner past my house where I stopped. "Oh Matt," I said. "I've just remembered, I have to meet my father at his work today. I'd better go. See you tomorrow … bye!" With that I ran off.

I looked back and saw Matt still standing in the same spot on the corner looking a little bewildered. I yelled out to him in French. "C'était agréable de te voir Matt. Is that right?" I hoped I'd said, "It was lovely to see you Matt."

I ran towards the lane behind my house, along the lane, back to the main road and turned into my street again. Essentially, I ran a massive circuit around the streets of Petone just so I could get back to my house without Matt seeing. "I wish our house wasn't such a dump," I thought grumpily.

Once home, I quickly changed out of my school uniform and into the jean shorts and tee shirt I usually wore to my factory job. I ran over to the factory and straight to where Queenie and Chrystal were working side-by-side.

"Why are you so late, Scarlet?" Chrystal asked. Queenie looked up at me from her work. I decided to come clean and tell them the whole drama of the past half hour or so.

"I had a big disaster with Matt, the nice boy who walks me home sometimes," I said. "I always leave him at the corner of our street and the main road, but today he walked with me down my street." I paused for effect, but Queenie and Chrystal clearly didn't get the issue this had caused as they both looked at me blankly.

"So ... I had to walk past my house as if it wasn't mine didn't I? ... otherwise Matt would see where I lived," I continued.

Queenie and Chrystal still looked at me blankly. "And we wouldn't want him to know where you lived now, would we?" Chrystal eventually said. Queenie giggled a little, but seeing my distraught look, quickly stopped and put on a straight face.

I realised I'd have to spell it out to Chrystal and Queenie. "Look, Matt wouldn't like me anymore and wouldn't want to walk home with me ever again if he saw where I lived."

The penny started to drop. "Only if he was shallow," Chrystal replied. Queenie nodded in agreement.

"I really don't think Matt is shallow," I said. "I guess it must be me then. Maybe I feel ... inferior."

"But why would you feel inferior, girl?" Queenie immediately asked. "You've got nothing to feel inferior about."

"Yes I do," I said starting to get a bit upset. "Matt lives in such a nice house in a lovely street in Petone and I live in a *dump* of a house!"

All my frustration over the events of the last few weeks came to a head in that moment. The Mean Girls. Me wanting to impress Matt.

Having to run around the streets of Petone so Matt didn't see where I lived. Chrystal raised her eyebrows at me and Queenie shook her head ever so slightly. She lifted her arms towards me, saying in her loving Queenie way, "Bring it here girl." I buried myself in her embrace and had the best Queenie cuddle. Eventually I sighed and we all got back into our work.

From then on, Matt always turned down my street when he walked home with me. And I'd always walk past my house as if I didn't live there, get to the next corner and then make up some excuse to leave Matt there. I would then run off, leaving Matt looking bewildered. After a while, I found I had to get creative with my excuses.

"Oh, I've got to meet Mum at the Petone shops." Zoom.

"Sorry Matt, I've got to go to the factory and take Chrystal's dog for a walk." Whoosh.

"I've just remembered I promised to help Matilda's grandmother." Zip.

As I ran off, I'd always shout the same thing back at Matt – "C'était agréable de te voir Matt." I'd then run the usual circuit, returning home to get changed and go to work. But now I ran with a smile on my face. I realised now I got to walk with Matt longer, even if I did have to tell him a little fib and ditch him eventually.

While I was getting changed for work on the days Matt walked me home, I'd play the same 45 on Chrystal's little record player. I'd pretend Matt was there, play this song and sing along. Have a listen to the lyrics if you're wondering why.

The Hollies – The Air That I Breathe

🐜 🐜 🐜

One of my favourite days on the school calendar was approaching – Mufti Day. I loved Mufti Days, a chance to leave the drab school uniform in the wardrobe and wear whatever I wanted to. These days came around only two or maybe three times a year, so the prospect of the day to come was terribly exciting. This particular Mufti Day was all the more exciting as it was also the last day of the school term.

I wanted to make a real impression on Mufti Day – an impression on one person in particular I should say. During the last school holidays, Matilda and I had gone to the Petone State Picture Theatre to see the movie Grease. Not only did we love it for the songs, but it also inspired me. I decided to take a leaf out of the book of Olivia Newton John's character Sandy, who transforms herself from ingénue to Greaser via a serious makeover to win her man, Danny. I started planning *my* makeover to coincide with Mufti Day.

I realised I needed some cash to do this, so I'd been saving like crazy for ages. The pile of overalls I had to process every day at the factory was much bigger than when I'd started working at age 10, so I'd been given a pay rise from $5 to $10 per week. Even though I had way more overalls to fold every day, I could still complete my work in just over an hour. I was a very experienced and accomplished overall-folder after all. If I ever got to work late for whatever reason, I'd simply work until I'd finished folding my pile of overalls and then lock up. Having a father who was Foreman had its advantages as I knew where all the keys lived.

It was time to initiate the four step makeover plan I'd devised. I began with Step 1 on a late night shopping night in Petone and made sure I finished my job bang on 4:30pm. The first thing I did after work was to visit the Petone Post Office to make a rather sizeable cash withdrawal from my Post Office Savings Bank Squirrel account. Step 1 of my plan was complete. Tick.

Step 2 was to get to an appointment I'd made earlier at the hairdressers in Petone to get my hair cut and styled like Farrah Fawcett-Majors. Her "do" was famous and I decided I finally wanted to tame my blonde curls and look like she did.

On my way to the hairdressers, my heart started to race when I spotted the two Mean Girls standing outside a store in the main shopping street of Petone ahead of me. As soon as they saw me, they predictably called out, "Hey Dump Girl, how's the dump going?" followed by bouts of laughter. Sometimes I really wished I could use my Karate on them, but I knew I'd get in big trouble with my mother and Sensei if I did. So I sucked it up even though my heart was pounding, walked right past where they were loitering as if I didn't hear or see them and carried on my way.

I really liked my hairdresser. She was a statuesque blonde lady who knew my father from the Petone Working Men's Club as her husband was a member there also. I asked her whether she could cut my hair like Farrah Fawcett-Majors'. "Of course Scarlet!" she replied. "Actually, you have the perfect hair for her hairstyle with all of your amazing curls."

"Awesome!" I thought.

During my hair cut, I was so nervous about what the finished product was going to end up like that I couldn't bring myself to look in the mirror. Finally the job was done and my hairdresser told me to take a look. I couldn't believe my eyes! My hair looked exactly like Farrah's and I had to restrain myself from jumping up and giving my hairdresser a huge hug.

"Is that really me?" I gasped.

"Yes Scarlet, that's really you. Didn't you realise there was a pretty teenager under that mass of blonde hair you came in here with?"

During the cut, I couldn't bear to look at myself in the mirror. Now it was done, I couldn't take my eyes off my reflection. My hairdresser held a mirror up behind me so I could get a full 360° view of my new do. "I love it, I love it, I love it," I kept repeating like an idiot.

"There are a few tricks I'll teach you so it'll look this good every day," my hairdresser said.

It turned out these tricks required a second trip to the Post Office as I needed to buy some Wella Balsam shampoo, conditioner and a blow-dryer. "Crikey!" I thought on the way to make my withdrawal. "This hairdo is high maintenance! But well worth the time, money and effort." Purchases made, I ticked off Step 2 and focused on the next step of my plan.

Step 3 involved visiting my favourite clothes shop. I'd needed a new pair of jeans for a while as my last pair was getting too short to be cool. The way I thought about it, buying a new pair wasn't really an extravagance, more like a necessity really. That's how I justified it to myself anyway.

After trying a few pairs of jeans on, I bought a new pair of dark blue flared Levi's, pretty much the same as the ones I'd bought before. I decided a new pair of jeans called for a new top and I'd seen just the one in the shop window. It was a pretty, light pink halter-neck number with pink lace around the edges. It went across my front and tied up at the back. Perfect. Step 3, tick.

Now onto Step 4. I needed some new shoes, so I went to a popular Kiwi chain of shoe shops called Hannah's and bought a pair of shoes with a 4 inch thick sole which were all the rage. The idea was for your jeans to be just long enough to rest on your shoes, which had to be big thick things. That was definitely the height of fashion back then. It took a little getting used to before I could safely manoeuvre around with shoes that thick, but I eventually got the hang of it. With my shoes secured, I could tick off Step 4.

Step 5. Step 5? The original conception of my plan had only 4 steps in it, but it is said "necessity is the mother of invention." As I was browsing around Hannah's, it occurred to me that now I'd bought my new pink top, I needed some matching nail polish as well. So I added Step 5 to my plan on the fly and walked a little further down the main street of Petone to the nearest chemist shop.

Step 5 involved buying some light pink nail polish, light pink lipstick and some mascara. I splashed out and bought a flash moisturiser called Oil of Ulan and a bottle of Formula 10-0-6 toner as well. I mentally ticked off Step 5 and my makeover plan was complete.

By the time Step 5 was over, the little Squirrel in my Post Office Savings Bank account had taken quite a beating and needed a lie down and a cup of tea. I'd used the last of my cash, but as I walked home with all of my purchases, I was on a real high having successfully implemented my plan. I was on such a high I made the fatal mistake of showing my mother everything I'd bought that evening. As in *everything*.

Mum almost had a fit.

No, let me reword that. Mum had an *actual* fit. It was almost as bad as the tirade she dished out to Sensei, but this time *I* copped it which made it ten times worse.

Mum was extremely angry with me. "I thought you were just getting your hair done and here you are with all this … this … other paraphernalia. Exactly how much money did you take out of your bank account?"

I thought I'd better tell the truth. "Well, the first time I went to the Post Office I only took out $100." Mum's eyes went as wide as saucers when I said, "only $100." "The second time I went to the Post Office I took out $50. So I guess that makes $150. Oh, and I also spent my wages from this week, so that's $160 all up."

My mother's face actually went white and I thought for a moment she was going to feint with the loss of blood. After she'd sat down and recovered, I thought I'd get the usual speech; "Do you have any idea what I could do with $160? Feed the family for a month, pay the power bill and car expenses," etc etc.

Instead, Mum looked at each of the items I'd bought and picked up my new Wella Balsam shampoo. "Why did you buy this Scarlet? What's wrong with the Apple shampoo I buy? You're just *wasting* money now! Just you wait until your father gets home."

Ok, now I knew I was in big trouble.

When my dad arrived home, I thought I'd try and head Mum off at the pass and get to him before she did. My mother wasn't born yesterday though and bailed Dad up the second he walked in the door. I only managed to get halfway from my room to the door and saw it all happening from the hallway. "Geez, she's good," I thought.

"Guess what your precious daughter has done now?" Mum said. The smile that had started to form on Dad's face when he'd arrived home turned upside down and he shook his head.

"Can't a working man even get his foot in the door before being hassled?" Dad said, but I could tell he was being playful.

Mum steered Dad into the living room and I could hear her telling him all about my shopping spree. Although I wasn't intentionally trying to eavesdrop, I'm pretty sure I heard the words "Wella Balsam" and "Apple shampoo" being mentioned. I rolled my eyes and shook my head in best teenager fashion. Dad re-emerged from the lounge a couple of minutes later and motioned for me to follow him to my bedroom.

Once there, Dad had a talk to me about the virtues of saving money rather than spending it. All in all, he made a pretty good case and didn't go off his nut like Mum had. I remember thinking at the time that both Mum and Dad were genuinely trying to help me and my brothers and sisters by creating a culture of saving amongst us all.

What I didn't know at the time and only found out years later was that my parents had a "savings plan" in which they put aside as much as they could, despite their limited means, with the endgame of buying a house of their own. Me outlaying $160 on my "makeover plan" must have seemed totally antithetical to that mindset.

"Your mother is actually right about this Scarlet," my dad said. "You must try harder to save money, not waste it."

I took offence at the word "waste," and with hands firmly on hips lashed out. "I am *not* wasting my money Dad. I don't spend money on cigarettes or alcohol like some girls I know at High School. I just wanted to get my hair done and keep it nice with some good products and buy a few clothes and other bit and pieces. I don't expect you and Mum to buy these things you know."

Dad jumped in at this point. "Talking about hair, what's with that Wella Balsawood shampoo you bought today? What's wrong with the Apple shampoo your mother gets?"

I had to giggle. "It's Wella *Balsam* shampoo Dad. Farrah Fawcett-Majors uses it. She's in all the magazines advertising it." I put on my best impersonation of Farrah Fawcett-Majors' voice. "'Beautiful hair just doesn't happen, it starts with Wella Balsam.'"

Dad shrugged his shoulders as if he didn't have a clue what I was talking about. But I could see him softening. "As for the Apple shampoo ..." I moved closer to Dad and lowered my voice in case my mother was listening, "... it's just *crap*! Look Dad. I promise I'll save all of the money I earn in the school holidays from the factory, ok?"

"That would make me happy Scarlet," my father said nodding his head.

As Dad was leaving my bedroom, he turned back towards me. "Your hair looks really good by the way Bubs," he said with a wink.

"Thanks Dad," I smiled back.

🐜 🐜 🐜

A few days after my shopping spree, I'd barely returned home from my after-school job when I heard Frank going mental in the living room. "Scarlet, Scarlet ... come in here quickly, you've got to see this!!" he screamed at the top of his lungs. I'd rarely heard Frank so animated and I quickly glanced at Mum as if to ask what the heck was going on. Mum was sitting at the kitchen table sipping on a cup of tea at the time. She didn't look up at me, but she was smiling one of her mysterious Sphynx-like half-smiles.

I quickly walked through the doorway connecting the kitchen to the living room and ... I saw it for the first time! It was magnificent, easily as good as everyone said it was. I think I even let out a little scream, it was *that* exciting.

So what was it everyone was buzzing over? It was only that colour TV had arrived in the Giesen household!!

Where once our well-loved black and white TV had stood, there was now a new boy on the block in its place. That new boy was a glorious Philips K9 26 inch colour television. Mum had placed the new set on top of a low-boy chest of drawers and it looked so big and impressive and, yes, colourful. I still remember the first image I ever saw on that colour TV's screen. One of those ubiquitous wildlife programmes was on at the time and there was a close-up of an Ocelot's face. It was very close-up indeed and it filled the entire screen. If I were watching it in black and white, I wouldn't have given it a second look. But in colour, that striking animal came alive. I'd never seen anything like it.

It wasn't as if colour TV was new to New Zealand. It had arrived shortly before the 1974 Commonwealth Games in Christchurch had begun. But as with any new technology, the initial cost of a set was way beyond many families' means back then, my own included.

I looked excitedly at Frank and then turned back to the TV. We were literally glued to the screen; even the ads were exciting in colour! I was so happy watching this marvel of modern technology that I didn't care when Frank informed me our old black and white TV now lived in his bedroom.

"Watch this Scarlet," Frank said in a smarty pants kind of way during a second batch of ads. He marched straight over to the TV and turned it off.

"Oh **no**, don't do that Frank," I protested. "It's going to take forever to start up again now." My only frame of reference in this regard was to our old black and white TV which took roughly three minutes to start displaying a picture once it had been turned on. With that TV, there was no "Quick! Turn the television on, such and such is on the news." By the time the set had warmed up and the picture finally came on, the next story, or perhaps even the story after that had begun.

But to my complete and utter amazement, the picture on the colour TV appeared almost as soon as Frank pushed the on/off switch again. "How … how does that work?" I said in utter astonishment.

"Don't know," replied Frank. "Must be magic, kind of like what they do across the road!"

We both laughed and laughed.

"Hey Scarlet," Frank said without taking his eyes off our new TV. "You know that Kiwi game show with Selwyn Toogood 'It's In The Bag'"?

"Yeah, of course I know it," I replied. "Why?"

"One of the top prizes is a Philips K9 colour TV, like the one we're watching now!"

"Wowwwww!" I gushed. It certainly felt like we'd won a lottery of some sort.

After the excitement had died down a little, my mind turned to something that had been troubling me a little since I'd first looked on the Ocelot's face. I turned to Frank and asked him the question. "Hey Frank … how much would this TV have cost?"

"Well, I saw a set like this one in Smith and Brown's in town a while back," Frank said. "I think it was 1200 bucks."

I just about fell off my chair! That was an enormous sum of money in 1978. By way of comparison, it would have amounted to around $8k in 2017 money.

Don't get me wrong – I was only too happy to be watching colour TV – but there seemed something slightly not-quite-right that only a couple of days ago I'd been hauled over the coals for spending $160 on hair and makeup etc, whereas somehow my parents had thought nothing about spending seven or eight times that much on a luxury item such as a colour TV set.

By now Mum had joined Frank and I in the living room and was enjoying watching the wildlife documentary with us. Over the space of half an hour or so I kept saying to myself, "Just shut up Scarlet. Don't say anything about it, just shut up." But eventually the inequity of it got to me, so I decided to be a stroppy teenager and turned to Mum.

"So Mum, how many months' food could you have put on the table for the price of this TV? Frank says it would've cost around $1200, so I expect you could've bought the whole dairy down the road for that. Or paid the electricity for a couple of years or something?" I glared at Mum in an accusatory way.

I could see Frank's face to one side as I challenged my mother. His mouth formed a very round "O" shape and his eyes almost bulged out of his head which he was shaking oh so very slowly from side to side.

My Mum remained expressionless for a couple of seconds, during which time I totally regretted saying anything to her. To her credit, when she did start talking, she spoke calmly and rationally.

"Do you know where these TV sets are made Scarlet?" she asked.

"Not really," I replied indignantly. "Probably in Japan or somewhere like that?"

"I'll tell you where they're made," Mum continued, unperturbed. "In the Philips factory in Naenae, down in the Hutt Valley."

I was starting to get the picture – pun definitely intended.

"You know that factory don't you Scarlet? Your father has a couple of rugby mates who work there. One of them managed to get the TV set you're now enjoying for your father for a really good price because it has a deep scratch down the left side of the cabinet – I don't suppose you've noticed that though have you? Your father thought it was a great deal, so we cut a few corners here and there for a few weeks and found the money."

I was rapidly dissolving into the chair in which I was sitting.

"Do you have any other questions while you're at it?" Mum asked with a tinge of sarcasm.

I tried to guts it out. "No thank you, I'm fine," I simply said.

I hugged my legs tight to my body to try and take up the smallest amount of space I could. I looked over at Frank who shook his head and mouthed the word "dick."

Yes, it was true – I was a dick. But a dick who was now watching a brand new colour TV – possibly the newest colour TV in our whole street.

Later that night, Frank and I settled in to watch the American TV show "The Man From Atlantis." Immediately prior to the start of the show, we were unexpectedly treated to something special – a first viewing of our favourite TV advertisement in glorious colour. The ad in question was known as the "Cadbury Crunchie Great Train Robbery" and graced our TV screens for 20-odd years winning awards along the way.

Unbeknowst to Frank and I, the ad was filmed mere kilometres from our house, somewhere up the Hutt Valley. Apparently, director Tony Williams had exceeded his small budget in the making of the ad and settled for a lawn mower as his fee. You can't get much more Kiwi than that! Frank and I didn't know any of this at the time though; we just loved singing along to the ad's jingle:

♪ *Have a Crunchie ... hokey pokey bar* ♫

You simply **must** take a look at the full version of this classic slice of Kiwiana in the video below.

nzonscreen: Great Crunchie Train Robbery (1:36)

Following the Crunchie ad, the main event began – The Man From Atlantis. Frank and I both loved this show, but watching Patrick Duffy in colour was a real revelation. On seeing a close-up of his face, Frank and I looked at each other in amazement. "Wow – his eyes are really really really green!" I exclaimed.

"Yeah they are," Frank agreed. "I don't get it – how did they do that?"

I shrugged my shoulders. "I guess they must've found an actor with super amazing green eyes."

🐨 🐨 🐨

The days leading up to Mufti Day seemed to drag by, but finally it had arrived! The night before, I painted my finger and toe nails light pink with my new nail polish. I had religiously been using the toner and moisturiser every night before bed in preparation for the big day.

As usual, at 7am I was woken up to the sound of the stereo blaring out one of my father's favourite songs. A tingly feeling raced through my tummy when I remembered it was Mufti Day and I jumped out of bed to join Dad in the lounge, pulling on my white satin robe as I went. I loved the song Dad played that morning and I still do. It's one of those songs that makes me feel warm inside whenever I hear it. As well as that, it always evokes wonderful memories of that most special High School Mufti Day.

Here is the song to which Dad and I waltzed that morning.

Andy Williams – Moon River

As soon as the song had finished, it was time for Dad to go to work and for me to get ready for the Mufti Day. First up was to have a bath, wash my hair with my new shampoo and then condition it like my hairdresser had taught me. Once that was done, I got out of the bath, wrapping one towel around my head and another around my body, just like I'd seen big sister Chrystal do a thousand times.

In my bedroom, I held my head upside down and blow dried my hair with my fingers, loosening up the tight curls as my hairdresser had taught me. Frank had heard the sound of my blow-dryer and he stuck his head around my bedroom door. "Oh Farrah," he teased. "I just love your hair – it's so wavy and shiny!" I resisted the temptation to smack him one thinking, "No, I'm a lady now."

When I'd dressed and finished getting ready for school, I looked at myself in my full length mirror. I hardly recognised the girl looking back at me. Usually I'd see my reflection wearing my frumpy school clothes, but today I was wearing a backless pink halter-neck top that made me look quite grown up. I so hoped I'd see Matt at some point during the day because he'd never seen me in anything but my school uniform.

As it had taken me so much longer to get ready that morning, I left home a lot later than usual. Add to that how slow I was in walking in my new 4 inch shoes and I was in real danger of getting to school late. Imagine my dismay then as I approached my school only to see the two Mean Girls up ahead.

My heart began to race and I considered crossing the road to try and avoid them. I was too stubborn for that though and decided to walk past them. "She'll be right, Scarlet," I reassured myself.

As I drew level with them, one of the Mean Girls fired her first salvo. "Where did you steal those clothes from Dump Girl? They're far too nice to be yours." Both girls started laughing.

Something snapped inside me and I turned around to face them, remembering Matilda had told me they must be ugly on the inside. "Hey, I may have been born poor, but at least I wasn't born mean and ugly!" I said assertively. It felt good to stand up to them and even better to see the stunned looks on their faces. I then turned on my heel – which is quite difficult in shoes with a 4 inch high sole – and started to walk towards school.

As I was walking away, one of the Mean Girls shouted after me. "Don't you turn your back on me, Dump Girl." After yelling at me, she hurled her school bag at me as a bonus. I have to hand it to her – she threw that bag with some force and it caught me square in the back. It must have been full of text books as it actually hurt a fair bit when it made contact with me. My initial reaction was to smash the girl who'd thrown the bag, but I ended up doing something even better. I kicked the Mean Girl's school bag all the way down the road to the next corner, not far from the school entrance.

I heard the sound of the Mean Girls running to catch me up and one of them was screaming, "You bitch, Scarlet. That's my bag!" I quickly turned around and instinctively adopted a Karate fighting stance. The two Mean Girls stopped dead in their tracks as they saw I meant business. And I did. I'd had enough of those two girls harassing me all the time. We stood looking at each other for a few seconds. Neither of us backed off, but neither advanced either. To this day I wonder whether I would have defended myself with Karate if they'd come at me. Given my state of mind, I think I very well may have.

Eventually, I put my hands down but maintained eye contact with the two girls. We'd come to some unspoken cease-fire for the time being, so I slowly turned around and carried on my way. It seemed like a miracle I'd managed to get to school in one piece.

The whole experience had shaken me up quite a lot, but I was glad I'd finally stood up to those girls. I went straight to D Block intending to unload my heavy text books out of my bag and into my locker. I also wanted to find Tracey, the friend from my class who'd joined me to watch Star Wars at the movies the year before.

I couldn't find Tracey and was still unsettled from my confrontation with the Mean Girls, so I decided to do what I always did in these situations – think of a song and sing it to myself. This always negated the bad thoughts and put me instantly in a good mood. Thanks Matilda's grandmother!

I was still hoping to see Matt sometime during the course of the day, so I sang the song in my head to him as I walked through D block towards my locker. As the music started up and I began to sing to myself, I suddenly didn't have a care in the world.

I sang this song for you, Matt.

Yvonne Elliman – If I Can't Have You

Walking through D block, it was as if the whole backing orchestra from this song was playing in my head in full stereo. Suddenly the music stopped and I got the shock of my life to see Matt ahead of me sitting on a bench seat with a mate, looking at the students going this way and that in their mufti outfits. I was shocked to see Matt calmly sitting on that seat because he was a year ahead of me and based – like Matilda – in C block. I hardly ever saw either of them at school during the day.

Matt stood up as soon as he saw me and walked towards me a couple of steps. I walked over to him and saw that his eyes were almost bulging out of their sockets, his mouth wide open like a loon. His friend was almost cracking up as he watched Matt.

After a couple of attempts, Matt managed to speak. "Scarlet ... you ... you look ... a-maz-ing!"

I couldn't stop smiling and was about to say something when Matt got in first. "I've been sitting here for a while, hoping to see you." He introduced me to his friend who, not surprisingly, was a really nice guy like Matt.

The bell announcing the beginning of the academic day was due to ring soon and I mentally kicked myself for taking so long in getting to school that morning. If I'd arrived sooner, I might have avoided the confrontation with the Mean Girls and would also have had more time to talk to Matt.

But for now the bell hadn't sounded, so Matt and I stood talking for a few minutes. That is to say, I let him do all the talking and stood there with a big smile on my face. Matt looked amazing. It was the first time I'd seen him out of his school uniform. He wore dark blue Levi's and a whiter than white t-shirt. He looked so handsome.

"I'd better go and put my books in my locker," I said.

"I'll come with you," Matt replied.

My locker was only a short distance away and as I was filling it with my text books, Matt alerted me to something with alarm in his voice. "Scarlet ... did you know you have a big red welt on your back?"

I quickly put two and two together and silently cursed the Mean Girls. "Oh yes," I said thinking as quickly as I could. "I backed into the door handle in the girls' loos just now. I'm *soooo* clumsy!"

All my life I've never been able to lie very well. When I do, it's written all over my face – I'm simply no good at it. Part of the problem I think is I can't come up with plausible alternative scenarios quickly enough. I mean ... I backed into the door handle in the girls' loos? Come on Scarlet! I think on balance not being able to lie is a good thing, but every once in a while I wish I could execute a little "white lie" convincingly.

Matt looked at me square on and I could tell he knew I was telling porkies. I couldn't tell him the truth because the truth was too painful – that I was being bullied because I lived in a dump of a house.

Matt smiled sweetly. I got the feeling he was thinking something like, "I know you're not telling me the truth Scarlet, but that's ok. One day you will. When you're ready."

"I'd better get going before the bell goes," he said. "But how about we meet at the school gates after school today and walk home together?"

"I'd love to!" I replied.

"Good, see you then. Don't be late ... looks like it could be a long walk with those shoes of yours!"

Matt and his mate ran off in the direction of C Block.

I was in heaven ... on Cloud Nine. Matt may as well have asked me out on a date. He had kind of hadn't he?

The school bell still hadn't rung, so I carried on looking for Tracey. I remembered she'd recently developed a crush on a boy who arrived at school every day on a bus from Wainuiomata. It occurred to me she might be waiting at the front of the school for his bus to arrive.

I hurried out to the school gates and sure enough, there she was waiting for the Wainui school bus which was pulling into the carpark. I stood with her as the boy she had a crush on stepped out of the bus and walked past the both of us. Nothing was said by either of them, but their eyes were locked on each other and ... he was gone. Tracey turned to me and gave me a look you could roughly translate as "so dreamy, yes?" I nodded my head in agreement. Even though they hadn't said so much as "hello" to each other, Tracey was happy to have made eye contact with this boy.

We ran off to class together as the school bell finally rang out. As we jogged side-by-side, I looked over at Tracey. I thought she was the best looking girl in my whole school. She always looked so beautiful and today on mufti day she looked more beautiful than ever. Once we'd found empty desks next to each other in our Home Room, I turned to my friend. "You look amazing Tracey!" I said.

"Thanks Scarlet!" Tracey replied appreciatively. "You scrub up really well too! Your eyelashes look so long!"

"It's mascara," I said proudly, remembering how Chrystal had introduced me to it when she'd lived at home.

"I'm definitely getting some of that!" replied Tracey. "But hey, what's with the huge red mark on your back? It looks nasty!"

I shook my head and spoke in a low voice. "I'll tell you about it later."

I have such vivid, happy memories of that Mufti Day. Tracey and I made pikelets together in Home Economics class, the last period of the day. As soon as they came out of the frying pan, we smothered them in butter that instantly melted and we gobbled them up immediately. So delicious! We made extra sure to tie our aprons on securely so we didn't mess up our mufti outfits. The white and blue polka dot dress I wore as a 4 year old flitted through my mind and I remember thinking how things had changed since then!

As soon as Home Economics class had finished, I hurried out of the classroom to meet Matt at the school gate as arranged. He was already waiting there when I arrived, but looking past him I saw the two Mean Girls dallying around in the distance. Luckily they didn't see me as I walked away with Matt. I would have been mortified if they'd yelled out any abuse in front of him. Somehow I didn't think they'd have had the courage to do that though, as I wasn't by myself this time around.

Matt was such a gentle, kind boy. As usual, he offered to carry my school bag for me. Back in the day it seemed like we had such heavy old hardcover textbooks and our bags were always full and a pain to lug around. That's why I made such good use of my locker at school. Matt carried my schoolbag as well as his and I smiled all the way home as we talked about nothing in particular.

On the way, Matt remarked that the red welt he'd seen on my back that morning had turned into a nasty-looking bruise. I shrugged and smiled. It really didn't matter to me – I was in heaven walking with Matt.

In no time at all, and long before I was ready, we'd reached my house. I could see my mother doing something through the window in Frank's bedroom so I instantly turned my head away in case she saw me.

I carried on walking as if it wasn't my house and soon we were at the next corner. I remember so many things about that day, but I can't for the life of me remember what excuse I gave Matt as I was about to run off as usual.

Over the previous couple of days, I'd been practising something new to say to Matt in French in anticipation of the next time he walked me home. I was only too happy to be able to try out my new farewell this Mufti Day. As I turned to leave I called out, "Merci de marcher à la maison avec moi, Matt." [Thanks for walking home with me, Matt.] I gave Matt my biggest smile and ran off in the direction of the lane behind my house.

When I say "run," I couldn't exactly do that with the 4 inch soled shoes I was wearing. Matt and I were roughly the same height when I wore those shoes and as I took off, I looked behind to see him smiling and watching me. "Don't fall over, don't fall over, don't fall over!" I said to myself repeatedly.

Guess what happened next? I fell over. I was so embarrassed.

Matt came rushing over to me, the concern plain to see on his face. "Are you ok, Scarlet?" he said as he helped me back to my feet.

I forced a laugh. "I'm ok, thanks Matt," I said. I'd actually twisted my ankle, but made out I was perfectly fine because I was so embarrassed. I limped home, all the way thinking "dick, dick, dick!"

My Mum hardly ever missed a trick and as soon as I arrived home, she asked me how I'd managed to acquire a limp *and* a large bruise on my back in a single day.

"It's these new shoes Mum," I said, trying out another little white lie. "I haven't learned how to drive them properly and I fell over at school today."

"Oh, do be careful Scarlet," Mum said worriedly. "You could do yourself some real damage in those blasted things!"

"Yes Mum," I replied hobbling down the hall towards my room.

❦ ❦ ❦

I didn't see Matt for a few weeks after the Mufti Day. He wasn't even in French class when school started up for the new term. Why hadn't I seen him? Was it something I'd done? I felt sadder and sadder as time went by and my tummy felt like it had a gaping hole in it.

Around this time, I was awakened at 3am for the third time by "the thing" that felt like I was being pulled down my bed. I was a bit calmer about it this time around and I really tried to shout out, but no sound would come out of my mouth. I quickly started to sing a song to myself as Matilda's grandmother had suggested. The song that came to mind was a Queen song I loved from an album in Frank's collection called "A Night At The Opera."

I think this song did quite well for them and you may have heard it.

Queen – Bohemian Rhapsody

When the force thing had gone and I could move again, I sat up in bed singing out loud and even played the air piano and air guitar to really get myself right there in the moment. Before long I was head-banging as I sang the heavy rock bit towards the end of the song. You could say I was doing Wayne's World long before that movie came out. I completely lost myself in the music and soon found I wasn't feeling scared anymore.

Still singing, I looked over at Little Sister Jane who'd slept through the whole thing ... again. "She can sleep through anything, that kid," I thought as I sang the last line of Bohemian Rhapsody.

"I heard you singing in the middle of the night last night Scarlet," my mother said over breakfast the next morning.

"Oh yes?" I replied innocently.

"You even sing in your sleep by the looks of things!" she said cheerily. Mum and Frank shared a little chuckle.

"You wouldn't be laughing if you knew why I was singing," I said to myself.

ঌ ঌ ঌ

Matt surprised me one day after school by running up behind me. "Hey Scarlet, can I walk with you?"

My heart just about popped out of my chest – I was that happy to see him. "Of course you can, Matt. Where have you been lately? I haven't seen you since the Mufti Day last term."

"Oh, I should've told you," Matt replied breezily. "I went on a trip with my family over the holidays that went on a bit longer than we'd planned. We went right up to the top of the North Island to a place called the Bay of Islands. Have you heard of it? It's amazing!"

I had heard of the Bay of Islands. The prior Christmas, my friend Tracey had asked me if I'd like to join her and her older brother who were hitch-hiking up there over the holidays. When I asked my mother if I could go, she started hyperventilating as soon as I said the word "hitch-hiking" and I almost had to call 111 – I was that afraid she was going to pass out. The closest I got to the Bay of Islands was listening to Tracey's stories when she returned home.

Of course I didn't tell Matt about this, but I wanted to sound knowledgeable. "Is that somewhere around 90 Mile Beach?" I asked.

"Yes, it is," Matt replied excitedly. "Oh Scarlet, I wish you could've been there. We drove right along 90 Mile Beach on a bus trip and stopped on the beach and had a swim in the sea and everything. It was so amazing! This bus trip took us right to the top of the North Island, to a place called Cape Reinga."

YouTube: 90 Mile Beach & Cape Reinga – Drone (2:36)

Matt asked me where in New Zealand I'd been. "Well, I've been to Masterton ... and Waikanae on the Kapiti Coast," I replied matter-of-factly. Matt laughed until he saw I wasn't joking. I think he was quite shocked by my answer given Masterton is only about an hour's drive from Petone along State Highway 2 and Waikanae is about the same distance along State Highway 1.

"You need to see more of our beautiful country," Matt said kindly without a hint of judgement in his voice. "Have you seen those ads on the TV – the ones put out by the Tourism people called 'Don't leave town till you've seen the country?' They even mention the Bay Of Islands in them."

YouTube: Don't leave home 'til you've seen the country New Zealand (NZ) (0:40)

"Tell me about the time you went to Masterton," Matt asked. He was always genuinely interested in learning more about me.

"Well," I started, thinking my story wasn't interesting or eventful in the slightest. "My father took my brother Frank and I over to Queen Elizabeth Park in Masterton one Saturday. We were just kids, so it was all very exciting. There was a little lake we rowed boats on and around this lake there was a little train that we went on a couple of times. There was a pretty good playground as well. We also went to a swimming pool not far from the Park which had a massive outdoor water slide. That was so much fun! We had a great day and it's a lovely memory."

YouTube: Queen Elizabeth Park, Masterton (1:10)

I finished talking. "Oh my God, what a lame story!" I thought. "I went to a park with my father and brother, we sat on a see-saw then went down a water slide! Matt will think I'm *soooo* boring."

To my surprise Matt reacted enthusiastically. "I *love* Queen Elizabeth Park!" he said. "My family and I went there all the time when I was younger. Usually on a Sunday. We still go there sometimes. I've been down that water slide too. Wouldn't it have been great if we'd been there at the same time?"

"What a lovely boy you are Matt," I thought.

Matt and I talked all the way home and my ear to ear smile was back. Before I knew it, we'd arrived at the corner where I usually came up with an excuse to run off. This day though, I didn't have to give Matt an excuse. As soon as we reached the corner, he simply handed my bag back to me. I secured the bag to my back and ran off calling out, "Désolé Matt, je dois y aller!" [Sorry Matt, I have to go!] He still looked a little bewildered as I took off into the distance, but I guess he was used to it by now.

𓃠 𓃠 𓃠

A new US TV show hit the Kiwi small screen late in 1978 called "Mork and Mindy." It was the first time we'd seen comedian Robin Williams and Frank and I loved watching him and his show. Robin Williams made the Orkan greeting "Nanu Nanu" famous and Frank and I adopted the saying to mean something weird or inexplicable.

Now, whenever Kemo Sabe barked at the wall of my bedroom or my new mirror, we had a word for it – Frank and I would look at each other and say, "That's a bit Nanu Nanu!" Soon it became simply, "Nanu Nanu!"

We also used the phrase to describe some of the strange events that took place over the road on Sunday evenings at the Petone Spiritualist Church. When the curtains in the front room were open revealing the giant banner with the motto "There is no death," that was Nanu Nanu too.

Frank and I always cracked up laughing when one or the other of us said our new saying and I liked how it brought a bit of light-heartedness to all of the strange things going on in our house. Even Mum knew what Nanu Nanu meant. If Frank or I saw or heard something strange around the house, we'd go and tell Mum. "That was a bit Nanu Nanu wasn't it?" she'd say playing along.

Take a look at this six second clip of Robin Williams in his red spacesuit saying the phrase he made famous.

YouTube: Nanu Nanu (0:06)

I loved the sound of "Nanu Nanu" and the meaning Frank and I associated with it. It always made me laugh when someone said it, including myself. It occurred to me that if I had another experience in the middle of the night in my bedroom, I'd simply say "Nanu Nanu." That would make me laugh and hopefully banish whatever was around.

There was another word from Mork and Mindy Frank and I used a lot – the Orkan profanity, "Shazbot." I didn't like swearing and still don't to this day. But saying the Orkan equivalent was somehow ok, maybe because the word was made up.

So, if I woke up in the morning and looked at my unruly hair in the mirror, it was "Shazbot."

If I'd done something wrong and Mum hit me with, "Just wait until your father gets home," it was "Shazbot."

And at school: "Scarlet, why haven't you done your maths homework?"

"Shazbot."

ೋ ೋ ೋ

Around this time I bought my first ever LP. It was "Rumours" by Fleetwood Mac, not a bad choice for a first album. Depending on which website you visit, sales of this album are quoted at somewhere around 40 million copies putting it in the Top Ten list of best-selling records of all time. That was in spite of – or perhaps because of – all the personal trauma going on in every one of the band members' lives at the time.

I played that record so many times the tracklisting is burned into my memory. Back in 1978, my favourite song was Side 1 Track 4, "Don't Stop."

"Don't stop thinking about tomorrow," I'd sing. Don't stop thinking about the next time I'd see Matt!

Fleetwood Mac – Don't Stop

The next time Matt and I walked home, I dropped into the conversation that I'd just bought an amazing album by Fleetwood Mac called Rumours.

Matt immediately stopped dead in his tracks. "No way … I've just bought that album and I love it as well!" he said excitedly.

"What's your favourite song?" we both asked at the same time, exactly in sync.

"Don't Stop," we both answered, again in perfect unison.

"Classic Nanu Nanu!" I thought.

We looked at each other, a little startled to begin with, then we laughed.

We carried on walking and talking about music and Matt spoke for some time about his other favourite album called "Bat Out Of Hell" by a guy called Meat Loaf. This became the second LP I bought which also happens to appear in the Top Ten list of best-selling records of all time. I instantly loved Meat Loaf's music and listen to this album to this day.

When I saw Matt next, I excitedly told him that I'd bought the Meat Loaf album. "Do you like it?" Matt asked expectantly.

"No," I replied. "I don't like it … I love it!"

Matt smiled. "It's *fantastic*, eh? I think Meat Loaf is a music genius!!"

I looked at Matt and smiled back. Matt was one huge ray of sunshine in my life and I could never stop smiling when I was with him.

As always though, I dumped him at the usual corner. This time I said, "J'espère vous voir demain, Matt!" [Hope to see you tomorrow, Matt!]

Matt stood at the corner, smiling his beautiful smile as he watched me run off.

🐞 🐞 🐞

I knew I liked Matt. A lot. But I wasn't sure whether he liked me in the same way. After work that day, I went next door to talk to best friend Matilda about this very important issue.

"How could he **not** like you, Scarlet?" was all Matilda would say. I wasn't particularly satisfied with this answer. After all, it's exactly what a friend would say, isn't it?

"What about you Matilda … are you interested in anyone at the moment?" I asked.

Matilda replied without hesitation, but a little tersely. "No, I'm not. You know how absolutely ***devastated*** I was when Donny Osmond married that Debbie woman earlier this year. I'm sure she's a very nice person … but anyway, I'm content with my Church. I don't need anything or anyone else."

Matilda and I were quiet for a moment, remembering the shocking news of Donny's nuptials earlier in the year. This unwelcome news had destroyed any remaining ideas she harboured of marrying the singing star.

"How about we go and play some tennis at the school that's put new courts in?" she suggested. "They have actual nets, so we could practise hitting the ball to each other with a real net between us rather than having to imagine one all the time."

"That's a ***great*** idea," I said enthusiastically. "I'll go get my stuff from next door."

The days were starting to draw out now and after we'd played a decent game of tennis, it was still light so we decided to cut through the Petone Recreational grounds to shorten the way home. There were lines of tall, dense trees by the front gate back then and as we were walking through them, a man jumped out in front of us, seemingly from nowhere. He was an older man and he wore a long, dirty grey coat. As Matilda and I looked on in horror, this man opened up his coat to reveal his naked body beneath. He looked at us two girls with a strange glint in his eye.

"Would either of you girlies like to touch my old fella?" he asked.

We were both well aware that "old fella" was code for "penis" and after briefly looking at each other, we ran the heck out of the Rec grounds as fast as we could without saying a word. We knew instinctively to get as far away from that guy as fast as we possibly could. I looked back to where the man was still standing, coat open, but he didn't chase us. Instead, he disappeared back into the line of darkening trees. Neither Matilda nor I stopped running until we got back to the safety of my house. Once there, Matilda told me in a quiet voice that she didn't think the man was the full quid while tapping her head with her forefinger.

Giggling about our experience now, we told my mum exactly what had happened. Mum didn't think it was a laughing matter at all, and she called the Petone Police straight away. When she'd finished her call, Mum told us the Police said they had a pretty good idea who the flasher was.

"What's a 'flasher' Mrs. Giesen?" Matilda asked.

I was so glad Matilda didn't know what a "flasher" was either as I was about to ask Mum the same question.

Mum looked a little uncomfortable at having to answer this, but gave it a good shot.

"A 'flasher,' girls, is someone – usually a man – who exposes his ... um ... ahh ... private parts in public."

"Why would anyone want to do that Mum?" I asked.

Before Mum had to come up with an answer to this one, Matilda grabbed my arm. "Come on Scarlet, let's go and tell my mum what happened."

I was about to protest that I really did want to know the answer to my question, but Matilda looked at me in a way that said, "Come on Scarlet, I'll explain it to you later."

As we were walking the short distance to Matilda's house, she gave me her explanation. "Didn't you notice that man had a hard-on Scarlet?"

"What's a hard-on?" I asked naïvely.

Matilda rolled her eyes. "It's a name for a man's dick when it gets ... you know ... aroused. That man obviously does what he does so he can get ... hard."

"Well, I've never seen a man's penis up close like that before Matilda ... and how come you know so much about all of this anyway?" I asked indignantly.

"It was in a book my mother gave me," Matilda replied.

"Of course it was – I should've known," I said. "You're such a book-worm Matilda."

We looked at each other and laughed hysterically.

"Would you like to have a look at that book Scarlet?" Matilda asked. "My Mum says all girls need to know about this stuff."

"I don't really think I want to read a book about men's penises," I said huffily.

"It's not *only* about penises," Matilda said. "It's also about puberty and how girls get pregnant and a lot of other things as well. Haven't you ever wondered why your boobs have got so ginormous in the past year or two?"

I looked down and blushed. "I don't think they're any bigger than anyone else's are they?" I asked.

"Oh no?" Matilda said. "Have you looked at mine lately? They have more in common with two aspirins on an ironing board – that's what my mum says anyway."

We had another good laugh at this. But I still didn't understand how Jane had got into Mum's tummy; no-one would ever give me a straight answer about that when I asked them. Matilda was so smart and if she thought I should read that book, then read it I would.

"Ok Matilda," I said. "Give me the book and I'll take it home tonight and have a good read."

Perhaps you can imagine the scene later that night as I retrieved the book Matilda had given me from its hiding place under my pillow. I was ready for bed and Jane was already asleep in the bed beside me. I opened the book – which looked like it had been read a hundred times before – and started reading. I had absolutely zero expectations as I began my little covert operation, but as I read, my eyes – and world – grew wider and wider.

Every page contained a revelation; I had more than one epiphany that night. I learned about puberty and sex and childbirth – the whole nine yards. There were pictures too and diagrams of body parts and processes I had up to now only heard in hushed conversations with friends at school. The book was clearly aimed at young people and in its later chapters there were numerous anecdotes written by kids my age and older detailing their own sexual experiences.

The more I read, the more thankful I was I'd taken Matilda's advice to read it. I finally learned how babies were conceived and born and blow me down if it had absolutely *nothing* at all to do with cabbage patches or storks.

Nowadays, schoolkids are taught about these things from the age of 11 or 12. There was next to no "Sex Education" in schools or any-where else in New Zealand back in 1978 however. My friends and I talked about this stuff, but we were almost totally ignorant of the facts and largely had to draw our own conclusions from the precious little information that was out there.

For example, I had a female friend at school who, like me, was naïve of matters of the flesh. In New Zealand in the 1970s, we were fed a steady diet of old movies on TV, usually American, where the story would play out something like this: man meets woman; man and woman develop feelings for each other; man grasps woman and they kiss passionately; picture fades out; picture fades in and we see woman holding healthy crying baby. My friend wasn't stupid, but having observed the plotline described above in multiple movies, she proudly announced to me one day over lunch she'd figured out that kissing was the reason and mechanism whereby women became pregnant. Because of this, my friend would never let her boyfriends kiss her for fear she'd get pregnant. I wasn't stupid either, but I didn't think this sounded right. I mean, cats and dogs and sheep and cattle didn't kiss, but they managed to have babies didn't they?

It didn't help that neither of my parents – and clearly my friend's parents also – ever broached the subject of s – e – x with any of us kids. And I mean *ever*. My parents' parents wouldn't have spoken to them about this sort of thing either and so the cycle continued.

I sat up reading Matilda's book until the early hours of the morning. There was so much I wanted to talk to her about! I marvelled when I thought she'd known about all of this for some time now but had never spoken to me about it.

"You're so smart, Matilda!" I thought.

The book I read that night was called "Down Under The Plum Trees" and was written by two Kiwi authors. It dealt with some of the subject matter covered in a slightly earlier book written by two Danish schoolteachers called "The Little Red Schoolbook." Much controversy swirled around both publications in conservative 1970s New Zealand.

Whilst I read the Kiwi book from cover to cover, I know little about the Danish book. What I do know is Down Under The Plum Trees was first published in New Zealand in 1972 and in 1977 was classified as "indecent in the hands of persons under the age of 18 years, unless such persons are being instructed by parents or professional advisers." This classification has remained in force ever since.

The Little Red Schoolbook fared somewhat better. It was censored in the UK and banned in France and Italy – go figure – but was classified as "unrestricted" (not indecent) in New Zealand. Maybe it didn't have pictures of "old fellas" in it like the book Matilda gave me did.

When I read Down Under The Plum Trees in my bedroom late into the night and early morning, I was actually in possession, unbeknownst to me, of a banned indecent publication. Oh well. I learned a heck of a lot. And it's all thanks in a way to a flasher in the Petone Rec grounds.

Tiredness eventually got the better of me and I wearily returned the book to its hiding place around 2 in the morning. I made a mental note to speak to my schoolfriend next time I saw her and let her know that kissing boys was actually ok.

🐛 🐛 🐛

Before I got the chance to talk to Matilda the next day about my newly acquired knowledge, she told me her once-scary grandmother had been rushed to hospital during the night. It turned out she'd had a stroke. Matilda said she and her father would be visiting her grandmother that evening if I wanted to go with them. "Of course," I replied once the situation had sunk in.

Back in 1978, visiting hours at the Hutt Hospital were between 7:30pm and 8:30pm and were strictly enforced, so we all arrived at 7:30pm on the dot to have as much time with Matilda's grandmother as possible. I had become very fond of her since our talk a while back and felt a great sense of trepidation as we walked to her ward.

We needn't have worried though. When we arrived, she was sitting up in bed complaining about the quality of the hospital food which she described as "barely fit for human consumption." She was a character alright. Not bad for 87 years old.

At one point during the evening, Matilda's grandmother sat up a little higher in her bed and turned to me. "So Scarlet," she said quietly. "How are things going for you at night in your house?"

"A bit Nanu Nanu actually," I replied without thinking. Matilda's grandmother looked at me curiously and I realised she didn't know what that meant. "It's happened once more since we last spoke," I explained. "But I'm not giving into fear. I'm staying happy and strong." Matilda's grandmother nodded and managed a slight smile.

Matilda and her father briefly looked at me and then at each other, but neither said anything to me. I didn't really want to go into the details of what we were talking about, but I found I didn't have to. I guessed Matilda and her father were used to the way this eccentric old lady spoke and they certainly wouldn't be getting in touch with the man in the white coat.

Even though Matilda's grandmother had suffered a mild stroke, she still managed to speak in her scary voice. "Everything happens for a reason Scarlet, even if the meaning isn't clear to us at the time. Keep singing and stay strong! Never give into fear. I've warned you many times in the past to watch out for the spirits, haven't I?"

The way Matilda's grandmother looked at me suggested she wanted to hear an answer. "Yes," I said quietly, "you have."

"Yes, that's right," she said with scary voice intact. "Now I'll give you another warning ... beware of the man in the white coat. You will, won't you?"

"Yes I will," I said nodding my head vigorously, knowing she meant I must keep my mouth shut about Nanu Nanu matters.

Matilda's grandmother was a Tough Old Bird alright and seemed more concerned about my situation than her own.

🐜 🐜 🐜

The next time I saw Matt after school, he raced up to me and took my heavy schoolbag off me without asking. I was always on Cloud Nine when we walked home together. Seemingly all of a sudden, Matt stopped talking and looked at me expectantly. Somehow, we'd walked all the way past my house and were now standing at the corner where I always ran off. It was as if no time had passed at all.

I got myself mentally prepared to say goodbye and run off, but before I could open my mouth, Matt asked me a question. "Voulez-vous alles au Cinema, Scarlet?"

My French was nowhere near as good as Matt's, but I was pretty sure he'd asked me out to the movies. I got as far as saying, "Did you ..." before Matt interrupted with, "En Français s'il vous plaît Scarlet, en Français." [In French please Scarlet, in French.] Matt stood in front of me with a big grin on his face, waiting for my response.

Realising he wanted me to speak in French, I thought for a few moments before replying. "Avez-vous me de mandez au Cinema?" [Did you just ask me to the movies?]

"Oui!" Matt said simply.

I didn't think it was physically possible, but now I had an even bigger smile on my face than before. I couldn't believe it – Matt did like me after all! Unless ... he simply wanted to go to the movies with someone? Hmmm.

"No," I thought. "He definitely likes me!"

I couldn't form the words I was after in French, so I spoke to Matt in English. "Yes, I'd love to go to the movies with you."

Still with a big grin on his face, Matt said he'd look in the newspaper and see what was on at the Petone State Picture Theatre this coming weekend. He suggested we meet at the school gates straight after school on Friday and we could make our plans then.

We stood on the street corner for a few moments, looking at each other. Matt then handed my heavy schoolbag back to me. "You'll be needing this!" he said.

I thanked him and then ran off as usual. I looked back briefly to see Matt standing on the pavement, watching me go. He looked the happiest I'd ever seen him and called out to him in English. "See you on Friday, Matt!" And I was off. This time I didn't fall over.

"Roll on Friday, only four sleeps to go!" I thought as I took off.

I was so excited when I got home that I turned Chrystal's little record player on and played a 45 I'd bought the previous year. I listened to the music as I got changed into my factory clothes and caught my reflection in the big old ornate mirror Matilda's grandmother had given me. I had the biggest smile on my face. And why not? I was the Happiest Girl In The World. I sang to the music filling my room, thinking about Matt until it was time to go to work.

Leo Sayer – When I Need You

Running across the road to the factory, I thought the first thing I'd do when I got there was to tell Chrystal and Queenie my news. They both knew the whole "I like him but I'm not sure if he likes me" thing. It was my drama *du jour* so of course I'd spoken to both of them at length about it. Maybe a little too much and a little too often actually. Anyway, I had something different to talk to them about today.

Once in the factory, I ran straight over to where Chrystal and Queenie were working. I must have had that huge smile on my face, because Queenie took one look at me and said, "So Matt finally asked you out did he?" I was so happy, I couldn't talk so I simply nodded my head. I must have looked like an idiot – a love fool.

"It sure is nice to get some good news from you for a change!" Queenie said. She looked up from her press and over to Chrystal who was laughing. Queenie had the biggest smile on her face and we all cheerfully got on with our work.

I still hadn't talked to Best Friend Matilda yet, so I went straight to her house after work to tell her my news. I barged into her bedroom yelling, "Matilda, Matilda! Guess what's happened?"

Matilda looked up from the book she was reading on her bed. "Um ... aliens have landed?" she said.

"No ... it's not that," I replied, a little mystified by her response.

I was about to tell Matilda my news before she quickly broke in. "Matt's finally asked you out. Is that it?"

"How is it that everyone already knows ... how the heck did *you* know?" I asked incredulously.

"Because you've got that stupid love-sick smile on your face, haven't you?"

"*Damn* you for being so smart Matilda!" I thought.

At that, Matilda tossed her book aside, leapt off her bed and ran over to me squealing all the while. We hugged and jumped around her bedroom until Matilda's mother poked her head around the door to see what all the commotion was.

We stopped carrying on and sat on Matilda's bed. Of course my best friend wanted to hear the whole story from the time I'd left school onwards. I had to tell her exactly what Matt said and then exactly what I said. Matilda thought it was so cool Matt had asked me out in French and she came up with a couple of French phrases I could have used which would have sounded better than what I'd actually said. "For next time," she told me.

Matilda was so excited for me – she truly was my best friend. "One day, Matt is going to get down on one knee and say, 'Scarlet, veux-tu m'épouser?'" [Scarlet, will you marry me?]

Before we knew it, we were planning my wedding to Matt.

"*If* he asks me one day ..."

"When Scarlet, not if, *when*," replied Matilda.

"*When* he asks me," I continued, "you'll have to be my Chief Bridesmaid, Matilda."

We both jumped up and down on Matilda's bed as if it were a trampoline. Like the teenagers we were.

❦ ❦ ❦

At my next Karate lesson, Sensei came up to me out of the blue and asked if I'd like to join the Sunday morning beach squad – the same squad I'd seen on Petone beach a few years earlier that had inspired me to start studying Karate in the first place. I remembered Sensei had said only the best, most passionate and dedicated students were invited to the Sunday beach squad.

I was a little overwhelmed by the moment and all I could manage to say was, "Yes Sensei" before he carried on coaching the other students. To fill my heart totally with joy, I was awarded my purple belt at the end of the lesson that Thursday night.

"You've earned this Scarlet, as well as your place on the beach squad," Sensei said. "Make sure you're there on time this Sunday, ok?"

"I'll be there at 9am on the dot with a big smile on my face Sensei," I replied.

"I wouldn't expect anything else from you," Sensei said.

My face was sore from all the smiling I'd been doing lately.

🐚 🐚 🐚

Friday finally came around. It seemed like four weeks since Matt had asked me out but of course it had only been four days. I walked to school with a real spring in my step and that big smile on my face. I was officially the Happiest Girl In The World and nothing was going to upset me today, not even the Mean Girls.

School dragged by but at last the final bell sounded. I packed up my things in record time and got to the front gates before Matt. As I was waiting, I saw the two Mean Girls coming up behind me and my heart started to pound. "Not today!" I thought.

"You're such a bitch Scarlet ... Dump Girl!" one of the Mean Girls said as they drew level with me. They had the look as if they were going to start up on me, but I just wanted them out of the way before Matt arrived. I would have been mortified if he'd heard them speak to me in that way. All I wanted was for this day to be about me and Matt, so I said nothing and watched as they walked past me and carried on their way.

I breathed a sigh of relief as they disappeared into the distance, leaving me standing there, smiling and waiting for Matt to arrive.

And so I waited. And waited. And waited. I waited until there was absolutely no one left in the school or the grounds. Even the Head-master passed me on his way home. "Are you alright?" he asked.

I nodded. "Yes, I'm alright Sir."

Watching the Headmaster walk away, I realised I had a huge lump in my throat and I felt like crying. Matt never turned up that afternoon and I was devastated. All sorts of thoughts and emotions raced through me. What had happened? Had Matt simply forgotten about our plans? Did he have the flu? Worse still, had he changed his mind? I went from the Happiest Girl In The World to the Saddest Girl In The World in the space of half an hour.

I walked home holding back the tears. In a pre-mobile phone era, my options of getting in touch with Matt were extremely limited. If I was a teenager today, I could simply send a text and say something like, "Hey Matt, Scarlet here. Are we still on for the movies this weekend?" But not in 1978.

When I got to my job at the factory, I went straight to my work station and started folding overalls. I felt so miserable and had to wipe away my tears repeatedly as I worked. Chrystal came over to me at one point. "Whatever is the matter Scarlet?" she asked. "You're crying all over your pile of overalls!"

This got Queenie's attention and she walked over to me as well. "What's happened girl?" she asked gently.

It's hard to talk when all you want to do is break down and cry, but I finally got my words out. "Matt didn't meet me at the front gate after school like we'd arranged. I waited there for ages, but he didn't show up."

Queenie held out her arms. "Bring it in girl," she said softly.

Wouldn't you know it, but right at the moment I was snuggling into Queenie and blubbing like a baby, my father walked past. "What's the matter with Scarlet?" he said to Chrystal in a low voice. Chrystal looked at Dad and shook her head as if to say, "She'll be ok." Dad nodded slightly and reluctantly walked away. "Let it all out Scarlet," Queenie whispered, so I did.

It took quite a bit longer to finish my work that afternoon. When I had, I went straight to Matilda's house to tell her the news. I told her the whole story and when I was finished, Matilda looked at me and laughed. "Good one Scarlet! You had me going there! You managed to get through the whole story with a straight face."

I broke down crying and Matilda realised that I was telling her the truth. "Oh Scarlet, I thought you were joking," she said, her face full of compassion. "I thought eventually you would stop and tell me you'd met Matt and you were going to see such-and-such a movie tomorrow night with him."

"I really wish I *was* joking Matilda, I really do. But Matt never showed ..." That's as far as I got before I dissolved into tears again. Matilda held me and tried to console me. "It's ok Scarlet ... everything will be ok."

Somehow though, deep inside, I knew something was terribly wrong and that everything *wouldn't* be ok.

I needed something to take my mind off my terrible afternoon, so I joined Matilda and her father when they visited Matilda's eccentric old grandmother at the Hutt Hospital. When we got to her room, I sat in a chair not far from her bed and listened to her tell us about the numerous bypasses she'd seen since she'd been admitted. She went on to tell us that there were a large number of spirits wandering the corridors, most of them confused as to what had happened to them and needing help to move on. "At least there are no Trolls in this hospital ... that's a positive thing," she said.

Matilda's father looked up at the ceiling. "Just watch who you talk to about that stuff Mum, or you'll find yourself in an entirely different sort of hospital, ok?"

"You don't have to worry about me Son," Matilda's grandmother said. "This talk is only for us, isn't it Scarlet?"

I looked up at Matilda's grandmother and nodded. She winked at me and I thought, "This talk is all a bit Nanu Nanu, that's what it is."

In normal circumstances, saying "Nanu Nanu" would make me laugh.

But not today.

🐾 🐾 🐾

The following Sunday morning, I attended my very first Karate beach squad training session on the Petone foreshore. This was a dream come true for me, but Sensei frowned when he first saw me. "I thought you were going to have a big smile on your face this morning Scarlet," he said.

I suddenly realised that my disappointment at not seeing Matt the previous Friday was affecting other aspects of my life and other people too. When Sensei said what he did, it snapped me out of my despondency and I made a conscious decision to put those feelings to one side as much as I could. "Yes of course Sensei," I said smiling. I loved that he'd chosen me to be in the beach squad and I felt very lucky to be there.

From then on, I put my best foot forward and ended up having an awesome session.

🐾 🐾 🐾

I couldn't wait to get to school on Monday, not so much because there was a Maths test I'd been studying for, but more in the hope I'd see Matt. I looked for him around school during the breaks but there was no sign of him. I even took my time leaving school when the final bell rang out and I walked home slowly – all in the hope Matt would run up from behind me and call out his usual, "Hey Scarlet, wait up."

But no. It was like he'd dropped off the edge of the world.

To give me a little kick while I was down, the Mean Girls saw me walking home and hurled their usual abuse at me from across the street. It was like water off a Duck's back though. Nothing else mattered except to see Matt and find out what was going on.

This was the pattern for the rest of the week. I'd walk the grounds of school during the breaks looking for any sign of Matt. I'd hope like crazy he'd come running up to me after school with his gorgeous smile as I dawdled my way home. He wasn't even in the after-school French class, but I reasoned he'd sometimes miss those so at least that wasn't unusual.

Halfway through the next week, I still hadn't seen any sign of Matt and he missed the French class for the second week in a row. Now that *was* unusual and the unwelcome thought that he was avoiding me grew ever larger in my mind.

I became convinced Matt had gone off me and had regretted asking me out to the movies. Two weeks had now passed and still no Matt. I was missing him like mad. He had been the biggest ray of sunshine in my life, but now that beautiful warm sunshine seemed to be covered by thick dark clouds.

At the same time as thinking Matt had gone off me, I started wondering whether he was alright. Had something happened to him? This was all very confusing for a 14 year old girl. I was heartbroken and couldn't understand why Matt was avoiding me.

I started playing the Fleetwood Mac Rumours album all the time. It brought back pleasant memories of walking home with Matt and our conversations together. I played one song in particular, a beautiful song I'd sing along with Christine McVie. I'd sing this song to Matt at least once a day, if not more; it was like therapy for me. "This song is for you Matt," I'd say to myself. "I miss you so much." I'd then play the track on the record player in my room and pretend Matt was there as I sang along.

Fleetwood Mac – Songbird

Three weeks had now gone by since I'd last seen Matt and I was really worried for him. He'd never missed three French classes in a row and I never once saw him at school or afterwards. All I could do was play "Songbird" and sing it for him in my bedroom.

Thank you for the music Fleetwood Mac. These were very puzzling times for me as a teenager and your music really helped me.

At the four week mark, I asked Matilda if she could ask around her year group at school if anybody could shed any light on where Matt was.

I asked her again at five weeks, but no one knew anything about Matt's whereabouts – not even friends of friends of friends.

One day into the sixth week, I was at home getting changed out of my school uniform and into my work clothes. Mum was the only other person in the house at the time, so I had Songbird cranked up on my little record player. Suddenly, my bedroom door slammed open and Matilda came running in.

"Scarlet, Scarlet, I know what's happened to Matt!" She must have been shouting at the top of her lungs to be heard over my music.

I quickly turned the record player off and turned to Matilda with a big smile on my face. "What is it Matilda, where is he?" I asked.

The look on Matilda's face stopped me in my tracks. She hadn't been crying exactly, but it looked as though she wasn't far off it. I knew her news wasn't going to be good.

My best friend walked up to me and took both of my hands in hers. "Matt has leukemia and he's in the Hutt Hospital. He's really sick, Scarlet."

The floor under my feet started to shift. I'd heard people say things such as, "It hit me like a ton of bricks," and that's exactly how I felt in that moment – like someone had literally whacked me over the head with a brick. I thought I was going to fall over until I realised Matilda was leading me to my bed to sit down.

Even though I was only 14, I knew having leukemia in the 1970s was virtually a death sentence. The statistics are much better today, but in 1978 the prognosis was not great.

I was absolutely devastated. I couldn't believe what Matilda had told me. I started to cry and soon Matilda was crying too.

I asked Matilda if she and her father were going to the Hutt Hospital that night to visit her grandmother who had suffered a series of mild strokes over the past few weeks. Matilda said they were indeed going to the hospital and asked if I'd like to get a ride with them. I jumped at the chance and we arranged to meet at Matilda's house at 7pm.

The last thing I wanted to do was fold overalls for the next hour or so, but I straightened myself up and walked to the factory. When I got there, I could see Chrystal and Queenie side by side in the distance and I knew I'd have to tell them my news – they'd been asking me whether I'd heard anything about Matt every day for weeks.

Queenie saw me first and of course knew immediately something was up. She went over to Chrystal and nudged her to let her know I was there. As I told the two of them what I'd learned and that I'd try and see Matt in the evening, hot tears were streaming down my face. Queenie didn't say anything as she put her arms around me. We stood there holding each other while I cried like a baby.

"You never know Scarlet ... Matt may get better yet," Chrystal said optimistically. But I knew deep down inside my heart that something terrible was wrong with Matt – somehow I just knew it. I realised then that somehow I'd *always* known it. From the day he hadn't turned up as arranged at the school gate, my gut was telling me something bad had happened. My head was putting all kinds of spin on it, but my gut was telling me otherwise. I should have listened to my gut.

Right on cue, my father walked past us just as he had the day Matt and I were supposed to meet at school all those weeks ago. This time it was Queenie who shook her head slightly as if to say, "Not now." Dad looked concerned, but kept on walking.

Chrystal had such a sad look on her face and was holding my arm. "I'm so sorry Scarlet," she said. "Think what Matt's poor parents are going through."

Chrystal was right. The thought there were other people involved in this tragedy seemed to pull me out of my anguish a little. I wiped my eyes and gave Queenie a final squeeze. "Thanks guys," I said gratefully. "I'd better get on with my work."

At 7pm on the dot, I met Matilda and her father at his light brown HQ Holden parked on the street outside their house. Matilda sat in the front passenger's seat next to her father while I sat alone in the back seat.

I remembered the day Matt had introduced me to Meat Loaf and the Bat Out Of Hell album. I'd played that record so many times and pretty much knew the lyrics to most of the songs off by heart. It's one of those rarest of records that doesn't have a bad song on it.

The words from the song Bat Out Of Hell floated through my mind. I started singing to myself in the back seat of the HQ Holden while Matilda and her father sat quietly up front, generously leaving me alone with my thoughts as we drove through the darkened streets of the Hutt.

Meat Loaf – Bat Out of Hell

When we arrived at the Hutt Hospital, I asked Matilda if she minded if I went and saw Matt on my own. "Of course not Scarlet, you go and find Matt," she said. "I really hope you get to see him and talk to him."

"Thanks Matilda," I said. "You're the best friend ever."

Like a bat out of hell, I was off. I managed to track Matt down relatively easily and before long I was walking up the long corridor of his ward. I spoke to two lovely nurses and asked them if I could see Matt. "That should be ok," one of the nurses said, "but we'll have to check with Matt first. Who can we say is here to see him?"

"My name is Scarlet," I said. "Scarlet from school. Can you tell Matt I've come to see him please?"

One of the nurses walked a little way down the corridor and into one of the rooms. She returned shortly with a white coat which looked like something a Doctor would wear.

"Matt really wants to see you," the nurse said, "but you'll have to put this coat on first."

"Course," I said and put the white coat on, helped by the nurse.

As we were walking to Matt's room, the nurse spoke to me in a quiet voice. "When did you see Matt last Scarlet?"

That was easy. I knew the answer to this question to the day – almost to the minute. "About six weeks. I only found out a few hours ago he was sick."

The nurse shot me a look full of concern, sympathy and sadness all at once. "In that case, you might get a bit of a shock when you see Matt. He doesn't look great, but try not to say anything about it and be as positive as possible. Can you do that?"

"Of course," I said. "I'm a pretty positive kind of person and I've been looking forward to seeing Matt."

The nurse smiled. "That's good then. Matt asked me if I could help him sit up so he can talk to you better, so I've put a few pillows behind him. Help him rearrange them if he needs to won't you?"

I nodded vigorously. By now we were outside Matt's room – my heart was beating so fast. "Here you go Scarlet," the nurse said opening the door. As I walked in, the nurse closed the door behind me.

I was glad the nurse had told me that Matt didn't look great so I could prepare myself as much as possible. I still got a shock when I saw him sitting up in his bed though. He looked extremely pale and had lost quite a bit of weight since I'd seen him last. He looked at me with sad eyes but still managed to smile his beautiful smile. My heart immediately melted and stopped racing.

Seeing Matt sitting up in bed like that with all the white pillows against his pale skin was heart-wrenching for me. I really had to hold back the tears but I put on my brightest smile and tried to talk as breezily as I could.

"Hi Matt!" I said.

"Hi Scarlet ... it's great to see you," Matt replied. "Come and sit down."

I sat down on the seat beside the bed and as I did so, Matt held his hand out for me to hold. I gently took his hand in mine and got quite a surprise to feel how cold it was. I put my other hand on top of his and held it tightly, as if I thought this would warm him up. I knew Matt wasn't in a great state and my eyes started to fill up.

"I'm so glad they let me see you, but I didn't think you'd be alone in visiting hours," I said.

"That's because visiting hours don't apply to my family," explained Matt. "Mum and Dad have been here all day and have just gone out now to get something to eat. They'll be back soon but I'm glad it worked out this way so I can get you all to myself."

I was glad too, happy Matt and I could share a special moment that was just ours.

"I didn't know I had leukemia until really recently," Matt said as if he was anticipating my questions. "My Mum kept taking me to the doctors because I was really tired all the time and had no energy, but they misdiagnosed me at first. Eventually they told me I had acute myeloid leukemia."

Matt's smile faded. "I'm so so sorry I didn't get to take you to the pictures Scarlet. I was really looking forward to it and then ... this happened." He said these words in such a loving, tender way and it touched my heart.

"Matt, there's something I really need to say to you," I said. "I'm so sorry for all those times I left you at the corner of my street and ran off."

Matt's smile returned. "Yes, I always wondered why you did that Scarlet. Why did you?" He squeezed my hand.

I sighed. "Oh, because I was embarrassed about the house I live in and I didn't want you to see it."

"But Scarlet," Matt said laughing, "I knew where you lived all along. I was always surprised when you used to walk right past your house as if you didn't live there!"

I was momentarily stunned by this revelation. "How on Earth do you know where I live?" I asked.

"Um ... it's called the telephone book Scarlet. I looked up your address in the phone book."

My mouth dropped open involuntarily and we both laughed and laughed.

"Oh, I didn't think of that," I said sheepishly.

"I thought you were acting a bit strange the first day we walked down your street. Then we got to the corner and you ran off, leaving me standing there. When I got home, I looked up your surname in the phone book and found your address. The next time we walked down your street, I saw your house but you walked right past it again. I figured you had your reasons for not wanting me to know where you lived, so I thought I'd wait until you decided to tell me. It's no big deal Scarlet."

I looked down at the whiter than white bedsheets on Matt's bed, feeling embarrassed and a little foolish. I looked back up at Matt and smiled thinly. "I really wish I hadn't done that now. I wish I'd invited you inside for a glass of milk and a piece or two of my mother's delicious shortbread biscuits. Even though my family are poor and can't afford a decent house, we always have plenty of food on the table – especially for treasured guests."

"I would've loved that Scarlet. Maybe next time, yeah?"

I remember thinking how strong and brave Matt was.

"How are the French classes going?" Matt asked.

"Not very well," I confessed. "We've just had a test actually."

"And ... what mark did you get?"

"I got 48%. I really mucked it up!"

"I'm sure you'll pass the next one," Matt said encouragingly. "You're really good at French Scarlet. Will you promise me to keep it up when I'm ... just promise to keep it up?" As Matt asked me this, he looked tenderly into my eyes and held my hand very tightly.

"Of course I'll keep it up ... for you," I said. "The after-school French classes aren't much fun without you there."

"You've still got Matilda," Matt said.

I nodded. "That's right, but it's not the same without you there with us."

I wanted to come clean and tell Matt the truth, that the only reason I'd persevered with French classes was so I could see him and try to impress him.

Before I knew it, the moment had passed.

We fell silent for a few moments, looking into each other's eyes and holding hands. I felt like I never wanted to take my hand away, never wanted to leave Matt alone in that sterile, cold, white hospital room.

Eventually, Matt broke the silence. "I'm so lucky to have met you Scarlet. I really wish I could have taken you to the movies. We would've had fun."

"It's me who's the lucky one Matt," I replied. "There will be plenty of time for us to go to the movies together when you get out of here, eh?!"

I sat still, smiling at Matt. There were so many things I wanted to say to him about how I really felt. I wanted to tell him he was the most beautiful boy I'd ever met in my life; that I felt warm sunshine whenever he was around me.

But I simply didn't know how to put these feelings into words back then. So Matt and I talked about this and that until I realised visiting hours were over.

"Matt, I have to go," I said. "I got a ride here with Matilda and her father. Matilda's grandmother is in hospital too. But would it be ok if I came and saw you tomorrow?"

Matt's face lit up. "Of course Scarlet," he said excitedly. "I'd love to talk with you some more. Come as soon as visiting hours start ok?"

I reluctantly let go of Matt's cold hand and stood up. "It was so lovely to see you Scarlet," Matt said as I walked towards the door to his room.

"It was so lovely to see you too Matt," I said. "I'll be back to see you tomorrow."

Reaching the door, Matt's final words to me were in French. "Tu es une jolie fille, Scarlet." [You are a beautiful girl, Scarlet.]

I smiled brightly. "Tu es belle aussi Matt!" [You are beautiful too Matt!]

Returning to the nurses' station, I handed the white coat back and thanked them for helping me. I then started on the long walk back to Matilda's grandmother's ward, all the while wanting to turn around and rush back to Matt's side.

There was so much left unsaid between us, so many things I wanted to tell him. Above all else, I wanted to tell Matt I loved him, that he was my first real love and I wished we had more time together.

It was true. I loved Matt.

I looked up at a big clock on the wall which said 8:40. "Only 23 hours until I can see you again Matt," I thought. "I'll tell you how I really feel tomorrow."

I returned to Matt's ward at 7:30 the next evening, excited at the prospect of spending the next hour with him. The nurses on duty that evening were different from the night before. They told me gently that my special, beautiful, beloved ray of warm sunshine had died that afternoon at 3:15.

I was shell-shocked. I said "thank you" to the nurses and walked away in a daze. It took a few seconds for the reality and meaning of it all to sink in before I completely lost it and had to sit down in the corridor before I fell down. Thoughts and feelings of all kinds were racing through my head; thoughts of regret that I hadn't found Matt sooner, feelings of loss – of not ever seeing him again, thoughts of what might have been between us and, most importantly, all the things I wished I'd said to him. My overarching thought was that this beautiful, kind, considerate, intelligent boy had been taken too soon and it just wasn't fair.

I cried and cried and cried. I cried all the way back to Matilda's grandmother's ward. Matilda saw me from a distance and came running over to me. She knew instinctively what had happened and wrapped her arms around me.

The next few days are a bit of a blur. The next firm memory I have is of Matilda and I going to Matt's funeral together. We saw quite a few of Matt's friends from school who we silently acknowledged before Matilda and I sat together quietly at the back of the church.

When the celebrant called on Matt's father to come forward, he stood up and walked to the front of the church. He spoke about his "beloved son" and how Matt had recently bought a record by an artist called Meat Loaf. He was crying as he said Matt had played this album over and over and that he loved one song in particular – Heaven Can Wait. Matt had played this song all the time, long before he ever knew he had leukemia, long before he knew he was going to die. These are the only words I can remember Matt's father saying.

At the conclusion of the service, Matt's casket was carried out of the church to the Meat Loaf song he loved so much. As the casket moved slowly past me, I mouthed a kiss and said softly, "I love you Matt." I watched Matt's father who was trying to keep it together – pain and grief written all over his face – and I wept for him, for Matt's mother and family, but mostly for Matt who had been taken so young.

As the congregation filed out of the church to the sound of Heaven Can Wait, there wasn't a dry eye in the place. Matt's funeral was so moving and poignant, perhaps because he was so young, his massive potential unfulfilled. "It's not right when parents have to bury their children," I overheard one lady saying to her husband. "It should be the other way around."

For me, the sadness of the occasion was due to the love I felt for Matt. I missed my beautiful friend.

Matilda and I walked outside, into the light of a perfect day. We saw that Matt's casket had been placed into a black hearse. The casket was covered with flowers and the back doors of the hearse were open. Matt's parents were standing either side of the casket as if reluctant to leave their boy. Lots of people were milling around them, their eyes fixed on the casket.

As I stood there looking at Matt's casket in the back of the big black hearse, I wondered whether I should go up to Matt's parents and say "hello" and tell them Matt used to walk me home from school and always carried my heavy schoolbag like the gentleman he was. I didn't know whether Matt had ever spoken to his parents about me, about this girl who would walk right past her own house and then leave him on the next street corner. I wasn't sure if I should intrude on their obvious grief – they both looked utterly devastated to have lost their son. I must have stood there wondering what to do for a good 30 minutes. I was so unsure of myself; I just didn't know what to do.

"We should probably go now Scarlet," Matilda said sadly. My throat had a giant lump in it, so I simply nodded as Matilda put her arm around me and led me away.

When I got home, I went to my bedroom, lay down on my bed and cried. Grief consumed me and I lay on my bed for the best part of the day, unable to move or think or do anything.

After a while, I felt I wanted to honour Matt and sing a song to him. I'd recently bought a 45 that seemed entirely right for the situation, so I picked it out of my collection and played it on my little record player. I sang it with all the love in my heart to my lost love. I sang it then and countless other times in the days and months after Matt's passing.

This song is for you Matt, from your High School friend who always dumped you on the corner of my street after you had walked me home. I loved you Matt, rest in peace.

Thelma Houston – Don't Leave Me This Way

After Matt passed, I threw myself into Karate more than ever before. I even entered a couple of tournaments. As usual, Frank was there on the sidelines watching and cheering me on.

At the first of these tournaments, I was about to start my fight when a strange thing happened. I bowed to my opponent and when I stood up to face her, I had the sensation I was no longer facing a human opponent. Instead, it was now the living incarnation of leukemia I was about to fight. I was literally going to fight leukemia and if I won, Matt would be saved. I won that fight easily and straight afterwards Frank came over to me. "Wow Scarlet," he said, "you really smashed that girl!"

From then on, all of my opponents became leukemia as soon as I bowed at the beginning of a fight. I'd bow and say to myself, "Leukemia, you are not going to take my Matt away from me," and I'd do my utmost to save Matt. There was no stopping me; I couldn't tell you how many times I saved Matt from leukemia in that way. I wish it could have been that simple in real life.

By the end of the year I'd been awarded my brown belt. "Only one more to go," I thought.

As if 1978 hadn't been filled with enough sadness already, more bad news arrived during the last week of the school year. My dear friend Tracey's mother died of cancer so Tracey was going to have to leave our High School and go and live with her sister and brother in law in Masterton.

We were both very sad she was going to be moving away. To me it felt like I'd lost two of my best school friends within weeks of each other; one male the other female. But Tracey pointed out that Masterton was only about an hour away by train and asked whether I'd like to come and visit her in her new home once she'd settled in. Of course I jumped at the chance and the plans were made for the new year.

The last day of the 1978 school year had arrived. I was so sad as I slowly walked to school by myself that morning. Matilda had broken the news to me a few days earlier that 1978 would be her last year at High School. Because she was a year older than me, Matilda had sat her School Certificate exams and already left school. We would find out early in the new year she'd passed her exams with flying colours. Who would have guessed? Matilda was soooo smart! She was eager to embark on a career and had secured a position as a trainee Teller at the Petone Post Office which she was to start shortly.

The school gates were ahead of me and my thoughts turned to Tracey. This was to be her last day at Hutt Valley Memorial Technical College. Soon she would be heading off to Masterton. This was to be Aroha's last day at school also. She'd told me two years of secondary school education was enough for her and she was going to start work in a clothing shop in Lower Hutt. My sadness deepened – I felt as though everybody who meant anything to me had left or was leaving.

As I walked through the school gates, I knew where I'd find Tracey. She would be waiting, for the last time, for the school bus from Wainuiomata to arrive. Sure enough, there she was and she smiled at me as I walked over and stood next to her. I wanted to keep my friend company one last time as she waited.

It wasn't long before the school bus pulled into the parking area and the Wainui boys and girls filed out. Finally the boy Tracey had a crush on, but was way too shy to talk to, walked past. He locked eyes with Tracey and they smiled at each other, but as always neither said a word to the other.

After Tracey's crush had walked past, I saw the two Mean Girls arrive at the school gates. This time though, my heart didn't race and when they called out, "You're such a bitch Dump Girl," I gently laughed and shook my head. After everything I'd been through that year, their taunts had no power over me anymore. The fact they'd failed to produce a reaction from me seemed to annoy them further, but just then the morning bell rang out and we all needed to get to class fast.

"What the heck was that about Scarlet?" Tracey asked me as we walked.

I shrugged my shoulders. "I'm not sure," I replied. "Maybe she's still upset from the time I kicked her schoolbag all the way down the road that Mufti Day." We both laughed as we picked up the pace to get to our classroom for the last time that year.

The school report I received for my second year at High School was a lot better than the one from the year before. For one thing, I got a B for the first time in my life. It was a B2 to be exact, in English. I was stoked. Overall, I was pretty happy with my marks and the progress I'd made in a year, especially in Maths. My father agreed, but nevertheless thought I could do even better.

My mother on the other hand thought my first B ever was something to celebrate. She was so proud and cooked me my favourite dinner. She went all out and even used one of Dad's beer flagons to made up some Raro orange juice which she chilled and placed in pride of place on the table at dinner time. This was a rare thing indeed; usually we drank only water at dinner. Frank was especially pleased because he was convinced he could taste the faint flavour of beer in the Raro, claiming Mum hadn't rinsed Dad's flagon out properly.

"Aw dream on Frank!" I said.

🐱 🐱 🐱

With High School done for the year, I went to work full time at the factory.

To try and avoid those testy conversations about money with Mum and Dad, I told them I planned to bank most of the wages I'd earn over the Christmas holidays but I needed to get my hair cut first. And buy a few Christmas presents. Mum and Dad seemed fine with a haircut and some Christmas presents, so I didn't push it any further and duly made an appointment with my lovely hairdresser.

While I was getting my hair cut, my hairdresser asked me if I was interested in earning a little bit of extra money. "Was I ever!" I said excitedly and asked her what she had in mind. She told me she and her husband also wanted to earn a little extra money by taking evening jobs at the Petone Working Men's Club. The club had now moved to its flash new buildings in Udy Street and was looking for staff to help ramp up its business. Both she and her husband had applied for jobs there and as these would require them to work three nights a week from 7pm to 11pm, she needed a babysitter to look after her two young children. The job was mine if I wanted it.

I absolutely jumped at the chance! My hairdresser lived only 10 minutes away from my place, so I could easily walk there after dinner and start work. During the school year, I could do my homework while I was babysitting – that's how I'd sell it to Mum and Dad anyway. The best thing was I could now save every last dollar of my wages from the factory and spend my earnings from babysitting. That would definitely get my parents off my back about saving, whilst also allowing me to focus on getting my grades up. It was a win:win:win situation.

Walking home from the hairdresser's, my mind was filled both with the upcoming all-important Fifth Form School Cert year as well as all the things I could buy with my babysitting money and no longer feel guilty about – things like clothes, make-up, records, you name it!

For the first time in a while I started to feel better about things. I found I was looking forward to 1979 and all the possibilities the new year promised.

🦌 🦌 🦌

1978 wasn't *quite* finished with us yet though.

A few days before the end of the year, my mother experienced something that was both strange and amazing.

Before I tell this story, there's one thing you need to know about my mother; she is a staunch non-believer in anything she can't see or touch.

Even though she'd play along with Frank and I when we said something or other was "Nanu Nanu," she definitely didn't believe in the Nanu Nanu one jot. She would never ridicule anyone for talking about or believing in aspects of the supernatural or paranormal – that wasn't her way – but she didn't buy into the unexplained either.

That said, on with my – or should I say my *Mum's* – story.

One night, Mum was putting the milk bottles out as usual. The Sun had long set and it was a beautifully clear Summer's night sky full of stars. Something above her caught her attention, so she looked up and couldn't believe what she was seeing. There was a mass of individual bright lights hovering high up in the sky, almost directly above her.

One by one the individual lights joined together until there was only one large ball of light. It hovered in place for a few seconds and then, without warning, shot across the sky at great speed in an easterly direction. Mum later described it as "heading due east, towards South America." She was quite adamant about this. Mum tracked the bright ball of light as it darted across the sky until it suddenly and completely disappeared.

The first I knew of this was when Mum came charging back into the house where she half-ran half-walked straight to the telephone stand in the hallway. "What are you doing Mum?" I asked. I could tell something was up.

"I've just seen a UFO so I'm going to ring the local radio station." Mum was so agitated and shaken up, it took her a couple of goes to dial the telephone number properly.

I thought this was all terribly exciting, although my first reaction was to laugh. "Yeah, whatever Mum!" I said. After all, this was my mother we were talking about, the Great Sceptic of the family. But I could tell she meant what she said, so I stood next to her as she waited for the radio station to answer.

Talkback radio had been around in New Zealand for at least a decade at this point and as luck would have it, there was a talkback show on air at the time my mother called the radio station. She was put straight through to the host of the talkback show and Mum proceeded to tell him exactly what she'd witnessed only moments before.

The host listened to Mum's story and when she'd finished, there was silence for a few seconds. Mum and I looked at each other expectantly, waiting to hear what the talkback host had to say.

It wasn't good. After he'd stopped laughing, he asked Mum whether she was pranking him and even had the gall to ask how many drinks she'd consumed that evening. It didn't seem to matter when Mum told the talkback host she didn't drink; he carried on making fun of Mum and cracking "jokes" at her expense for some time.

Mum was devastated. Consider it from her perspective – here was this great nonbeliever who had seen something unexplainable in the sky and then had the guts to ring up a radio station to report what she'd seen. Now this fool of a talkback host was roasting her over her story and was basically questioning her sanity.

Eventually, Mum butted in and told the host this was no joke and everything she'd said was true. She reiterated that the large ball of light had darted across the sky due east, straight towards South America. The radio guy started laughing again and suggested that maybe the little green men wanted to have a go at learning some Latin dancing – the rumba, or the tango maybe.

Mum had had enough. She simply said "Goodnight" and hung up on the talkback host by thumping the receiver down on the phone's cradle. She was so upset by the treatment she'd received and was visibly shaken.

I asked Mum if she was alright. "Scarlet," she replied, "I'm absolutely disgusted by the way I was treated just then. All I did was to describe exactly what I saw outside only minutes ago and that radio … person … could only make jokes about it."

Mum was getting mad now. "Bad move, radio guy," I thought. "You wouldn't like my mum when she's angry." I felt bad for Mum. I knew she was a huge sceptic of anything even slightly paranormal.

"I believe you saw what you said you saw Mum," I said kindly. "I know you'd never make that sort of thing up in a million years."

"Thanks Scarlet. Come on, let's have a cup of tea."

"Good idea Mum. I'll make it."

So I did ... but this wasn't the end of the story.

Early the next day, Mum went outside to bring in the milk and The Dominion morning newspaper as she had a thousand times before. She always read that newspaper from cover to cover and this morning there was something in it especially for her.

On the front page, and in several pages into the newspaper as well, was story after story about a UFO sighting in the skies over Wellington the night before. Apparently, hundreds of people had come forward and told their stories to the newspaper which had obviously taken it way more seriously than the talkback radio show host had. There were even a couple of very blurry looking photos of the event which, to be honest, could have been anything.

The main thing was that my mother had been vindicated! Yay!! She had been one of the first to tell her story and had been treated very badly because of it. But the sheer number of witnesses who all described seeing the same thing at the same time was very persuasive and could not be ignored by the media.

To cap the whole thing off, stories of UFO sightings emerged the very next day from the Arizona desert and South America – exactly where Mum said the lights over Wellington had headed. Now that was a bit Nanu Nanu; even Mum thought so.

I couldn't say seeing those UFOs made Mum a believer in *all* things supernatural and paranormal. She still was a huge sceptic and remains so to this day. The difference is she now believes in UFOs.

Why? Because she saw one with her own eyes.

There have been numerous UFO sightings around New Zealand over the years. Perhaps the most famous and celebrated sighting took place around the Kaikoura Coast in the South Island in the late evening of December 30th and the early hours of December 31st 1978. This was only a matter of days after my mother's experience. Could the two be related?

YouTube: The Kaikoura UFO sighting continues to baffle, 30 years on (5:57)

New Zealand can also lay claim to its own rock star in the UFO community. He was Bruce Cathie, an airline pilot by day and UFO researcher and author by night. After witnessing a UFO over the Manukau Harbour in Auckland in 1952, Bruce dedicated more than fifty years of his life to UFO research writing half a dozen books on the subject, perhaps the most well-known being "Harmonic 33" which was published in 1968.

He developed a number of theories over the years using complex mathematical equations and calculations, around the core idea that the Earth is covered by a grid-like energy pattern now referred to as the World Energy Grid System. The lines making up this grid crisscross our planet and the points at which they intersect tend to be UFO hotspots.

It's fair to say that Bruce copped a fair bit of flak from sceptics over the years, some keen to discredit his work. Unperturbed by this, he ploughed his own furrow for over five decades until his death in 2013.

A true Kiwi trailblazer, I hope one day Bruce Cathie will receive the worldwide respect and recognition he deserves.

🐾 🐾 🐾

Two days after Christmas, I celebrated my 15th birthday. Five days after that, it would be New Year's Day 1979.

Neither the festive season, nor the factory Christmas party, nor my birthday celebrations filled me with much joy this year. My heart had been rent in two and I was still grieving over the loss of Matt, my ray of warm sunshine.

It was late afternoon New Year's Eve, just a day or two after my Mum's experience with the UFOs. I was feeling particularly down this afternoon and was missing Matt a lot. As I often did when I felt this way, I quietly slipped into my bedroom, pulled my door half shut behind me and retrieved my 1978 copy of "The Pitonian," my school's annual yearbook.

Sitting on my bed, I quickly thumbed through the magazine to the pages containing the class photos until I found the one Matt was in. There he was, frozen in time, standing in the middle of the back row, smiling his special smile. With tears in my eyes, I touched his image. "I miss you Matt," I said sadly. "I miss your warm sunshine. I wish you were here with me."

No sooner had I said these words when a flash of something caught my attention. I looked over to the entrance of my room where I saw a long vertical shaft of gold light shining brightly on the scrim just inside my half open door.

"That's really odd," I thought. "I've never seen anything like that before." Without warning, the shaft of light disappeared.

I looked back at Matt's picture in The Pitonian and imagined in my mind's eye that he was in my bedroom with me. "Shall we dance?" I asked playfully. I got up from my bed, turned on my little record player and played the 45 that was already on the turntable.

Closing my eyes, I imagined Matt was next to me as we slowly swayed in time to the music. I didn't want the dance to end.

Nazareth – Love Hurts

When eventually the song had finished, I came back to reality to find I was facing directly towards the large windows which looked out onto our small front lawn. Without warning, a vertical shaft of bright gold light flashed across the entire width of the window moving at speed from the left hand side and disappearing upwards and off to the right. Realising the light had appeared **outside** the house, I rushed over to the window as quickly as I could until my nose was pressed up against the glass pane.

The shaft of light was nowhere to be seen.

My mind was in the process of trying to convince me that I'd seen some sort of trick of the light, until I looked down at the small patch of grass outside my window.

There was Snoopy the cat, his back arched, hackles raised and the fur across his entire body puffed up looking all the World as if a bolt of electricity had passed through him. But it wasn't these things that intrigued me the most. Snoopy's ears were as flat as they could be and he was looking wide-eyed up and off to his right, exactly where I'd seen the shaft of golden light disappear.

I followed Snoopy's gaze off into the distance and felt a warm glow spread inside me. "Bye Matt," I said, joy returning to my heart.

So ended 1978. A year I will never forget.

🐈 🐈 🐈

It has been so very difficult writing about this part of my life, recalling the short time Matt and I had together. Even though these events took place almost 40 years ago, tears are streaming down my face and I feel my heart is breaking all over again just as it did in 1978 when I was only 14 years old.

I couldn't have known back then that one day I'd be a Mum. As a 53 year old woman with a 13 year old son of her own, I simply can't imagine what Matt's parents must have gone through when they lost their beloved son. I wish I'd had the courage as a 14 year old girl to go and talk to them at his funeral. I would have told them about the time we'd spent together; the French classes, the walks home, our plans to go to the movies together which were destined never to come to fruition. The courageous version of me would have told them I loved Matt and missed him like crazy. And I would have told them he was like a warm ray of sunshine in my life.

My story about Matt would have ended here had it not been for a series of strange events that took place immediately after I finished writing about 1978.

The first happened around 9pm on a Sunday night as I was sitting in bed writing, literally as I'd typed the words "So ended 1978, a year I will never forget."

At that *exact* moment, I heard a boy's voice in the hallway directly outside my bedroom say "Hello" firmly and clearly. I got out of bed straight away expecting to see my son in the hall.

No one was there.

I walked on down the hallway to my son's bedroom only to find his door shut. I chuckled when I saw his hand-made sign announcing "Led Zeppelin Rules" which he had Blu-Tacked to the door.

I opened the door to see my son sitting on the small couch in his room, playing "Stairway To Heaven" on his acoustic guitar. He casually looked up at me and stopped playing. "Hi Mum, what's up?" he asked.

I was taken aback not to find my son in the hall, let alone to find him in his bedroom with the door shut. It then occurred to me that the voice I'd heard didn't *quite* sound like my son's – it was deeper in pitch – but I needed to ask him the question anyway.

"Did you say 'Hello' to me from the hallway just now?" I asked.

My son gave me a strange look. "Nup. How could I? I've been here in my room playing guitar for the past hour or so."

"Right," I replied unsurely. "I could've sworn I heard someone say 'Hello' to me just now, right outside my bedroom door."

My son looked at me like I had two heads. "Well that's a bit Nanu Nanu isn't it? Deffo wasn't me Mum."

I nodded my head slowly and told my boy it was getting late and that he should get to bed. I copped the usual teen attitude but he's a good boy and I know he'll do as I ask once he's finished playing Stairway To Heaven.

Walking back to my bedroom I had to giggle. "I've even got my son saying 'Nanu Nanu' now!" I thought.

I climbed tiredly back into bed and contemplated what had happened. Could that have been *Matt* saying "Hello" to me? I shut down my laptop and drifted off into an uneasy sleep.

In the early hours of the morning, I woke up from a vivid dream in which Matt and I were at the movies together. Sitting in the back row of the Petone State Picture Theatre, Matt had his arm around me while I rested my head on his shoulder and smiled the same huge smile I wore whenever I was with him. We didn't kiss; we were content to simply watch the movie and hold each other. In my dream, I felt an overwhelming sensation of peace and love.

The dream seemed so real that the feelings of peace and love stayed with me for a few minutes after waking up. When it finally sunk in that I had been dreaming, those feelings were replaced with an aching loss. I wondered whether Matt had given me that dream knowing how very much I would have loved to have gone to the movies with him in real life.

For me, the strangest episode took place later the same morning. I'd found it difficult to get back to sleep after being awakened by the dream of Matt and I at the movies. Dawn wasn't far away, so I decided to go for a run down to the beach and around the bays.

I quickly changed into my running gear and started off. I ran down the hill from my house to Worser Bay, around the twisty turns of Karaka Bay and towards the sandy beach at Scorching Bay.

YouTube: Scorching Bay, Wellington, New Zealand (0:17)

Running along the pavement adjacent to the beach at Scorching Bay, the dark of the sky was giving way to a glow in the east announcing the Sun's imminent arrival. There was absolutely no one around except for an elderly man walking his dog by the water's edge.

Scorching Bay has a number of bench seats dotted along the beach front looking directly out towards the sea and as I jogged past one of these benches, a single red rose lying smack in the middle of the seat made me stop in my tracks.

The rose looked in perfect shape, as if it had been freshly cut. It was an extraordinarily deep red colour with a very long vibrant green stem. Droplets of water were dotted here and there on both flower and stem as if recently applied. I scanned the landscape to see who could possibly have placed the rose there at this hour, but there was no one to be seen. Even the elderly man and his dog had disappeared.

I sensed strongly that the rose was meant for me – I'm not sure **how** I knew this, but the feeling was very powerful. I carefully picked it up, held it to my face and inhaled its exquisite fragrance.

As soon as I touched the rose, the first delicate notes of a Piano began to sound in my mind. Gently growing louder, I recognised the song playing instantly. As the first pink rays of the Sun began to reach out like fingers into the eastern sky, I sang Heaven Can Wait along to the music in my head.

♩ *Heaven can wait … ♪*

I stood by the beach in the calm and quiet of the dawn, looking out across the flat waters of Scorching Bay, smelling the gorgeous rose and singing Matt's favourite song to him wherever he was.

♪ *Heaven can wait … ♫*

Almost at the end of the song now, it was as if all my senses were heightened. I could hear the sound of tiny waves lapping on the seashore and the call of Seagulls from way across the harbour. I could feel the warmth of the Sun on my face and the sharp taste of salt in my mouth. Above all else, the intoxicating fragrance of the rose was all about me. With tears flooding down my face, I closed my eyes and sang the last words of Meat Loaf's beautiful song.

♪ Heaven can wait ... ♫

I reopened my eyes and looked around me one last time to see if there was anyone who could possibly have placed the rose I was holding on this particular bench seat at the crack of dawn. Again, there was no one. I wanted to give the rose back to the Universe so I tenderly kissed it before replacing it on the bench and running off.

Wiping the tears from my face as I ran home, I thanked Meat Loaf and Jim Steinman for creating the incredible music on their Bat Out Of Hell album, music that had comforted my precious Matt in his last days.

Thank you Meat Loaf and Jim for making the Bat Out Of Hell album a reality – I'm aware of the intense struggle you faced in bringing it into the world. Your music made a dying teenage boy really happy here at the Bottom Of The World.

Meat Loaf – Heaven Can Wait

18

July 2017 - My Ghost Revisited

"Scarlet, wake up.

"Scarlet, wake UP!

"SCARLET! WAKE UP!!"

I open my eyes and try to clear the sleep fog from my head. Standing silently beside my bed, I see the black and white slightly distorted image of My Ghost. I sit up and look at the time – it's 2 in the morning ... as usual.

"MG must be here to congratulate me on the progress I've made on my book," I think excitedly. It was only a couple of days earlier that I'd finished writing about my personal *annus horribilis*, 1978. I was pretty chuffed I'd reached this milestone after the best part of half a year's work and was expecting a pat on the back – figuratively speaking – from MG for getting this far.

How wrong could I be?

"There's no time for resting on your laurels yet Scarlet," MG says petulantly inside my mind. "After 6 months of writing, you're only up to 1978 – when you were 15 years old. At this rate you'll be lucky to finish before 2020. It's absolutely ***imperative*** you complete your story by 2020."

This was something new. "Why is it so important to finish my story by 2020?" I ask. "You've never said anything about 2020 before ..."

MG quickly cuts me off. "No arguments Scarlet. It is of vital importance you continue writing your book immediately. Time is of the essence!"

"But I don't get what's so important about 2020?"

I can just make out MG's disapproving look that I've become all too familiar with. "You'll get the answers you need Scarlet ... in time. All I can say now is dark times are coming. You need to carry on with your book *now*! There is so much more to write and no time to waste, so ... get moving!!"

MG vanishes.

It's my turn to be irritable. After all, I've managed to fit my writing in between everything else life has thrown at me during the year – but this clearly hasn't been enough for MG.

"I'm absolutely buggered MG!" I announce to the empty bedroom. "I've just finished writing about Matt and it's been a real emotional Roller Coaster to bring those memories forward and put them down on paper. I need a break ... only a little one. It's school holidays, so I've arranged a couple of days skiing up at Mount Ruapehu with my son and some friends. I'm sure that'll be enough to recharge my batteries and I'll get on with my story after that ok?"

MG's voice in my head is as ominous as it is disconcerting. "Alright Scarlet. Take your break. But no excuses afterwards ... get on with your book as soon as you get back. There is no time to waste!"

"Ok ... ok," I say tiredly. "I promise I'll carry on writing as soon as I'm back from skiing."

I yawn, lie down in my bed and try to get back to sleep.

Any thoughts of that are hijacked by the mental list I start making of the things I need to pack for my ski trip.

Mount Ruapehu here we come!

19

Coming Soon

Thank you, Dear Reader, for reading the first book in my series, My Ghosts At The Bottom Of The World – I hope you enjoyed it. I would love for you to join me as I continue on with my journey of self discovery.

Watch out for the next volumes in my story ... coming soon!!

Volume Two - The
Journey Continues

Volume Three - My
Secret Calling

Volume Four -
Gnothi Seauton
(Know Thyself)